THE
AMBER
SHADOWS

THE AMBER SHADOWS

LUCY RIBCHESTER

PEGASUS BOOKS
NEW YORK LONDON

The Amber Shadows

Pegasus Books Ltd
148 West 37th Street, 13th Floor
New York, NY 10018

First Pegasus Books hardcover edition August 2017

First Pegasus Books paperback edition June 2018

10 9 8 7 6 5 4 3 2 1

ISBN: 978-1-68177-748-1
Printed in the United States of America
Distributed by W. W. Norton & Company, Inc.

For my family

'War is very like a bad dream in which familiar people appear in terrible and unlikely disguises.'

Graham Greene, *The Ministry of Fear*

Prologue

'Damned engines. The way they shudder when they're pulling to a halt. Sets one's teeth on edge.' The man in the navy blue suit moves his hands down the serge on his thighs, pulling at the trouser creases. Though it is cold in the carriage, and they are the only two in this compartment, it is also airless. Horsehair stuffing pokes through cracks in the leather seats, making his legs itch. When his trousers are straight he fluffs the collar of his shirt.

Outside the train window the light is starting to fade. A tiny slash of fire signals the end of the sun; the rest of the sky is uniform navy. Where are they? Kent? Have they been rerouted? Have they left Buckinghamshire yet? They must be hours still from London, the fields are too pretty, the air is still too full of pollen.

Opposite him, the other man in the carriage stirs. His suit is cream linen, his hair blond; his voice when he speaks comes out slow and lazy. 'You know Stravinsky spent months, perhaps years of his childhood on trains. They say it influenced his music. The rhythms.'

There is a pause of seconds. The man in navy pouts his lips; he wants to think of something to say to this, he wants to reply, but he doesn't know if the other wants a reply. Then fate presents him with a new outlet.

'You've dropped your book.' He reaches to the floor.

'How clumsy of me.' The blond sticks out his hand. 'Thank you.'

'*Figley's Book of Ciphers*. Ha. Not planning on fighting Fritz with that, are you?'

'Gracious, no.' The blond man laughs. 'Gift from my father when I was a boy. I always take it on train journeys. Flick through it every now and then. Passes the time.'

'I see. Family bringing you to these parts?'

'As a matter of fact, yes. Relative of mine working at some godawful Foreign Office outpost in the middle of nowhere. A manor house full of bored typists. I can't imagine anything more torturous. You?'

'I . . . work in Bletchley village. It's small, sort of . . .'

'Yes, I know the one. That's where she works. Funny. Small world, isn't it? Are you from there?'

'No. London.'

'Same.'

Silence folds back in. The blond man closes his eyes. When he opens them again, just a peep, the man in navy looks sharply down and fidgets with the things in his pockets. 'Suppose,' he says, still fidgeting, 'suppose we're going . . . to be here all night. Night in the sidings. Mother's roast'll go to ruin. If there was only some way of telegramming while on the train. Suppose . . . at this rate . . . Do you know this happened last time I took the train? Got re-railed and ended up in Maidstone. What do you suppose causes these wretched delays?'

The blond shrugs. 'War.' He wishes this navy-suited woollen agitator would shut up. He is putting him off his daydreams. And they are good daydreams. They are dance dreams. In his head, he is not in linen but silk stockings – thick, defiant, bully-for-you rationing – and a taupe velvet doublet with slashes of tawny silk. He is doing fouettés, foot cocked nice and tight on thigh, spin, one, two . . . seven, he is Basil from *Don Quixote* – no, he is Stravinsky's Prince Ivan – and the orchestra is blisteringly loud.

But the man in navy must talk. Strangers must talk to other strangers, when they meet like this, on trains, in the middle of a war. 'Stravinsky, you say . . .' the navy man gabbles. 'Now there's a funny thing. I haven't heard his music in a long time, but you know, you remind me of someone I once knew. I'd only have been a boy myself. But he liked Stravinsky too. He was a ballet boy.'

Now the blond looks up, takes in the other's face: the gristly cheeks, the eyes blue, sunken back and a little darting. Does he know this man? He tries to remember who got in the carriage first. Had he been there already? But no, perhaps they got on at the same time. 'I don't think so, old chap. Don't recognise you.'

'No, I'm sure. I do remember. I used to work in a theatre in the West End. You're from a musical family, aren't you? You have a very lovely . . .' He blushes beet, and that's when his voice stops and he leans back in his carriage seat again. 'Very well.' He stares for a second longer. 'Probably a different boy.'

'Probably.'

He takes from his navy breast pocket a silver case. 'Probably been sent to the front by now for all I know. Cigarette?'

The blond man sits up cautiously now, for the question is coming. He can taste it in the air.

Two men, of fighting age, neither in uniform.

What can the possibilities be?

He shakes his head softly at the cigarette case. 'No thank you.'

The train creaks, settling in for the night. Steam fizzes into the dusk.

But the man in navy doesn't ask about what he does for the war effort. Instead he says, 'I say, how do you know that fact about Stravinsky, and the trains? That's an odd fact to know.'

The blond man hesitates. It is a story he has not told for a very long time, and he does not know himself quite why he said that about Stravinsky – unless it was because he wanted to tell. And if these encounters we have with strangers – these days, these hours now with nothing to lose – are not for telling the story of the person we want to be, what are they for? What time might we have left now to tell that tale or be that person?

The blond man takes a breath. He watches his daydreams fly out of the train window and dance into the coal steam and the sidings clouds, and he begins to talk.

EIGHTEEN MONTHS LATER

BLETCHLEY, 1942

Chapter 1

The air was December cold, and Honey Deschamps turned
the collar of her coat up as she left the Ritzy's soggy warmth.
If she hadn't been quite so self-conscious, sitting between
the courting couple in RAF and WAAF uniforms and the
old smoker with the phlegmy cough, she'd have stayed for
a third viewing. Partly because she had paid for a ticket, and
merry-go-rounding it at the flicks was a way of staying out
of the cold. Partly to put off thinking about work the next
day. But mainly to reassure herself just one more time that
Joan Fontaine was right to stay with Cary Grant and he
wasn't trying to murder her after all. Because the first time
around Honey hadn't been convinced.

Mr Hitchcock had ended it all so abruptly, on the edge of
that cliff. That happy little twist, after all that *suspicion* Grant
wasn't a bad fellow after all. Honey thought that really,
really if Mr Hitchcock had played the movie out for just

another ten minutes, if you could have only seen the two merry lovers after The End credit, after they'd rounded the corner of that sea-top road and were on their way back to town, just when Joan Fontaine really was satisfied that Cary Grant wasn't about to kill her, *that* is when Honey thought he would have made his murderous move. Perhaps taken out a pistol, or simply shoved her over the edge.

She had kept a closer eye on him the second time around but even then she wasn't convinced. She thought that if it had been her in Joan Fontaine's position, she might have just played along with him for a while longer, let him drive back down that winding road, perhaps even all the way home. But she certainly wouldn't have trusted him. She'd have made her plans to get out at the earliest possible chance.

Oh, it was only a silly film. But then, she thought, as she crossed the street – just missing the bumper of a car that had sped up with its slatted blackout lights dipped – that was what happened to you now: that was what had been happening *a lot* recently. The most important thing in the world was going on all around and all she could do was fixate on a silly film. She dodged her way past a line of Home Guard soldiers and her mind looped again in tangles over whether Fontaine had been right or wrong to stay with him. And what it probably was, at the end of the day, it was probably actually if she thought about it, the fault of the writer. They had over-salted the sauce, made Cary Grant too villainous for cheap effect. There, it had backfired. They should have had Gregory Peck instead. She was not convinced of Cary Grant's innocence, and Joan Fontaine couldn't be that much of a fool.

She ducked into the grocer's on the corner of the high street, fumbled for the coupons Mrs Steadman had given her, bought bread and bacon for the household, and started off down the little Bletchley lane towards her billet. The town was quiet. There was a neat winter stillness in the air, a dogged calm that turned a blind eye to war anxiety, and lit its candles and drew its blackouts and sent warm smells fogging out of red-brick chimneys no matter how much rationing of food was going on.

Honey's eyes had grown more and more accustomed to the dark over the past few years. Was it the carrots? Mrs Steadman certainly seemed to think so, boiling them into pulp, mashing them into soups, baking them into cakes. She could see her own ice-breath as she strode, and it was curiously pleasing. It reminded her of childhood and Christmas, snow and pantomimes. She remembered the poster she had seen for the Park's Christmas revue, and like a magic trick it dropped the curtain on her happiness, the frosty pleasure of the walk, the finicky problems of Joan Fontaine.

Tomorrow she was back on day shift. She would be back at the Typex machine, trying to block out the tower of paper that fluttered taller the more she churned through it, filtering out footsteps and noises, curt calls from one room to another, the shunt of the wood pulley dragging messages between huts, tweed legs, ladies' chatter.

She sighed. Not all days were frantic, not all tweed-wearers were curt.

She had passed the dusty terracotta brickworkers' houses and was almost at the front gate to the cottage. The wobbling weft of the thatched roof was swimming out of the dark. Ridiculous billet. Like something Lewis Carroll would have imagined. It was called Yew Tree Cottage and was set in a clutch of three ancient buildings huddled together like witches, all wattle and daub, probably tradesmen's dwellings when built, but swelled through time into antique curiosities. How an odd couple like the Steadmans had ended up in such a place she had no idea.

She was so deep in her own thoughts that she almost didn't see the figure leaning against the blacked-out lamppost in front of the gate. In fact she didn't see him until he coughed and said 'Excuse me' in a soft voice. And even then it was not his face but the sense of another face much lower down that Honey's gaze was drawn to. Two bold wet eyes and a worried expression gazed at her from either side of a thin pointing nose.

'Dear me.'

'Sorry, Miss Deschamps, I didn't mean to startle you.' The man took a step closer and Honey saw in the glaze of cloudy moonlight that he was dressed in an overcoat, with a frayed trilby shadowing his brow. At his feet, on the end

14

of a long ribbon, was a greyhound, sniffing the air in short bursts as if tasting the smoke from nearby chimneys.

The first thought that came flooding in was that they were hauling her in for an emergency midnight shift. It would just be the night for it to happen, when her brain was foggy from too long at the Ritzy. The second was that there was a problem with Dickie. Every time some stranger called her name or startled her, she assumed it must be some hot water or pickle her brother had got into. And thirdly at the back of her mind were warnings about fifth columnists and perverts. But this man had a dog, and villains didn't usually have greyhounds.

'What a darling thing.' She dropped to her haunches, pulled her gloves off and ran her fingers into the silk behind the dog's ears. It turned its worried eyes on her, stuck its nose close and began sniffing her breath.

'Nijinksy.' The man smiled and tugged gently on the ribbon. 'He is something of a tart, you know.'

'Nijinsky.' She almost snorted. She gave a little shivering laugh. 'I never heard that for a dog. But it's perfect. Have you ever seen the real one?'

'As a matter of fact, yes. With the Ballets Russes. Could only have been two or three at the time.'

'Really?'

'Really. Look, I'm sorry I startled you.' The man reached under the belt of his coat, ran his hand up his torso and pulled out a brown paper package. Even in the gloom she saw the faded red of an airmail stamp and the black crown of the censor smearing its top surface.

'You are Honey Deschamps? I mean Miss Deschamps?'

'You're an odd sort of postman. Is that for me?' He didn't seem in a hurry to hand it over.

'Sorry,' he said again. 'I just rather thought it might be urgent, and was finishing a shift anyway.'

He must have seen the confusion on her face. 'It came to our hut, by mistake. You know that messenger girl. The one with the . . . I'm terribly sorry, I should have introduced myself. It's just I've seen you around the Park so very much I sort of feel I know you a little already, isn't that strange?' He spoke quickly, his eyes flicking to and fro. He still hadn't yet introduced himself, but she clocked him right then and there for who he was.

It would just be like one of the Hut 3 boys to call his greyhound Nijinsky. Very well, at least he wasn't Cary Grant come to murder her.

She drew in a breath and extended her hand for the package. This time he gave it to her. It was too dark to see anything properly but the government stamps, a faint address in a flourishing hand and the traces of a postmark in the top corner. It was heavier than she expected for something the size of a bar of shortbread, and there was a faint scent about it. Or perhaps that was coming off him. Most likely it was broken soap samples from her stepfather's factory.

His mission complete, the man looked lost. 'I got your billet address from Winman, in 6. I hope you don't mind.'

'Ah.' Winman was Head of her hut.

'It's a funny little cottage, that.' He peered past her down the garden path. The dog had taken an interest in the gate, sniffing it thoroughly with a low whine.

'Rabbits.' She pointed backwards with her thumb. 'They keep them in the hutch.'

'Ah. Lean times.'

'Well, not really with a hutch full of rabbits. And they breed like . . .'

'Badgers?'

'Exactly. Badgers. I was going to say bears.' The silence was awkward. 'But rabbit pie does get a little dull after a while. Do you hunt with him?'

'No, he belonged to the man in the farm where I was first billeted. He didn't want him. Nijinksy, wait.' The dog was pulling towards the edge of the garden fence, roused by the rabbity scent.

'I bet he didn't give him that name either.'

The man smiled. His face was blurred by the dark, but he looked handsome underneath the shadows of that hat. The muscles of his face were exaggerated, clinging to his cheek-bones like gristle. Honey thought for a tiny second, with the cold and the late hour and the act of kindness, that she might invite him for a cup of cocoa. But as soon as the thought hit her she batted it away. Ridiculous. Hut 3 man, steady on, Deschamps, she told herself. Smelly tweed most likely lurking beneath the coat. A chessman's brain, a mathematician? Worse, a *classicist*? Added to that Mrs Steadman would most likely hound him back down the street as far as the Eight Bells, holding her broom at a threatening angle.

'Well, thank you very much for coming out of your way. For a parcel. I mean, I could quite have got it tomorrow morning.'

'Pleasure.' He touched his frayed hat brim, and tugged on the ribbon of the dog, and they both walked away in the direction of the brickworkers' cottages. She watched the funny dainty jog of the greyhound's hindquarters making double-step with the man. What an odd couple they were. It was as his pace quickened into its natural rhythm that it struck Honey she had seen him before. There was something in his walk. But she couldn't think where. It wasn't the Park, she was certain. But Bletchley was tiny. It could have been the station or the butcher's or outside the Eight Bells.

'Oh,' she cried out. 'Excuse me, wait, will you?' A short trot in her corkboard heels and she had closed the distance between them. The parcel hung heavy in her left hand while she reached into her pocket with the right. She felt her fingers touch brown paper, then grease. With her fingernail she split off a tiny sliver of bacon rind. The dog had smelled it already and perked up. Honey dropped it into his mouth. The ridges of his teeth snagged on her fingers but he took it gently, swallowing it with a snap.

From the short run, her cheeks felt hot against the cold air. 'Can't resist a hound. My grandfather used to race them. Bigger ones, mind.'

The man was smiling, a fond, tight smile. First he looked at Honey, then at the dog. He suddenly extended his hand. 'Felix, by the way. Felix Plaidstow.'

She accepted his clutch. His palm was textured and dry, dead cold. 'Honey Deschamps. Well, you know that.' She wiggled the parcel. As they touched she became aware of the bacon grease still on her fingers. He really had very handsome eyes, the sort of eyes she imagined Russian men might have, cut like gems. Blue perhaps. The thought made her begin to witter. 'Of course you know my name, from the parcel. Or you wouldn't have sought me out, which was extremely nice of you. I'm excited to see what's inside. Must be better than rations. Early Christmas present, I don't doubt.'

She let go. For a second his hand stayed poised where she had left it. Then it faded back into the gloom by his side.

'I really had best be home, I just wanted to give the bacon to the dog. It was extremely, awfully nice of you. People do such small kindnesses these days, I mean, if one was to say the war had a silver—' She finally managed to rein in her tongue. He was staring at her with an unreadable, tilt-headed amusement.

'Goodnight,' she said, brightly like an idiot. 'Thank you again.'

19

'My pleasure. Again.'

The dog looked back at her over its shoulder this time, as they marched off.

Nijinksy, she thought. And he was so like a ballet dancer with his high-stepping paws and his moody eyes. Dickie would love that; she would have to write to him. But what a name for a hunting dog. So very typical of Hut 3, she thought, turning towards the cottage gate. The intelligence hut. If she'd been asked that night to make a play of Hut 3 she would have her cast already mapped out. A stout army man with a bristling moustache whose plain clothes weren't fooling anyone. Two or three Felixes – handsome Cambridge boys, wanting for soap but sensitive enough, good at languages. Not codebreakers. An American, some impossibly leggy eighteen-year-old girls, gooey. Then she wondered what the Hut 3 watch would come up with if asked to make a play of 6.

Mathematicians, male and female, tweed, fearsome women with the keys to the indexes round their necks. And in the Decoding Room, a frazzled typist with scarlet hair. That would be her. They would have to hire a costumier to pick holes in the woollen jumpers of the actors playing the cryptanalysts. There was a man in Honey's hut – Geoffrey Bald, his name was – who sometimes came to work in his pyjamas.

She held the parcel close to her face. The postmark was foreign; that was what was different about it, the alphabet.

The Amber Shadows

She looked up the street to see if she could spot Felix Plaidstow or the dog but they had melted into the blackout.

At the front door she turned her latchkey stealthily. The smell in the hall was moist and sharp; tinned mandarins and suet. There would be a tray left in the kitchen, that was the evening meal way. She jumped, as she always did, when she caught the glow of Mrs Steadman's luminous bird hanging on the hatstand. It was removable and could be pinned to any number of headpieces, or, in an emergency, used as an enormous brooch; a precautionary measure to being run over by cars or bicycles in the blackout, government advised.

Mr Steadman was lurking under the stairs in his dark overalls, fiddling with one of the narrow shelves that served as bunks in case of air raids. Bletchley had taken only three hits during the months London was battered, none of them this far south. But every night Mr Steadman muddled with his sandbags and his bullseye lamps and his ration boxes under the stairs. In those three raids, Mrs Steadman had crowded them all into that poky cupboard armed with bowlfuls of raw carrots. She held no truck with the Anderson shelter in the garden or the Morrison shelter in the kitchen. She didn't believe in corrugated iron or wire cages. Her aunt had been killed in an Anderson shelter that took a direct hit in Southampton. Going to the communal shelter at the brickworks was out of the question. The Steadmans despised their neighbours.

Mr Steadman grunted something that might have been a question, and Honey muttered back something about the

Ritzy being full and made towards the kitchen. She took the slippery bacon in its brown paper from her pocket and left it in the cold cupboard. From the front parlour she could hear the hum of the wireless, and the crack of knitting needles. On the hall table was a pile of balaclavas, every shade of pink going, next to a box labelled up with a War Office postal address. She wondered how the soldiers in the African desert would take to magenta.

On the upstairs landing she noticed a sliver of pale light coming from underneath Rebecca's doorframe, and wondered whether she should knock for once, but hadn't the energy.

Her own room was freezing, its spartan space filled only by a bed, a wardrobe, a small table and a chest of drawers. There was little upholstery to keep in the heat and it always felt cool, which was a boon in summertime but not now. The parcel still in her hand, her coat still on, she turned up the gaslight. She flicked with her foot the coloured rag-knot rug that lay across the centre of the room. It shifted back easily from the polished boards. One thing that could be said for Mrs Steadman, she kept a charwoman and she kept the place spotless. But that was where her hospitality ended. Honey dropped to her knees, then her bottom, then extended her long legs along the floor. The wood was warm, an oasis in the cold room, sitting directly above the parlour hearth. Downstairs Mrs Steadman nursed a glowing fire every night for herself and her husband at which 'guests', as she called her billettees, were not welcome.

Honey stretched out until she was lying flat on her back, the heat seeping through the wool of her coat. It was growing thready in patches but the clothing ration meant she couldn't purchase another until the New Year. She would have to ask her friend Moira to help mend it, she was clueless with a needle.

After a few minutes she had thawed enough to undo the belt. She sat up and took the parcel onto her knee. Its wrapper was an odd sort, thicker than British brown parcel paper, and with that strange postmark in the corner that she now saw bore Cyrillic lettering. The paper had been stamped twice, by two separate censors, one of them British, the other with the same Cyrillic. For a second it popped into her head that it might be a bomb. She took it gingerly to her ear, to her face. The phrase *curiosity killed the cat* entered her mind very slowly. But there was no ticking, only the sweet woody smell.

She slid her finger under the corner and carefully tore the top rim. Whatever was inside was wedged tight. She could feel the soft smudge of newspaper padding under her fingertip. Tearing the rest of the wrapper off, she found herself holding a tin; a gaudy red and white thing with nothing front or back but a picture of coloured pencils fanned out as if inviting you to select one.

She frowned. Pins and needles had begun to settle in her legs and she shifted her weight. Moving sent a shiver of cool draught down from the window. She ran her finger round the rim of the tin but it was sealed. Funny, because there was something a little old-fashioned about it. Perhaps the design looked dated, or perhaps it was faded, she couldn't tell in the light. She dug her nail into the sealant, just as she had done with the bacon in her pocket, and sliced efficiently around it. With a small pop came that smell again, sweet and musty; an older woman's perfume, almost like her mother's.

She pulled away the lid and saw more paper; this time carefully pressed tissue. Thinking it to be the strangest game of pass the parcel she had ever played, she smiled as she tore the final wrapper off, the thought of the man in the dark coat, with his greyhound at heel, melting into her mind.

In her palms was a cold, solid lump.

It looked like a square of glass, heavily smoked, shattered, then mosaicked back together, and brown, held together by a thin foil square of steel or tin as the sandwich filling in the middle. It was only slightly larger than the width of a deck of cards, and about a quarter of an inch thick. She turned it over. On one side it was hard and glossed to a shine, on the other the surface was softer and more pliable.

She snorted in disbelief. Was it some sort of giant brooch without backing? An ornament someone had forgotten to carve?

The packaging sat at her feet, and she reached for it. The Russian alphabet, the boxy backwards R's and diagonal H's and hard Y's. She saw it now in the postmark 'Ленинград'.

One of the few Russian words they all knew in Hut 6 from books and newspaper reports. Leningrad. Where the Nazi army had arrived over a year ago. Where they had begun their assault on the structure of the east. So many decrypted signals had travelled through her hands bearing that name, it had become a keyword for the cribsters in the room across the corridor. But who in Leningrad would know her name, let alone have the will or wherewithal to smuggle a parcel past the censors and onto international post routes? And what the devil was it? Just a slab of broken smoked glass?

She turned it in her hands, still half-fearful that it might after all be some kind of ingenious bomb, bracing the sharp corners of the square rather than the flat sides. She raised it to her nose to breathe in more of the scent. On the way up it caught the glow of the gaslamp, and a silent firework of mosaic red sprang to life; a network of cracks and veins, bubbles and pools, an impeccable tawny jewel. And that was when the pieces dropped into place in her mind, and she suddenly felt – even if she did not yet know – what she was looking at.

Chapter 2

There were two things that separated the Park estate, that sat along the lane from Bletchley station, from others like it. The first was the eight-foot chain-link fence that surrounded the perimeter, topped by curls of barbed-wire. The second was the people.

The Park buzzed like a university campus at most times of day, but it was something else to watch at changeover time, which came every eight hours. Quarter to eight in the morning and a patch of land no bigger than the Buckingham Palace grounds would be transformed into the like of London's Piccadilly Circus. In each direction, to and fro, close to a thousand people poured past the gates, on foot and bicycle, waving papers at the red-capped staff of the Military Police, spilling out of khaki rusting buses and grey jeeps and old glossy black Rollers requisitioned for the purpose. When the incoming buses had emptied, the night-shifters would spill onto them in the opposite direction. It was exactly like a spilling, coming off night shift, the feeling of pouring your jellied limbs into a leatherette seat, turning down the bus blind and cranking down the dirt roads to the out-of-town billets.

You could tell the ones coming off night shift even before they got onto the buses by their faces: brains leeched of energy but still doing the jitterbug overtime. Their clothes would smell of the coke stoves kept inside the Park's huts and sometimes the steak and kidney pudding they'd been offered at three a.m. break in the cafeteria. The Wrens – the Women's Royal Navy Service – could be picked out by their blue uniform, skewed after a night doing whatever furtive and noisy things they did inside the wood walls of Hut 11.

The entrance gates stood to the left of the estate, and led sidelong towards the mansion. To get the proper postcard view of the house – the sepia one that had sneaked into gift shops while the old aristocratic owners still had it – you had to wander down past the lake, towards the front perimeter. Standing, looking across the water's cool surface, you could see the red-brick and sandstone building emerge hodge-podge beyond a bank of lawns. It was oddly shaped, made from memories of its owners' travels: a loon-eyed gryphon, a half-barrel of faux-ancient windows, a little bit of medieval cloister taking up part of the front wall. A nub of conservatory came poking out at one side and somewhere behind it a bronze roof dome had faded into a frivolous mint green hat.

Honey had joined the Park in late spring 1941, a year and a half ago. Then, the odd angles had looked beautiful and eccentric; Sahara gold and hot red. But in winter, on an overcast day like today, it had the look of a joke out of season; a jester's costume in an old wardrobe. Soon after she'd arrived she'd found herself pressed at lunch between a debutante scandalised at its vulgarity and a messenger girl gaping at its glamour.

It was to the right of the mansion, as you stared at it, that most of the wooden huts had sprung up; giant rabbit hutches for burrowing workers. Everyone employed at the Park had to stay within their own creosoted boundaries; to go into any hut other than your own was forbidden, except to the beer hut for refreshments, the administration hut with permission, or the mansion, to dine, for recreation or because you had been summoned.

Winman, Head of 6 – Honey's hut – liked to paste on a noticeboard in the entrance to the hut morale-boosting achievements that came from their work, and because of this Honey did have a vague mental map of what went on where. But it had its limits.

Everything started with the raw intercepted signals that came in to Hut 6 from listening stations around the country, brought by motorcycle – she knew this as she'd had a brief stint as a motorcycle dispatch rider early in the war that had ended in tears when the roads became frosty. Or sometimes they came in by teleprinter. After the messages were logged, the ciphers were broken using cribs – snippets of messages deduced through guesswork – and other cryptanalytical hocus-pocus. It was then that the stack of intercepts would come to Honey and her colleagues in the Decoding Room. Usually there were four or five of them on shift, each with a Typex machine rigged up to the decryption settings of that particular broken key – for there were many German keys in a day – and they would churn their way as fast as they could through the pile of intercepts. Hut 3 was where the final decoded messages went, for assessment or analysis for action in the field. Sometimes the men from Hut 3 would come through looking for a duplicate or missing message. More often than not the two huts communicated only by a wooden pulley and box, linking them.

Between them 3 and 6 dealt with army and Luftwaffe signals. Hut 2 was where the beer was found. Or black tea or powdered milk or sometimes horrid scones made with currants – dry fly cakes. Hut 1 was where you went if you had a problem with your billet. Hut 11 was the noisy hut. (No one knew what the machines did but according to a cribster called Wilf the Wrens who operated them all got so hot in there that they worked in their underwear. This had not been verified.) Huts 4 and 8 were connected in the same way 3 and 6 were. Huts 5, 7, 9 and 10 did God knows what. She didn't think there was a Hut 12, but there were other small toilet huts and garages and cots at the back of the mansion where they kept pigeons. Perhaps Hut 7 was for the pigeon boys.

She creaked open the door to Hut 6. The air inside was even colder than outside, a stale coldness like a cheese store. The windows in the hut were closed and blacked out, and coke stove fumes seeped out from under each room door into the main corridor in acrid channels. On the notice-board directly in front of her a blotter sheet had been torn out and in pink pencil was written in capitals, 'SOUTH-HAMPTON RAID DIVERTED', and below 'intelligence from the YELLOW 12 December allowed RAF from Chicksands to be scrambled and German targets foiled. Winman.'

Like everything in Britain now, signage was the enemy and the doors that branched off the hut's main corridor were blank – you simply needed to know where you were going. Honey's room was last on the left. There were four women in already, bent over cups of black tea steaming perfumed ribbons. At the end of the room Miss Mooden, Head of Room, sat at her neatly stacked desk beside a black Bakelite telephone. Honey took the desk nearest the door. Beside her Typex, underneath the lamp, someone had left a magazine open: 'Ask Sister Mary: Headaches and Boils.'

No one had started yet. The machine in front of her sat like a grumpy toad, waiting. The Typexes were clumpy plastic-and-steel typewriters, about three and a half feet wide, with extra cogs sprouting from the sides and a reel on top that formed the toad's hump. Coiled around this reel was a roll of thin white tape that spat out the letters as you typed. She ran her fingers around the mechanics to check nothing was loose and everything was oiled. The in-trays were empty, which meant the night shift had worked through the previous day's keys, and no one had broken into the next day's yet.

In a quiet voice Mooden was explaining the work to a new girl standing by her desk. 'You can do the pasting today. It'll be very fast once they get typing. But the pasting's easy. You don't need to think about anything, just cut the tape they give you into strips and stick them to a piece of paper with that brush.'

'Can I ask what's a crib? And is it the same as a menu?' the girl asked.

'Oh.' Mooden's face froze. She looked round to see if anyone would jump in to help her, or perhaps if anyone was going to listen in while she muddled through an explanation. Honey saw her eyes land on Moira Draper, sitting at the next station.

'Moira, could you . . .?'

'I've not even had my tea yet.' Moira had her hand round the back of her own machine, straightening out the wires. 'You don't need to know what those are, love, it'll come with time.'

'We'll just stick with the pasting today, I think, since it's your first day. Don't worry if you hear any funny words. Moira can help you if you get stuck.'

'Anyway,' Beatrix Loughborough – Lady if you believed the rumours – was saying, across the table from Honey. 'What I heard was that she was followed by a man all the way from the station. No one knows whether he'd come into the town from outside, or if he was from town.' Beatrix was at the machine directly opposite, bent forward whispering to the others. Next to her Sylvia, a quiet girl from Aberdeen, was picking around the edges of her cuticles, pressing back the skin.

'But surely . . .' interrupted Moira, then trailed off as Beatrix steamed on.

'*She* said, or rather what I heard she said was that she knew he was following her for some time. She turned a street too early, and he did the same.'

'Who's this?' Honey asked.

Moira leaned over. 'Some girl in another hut says she was followed home by a man, couple of nights ago.'

Honey felt her neck prickle, a draught passing.

Sylvia said, 'And she didn't blow her whistle or run?'

'Do you carry a whistle?' Beatrix asked coolly. 'Anyway, he asked for her *papers*,' she mouthed the word, 'and she showed him her identity card, and then he said, "No, your Bletchley Park papers. Show me your 1250, your BP papers."' Beatrix paused.

'I heard—' Sylvia said.

'So she showed him,' Beatrix went on. 'She dug in her pocket and pulled them out. She said at that point if she'd had a torch she would have shone it in his face. As it was, there was enough moonlight for her to see he had RAF chevrons on his shoulder. Not sure how many.'

'No torch, no whistle,' Moira murmured.

'And then,' Beatrix said, 'he looked at her papers and said, "You shouldn't have shown me these."'

Mooden at that moment finished a point of explanation to the new girl and there was silence.

'But then what happened?' asked Moira.

'What do you mean?'

'Did he give her back her papers?'

'I assume so.'

'So he didn't arrest her or . . . drag her into a bush?'

'I don't know,' said Beatrix, leafing through a pile of loose red-stamped sheets. 'I didn't hear the end of the story. But I mean the point is: don't talk to strange men. No matter what they're wearing. Or not. Like that man fiddling with himself on the train last week.'

'Did you say he was RAF?' said Honey. 'Uniformed?'

'Mmmm.' Beatrix was dropping oil into the back of her Typex.

'Can't trust Raffies,' said Moira. Beatrix looked up sharply and their eyes met. She was wearing the map scarf again. It was stuffed low under her cardigan but Honey could see it, they all could, ruffled at the base of her pale neck. The silk map she wore. Round her black hair, at her throat, threaded round her shoulders on top of her coat. Beatrix's fiancé had been an airman, shot down during the summer. He had given her the silk map of Italy, a memento of a previous trip, standard RAF issue, the silk being easier than tough paper to bunch up in their pockets. Moira looked away but didn't apologise.

'Did he . . . he didn't have a dog with him, did he?' Honey asked softly. A blush was creeping up her neck, along with a crawling shiver.

'No idea. I only know what I heard, that's it. But the point is, official or not, just . . . just don't show your papers to anyone. Even if they say they're official. They're probably not or they wouldn't ask for them.' She added after a pause, 'She's being disciplined. By Captain Tiver.'

There was a sharp bang down the corridor. Fist on wood. Raised voices began to filter through the walls. It meant another key was on its way to being broken. They didn't have long before the rush of paper messages would come. Chatter changed rapidly to whisky and Americans.

'One of the Wrens smuggled in a case, because of course they're trained in the Scotch Highlands. They have a whole crate of the stuff at the Woburn Abbey billets, you really didn't know? It's common knowledge.' Beatrix was baiting Moira now.

'You'd brave the rats and the broken loos for a splash of whisky, would you? Woburn's a dump.'

'It's a country manor, of course there are rats! It doesn't mean they're crawling over people's laps while they take tea.'

'Take tea, do they? The Wrens take tea? And I thought they were here to work.' Moira stretched back in her chair and sucked on a Player's. She leaned forward and dropped ash on the blotter in front of her, right on top of His Majesty's Service. 'I know this: they have a throne at Woburn on which to do their business. The toilet is actually raised on a dais.'

'I heard they sunbathe naked on the roof,' said Sylvia.

Moira threw back her head and laughed. 'Not in this weather. Your nipples would turn to rock. Honey can tell you all about that.'

It was like this with Moira. 'Honey can tell you . . . Remember when we . . .' She was a great chronicler of activities; she remembered everything. And she remembered it so that you were both having as much fun as each other, or both in as much trouble as each other. That time we took off our clothes and swam in the quarry (Honey had been petrified). That time we got our knuckles rapped for having bicycle lights on in the blackout (it had only been Moira with the lights on). Remember last summer when the Wrens were sunbathing on Woburn Abbey roof and we all took our tops off and some of the Eagle Squadron flew low over. Honey hadn't been able to look anyone in RAF uniform in the eye for a month afterwards. But

Moira had roared with laughter, it had poured out of her red mouth.

Moira had been in the Research Cottage in the Park's early days, one of the original Dilly's Fillies, the brainbox women Professor Dilly Knox had handpicked for his Bletchley Park staff. She was educated at St Hilda's, Oxford, mathematics, top of her class, a grafter with a pub landlord for a father, a string of scholarships and a Northumberland accent. The rumour was that while she was working there she had made some breakthrough that saved a pack of merchant ships from German U-boats. But as Winman had said, 'No one would believe a twenty-year-old girl could have saved them anyway,' so it didn't matter that the credit would never come. No one knew why she was working now in the Typex room with the decoding girls. It was one of the Park's mysteries.

A telephone rang down the hall. 'Job up!' The cry pierced through three walls' worth of flimsy wood.

'Want tea?' Sylvia had scraped her chair back.

Beatrix rolled her eyes. 'Don't put the kettle on the stink machine.' She eyeballed the coke stove. 'It takes on the flavour.'

After a few minutes of shivering Honey decided she wanted her coat back on. She had just rucked it off the hook when the door slammed back.

'Got Vulture.' A boy with sandy hair, extravagantly long at the fringe, thrust out a sheaf of fresh cold intercept papers.

Blocks of capital letters, scrambled nonsense language, were scrawled in pencil across each foolscap gridded sheet. Coloured underlining – grey in this case – marked them in parts.

Beatrix stood and reached across. 'Thank you, Poo.'

'Who broke the code this time?' Sylvia still had the kettle in her hand.

'Me.'

The women made merry hell at him, rubbing his hair, scoffing and tickling his ribs until his pullover rode up to his belly button. He roared at them to stop. The new girl stood a few steps away, bracing a smile. Mooden pretended to be busy.

'You lying scamp.' Beatrix flicked his ears.

Poo caught his breath. His freckled face burned. 'All right, it was Geoffrey Bald. But don't give him credit.'

'It's the pyjamas,' said Moira.

The tea was forgotten. They sat down at their desks, took a second to shake their shoulders and crack their necks. The Typex machines were unwieldy and stiff and one had to adopt a sort of hunched position to get any sort of purchase or speed on them.

The intercept papers were distributed, settings were given out for that day's Vulture key, correspondent to the Enigma settings that had just been broken. Poo helped Beatrix set her machine so she could pass it on to the rest. They shifted and clicked the cogs.

Though the Typexes were British-built they had been set up to replicate the German Enigma machines used to encrypt signals by the Nazi army, navy and Luftwaffe. Enigma – the unbreakable cipher machine that, among others, the 20-year-old Northumberland girl next to Honey had cracked – could be set to any number of keys, each for a different campaign or regiment. Vulture was used by the military on the Eastern Front, named because they – at the Park – used a pencil the shade of a vulture's plume to mark the decrypts in that particular key. There were also Red, Yellow, Light Blue and Green. They had run out of colours after that and called the next one Ermine.

Honey had what she always told people was 'poetry German'. 'I have poetry German,' she would say and even as she said it feel the little cringe inside because it was the kind of thing her mother would come out with. But she didn't have any better way of putting it. Four years of studying Goethe and Nietsche and she still had only 'poetry German'. But it meant she could read the plain text coming out the other end of her Typex, even when she didn't want to. It meant that last year when Luftwaffe Yellows were being broken daily, she was one of two on her watch who knew what was coming to Britain before it happened. The coded intercepts went in, the decrypted plain text came out. That time it had been about supplies, manoeuvres, incendiaries, strategy. Sometimes they'd name the towns that were their targets. *Korn*, they all discovered too late, was code for Coventry.

The Amber Shadows

Sometimes she'd have to wait for the newspapers to find out if the messages she had seen had been passed on in time, and the bombings stopped. Sometimes they weren't stopped and there would be photographs in the next day's newspapers. The worst of it was connecting it back to what you had seen in the intercepted messages; when you noticed 'ten kilos of gunpowder' in one message, and then the next day the fish factory in Putney went up and the south of London stank like a chip shop for days.

There were the wheels to shift, plugs to adjust, wires to be connected correctly. All was done quickly and quietly. Honey took one of the papers from the top of the pile and began to type. It was five past eight.

After a few minutes she checked that the strip of type coming out the other end looked German. Poo – Rupert Findlay, his parents had named him – was still hovering in the doorway. The cribsters always had a buzz just after breaking a day's key. 'How's your mother, Honey?' he shouted above the din. Her fingers faltered for a second.

'Still too old for you,' Beatrix shot back crisply.

Honey turned her neck to show him she was smiling, a friendly smile, not a nasty one, and in return the boy's face turned crimson. Surely it was she who should blush, she thought. All the boys, ever since she could remember, every single one of them had a fancy for Martha Deschamps. She turned back to the typing, picking it back up like a pianist who'd slipped a note, and saw Poo from the corner of her eye wriggling out of the room.

It was an hour or so into the pile when a low gasp across the desk next pierced her concentration. Beatrix had stopped. 'My God,' she said. The clacks around them faded a notch. 'Are you reading what's coming out?'

Honey could see the German but she wasn't making sense of the words. It was tough to read when they were bunched into groups of five letters, regardless of the word breaks. She shook her head dumbly.

'"FYDOR ROKATOV, WOOD, GOLD, OIL, CANVAS, KONIGSBERG, MELTZER, THIRTY-FIVE KILOS, WOOD, GILT, KONIGSBERG, TWO AMBER CLOCKS, TEN KILOS". What does this remind you of, Honey?'

Honey froze as the key clatters dropped away. She felt beneath her hands not the round lumps of the letter hammers but instead, growing slowly, one flat, tiny slab of amber, hard as burnt sugar, sticky as burnt sugar, leaving a glue on her skin that the others in the room couldn't fail to see or smell. She looked down at her hands.

They were empty.

Beatrix was answering her own question, pleased with herself. 'They're looting more of Leningrad. Do you remember this time last year . . .?' But Mooden had caught her eye and even now Beatrix was reaching over, slicing the strip of message in two and passing it on to the desk of the new girl with the jar of paste. 'Grab hold of that one.'

She started up again. The hammering of the keys throbbed at Honey's temples. On her first day here, in the Decoding Room, Beatrix had told her that she was replacing the seventh girl who'd had a nervous breakdown over the noise. 'The seventh!' Beatrix had said, firing the words at Honey like cannon, like a challenge.

They were looting around Leningrad. The palaces. The houses. Just like last year, just like the signals that came through this time last year, when they had looted . . . she knew she remembered.

Her stomach dropped. She stood up. Mooden's eyes flicked onto her.

'I think I just need . . .' she began to say, then the gazes of the workers around the table all trailed onto her one by one, each woman's machine pulling to a halt. She looked down at her hands, imagining again the weight of the little slab. She felt its weight pressing on her, pushing her back down into her chair. 'No, I'm fine.'

'One of the boys,' said Mooden without looking up, 'got hold of some coffee. I'll get you one – when it's time for break.'

As Honey threaded a new intercept paper into the front of her machine, she felt the warmth of a gaze on her, looked up and found Moira staring sidelong before returning to her own typing.

Chapter 3

The Index Room was on the right, close to the hut's front door. As she walked the corridor, passing each chamber, little noises filtered out: pencil scrapings, hushed voices. The Typex racket was still audible even at the furthest end of the corridor.

Honey smiled, then worried that her smile was frozen, as she asked the girl on the reception desk to find her the intercepts from last year, filed under the word she was looking for.

It did not mean anything. It could not. How could anything have passed a Russian censor and made it as far as Britain without being intercepted? How could anyone have known to reach her at the Park's London PO Box? Who would have told him she was here? Her mother? Unthinkable. Dickie then? But if Dickie knew he was alive, then Dickie himself would have told her. Dickie would have shrieked it down the telephone, he'd have turned up on her billet doorstep. He knew where she lived.

The girl came back with a stack of files and slapped them down. Honey tried to focus on not sweating. Her forehead felt sticky despite the cold. Perhaps the coke stove was more powerful in this room. It certainly felt close, and acrid, and now, there, she had left a sweat fingerprint on the file's card covering.

She turned towards the corner of the room.

'Excuse me.'

She turned back. The girl cast her eye curiously up Honey's face. 'You have a lipstick mark on your cheek.'

Honey's hand shot up to rub it off, and she felt the burn spread across her face. *Burn.* The feeling became the word, and then the word became . . . *burnstone. Bernstein. Amber.* Once again, the fragment of smoked glass began taking shape in her hand. She could feel it. She looked down and saw the brown index folder in her palm shape-shift, its manila shade darken. It began to feel cool and brittle.

'You have to sign for those.'

'Oh?' She looked down again. She was holding paper. Paper and card only. 'I just want to check something for a second.'

'Doesn't matter. Rules.' The girl chewed her pencil end and shrugged. 'Thank you.' She clipped the word as Honey scribbled her name in a register.

'I don't know who reads these anyway,' the girl muttered, taking back the book. Behind her several women were bent over box files, raking through library cards, making notes. Honey retreated to the corner of the room and opened the file. There were six cards listed under the keyword. *Bernstein.*

Last year, she had blocked it out while it was happening. It was too much to think of. But while the siege of Leningrad raged on through encrypted messages – calls for ammunition, troop commanders, names of the dead, names of the captured – there was another list that had slipped through, and she held it now. Creased from the Park hands it had passed through, the men who decided how to act upon it, the typing at the crease was almost rubbed blank, just as one day the contents the message spoke of had been blanked out, removed from the Pushkin Palace, the Detskoye Selo, the old Catherine Palace in Leningrad.

'BERNSTEIN SECHS TONNEN. FUNFUNDDREISSIG PLATTEN, VERGOLDET UHR'. *Amber, six tons. Thirty-five panels, gilt clock* . . . She had remembered. A year ago, after blazing into Leningrad, the Nazis had dismantled the Amber Room from the Catherine Palace and shipped it to Konigsberg in Germany. *The Times* had run a piece. 'Eighth Wonder of the World: Suspected Looted.' Their special correspondent had seen a goods train piling out of the palace complex, and the messages that came intercepted to the Park confirmed it. Six tons of amber panels, forty-seven chairs, eight kilos of bronze and gilt, all stolen and relocated to Konigsberg Castle.

The Amber Shadows

The Nazis had it. The Nazis had the pieces of the Amber Room. She turned the thought over in her mind, trying to turn it backwards, trying to wipe the sticky stolen sugar feeling from her palms. Why was it sticking in her mind, the idea that was what it could be? That small flat piece of brown gemstone. Could it be amber? Could it be *stolen* amber? If the man she was thinking of, the man who had once worked for the Pushkin Palace, if he was still alive, had he taken it before the Nazis came? Where had he sent the piece from? And what was it to her? A keepsake? A memento of something that had been destroyed? She had to talk to Dickie.

'The index? What are you doing in the Index Room?'

Honey hadn't realised she was standing in the doorway, the back of her head visible from the corridor. She felt a cold rinse over her skin. 'Moira.'

'Did I startle you? I am sorry. You don't look well today, if you don't mind my saying.'

'I needed to find a duplicate, for one of the messages.'

Moira's eyebrows pulled back a little. 'Gap in one of yours, is it?'

'Yes.'

'Well, you might be better trying the Registration Room first. If it's one of today's intercepts they won't have indexed it yet.'

'Ah.'

'Registration's that way.'

'Yes, I know, I might just try . . .'

Moira started to move past her, then looked back over her shoulder. On her lips was a faint friendly smile. 'Name of a soldier, is it? I'm sure he'll be home for Christmas. Don't worry too much. You can put your head in all sorts of spins here looking out for those boys. By the way . . .' She broke off. Her face was an opaque mask. Behind it hovered some mischief or excitement trying to slip through. 'No, nothing. I have something to tell you. Have to go for a jimmy riddle first. But I'll see you across at the beer hut.'

Honey's arms were shaking as she pressed shut the door to Hut 2. She spied Moira already ahead, hanging from her fingers six empty blue-rimmed mugs like enormous rings. Pasted to the door was a notice: 'Crockery shortage – bring your own. Mrs Crisp.' She took a moment to acclimatise to the sweaty air and entered the squeeze bubbling outwards from the serving station.

On the gloss green paint on the walls, condensation had gathered in thick dribbles. Men in tatty woollen jackets were clustered, debating the rules of backgammon. When she caught up with Moira, Honey was trembling so hard she thought it must be visible. Every piece of her wanted to shout out her secret, what she had been given, what she had discovered. The only way to plug it was with small talk. 'That's a nice blouse. Did you make it?'

'This?' Moira pointed at her red silk. 'It's my mother's. Well, mine now. Here.' She shoved three of the empty mugs into Honey's hands.

To her annoyance Honey began to blush. 'She's got nice taste in blouses,' she said, struggling to get her fingers through the handles. The queue moved forward and she felt the pull of Moira's fingers on her sleeve. 'You were miles away this morning. Someone special?'

'Could say the same to you.'

Across the hut wall, behind the serving lady, was a picture of a woman in a knotted turban with black lashes and scarlet lips. The words 'Beauty is your Duty' floated beneath her in pink, then it listed all the things you could do for the war effort. Wear rouge. Put your hair in a silk scarf or glamour band to save washing it. Buy 'Mitchell's Stockingless Cream'.

Moira smiled, her eyes lowered a fraction and she shook her head. A laugh escaped her. 'All in good time. Not here.'

The canteen woman slopped teaspoons of powdered milk into their cups, displacing brown liquor onto the floor. Next to her a lady in slacks and a tabard with a bent back was brandishing a sugar spoon.

'How many?'

'Six,' Honey said.

The woman widened her eyes.

'I mean there are six teas. One spoonful in each.'

'Toast? Jam?'

'Is there jam?'

'Marmite. Is there Marmite, Dolly?'

'There's Marmite. Just a scrape each, mind.'

'No thanks.' Honey shuddered.

'Bring the cups back,' Dolly, in her slacks, shouted.

'They're our cups,' said Moira.

Honey felt a jab in the ribs. 'That,' whispered Moira, drawing so close Honey could smell her face cream, 'is Alan Turing over there. Do you know who he is?'

'No.'

'He's—' She broke off. Moira was in the habit of opening her mouth before thinking. 'He used to work in the Cottage.'

'Oh yes?'

'Yes. But mad as a fish. They say he's buried treasure in the grounds of the Park. He's taken his bonds out in silver and buried them. Because he doesn't trust the banks any more. Do you believe that?'

'I don't know.' Honey blushed again. The story had tripped a memory, and now things were beginning to materialise in an odd pattern in her head. Buried treasure. Things hidden.

Moira continued towards the door. She was anxious and keen today, jolly. Her manner was putting Honey on edge. They were halfway across the room when a girl dressed in cat ears interrupted them, selling tickets for the Christmas Revue. She looked familiar. Honey remembered her doing a similar turn in the canteen when the auditions were on. She had singled Honey out: 'Perfect for a Principal Boy with that chest.'

Moira's eyes were already gleaming. 'Christmas Revue! What do you think? It'll be a giggle. Are there songs? Do they sing? Do they do jokes about the Park? Has it been written specially? Is there Scottish dancing?'

The girl tackled Moira's questions like a batsman, wielding an iron sell in BBC English. Honey looked down and saw she was wearing Tudor pantaloons and tights stained carrot-tan. Katie Brewster, that was her name. She was a secretary. Well, they were all secretaries, officially. Moira delved into her purse. 'We'll take three.'

'Three?' Honey said.

'You're coming, I'm coming, and someone else is coming.'

'Who? Beatrix?'

'Beatrix.' Moira snorted. 'Not Beatrix. Someone else.'

'Who?'

Moira ignored her while she handed over the money and tore off the raffle-style tickets with printed numbers on them. When Katie had gone, she dropped her voice. 'Do you believe in real, hard, smack-you-on-the-nose love? The kind of love in the flicks?'

Honey was about to say, 'Like Cary Grant and Joan Fontaine?' Instead she said, 'I thought you didn't like the flicks.'

Moira shook her head impatiently. 'There is someone. Someone special. I think. I sort of know. If you know what I mean.'

'Is he at the Park?'

She thinned her eyes. 'You'll see.'

For some reason, at that moment a terrible blow of anxiety struck Honey. She thought immediately, with no foundation and yet with absolute conviction, that Moira must mean the man she had met last night: Felix Plaidstow. And the thought winded her with an intensity she did not expect. She hadn't even seen his face properly. He had only told her his name as he was leaving. And yet when she thought of him, when she thought of Moira's secret, and when she connected the two – when she thought of the possibility that the two might be connected – it had a strange, dreadful effect. She felt as if she might be in the grip of fate, as if fate had placed Felix in her path for Moira to steal him. The room seemed to distort a notch, as if the world had been tilted very slightly diagonally, or she had crossed into another realm and was having a bad dream.

Two women in WAAF uniform were standing there with a paper bag, offering something, and again Moira was laughing – by God she was jolly today. She had put down one of the mugs and was popping something into her mouth. She put her hand back into the bag and pulled out a sticky white lump then held it to Honey's lips.

'Go on, go on,' Moira was saying. She was holding her own expression very tightly. Her eyes were baited with sparkle.

Honey opened her mouth for the sweet. It tasted foul. Chemical, nutty and sour.

She felt her face sieze. They all guffawed.

'It's bloody horrible. You lot are trying to murder us.' Moira spat hers into her hand now.

The women laughed, open-mouthed. Both had shiny scarlet lips that contrasted prettily with their khaki.

'What is it?' Honey asked.

'Cobnut marzipan. We gathered the nuts ourselves. There's hundreds of them around. Thought we'd be clever, you see, for the Christmas cakes. Now the government have outlawed icing.'

'What?'

'Marzipan on cakes. It's illegal now. Too much sugar. This is cobnuts and saccharine.'

'Tastes like nail polish and the custard they serve here,' Honey said.

'Inventive though, aren't we, duck?'

'My thumbs are burning from these cups. Honey, let's get back to work. You hold this one for a sec and I'll grab the door.'

Outside Moira hurried back in the direction of Hut 6 in sure footsteps, steady on the frost. Honey's skirt was too tight to keep up but she tried, in skating waddles. The lake in front of the manor was cut through with white ferns of frost; doilies floating on slate murk.

'Can skate on that in a few days if it keeps up. God, you do like a dawdle, don't you? Is it that skirt? I could put in a slit and widen it for you. No point dawdling in this weather.'

They passed two girls on a bench in front of the lake, one of them trying to light a flimsy cigarette for the other. Honey didn't recognise either. It was real then, it was true that you could see people every day here you had never set eyes on before. It didn't matter that she hadn't seen Felix Plaidstow here at the Park before, even though he said he worked in Hut 3. It didn't matter that he had given her that strange gift. Why did she have this doubt in her mind about him? Why had she connected him to Moira, and why couldn't she stop thinking . . .

Suddenly she couldn't take it any more. She began catastrophising: his tilted head, his greyhound, Moira's new beau. 'This chap of yours,' she said slowly.

Moira stopped in the thicket of bushes that connected the lake to the cluster of huts. As she turned her eyes flamed. 'Honey, I never thought I'd say it, never in a million years. But he's . . .' She paused and rubbed her lips together, then said the word quietly like it was the most secret part. 'American.'

'Really?' Honey's stomach sprang. 'How . . . how lovely.' She felt lighter almost instantly.

'Do you like their accents?'

Honey hadn't time to answer, before Moira, turning the path and emerging first from the bushes, said, 'That man over there is waving. Do you know him?'

Honey recognised the shape of him before the rest. Something about seeing the uneven cut of the coat, the belt, the gait of the legs, sent her out of herself for a second. He was carrying an unwieldy black leather case. It dragged on his right arm. Shoving all the cups not very steadily into one hand she waved back.

The relief caught her off guard; she realised then that part of her hadn't trusted him at all when he said he worked at the Park. A tiny part of her was suspicious not just of that slab of glass, amber, whatever it was he had delivered, but of him. How silly; she must have Joan Fontaine on the brain. But there he was, unmistakable; here, giving her a light, polite smile.

She smiled back, opening her mouth. He broke his first, and continued in the direction of the back of the manor, a place Honey was not permitted to venture.

'Who is he?' Moira asked. She was watching Honey carefully, the way she had outside the Index Room.

'No one. I think he works in 3.'

'Oh.' This last bit interested Moira. She nodded, happy with the trade of secrets, then scurried on her way in dogged strides. 'Handsome little scruffball, isn't he?' she called back.

'What do you mean, scruffball? Do you think he's scruffy?' She had not considered Felix Plaidstow scruffy. He might have been louche, the greyhound vouched for that. Perhaps there was something a little unkempt about him. Weren't they all like that in Hut 3?

As she reached the door she accidentally bashed the trio of mugs against the frame and realised she was distracted, that her cheeks were still pinched with the heat of blushing.

Chapter 4

'Which of you ladies wants to find me a kiss?'

It didn't take long to work out who the American was.

The new girl looked horrified.

Moira sighed – a knowing sigh – and scraped back her chair.

'Don't bother,' said Mooden, beating her to stand. She patted down her brown wool skirt and tightened her necktie. 'I'll fetch it.' The American looked as if he'd been slapped.

'Kisses,' Honey leaned over to the new girl, who was dabbing paste onto the latest decrypt, 'are what you get when a message is duplicated. Sometimes two wireless operators in different stations take down the same message. If you find a gap in a message you're typing when it comes out the German end, it's worth looking to see if there's a duplicate been taken down from a different Y station – wireless station – in the

Registration Room. Otherwise . . .' She gestured with her head at the man behind. 'They come looking. The indexers mark them with an X. Kisses.'

'The gentlemen in Hut 3 like their kisses,' Beatrix said.

'When they can get them,' said Moira. She was avoiding the eye of the chap. He leaned against the wall. The clattering of fingers resumed.

'Sweet music,' he said.

'Watch it.' Moira flicked her neck round, making her chestnut set bounce. 'How else do you get your decrypts?'

'I wasn't kidding. They're changing the walls round in there. Got carpenters in from the local coffin works. This is sweet music compared.'

Honey saw from the corner of her eye the man take out a Woodbine packet, slice into the foil with his fingernail and remove the first cigarette. He was wearing olive green serge with epaulettes – US Army Airforce. His hair was parted sharply down the side, grey and thinning on top. He blew the smoke towards the back of Moira's hair and it hung in a cloud between them.

When he left Beatrix muttered, 'They're a little bit coarse, aren't they?'

The bruising came on like clockwork, three p.m. every day, afternoon-tea time (seven in the morning if she was on night shift). Honey's fingers were better now than when she had arrived, but the typing still brought an acid pain. She stretched her fingers, making a small crack along each knuckle.

They must have battered out over a thousand intercepts between them; the majority of the day's Vulture key. The keys changed at midnight every night, so there would be a new set tomorrow, and when they finished this lot they would start on Red or Yellow or Chaffinch, intercepts from Africa, France or the Netherlands. Honey caught Moira's eye and they both blinked, then widened their eyes, then smiled blindly like they were sharing something.

'There's a dance Thursday night, isn't there? Over Wavendon? The American airbase.' The way Beatrix directed the question it seemed as if it was meant for Moira.

The typing was replaced by a shuffling of papers. Mooden was rolling up a wad of messages. Connecting Huts 3 and 6 was a thin wooden bridge, with a pulley system operating a tray that slid along it. Usually when there were enough messages decoded, one of the decoders – Mooden more often than not – would bind up a load into a red leather tube, dump it into the hatch, tap with a broom handle and fire it through. She shoved through a roll now. But this time, after a few seconds, the wood tapped back.

Mooden's head snapped up. 'They're sending something our way?'

'Maybe returning the kiss?' the new girl ventured.

'No, they usually bring them back by hand.'

'Any excuse to get off their botties for a flirt,' Beatrix said.

For some reason Honey's stomach lurched. The knocking seemed portentous. They all listened as the tray slid along the bridge, bumping on the wood knots.

The trapdoor rattled and out crept the tray. Mooden was closest. 'Deschamps,' she said. 'Is it your birthday or something?'

'What is it?' Moira craned her head.

Honey had stopped listening. She was staring at an intercept, the last one of the day, hanging out of her machine, the words split as usual into five-letter blocks. She was staring at it because she couldn't stand to look at the pulley drawer. She knew, she could feel it, what was in that drawer. It was all too strange. She thought she might cry or vomit or blurt out what she had been given last night.

'Deschamps. Honey,' Miss Mooden said again. 'It's for you.' Mooden dumped the package on her desk, obscuring the pile of tape strips.

'*Is* it your birthday?' Beatrix asked.

'You should have told us, we'd have baked you a cake with cobnut marzipan,' Moira said.

The others looked questioningly at Moira and as she explained about the WAAF girls in the beer hut Honey's gaze moved onto the package. It was addressed the same way, London PO Box 222. All their post came through the London box. People had had all sorts delivered this way:

food parcels, books, a grand piano. The handwriting was the same, and the Cyrillic letters on the postmark.

She reached down, feeling the brown paper. The edges were soft and frayed as if they had been wet then dried again. Scribbles were drawn across it, faded by passage.

The room seemed like one great tentacled creature watching.

'What is it? Care package from home?' Moira nodded at her lap.

The blush rose fast. She slid the parcel to her feet. It smacked the ground. 'Chocolate. From my brother.'

'What does he do again? Is he out in the forces?'

'No, he's . . .' She hesitated. This could go one of two ways. 'He's with ENSA now. He's a ballet dancer. He was a CO,' she added quickly, as if she had to admit to it so that no one could accuse her of lying. But saying the full words – Conscientious Objector – was too shameful. Dickie the pacifist had done his time, five weeks up in Wakefield prison, and now he was touring for the troops as part of a tribunal deal.

There was a pause.

Then Moira murmured, 'Musical family.' The door opened and the four o'clock back shift began to filter in.

'Oh . . . I . . . think that I shall never see, a sight as curious as BP.'

The revue cast were warming up. Blackout fabric had been draped between pillars in the hallway of the mansion, makeshift dressing rooms. As they passed into the warmth of the house, letting the front door slam, Honey heard a hefty groan through a gap in the curtains. A woman was shrieking, 'Oooh, somebody's not been using his ration book! Breathe in, they fitted you three weeks ago.'

Moira was busy explaining to the American the point of British Revue.

'So it's not a review of other people's shows?'

'It's . . . they must have revue in America.'

'They have critics.'

'Honey, help me out. Your mum's a singer. What do they call revue in the USA? Vaudeville.'

'Oh, *revue*. I thought you said review. Your mother's a singer? What's her name? We saw some singers at a base on the coast last summer.'

The two men on the other side of Lieutenant Reuben MacCrae bent forward. One of them wore a dark twill suit and an old striped cricketing tie with a tight little knot; the other was in brown wool, many shades.

'Martha Deschamps,' Honey said. The package she had received in the afternoon was weighing down one side of her coat, and she had to concentrate to keep herself balanced. She hadn't had time to go home between ending her shift and the revue, and didn't much like wandering around in the blackout on her own anyway. They had taken a light supper at the Eight Bells, watching through a crack in the curtains as a different kind of cast warmed up; the dancing girls limbering and rubbing face powder onto their legs. In the toilets, Honey had unpicked a small section of the lining of her coat and dropped in the parcel, unopened. But it was making her walk funnily, and she felt she must be drawing strange looks.

'Martha Deschamps.' The man with the cricketing tie was pondering. Both men were English. He had introduced himself as 'Bugs'. 'Oh, she's wonderful. I saw her singing "White Cliffs of Dover" down on the Kent coast. Brilliant woman. Unstoppable.' Honey thought it perhaps prudent not to mention that her mother had thrown a carriage clock at the wall when her agent suggested she should be singing Florrie Forde to the troops instead of Wagner.

'They're putting her to good use,' she said.

'Still, secretary work must be a bit different from singing, though?' He posed the question the Bletchley way – the assumption that what you did was boring, manual, secretarial stuff.

'I suppose,' Honey said. She looked around her as they walked into the cafeteria. The tables had been taken away and the seats arranged lecture-style.

'Still, it's awfully valuable, being a secretary,' he said with a twinkle. 'What's your name?' They all shuffled along a row to the middle.

'Deschamps.'

'Oh yes, you said that, but I mean not that name, your Christian name. Ah, I see, you don't want to tell me. Old-fashioned are you?'

The woollen man spoke up. 'She called her Honey.'

'Honey, is it?' Bugs sat peremptorily, letting Moira and Reuben MacCrae wiggle past. He patted the seat next to him. 'You don't look like a Honey, if you don't mind my saying so.'

'Say what you like.'

'I mean you don't act like one. Mind if I smoke?' He took out a pipe.

'How should Honeys act?'

'Well.' He waved his arms around as he lit his pipe. 'Sweetly. I'd say you're more like a cider. Or a milk, I'd say. Maybe a sherry.' He didn't explain what he meant, but he laughed until the first smoke made him cough.

Lots of people told Honey she was not like a Honey. Carrot; she'd had that a lot. Tomato. You should be called Carrotina or Tomata. It was the colour of her hair, a very vivid ginger, mixed with auburn. Orange was the best description.

'And Deschamps.' He was getting a good puff going; the smoke smelled of vanilla. 'I know the name Deschamps too. Your father's called Henry.'

'Stepfather.'

'He's a soap baron.'

'Yes. Deschamps Soaps, of course.'

'So your mother's a singer and your father's a soap baron. And Dickie Deschamps, the ballet dancer with the Vic-Wells, he's Martha's son, so that makes him . . . your brother.'

The Amber Shadows

It was always like this. People grasping details of her family and presenting them to her.

On the stage, they had lit lanterns and a market street scene glowed to life. Three square-paned windows propped up against the backcloth burned golden. It looked warm and medieval, fragments of shadow-puppet living going on behind each window: the butcher's, the blacksmith's, the dairy. It reminded Honey that for over a year now she hadn't seen lights in windows on market streets. The blackout was a strange thing, but you got used to it.

'Of course, Honey's not her real name. Her true name.' Moira leaned across.

'What is your true name?' The man was smiling.

Honey shot Moira a look. 'Never mind.'

The man was looking over the heads of the incomers, watching them all like counting off beads on an abacus. 'So many gels,' he said. 'Do you know, Honey-that-is-not-your-true-name-Honey, one in three people at the Park's now a woman? It's amazing we're managing to keep the secret from Jerry with all those gossiping tongues.'

There was a single trumpet note from Katie Brewster dressed as Puss in Boots, and the show began.

At the interval, there was a squash for the drinks table. One of the women from the beer hut – Dolly with the blue slacks – had been requisitioned to man it.

'Gin and French or Gin and It?'

'What's the diff?' Bugs asked.

'French's got an olive. It's got a cherry. Both vermouth.'

'Italian,' Moira explained.

'I say,' said Bugs, 'should we be drinking drinks with Italian in the title?'

'Bit of a rum name,' the woollen friend said.

'It's not rum, it's gin.' They both threw back their heads and guffawed. Dolly – who looked like a woman who ate her porridge every morning without fail, or sugar – pointed her eyes to the queue behind them and back. Honey looked over her shoulder to see Reuben and Moira. Moira kept inching closer to him in the queue but each time she did so he moved his shoulder very slightly away. Moira took out her cigarettes and looked about her, patting her hair. Reuben examined all the bottles on display on the table, very carefully.

'So what's it to be, Honey-not-Honey?'

'Nothing, can't stand gin,' she murmured and moved away. Her mind had already begun swimming another route. Felix had been at the Park that afternoon. She had seen him in his overcoat, with his giant bag. And anyway why would she have thought him a liar? There had been nothing about the way he stood, nothing about his accent, his words – anything he had said or done – that would mark him as a liar. He was neat like the boys at the Park, awkward like the boys at the Park, young, soft-spoken. So why did she keep having to go over ground, to convince herself – like Joan Fontaine . . .

'I said with hair like that I'd have put you down as a Scotch girl . . . is she listening?' This last was addressed to Moira, and Honey realised she was staring at the beer mats on the drinks table.

'Scotch as in place or as in drink?' Reuben asked. They began squirming back along the row to their seats.

'Scotch is only ever a drink,' Honey said, sitting. Her coat lay folded on her lap. Through the lining she picked idly at the shape beneath the brown paper.

'If you have such an arty family,' said Bugs, 'perhaps you'd best help me with a little puzzle I'm having at the moment. Do you like paintings?'

Honey watched the stage transform before them, aided by men in Home Guard uniforms, into a battleship's deck. They draped blue netting where the glowing street-scene windows had been. In between it had been a Victorian drawing room, complete with doors.

'I don't like painting myself, if that's what you're asking.'

'That's not what I'm asking. There's a chap who's offered me a charcoal Dalí. It's a good deal but I'm damned if I know an original Dalí from something drawn by the local drunk. Would you mind having a look? Perhaps you could . . . swing by my billet?' Beyond him, the man in brown wool was making a show of not listening, filling his pipe, packing it tightly, reading the bottom of the box of matches.

Honey looked back at Bugs. He was taking a sip of his drink. Before his lips touched the rim of the glass his tongue hung out a little, cupping the fluid as he poured it backwards.

'Will you excuse me?' She stood up. 'I have to make a telephone call.'

'Now?' Moira leaned across the row and pulled on the hem of her skirt.

'I'll be back before it starts.' She picked her friend's fingers off and squeezed out of the row, out of the room, until she was back in the hall.

In the cooler air she made towards the telephone kiosk in the lobby, and dialled seven. 'Trunks? Can I place a call to London?' If she could catch Dickie before the second act there might be time to explain. Or at least to ask what he knew. 'Sadler's Wells. It's for one of the Vic-Wells ballet members. Dickie—'

The operator cut her off. 'Sorry, my apologies. No trunk calls from this line.' The woman hung up. A lifeless buzzing replaced the bustle of the background exchange. Honey waited for a second with the smooth receiver in her hand, weathering a sigh. Then she dumped it back on the hook and returned to her seat.

There were rationing jokes. An ogre wore a squander-bug costume with a swastika armband. When Woolton Pie was mentioned he shook and cowered and wept, and the audience roared. Afterwards came invitations to the American base.

'Can't. I'm tired.' Honey rubbed her eyes to back up the lie.

'That's the problem with the Hut 6 gels,' said Bugs, leading the way outside into the cold blackout. 'Brains like pie meat after a day's work. The men give you too much to do.'

Honey drew her coat around her and dodged her way through cheek kisses from Bugs and the woollen man. In the end it was the woollen man whose hand tried to ambush her buttocks as she said goodbye.

As she waved to the Military Police on the gate she thought again about the glowing windows on the stage set and wondered what her mother and Henry Deschamps were doing right now. Were they in their London house, listening to the hornets dropping their incendiaries, counting to ten when the shadow came overhead and the noise stopped, in case finally the blow was about to strike? Or were they down on the coast? She could never keep track.

'Honey, wait!' Moira's voice rang out in the dark. Footsteps came hammering from somewhere, the skidding of grit and a squeal. 'What do you think of him?' She took Honey's arm. 'Ooh, your coat feels funny. Do you need the lining fixed?'

'Probably.' Honey hurried to tighten her belt.

'Do you like him?'

'Bugs. Verb, is it?'

Moira laughed. 'Sorry about him. I don't think Reuben knows him. I don't know where they got him from.'

'Never mind my mother, I'd like to have a word with his mother.'

'But Reuben . . .'

'I didn't speak to him.'

Moira's silence said this was not the answer she wanted.

'He likes Shakespeare. I think revue was a bit beneath him.'

'Great.'

'He's from North Carolina. He has a horse at home.'

Honey nodded but the gesture was lost in the dark. 'Who's looking after it?'

But Moira had already begun to say, 'The scruffball . . .?'

'He's not my sweetheart.'

'Have you ever had a sweetheart?'

Honey paused for a moment and thought briefly about the sailor she'd met in Kent last year when the train got diverted on the way back to Bletchley. They were chatting in the carriage one minute, the next spending the night above a restaurant, pretending to the landlady they were engaged, covering her ring finger craftily when she signed the guest book. It had felt extravagantly naughty although he was two years younger than her and his timid fumblings hadn't really constituted sweetheartdom. Come to think of it, she didn't even know if he was still alive. But there hadn't been anyone else, ever. 'How is there time for a sweet-heart?' She knew this was a silly question.

'I sometimes wish this war would go on forever.'

'You don't mean that.'

'But what else would we be doing? I'd be a bloody cleaner like my granny was. Or married.'

'You have an Oxford degree.'

'Hmmm.' Moira was silent for a second. 'Did they approach you through the university?'

'No. I studied languages in London.'

'It was your mother, wasn't it?'

'My father. Stepfather. One of his friends in the club was asking around. I think the Park get their typists that way.'

Moira made her funny 'hmmm' noise again. 'Don't worry about what Bugs said. About you just being a secretary.'

'Nothing wrong with being a secretary.' Winman liked to tell them from time to time that they were the country's brightest minds, handpicked, each and every one. Sometimes he'd write it out in coloured pencil and pin it to the noticeboard.

Moira began to hum a little tune as they walked. Honey had never asked her about her time at the Research Cottage. But sometimes she wondered what that breakthrough was. Who were the boys on that ship, who would one day go to their graves never knowing that they had a guardian angel with a chestnut set who liked to mend clothing and say 'hmmm'?

'I really mean it. Your coat looks odd, Honey. Even in the blackout I can see it's lumpy on one side. It's probably frayed a thread. Turn around.'

'I've got stuff in my pockets.' She moved a pace away. Then half a pace back.

'Beauty is your duty,' Moira mused. She sounded distant, sort of sincere. 'I mean if you really love someone, it'll go on beyond the war, won't it? It'll have to.'

They stopped walking. They had reached the corner of Wilton Avenue. At least it felt like Wilton Avenue, only it was impossible to really know because the street signs had been removed. 'See you tomorrow.' She squeezed Honey's arm. 'Fix your coat, love.'

'Think you'll marry him?'

The voice came quietly out of the dark. 'I might have to.'

And then Honey was alone, with the moon and her thoughts. That was when the day began to crystallise. Its twists and veins hardened.

How many times she had idealised, demonised that man, through childhood? Her mother refused to talk about him; she'd had to learn everything from Dickie. Henry Deschamps – her stepfather, the soap baron – sometimes let slip remarks in the middle of fights: 'There's some men fine for a fancy but leave you when the wind changes'. That was how Honey from her earliest memories had the impression her father must have left her mother. She must have been seven or eight when Dickie changed her mind. Dickie would have been eleven or twelve.

There had been no marriage, of the official, legal kind. Their mother and he were bohemians – there was nothing to keep them together but their own love. But she had used his name, Dickie said. Only on Honey's birth certificate, which she had seen when she needed it for matriculation at university, it had said something different.

Dickie said he had been a musician. He had come from St Petersburg, as it was back then. He had worked at the Russian Imperial court before the revolution, but he had been a rebel, he was one of the reds under his fine clothes. His family were artists and they had been itinerant too. They were the real bohemians, the real ones, Dickie said, though he never explained who the false ones were. Her father had conducted the orchestra for the Ballets Russes in 1910 at Paris in an opera house so important Dickie said it was haunted. He loved Stravinsky, and they were great friends. He was a renaissance man, and as well as composing music and conducting orchestras, he was a great painter, a collector of art. This came in handy after the revolution, Dickie said. After his escape back to Russia he became a custodian of all that was beautiful, all that was important, Dickie said, in the world. His mother – Honey's and Dickie's Russian grandmother – had been a cherished prima ballerina of a golden age. Her slippers hung in a museum, somewhere.

It was around 1910 that their mother Martha had been peddled over the sea from London to Paris by her agents. She had, going by the photographs, been a striking cat-eyed woman even back then. 'Born to play Carmen!' the *Evening Standard* screamed of her in the twenties. Some of the older photographs had been tinted, but you didn't need colour to see the drapes, the patterns, the textures all layered on her, all worn like skin, like she grew them branch-and-leaf style from her shoulders and hips, and the beads and her dark round eyes. In some photographs, she looked like a little wooden doll. She was always smiling the same smile. The earliest commercially available postcard of her was dated 1911. She was still calling herself by her maiden name back then.

The stories varied depending on Dickie's mood as to when exactly they had met. There was an empty houseboat on the Seine where they paid a watchman to turn the other way. There were cakes in Vienna. The unofficial wedding was a gypsy affair in Budapest, presided over by an ancient woman who was their great-great-aunt. Martha kept a beautiful embroidered skirt in her wardrobe that she would sometimes let Honey play in as a child, and Honey had decided without consulting Dickie that this must have been the skirt their mother wore at her wedding.

Dickie had been four years old, he said, when they came for his father. Honey was in the womb. In some early accounts he was a Conscientious Objector. Other times Dickie had him as a spy. The one time her mother had spoken about it – tearfully, after a row, through the locked bathroom door when Honey was threatening to throw herself from the window into Bloomsbury – she said he had left in the middle of the night accompanied by two English men and she never saw him again.

She wouldn't say any more because by that point Honey had decided not to throw herself from the window. Dickie always said their father had fled back to Russia, that he had been given sanctuary with the Red Army. Leningrad was the final place he ended up. Occasionally he would show her a newspaper article from the stand in Soho that sold Russian papers. He said, there was his name, there it was, curator of the Detskoye Selo, the museum created for the public in 1918 after the revolution, keeper of the country's most precious public art, pianist, conductor, bon vivant, ballet lover. Ivan Korichnev; custodian of the famous Amber Room.

She walked with an uneasy gait, torchless on the cloudy night. Sometimes slatted blue headlights from passing vehicles made strange ripples of objects come in and out of focus: now a pile of brown wet leaves banked on the path; now a cat; now a red telephone box. It was easy to forget there was a war on, on a country lane, in the dark. She almost smacked into the corner of the Eight Bells but the sensation of cold stone and the malt smell from inside stopped her in time.

When she reached the squat little cottage that looked like a hay barn, just outside the churchyard, she thought she heard laughter. It was an odd place in daylight, a little like Yew Tree Cottage and its sisters, a relic from a time when Bletchley village was another thing entirely.

'Mother of bumpkins. No wonder they picked here. It's the last place you'd bother to bomb if you were a Jerry,' Beatrix had said once, when they were out on a bicycle ride.

Honey listened out for the laughter again, but the building was quiet. Smoke was pumping out of the chimneys on both sides. She walked on, drinking in the smell, enjoying it. She closed her eyes for a second, trying to imagine what the lane might have looked like lamplit, a few years ago. Then she heard the soft crack of a car moving slowly over pebbles, and if she hadn't been frightened of being caught in a smash, she might not have opened them again quite so soon.

But she did. Brightness brushed on her lids, her eyes snapped open, and the scene that greeted her through the cottage window was as strange as anything she had seen before or since the war began. The blackout curtain inside the pane was halfway through falling down. But even before the thump reverberated through the old thin glass, she saw what was inside.

The Amber Shadows

From the light in the room the whole front of the white building was lit up. The wash on the stone that had been blacked out before now turned creamy gold while the window itself blazed bright, leaking light round the edges, a stage curtain lifted and brought to life. Through it Honey saw a table full of people. There were at least ten of them gathered round a very grand old dark-panelled dining room. Candles stood in the centre of the spread. Dishes steamed; a ham, crystal glasses full of port or wine. Paintings lined the wall behind, crammed and hooked onto every inch of space, leaning against the mantelpiece, jumbled one on top of another in some places. The faint, rich colours blurred together and faces from captured moments in various centuries were frozen.

At the table, though, there were no faces. Every single person seated round it had a bright white napkin draped over their head. It looked like a banquet of upright corpses, all motionless, all waiting for something to happen.

Honey's mouth began to drop, but she couldn't scream.

Swiftly, very swiftly, a smear of a man's shape shuffled into the frame of the panes and wrestled the fallen blind back up.

The spectacle vanished. The dark folded in. But still she stared.

It had been real. It – they – had been real. She recreated the image in her head immediately, placing each object, each curved hump, each glance on each painting's face into a picture, until she thought she had a grasp on what she'd seen. But as the night reached back round her the details began to falter. Had she seen men seated round the dining table, or was it just the paintings? She had thought in that moment she knew what she was looking at. But now she was not so sure. Her heart was going like the clappers. The rush of blood to her hands and head told her it had been real. She looked up; the chimney continued to pump smoke, the cream walls were leaking again sounds of talk and laughter.

As she completed her walk home to Yew Tree Cottage she felt queasy. Her fingers fumbled on the gate's catch. She removed her gloves with her teeth and fiddled with the icy iron.

In her bedroom she switched on the wireless and turned the dial until she found music, enough to drown out the play Mrs Steadman was listening to below. She could hear Rebecca's footsteps in her room across the hallway, Mr Steadman coughing catarrh in the bathroom and spitting. With a still-thudding heart she reached into the lining of her coat and retrieved the parcel. Carefully she untucked the ends of the paper. This time the tin was French: Butter and Fruit Satines. Inside it had been padded with tissue. The shape was the same, a small square of brown hard gem, snapped into mosaic shards then stuck and sanded back together. Like the other tablet there was a sandwich of fine foil between the two mosaic sides, a rougher, stickier coating on one side and a high gloss on the other. Now she shivered. On the wireless the pips beeped in preparation for the nine o'clock news, and they somehow felt shocking against the raw, secret ancient amber weight, shadowed in the naked palm of her hand.

Chapter 5

By the time the third parcel came along Honey hardly felt surprise, only a queer stab of something anticipated with fear.

That afternoon they had broken the Vulture key again. In the wave of intercepts came numbers and names of ammunition, weaponry, unit commanders. Then as the tapes hammered on, other lists came firing out. KLEIN 175, DRESSLER 150, HUBER 5.

It reminded Honey with chilling precision of the decrypts that had come through last summer, as Hitler broke his pact with Stalin and the Nazi armies moved into the east. The lists had begun then, pouring into the Park, German commanders recognisable by name, each followed by a number. She had seen them then as she did now for what they were: the killers had names, the murdered only numbers.

The Amber Shadows

She felt ice in her blood when she saw the parcel in the messenger girl's hands, wet from the drizzle outside, cross-tied with string and creased at the corners. The smudge of the censor's crown was there again in the middle. The parcel was bulkier this time. As she took it she felt through its wrapper soft newspaper or butter muslin distorting the shape inside. The messenger girl handed over the rest of her goodies to the others and left.

There was a box of coffee for Beatrix from home and a card from Mooden's aunt with an ice-skating snowman on it. She pinned it on the board. Its head looked like a frosty Halloween pumpkin; pebble teeth, coal for eyes. The coffee took precedence for excitement. Beatrix opened the bag and they passed it round, closing their eyes, shutting out the messages from the machines in front of them, inhaling.

'Early Christmas present, Honey?' Miss Mooden asked. 'You have a thoughtful family. You got one yesterday too. You can open it here if you like. Don't be shy.'

Honey's hand slid over the Russian lettering on the stamp. She tried to look nonchalant but she wasn't slick enough. Moira caught her eye, opened her cherry-red mouth, then closed it again. There was a question on her face. Honey's throat froze; she couldn't think of a lie. Words had just about formed in her head when Moira said, 'Smells like soap. Doesn't your stepfather own a soap factory?'

'Yes, it does rather, doesn't it?' She breathed out.

'Are you going to open it?' said Mooden.

The clock seemed to halt for a second. Once again panic dried out her tongue.

But Moira jumped in. 'You can't tell her to open her bloody Christmas presents early! What kind of person does that? Few enough presents this year by the looks of the shops.' She flicked her hair over her shoulder and went back to typing.

Honey dropped the parcel out of sight, underneath her chair, and went back to her own pile of work. She caught Moira's look from the corner of her eye, so swift she could have missed it. And a tiny smile too. But she knew that look. Moira thought she had a secret sweetheart. Silk knickers from the front line or some American with black-market chums, that was probably what she thought. No matter, she had saved her blushes and that was all that mattered.

At lunch Honey managed to swallow a crumbling corned beef and mustard sandwich and some of Beatrix's coffee, black. As soon as four o'clock changeover arrived she slipped from the room like a thief.

Wednesdays were bath days. Honey had forgotten until she opened the door, smelled zinc and saw Mr Steadman's oily overalls steeping in a bucket just inside. The water was still warm and filled the hall with a tepid cloud. Even the beak on Mrs Steadman's luminous bird had curled upwards as if in disgust.

The Amber Shadows

'There's water if you want a bath,' Mrs Steadman shouted through the crack in the parlour door.

Honey had thought this was a joke when she first moved in. The idea that Mr Steadman's oily water was to be used for bathing once it had stripped his clothes of grease seemed worse than ludicrous. She soon found out that Mrs Steadman never joked, especially where household matters were concerned. Rebecca, who had arrived first, had slipped a note under her door – 'There's a bath house in the manor, free to use'. Honey bathed there once a week now, on Sundays before or after shift. Still every Wednesday the pageant had to be performed.

'Lovely, Mrs Steadman. I'll prepare the bathroom.'

The Steadmans were proud to have a fully functioning bathroom, built in a lean-to off the kitchen – the 'scullery' Mrs Steadman called it – by the man of the house, with his wife as chief decorator. Their tastes had clashed on certain things. The toilet bowl was chintzy, with painted flowers and a delicate neck. But the hole hacked into the floor was too wide, meaning the linoleum flapped a few inches around its edges. Occasionally you'd hear or see a spider or mouse investigating the gap.

Half of the bathroom had been carved from the old pantry and they'd left that part of the wall as it was, backed with sticky lino and oilcloth printed with pastel flowers. The old crockery sideboard now formed the linen closet. Behind the skirting boards on the outside wall beetles and more mice scuttled. The toilet flushed, but there was a flush curfew and you couldn't use it after eight p.m. or Mrs Steadman's bedtime, whichever came first.

Honey went in and dragged the copper tub into position, close to the bathroom door. She propped it so it half-blocked the entrance. Mr Steadman had once walked in on her, and though he had apologised he hadn't blushed.

Upstairs in her bedroom she fetched a towel, some lavender soap from the factory, and a tub of cold cream; accoutrements of the Bathtime Lie. She took the pencil tin with the first piece of amber from where she had hidden it under a pile of laundry, and the satines tin with the second piece from the bottom drawer of her chest.

Downstairs she could hear the wet overalls being removed from the zinc bucket, and the terrifying scrape of the mangle on the scullery linoleum. Mr Steadman was groaning as he heaved the bucket towards the bathroom. She arrived just in time to see him slopping it over the piece of carpet on the threshold.

He pushed back the door. 'Bloody hell,' he said, waddling in inch by inch. As he tipped the horrid contents into the copper bath, splashes rained up onto his pullover. He dried his hands on his front, leaving dark fingerprints, and backed out of the room, the bucket rattling.

She smiled, thanked him again and closed the door.

With her knees she nudged the bathtub until it crept over the doorframe and was flush against the warped wood panels. She hovered her hand over the surface of the water; blood temperature, on a cold day. Grey particles and ribbons of oil swirled on the surface. Where the copper shone, the water looked brown.

Usually at this point she'd light a cigarette and pull out a mystery novel – Ethel Lina White or John Dickson Carr. There would be a twenty-minute window during which she was supposed to relax and bathe, but instead she'd try to solve a murder and forget she had filthy skinflints for billeters. Tonight however she squatted down on the lino and braced her back against the frigid ceramic of the toilet bowl. The windows on the lean-to wall had been pasted over with brown paper for the blackout. A blue glass shade covered the gaslamp on the wall above the bath, giving the room a cold romantic glow, the strangeness of something on the silver screen.

The latest package the messenger girl had given her had dried out now, the paper stiff and salty. As fast as she could she tore the wrapper away and found buried inside layers of tissue paper a red Brussels-branded Turkish delight box. The gaudy rose colour turned violet in the blue light. She sliced the wax seal open with her nails and pulled the lid. The panel tumbled out hard.

Now there were three.

Honey picked them up one by one, rolling her palms over their smoothness. She propped them against the side of the copper tub. The capillaries between the shards took on a new colour in the colder light.

Four by four inches each; brown; honey-coloured, the mosaics all glued together then smoothed. She got to her feet, picked one up and held it closer to the blue lamp. Hazy browns and umber knots burned through the tint. Her finger came to rest on a rough ridge running along the bottom of the square. She picked at it for a second, then brought the panel closer. Along one side of the piece, about an inch from the bottom edge, ran a straight line, grooved, not very deep and not very wide. She tilted it and checked the opposite edge. There was the same groove. On the third side she found the same, but the fourth was smooth.

She picked up the other two pieces. They too were each gouged, this time only with a single tram-line, gritty and hidden by their pattern, along one edge. She placed them down on the floor again, beside one another, standing on end, then fiddled to see if she could slot them together. It took a bit of wiggling but it worked. Now she was faced with three sides of a box, and a groove running right round the base, as if it was missing its bottom. Carefully she turned it topsy-turvy. Maybe it was missing its top too.

Either way, there were more pieces to come. Bracing it in both hands, for the joints were not steady, she held it closer to the blue light.

Sounds were travelling through the warped door. Mrs Steadman was cranking the mangle, pinching the water-logged overalls between its rolls. She was humming 'South of the Border'.

The Amber Shadows

Honey leaned an inch closer to the lamp and her heel slipped on the lino. She was flung forward just slowly enough to glimpse the splodge of rainbow-silvered petroleum on the surface of the water that came looming towards her. Her tendon yanked and her knee crunched on the floor. The amber flew out of her palms, spiralling upwards, separating out into its three flat panels, and making three flat wet smacks in the filthy bath. She managed to grab the edge of the copper tub just in time to stop her face from following them.

'Rats!' She pushed her leg out in front and stretched her ankle until it crunched. She rubbed her knee, then peeled up her sleeves, tucking them beyond her elbows.

The feel of the oil on the surface of the water was appalling; a horrendous festering grey. It gave her the shivers not to see what she was wading her hand through. Imagination conjured water voles, a tropical snake, a piranha – the water was the right temperature for one to lurk – waiting to snap off her fingers. After a few swills she swallowed her revulsion and plunged for the gritty bottom. Her fingers landed on a hard corner. She pulled the piece out. Oily water dripped down its surface.

Keeping it at arm's length from her ivory blouse she reached for the pile of newspaper squares on the spike beside the toilet bowl, and tore free a handful. She left the papers blotting the slice while she went fishing for the second one. This time round she found gummed papers and saturated tickets near the bottom; things the old man had kept in his pocket and forgotten to take out before handing over the overalls for their wash. In the crevices of the copper base there was a sludge of crumbs. She held back her nausea, ignored the smell and slid her palm flat to the far end. There it was. As she began to withdraw her arm from the murk, the panel slipped again, and slapped the water. She caught it floating and scooped her palm underneath to stop it from slipping. There was something very slick on the surface of this one, the texture of butter, stopping her from gaining purchase.

As with the other, once it was out of the tub she snatched off a wodge of cut newspapers to wipe it down. She placed both in the sink and cranked open the stiff tap, letting a trickle of cool water spill down into the bowl. Carefully she rinsed each piece, turning them over to clean both sides. It was only then that she noticed the buttery substance was on both, and was not washing off but beginning to turn firm and smooth again. She took her index fingernail and scraped it down the surface of one of the slabs. It brought with it a little fragmented curl of brown.

Wax.

She tried again. More scraped off. The second piece lying underneath was still warm, having only had the slopping dregs of the clean cold tap water. Honey smudged the surface with her thumb. The coating shifted easily. She rubbed harder and a sleek section of amber became clear.

She held it cautiously to the gaslamp above the bath. Tinted paraffin wax was spread in a messy map of fingerprints across the surface.

Hastily she dipped both pieces back in the tepid water and swilled them around, scratching with all her fingernails to remove the coating. It was sticky but her nails were sharp and it came off in small drifting parings until the surfaces felt more or less smooth. There was some alcohol or chemical in the water, coming off Steadman's overalls, that seemed to help dissolve it.

Not caring about the mess any more she took her towel and dipped it underneath the surface and scrubbed hard until she felt the polished amber flush on each piece. She found the third part, still lurking in the filthy water, and tried that one too. When she was done, her flannel towel was fungal brown. But beneath her fingers each small slab of amber had sprung a texture.

She took the pieces out and lined them up again as she had before, against the copper. Now they all looked polished, as shiny and hard as marble. But here and there when she placed her fingertip flat, there was a roughness, a scratch, a lip.

She dragged the slopping tub out of harm's way and held one piece as close to the blue lamp as it would go. The lamp was curved, and ended in a glass bell, but up close its beam was strong, spilling fish-silver rays into the amber, making a stained-glass window of the piece. She did it to each in turn, her breath quickening by the second. As the blue glow leeched and spread its way through the hard ancient sap, it lit up each carefully made slice with a kaleidoscope of images, a labyrinth of patterns that made Honey's flesh prickle hot and cold at the same time.

There were letters.

Chapter 6

Since the spring of 1941 she had spent six days a week staring at blocks of scrambled letters. But to see before her this
calligraphied gobbledygook, carved with care and effort –
for the amber was not soft – struck her dumb.

The letters traced a path up and down, curling round
loops of vines, leaves, feathers and long-tailed birds shying
behind creepers. It was effortful, it was intricate. As she
followed the path with her finger, she picked out the spare
bits of wax gummed into the ridges. Someone had created
the route lovingly, then covered it all away. There was
beauty in it, even without any meaning; a surface image,
then an invitation to something else. Lift the carving of one
of the leaves and see what you find – something on the
forest bed, something closer to the roots.

The script the carver had used was gothic, tailed and
tapered on the ends of the letters. There was something arch

about it that fitted its mystery. Whatever was written there wound and turned when you least expected it to change direction. The back panel was free of letters but covered in images of birds, long-feathered, drawn thickly, haughty-necked and with wise human eyes. It had the look of medieval woodcutting. The path picked up again on the other side with the same curling letters. It reminded Honey of a theatre's proscenium arch and curtain, framing for now an empty space.

'Have you drowned in there?' A broom beat against the door and her heart sprang. Her thoughts shook to the ground. Trembling, she dismantled the panels, bundled them into the stinking towel, and slipped off her stockings. Time for the most unpleasant part of the deceit.

She lifted each leg in turn to the icy trickle from the tap and wet her feet. With her spare hand she flicked a bit of freezing water through her hair. The cold shocked her scalp. She looked down at the bundle of amber poking out from the towel. It was still there, still carved. She hadn't dreamt it.

'Finished,' she shouted back. She rattled the tub, shaking the water about, and made two thumps of bare footsteps; code for 'finished'.

'Knock Rebecca on your way up. She'll want the water.'

Honey's breath was still running fast and short when she closed the door of her bedroom. She could hear Rebecca padding the landing; her turn for act two of Bathtime Lie.

The Amber Shadows

The patch underneath Honey's rag-knot rug had already been toasted warm by Mrs Steadman's fire. Now the house was silent. Mr and Mrs Steadman never argued about silly things, the way her mother and Henry argued when she was little, the way they continued to fight always, on trips or at picnics. She wondered at what stage a couple stopped arguing and simply ceased to talk.

She drew the blackout curtains, sealing the join with buttons, pulled her electric lamp on its thin flex towards the middle of the room and sat with her legs splayed wide.

There was no way in any language the letters could make sense. There were repeated consonants, quadruple consonants, double Qs. She took paper and a biro from the bureau and scribbled them down:

XWCWPTWDRQJSMZVGTNRQJZVIFUZHPZV
on one side, then
YWXIUUZAJLLTJVGRQQKMDAZVWCZRBBZRSNFVBZK

The first thing she noticed – the only thing she noticed – was that there were no breaks between the letters. Enigma intercepts came in blocks of five. But that could just have been the way the wireless operators took them down. These letters on the other hand kept a continuous path with no space for word gaps. It was as if they were part of the picture. They seemed to be winking at some meaning that was staring her in the face.

With a start she realised she was biting the inside of her cheek, and as the pain hit her suddenly, so did a thought. It was a shocking, horrid thought, but one that must be confronted. No matter who had sent it, no matter what their purpose, sending coded letters to her was as fine a message as waving a red flag at a Spanish bull. And within that message one strong, sickening, unthinkable question had to be asked: this person, this cryptologic amber crafts-man, whoever they were, wherever they lay low – did they know what she was doing at Bletchley Park?

That Honey had ended up at Bletchley Park had always seemed to her to be a matter of fate, the origins going back far further than that meeting between Henry Deschamps and the man he called K. Although the official story was that K had struck up conversation over a game of black-jack, and made discreet enquiries at the table as to who might possess a trustworthy, stout-nerved daughter they could spare for the war effort, Honey believed the true reason she had ended up there was set in motion before she was born.

There were no possessions left in the house as mementos of Ivan – or was it Ivor? – Korichnev. Even his name had been obliterated as far as she could trace. All the old programmes she went digging for had Martha down by her maiden name, or the name on Honey's birth certificate, until she became Deschamps, round about Christmas 1918.

The Amber Shadows

But there was a playbill for a production of a Stravinsky ballet at the Coventry Opera House, undated, with no names on it. And at some point there had definitely been a book.

She must have been eleven or twelve and Dickie fifteen or sixteen when he stopped telling stories about his father and shut up shop whenever she asked. Before then however he had given her plenty of scraps, enough to paint a picture. It was an impressionist's picture, made of parts that didn't quite fit. But then it had been the era of cubism, and Honey had not found it strange that an ear could sit in the middle of a face, a room could be made of triangular shards, and one's family history could be splintered into pieces here and there. According to Dickie, Ivan Korichnev had come from a political group of artists, for whom destabilising the bourgeois was art's calling: art that threw light on its own construction; art that broke rules; art that provoked you to find it ugly or cruel. Dickie said he hadn't had much success as a composer, and it had driven him mad. He trialled new ways to approach composition, and in doing this he had stumbled on the idea of the cipher.

Ivan – or Ivor – had composed a piece using words from the Bible substituted for musical notes. According to Dickie he had followed this up with a piece based on the Communist Manifesto, and one using poems by Pushkin. Dickie's explanation for the absence of manuscripts for these was that their mother had burned them in the days after his flight.

This was plausible. Martha had no tolerance for atonal music. She was a woman whose flesh was built from emotion. People who loved her called her 'whimsical', 'capricious', 'diva'. Directors she had crossed called her 'bitch', 'vixen', 'dragon'. She loved the giant arias: Puccini, Bizet and Saint-Saëns. She had little time for Mozart. She sobbed when Wagner was adopted by the Nazis.

The more wild and swollen Martha's emotions grew, the more introverted and mathematical grew their father. He reached back further in time. He travelled into worlds of alchemy and algebra. He began making ciphers into music. At some point in their childhood Dickie had produced his copy of *Figley's Book of Ciphers* as evidence. He had shown her the inscription 'Love from Papa'; the florid signature that followed. It was all that was left as a memory of their father, and it was Dickie's constant evidence of his existence. Ivan had been trying, through naming musical notes by their Latin letters and scrambling those letters into a cipher, to create something honest, whose purity lay embedded in its form. 'If a note,' Dickie said, 'relates to its alphabetical representative, then music can be enciphered just as letters can. Unravel the music and you'll find something that is true.' It hadn't made sense to the child her, and she wasn't quite sure it did now. She couldn't remember how the book came in, but it did.

According to Dickie their father had written a masterpiece for piano, voice and dancer in this way. But nothing remained of this work. He'd destroyed it somewhere down the line. If it had survived, it would have been too dangerous for the masses, Dickie had said. No, *Figley's Book of Ciphers* was all that was left, and Honey, when she grew into an introverted child who chewed her dress hems and wouldn't speak at nursery, was proof, said Dickie, of their father; she was her father's daughter. Dickie on the other hand was proof of their Russian heritage, for he was a great dancer – indeed Madame . . . what was her name? The woman with the black bun and the wooden cane, Dickie's Russian ballet mistress – had said so. Dickie was the finest little ballet boy in his class. Dickie rarely got the slap on the calves. Dickie was destined to greatness. What was that if not a sign that Russian music was in his blood?

This cipher book. *Figley's*. She couldn't remember what the cover looked like but she remembered its fudge-scented paper. Dickie always used to have it with him on trains. It was some kind of totem for him. It had spurred her on to learn to read, to look over his shoulder when he was absorbed in it, to try to grasp its meaning. She fixated on it during those journeys, taxi rides, at the back of the theatre while their mother was rehearsing. But always the ideas had remained just out of reach. She couldn't grasp the concepts, she was a year or two too young. And then one day the book disappeared. Perhaps it had been victim to a spring clean, given to a charity bazaar, or sent overseas with the Red Cross. Perhaps her mother had found it and burned it.

Honey had never seen it since.

When she learned to love crosswords, when she took up languages and studied their sounds and tones, which used the same building blocks as English but created different results, she hadn't thought of *Figley's Book of Ciphers*. But she'd had it there, in her mind, a skewed corner of the picture that you couldn't see properly unless you turned the whole thing upside down or on its side. She knew the book was there somewhere in her childhood memories, but only the way she knew about uncles in far-off countries, and her father, and God.

She ran her hand again over the carved letters vining the amber panels. Amber, postmarks, codes. It pointed in one direction. But directions, if you didn't read them right, could always mislead.

The difference between a code and a cipher was a matter of words. Codes replaced words and phrases with one alternative that only the two parties on either end could understand. Ciphers were what Enigma produced, letter-for-letter substitution. The advantage of a cipher was that there were potentially limitless keys. Finding the right one was about trial and error, knowledge or machinery. The disadvantage of a cipher was that the interceptor almost always knew they were looking at one. Codes on the other hand could replace whole words for other meaningful words. The clock strikes in spring. Hand me the blue folder. Keep mum.

On her first day at the Park, after she had replied to and signed the letter her stepfather had brought home; after she had followed the instructions and taken the train to Bletchley; after she had made the telephone call from the station, waited for the car, sat freezing in the back while it crawled a slow path towards the mansion; after she had paused at the gate while the Military Policemen checked the identity cards of everyone inside, their rifles pressed flat between their bodies and the car doors; after she had stepped out onto the gravel, taken a seat opposite the man in the oak-panelled room who introduced himself as Captain Tiver; after she had taken his expensive pen, tried not to sweat on its enamel octagonal casing, placed her quivering hand so that nib met paper and scratched a leaky signature across the Official Secrets Act; after she had done all that, Tiver had taken a revolver from his desk, thumped it on the wood, and said as calmly as if he was ordering sherry, 'If you break the Official Secrets Act, I'll shoot you myself.'

Keep mum. What ran through her mind now was the foolish Wren who had dug out her papers for the RAF man in the dark of the street. 'You shouldn't have shown me those,' he'd said. But he'd asked for them.

What if someone was asking for her papers now, using these little elaborate nuggets of amber? 'You keep your mouth shut,' Tiver had said, 'and you'll do fine here. But shut means shut, about everything. If someone in Hut 8 knows what colour the walls are in Hut 3, I'll know they've been talking, and I've already told you what I do with people who talk. In medieval times they'd have cut out your tongue. Now any fool can write we have to cut out more than your tongue. Britain doesn't mess around with traitors; never has, never will.'

She saw a sandbagged cubbyhole, a leather brace, the short muzzle of Tiver's gun. Did they blindfold you when they shot you for treason? Or did you have to stare at the flash that shot out the front of the muzzle just before you lost consciousness?

No, she must not tell. She must not tell a soul what was sitting in her hands. Still, as she settled on that thought it scalded inside.

Bletchley had filled her with secrets from her very first day, until she itched. But the secret of Bletchley was nothing in that moment compared to the secret in her hand, something too close to her heart to even make sense of. Why would her father be trying now, to reach her? Why now?

The numbers of those murdered Soviet men she had read in the day's intercepts flashed in her mind. If he lay dying in another country, and he knew that he had just this tiny window of time . . .

There was no talking between huts, it was true. But there was someone she could talk to.

Honey heaved herself to her feet, kicking back the rag

knots onto the warm patch of floor. She pulled open her stiff second drawer and found a pair of stockings to replace the ones she had taken off – she hated to redress in dirty stockings even if taking them off only for a second – and tugged them on. She slipped her feet into tennis plimsolls, scraped her hair off her face into a beret and wrapped the amber slices in a bitten old fur muffler. She put on her coat, and put her ear to the door.

One of the Steadmans was snoring in the parlour, the other was clattering in the scullery.

If she were to leave to go wandering in the blackout they would want to know why. It was too late for the cinema, and the Eight Bells would have the dancing girls on by now. If she said she was going to the British Restaurant they would want to know why she didn't eat her cold tray supper. If she said she was meeting a friend from the train they would want to know where they were going to stay.

She went over to the window. The flower beds below looked soft but the frost was deceptive and besides it would be muddy and she'd make a noise. Within arm's reach was the top of the apple tree.

She climbed onto the sill and stuck out her leg towards the tree. Her mother had made her take ballet as a child, with the same terrifying Russian ballet mistress with the scarlet mouth, and she was still supple. She stretched her foot to reach the most promising branch. It bowed and bent, but then it held. With the muffler spilling fur out of her pocket she reached with both hands and found dead leaves that allowed her just enough purchase to pull a small tangle of branches forward. Clinging with faith she brought her other leg into the tree. Her window remained open. It would be chilly when she returned. But that didn't matter. It was more important she see Moira.

Chapter 7

A military van loomed close, invisible until it was almost touching her side. Its louvre eyes made tawny stripes on the grit. As she looked up she saw the canvas and rope ties, the bulk of the bodies travelling inside, the faceless driver in a tin hat. The crackle of tyres yawned, then retreated.

She should have been used to it by now, these things, these vehicles that came creeping out of the darkness with their military cargos shifting round the country, but she wasn't. She checked her pocket, but she'd come out without her torch.

She had not become used to any of it in fact; not the butter ration, not the signless railway stations, not the sparseness of toy displays in shop windows – no metal trains or aeroplanes this year, only wood, wooden soldiers – and, most of all, not the boys in uniforms that didn't quite fit. Skinny forms, awkward hips in khaki bulk, an actuary's sloped shoulders in an Air Raid Warden's jacket, her dentist passing on Home Guard parade, someone else's son with a rifle chafing his shoulder, and then the men in plain clothes – nice suits – who were the most furtive and frightening of all.

The high street was a muddle of shapes. She picked her way like a goat up a mountainside, stepping high where she thought pebbles and kerbs might be, feeling walls of moon-lit stone. No sight of diners in the restaurants behind the walls, no steamed-up pub windows showing customers with pints of froth. Her lips braced against the cold breeze and she walked on.

She had to count off the lanes. Moira's was the third. Her iron gate needed oiling; the sound nearly shot Honey out of her skin.

She thought for a brief second about throwing a stone against the window, but after a quick vision of an awkward explanation to the emergency glaziers she settled for the door. It was answered by a woman with a round pink face under a white cap, and a baby barnacled to the side of her body. Her brow creased in surprise.

'Is this where Moira Draper lives?'

The woman's frown deepened, then she peered closer. 'Are you creeping around in the blackout? In this chill?' The idea seemed so preposterous that Honey felt foolish.

'Work matter. Rather urgent.'

'Ah, she's just back, you see.' The woman all but winked. The billeting officers had done their work well. Not like the man above the baker's who had pestered so ferociously his billettee girls about the work they did that they reported him and he was banned from hosting more – which might, all along, have been his plan.

Moira's landlady tipped her head back and rolled her eyes towards the stairs. She never asked what the girls at 'the Park' did. She widened the door. The baby cawed and she pushed its fist gently into its mouth.

'I'll call her down.'

'No, don't. I'll see her in her room.'

'You don't want the parlour?' She seemed almost hopeful. Honey looked beyond her past the open door that led off the hall, and saw a case of ornaments on different levels of shelving. There were china spaniels with golden chains, a woman with a shepherdess's crook, clinging on to her bonnet. The wallpaper was new, little coloured spirals and splashes, blue, red and mustard. The hall smelled gluey and clean. In a frame on a dark wood plant stand was a picture of a young man in dress uniform.

'It's you.' Standing at the top of the stairs Moira's cheeks were flushed – or rouged, Honey couldn't tell from the distance – and her eyes looked energetic. She leaned on the bannister. She was wearing a long cream silk robe, of the style popular in the twenties, her arms swimming in the wide sleeves, frayed at the collar and hem. 'You'd better come up.' Her hair was frizzy, as if she had been bathing and had forgotten to wrap it in a towel.

As Honey passed her into the bedroom, she whispered, 'You have wood bark on the hem of your coat.' So that was the sort of thing one spotted when one had a cryptanalyst's brain.

Honey brushed herself down. Moira swooped in and caught the debris before it fell on the rug then dusted it between her palms into the waste paper basket.

Honey stood in the centre of the room, feeling brutally exposed. Quickly, before she changed her mind, she reached into her pocket and pulled out the fur.

Moira looked at it. 'Don't tell me you came picking your way through the blackout to ask me to darn some roadkill.' She laughed and sat down on the bed on top of a satinette pillow. She picked up a lipstick case from the table next to her and with a butter knife began scraping out the remnants and packing them into a second case. A selection of other cases was scattered at her side. Underneath them a magazine lay open at an article: 'Death of a Dinner Gown'. There was a how-to section on taking your debutante nan's old ball dresses and making them into glamorous draping slacks. On the walls were torn pictures from more glossies, Cecil Beaton shots of very lean women in Make Do and Mend. A pillbox of marge coupons lay open by the bed along with reels of cotton, needles and scraps of haberdashery. *Beauty is your Duty. Never forget that good looks and morale go hand in hand.* So this was what she did for the war effort now. A picture came to life in Honey's mind of the first time she had seen Moira, scraping and scrabbling through the cool spring woods beside the Park lake, gathering bluebells for a sick man she'd been in love with back then. She'd torn her high heel in the undergrowth and had waded back into the sludgy muck to retrieve it. She had always taken that much care in her appearance, but looking at the spill of sewing stuff and magazine patterns it seemed as if it had become an obsession.

Honey let the fur fall open. The amber pieces tumbled out and she caught them with her palm, one by one, with tiny clacks.

Moira put down both knife and case and leaned in.

'Caramels?'

'Caramels?'

'Well, I don't know, what the devil are they? They look like slices of the caramel that came out when my granny used to try and make toffee.'

'Smell.' Honey stuck one out towards her.

Moira sniffed. 'Soir de Paris.'

Honey snatched it back. 'Perfume on the brain. It's amber.'

Moira was shaking her head lightly. There was a fizz in her tonight. Her hands moved quickly over the lipstick cases, as if by staying in one place for too long they might be caught at something, by someone. She reached over and took the first piece by its sharp corners, wincing as it pricked her, and looked it over with calculating, logical eyes. Honey watched her. In the bright electric ceiling light the flaws on the carvings showed up: bits of dust clotted in the gaps, wax still clinging to the face. There were tiny slivers where the glue had not quite settled between the mosaic shards, and others where it had oozed a little and hardened, where the sanding hadn't been quite flush.

'I don't understand what I'm supposed to be looking at. Where did you get these from?'

'I don't know.'

Moira looked up and stared at her. 'What's written on them?'

'I need your help to find out.'

Downstairs the baby had begun to scream, ungodly bursts in boiling waves, surging up, down, up again, then a quick pierce of lung. Moira stood up and put her hand to her brow. 'Does my nerves in. Where did they come from? Is this what you were sent today in the hut, and the other day?'

'By the PO Box, 222, the London one.'

Moira shook her head. 'No, no. These wouldn't get past the censors. Do you see these?' She pointed at the letters. 'Don't you know what happened to Betty . . . Betty . . .' She snapped her fingers but the name didn't come. 'Well, Betty Somebody. Betty Somebody was writing to her boyfriend in code. He was in another hut and was writing back in code, it was all just supposed to be a bit of romantic fun, but they both got hauled in front of Tiver.'

'Where's Betty Somebody now?'

Moira shook her head. 'Don't know. Not at the Park.'

Honey looked at Moira. Her brown eyes had stilled. Her mouth was small and straight.

She leaned forward and rubbed her finger on the panel. 'They didn't look like this when I opened them. They all had wax on them, a layer covering up the carvings. You wouldn't be able to tell just at a glance if you opened them.'

'Oh, bloody hell.'

'That's why I need you to help me find out what they say.'

'So we can both be shot.'

'I'm not a fifth columnist.'

'Keep your voice down,' Moira spat. 'She's got ears like a wolf. If that baby makes a babble three rooms away and she's cleaning up here she's down the stairs like a rat.' Moira grabbed the other two pieces, laid them out on the floor, and dragged the flex of the lamp closer. Honey could see her brain beginning to warm up, clack clack clack like a sewing-machine needle it went, over and under the pieces. She ran her finger along the pattern. 'Who is he, have you any idea?'

Honey hesitated. 'No.'

'What was the postmark?'

She stalled.

'Spit it out.'

'Are you ready?' She looked down and focused on the vines. 'Leningrad.'

Moira's finger stopped. Honey held her breath. In the silence she lowered herself carefully down onto the floor, crossed her legs and loosened the belt of her coat. Still Moira was staring at the amber. After a while her face turned up and she frowned very close to Honey, appraising her make-up, first round her eyes then her mouth. The sewing-machine brain was going clack clack clack again. Then she began to laugh.

'What?'

She put her hand to her mouth and spittle came bursting through her lips. 'God, you know how to make one shit one's knickers.'

Honey snatched the piece from her. 'What?'

'Leningrad? Honey, no one is sending you codes from Leningrad. It's besieged. You've seen the decrypts. Come to think of it, you've got a wireless, haven't you? You can read a newspaper. The Nazis have surrounded it.'

'That's what I'm frightened of.'

Moira scanned her face again and saw that she was serious. She took the piece gently back out of Honey's hands. 'Wax or no, I don't even know if they have a postal service left, let alone . . .' She shook her head and leaned forward. 'He's not a Russian, that's for sure. But you're too pretty for your own good, Miss.'

Honey felt tears of shame gathering at the top of her nose. She had an impulse to crunch the piece in her hand. Was this not mockery? Was her father not there, among the occupied, reaching out to her with whatever he could? Moira had to be wrong. She opened her mouth to say as much, but sense caught her at the last second.

Moira was untucking the collar of Honey's blouse where it had folded in. 'You know the boys in our hut have a funny sense of humour. Someone's bashed up the family chess set and glued it to tin foil, or painted and scratched out a bit of glass. It's a token.'

'I can see how helpful you're going to be.' Honey began wrapping the panels back in the fur.

'Don't get a cob on. I'm not the one using bits of tat to flirt.'

Honey couldn't face looking up. Her cheeks were warm. Her nose felt swollen.

'You should be flattered. Half a minute ago you were a fifth columnist, now it's nothing but a silly boy with too much time on his hands. Look, a codebreaker wants to woo someone he thinks is a clever girl – probably put the shits up her as well because they all like a bit of that, you know some boys think frightening a girl is the same thing as seducing her. I mean, it might even be a Hut 3 boy, they're off their rockers, Reuben said as much.' Moira prised the pieces back out of Honey's hands, calmly but firmly, into her own warm fingers. Her nails were painted red, a brilliant thick lacquer.

She lifted one of the slices to the lamp again. The lamp bulb was dark orange and flattered the amber. She examined the curled letters. 'It's very pretty. It's not perfect but someone has an artist's eye. How did you know to scrape the wax off?'

'It fell in the bath. Mr Steadman's overalls had been in there.'

Moira made a face. 'I don't know why you put up with them, you could put in for a change of billet.'

'Well, there must have been some kind of solvent in the water or maybe just the warmth because it melted the wax off. I cleaned the rest.'

Moira picked up her lipstick and butter knife and went back to stuffing the case. 'Listen, you're not completely safe just yet. Whoever sent these could still be disciplined. You could be disciplined for having them. You should probably get rid of them somewhere and just hope he comes up with a more sensible way of asking you to a hop.'

She wanted to tell Moira about her father, about Dickie and the book of ciphers, but the words wouldn't come. Every time they drew close to her lips they began to feel foolish. 'Can you help me find out what they say?'

Moira sighed and leaned against the frame of her bed. 'It's not as easy as that.'

'But you were in the Cottage.'

She looked sharply at Honey.

'Didn't they teach you some techniques?'

110

The Amber Shadows

Moira paused. She looked down, frowned and wiped a smear of greasy red from her thumb. She sighed a little huffily and eventually said in a dropped voice, 'You need multiple messages. Or at least an idea of what you're working with. Traffic analysis comes first, place it in context before you can begin to think about cracking it.'

'There are multiple messages. There are two.'

Moira put down the lipsticks again and pointed with the knife at the panels. 'Look, you are at an advantage over us because the person sending you these obviously wants you to read them. When we intercept a cipher we're interlopers. They don't want us to know what's written; they're deliberately disguising it from us, so we have to start from the very beginning to try to crack it. Figure out where on earth it's coming from, or what context it's been sent in. Whoever sent you this wouldn't have done it if they didn't think you'd be able to read it somehow, in the end.'

'So they think I have the key?'

'Or it's a challenge to you to find it.'

'Would be too easy if they just sent the key.'

'Maybe.' Moira paused. They looked at each other. For some reason Honey knew Moira was thinking about the crossword competitions too. Rumours were going round about the new recruitment methods; they put crosswords in the newspapers and invited people to submit their answers to a PO box. The ones who completed it all were summoned to London, to further tests. Some said Mooden had come

111

via that route, and a girl called Sarah who worked in the Machine Room. The ones who passed highly were given senior positions.

'But why you?' Moira said, and Honey caught the flash of something in her eye. It wasn't jealousy but something else, more melancholy.

Honey shook her head. 'If it is a test, it's not just for my brain, it's for my loyalty.' She thought of the gun muzzle, the awful firing squad chair. Blindfolded. The baby began to cry again downstairs.

Moira sighed deeply. 'Then let's hope it's nothing but a smelly tweed boy playing a love prank, shall we?'

Honey swallowed, still hoping in blackest hope that it was the other option instead.

'With a single cipher like this you have no inroad. There's no pattern to place it in. The more letters you have in a message, the more tools you have to work with, the easier it is to crack.'

They were spread on the floor, stomachs down, the three pieces lined up in front of the lamp.

'With more letters you can start to develop patterns. The first and simplest of those analyses is letter frequency.' Moira pointed to the first sheet of amber. 'Count the B's then the F's then so on . . . If you have enough of a message *and* if it's a simple letter substitution cipher – A always equals K, B always equals S, the easiest kind – you should start to see patterns emerging that correspond to the way the real alphabet is used. Say there are the most Y's in your cipher text. What's the most common letter of the normal alphabet?'

'S?'

'No, S is seventh after E, T, A, O, I and N.'

'Nations,' Honey mused. 'No, that doesn't quite work. I'm useless at anagrams anyway.'

'It's not an anagram, it's a cipher. You count up the most frequent letter in your cipher and the likelihood is—'

'It will be E or T. Possibly A.'

'Yes.' Moira looked at her cautiously. 'Then it becomes a case of guesswork. Where are the letters you think you've cracked placed, in relation to other letters? For example, say X equals T, and you think that B equals E. If you have the pattern XFB repeated throughout the text, what does that make F?'

'H. The.'

'Exactly.'

'But you don't do that with Enigma.'

'You can't do that with Enigma because the letters haven't been scrambled once, they've been – you don't really want me to explain Enigma, do you?' Moira was screwing one brow up.

'But this can't be an Enigma cipher because whoever sent it wouldn't have access to a machine, or at least they wouldn't know if I did.'

Moira raised an eyebrow. The Typexes.

'All right then, but I wouldn't have access to the key. And Enigma has – well, many keys.'

'You would need to find the key, certainly. But I don't think this is Enigma. This is—'

Honey felt it floating up in her, staying just behind her mouth: *the amber itself is part of the code. It's the last place he worked.*

'The next thing we have to think about,' Moira went on, 'is traffic analysis. It was weeks before we even began looking at the individual messages in the Cottage. What we'd do is make tables of where the messages were coming from. What their callsigns were, what time of day they were logged, the length of the message. Then we'd separate them out into groups. This data, shall we call it – this tells you a dozen things about a message before you've even looked at its contents. Say you get a report sent from a ship at six a.m. every single day without fail. Same number of letters, same callsign. What could it be?'

'General report.'

'About what?'

'I don't know, supplies?'

Moira looked out of the window.

'Weather.'

'Yes.'

'So then,' Honey said, 'like a crossword clue you can take that information to the intercepted message and work out where the words "weather report" might go. The words

114

"weather report" become your crib – your guesswork of the solved bit.'

'Indeed. And sometimes it's "nothing to report". Sometimes they use the same sign-off, "Heil Hitler", or they always write the full name of a General, that's for certain, which they should never do. The Italians like to say "*fine messagio*", end of message. One of the girls used to think this was terribly arrogant – to declare their messages fine. But you see repetitions are the cryptanalyst's best friend.'

'You shouldn't be telling me this.'

'You shouldn't be showing me your little trinket box, should you?'

Honey sighed and picked up two of the pieces. She chinked them against each other. The noise was musical; pleasing, distracting. She did it again. 'Did you like working in the Cottage?'

Moira stared at a tiny red blemish on her calf, emerging between the slashed leaves of the gown. Then she rolled over onto her side and picked up a piece of fluff from the carpet. 'Same. Same as the hut.'

'You saved a ship, didn't you?'

Moira picked up her lipstick tube and began wiping the sides with her index finger, where the red had smeared over the rim. 'Well, I'll never know them and they'll never know me so that's really that, isn't it? I prefer the Typexes anyway, it's better for my nerves, so the doctor says.' She threw the lipstick onto the bed and reached across for a

skein of tissue paper. As she pulled it towards her it crackled open to reveal a silk flower; a cream rose, floppy and
soft, fashioned from what looked like parachute material.
There was a card lying idle next to it. 'Listen, I can take a
rubbing of these patterns and have a look. Can't promise
you anything though.'

'Be careful with them.' Honey began moving the torn
muffler back towards her.

'But there's something you also have to do for me.' Moira
grabbed her wrist. 'That dance, tomorrow night.
Wavendon.'

Honey began to shake her head. Visions of Bugs and the
woollen man took slow shape in the shadows on the wall.
'Please, no.'

'I'll find you something to wear. Please, Honey, I need
someone to come with me.'

'Reuben will go with you.' She pointed at the silk flower
on the bed. Moira coloured up to her brow and pushed it
under the quilted bedspread. 'It's pretty, isn't it?' She got to
her feet and moved over to the wardrobe. Peacocks and
lilies were carved in hard dark wood on the doors. 'Look,
he's going to make it official, tomorrow. He said about as
much tonight. Or hinted. That thing at the revue, not really
talking to anyone at the interval, that was just a little mood
he takes. But I can't go with him to the dance until it's official. Do you know what I mean? Wait till you see what I'm
going to wear.'

She wrestled with the closet's crammed insides until Honey heard the noise of fabric rasping clear. 'What do you think?'

Honey looked down at Moira's painted toenails, then up all the way to where the fabric reached her shoulders and brushed against her hair. She had a look in her eye that was unstable, wild. She dropped her lashes to gaze over herself, over the way the fabric settled on her figure. She had a beautiful figure; the kind certain types of men felt entitled to stare at. All those brains up top, thought Honey, and what she wanted to do now, all she wanted to do now, was make and mend, hoard lipsticks and flowers. Sometimes she wondered what had really gone on inside the Cottage. Moira was holding against her body a siren suit, a long scratchy felt all-in-one with a turquoise hood draping behind it and a zip up the front.

'You're going to wear a siren suit to the dance?'

'Why not? No danger of anyone turning up in the same outfit. And it'll be bloody freezing in a field outside Wavendon. It's on an airbase.'

'But you'll roast inside the hall.'

Moira danced a couple of steps closer and Honey reached out and took the felt hem of one of the trouser legs in her hand.

'I'm not planning on doing much in the way of dancing.' Moira's eyes lit up. 'I have a beautiful patchwork dress you can wear. Scarf silk. I'll put your hair in a turban.'

Honey gathered together the pieces.

'Hang about, I haven't finished rubbing them.' Moira dropped down onto the floor again, the siren suit cast onto the bed. 'Please come,' she blurted. 'Tonight, he took me to one of those places, by the station. You know the ones the Tommies go to.' Honey knew the ones. 'But you could forget you're in one of them when you see him, when you feel him.' She paused. Behind her eyes, in the lines of her face Honey saw it plain, the waters of the dam rising to breaking point. Then all Moira's secrets came flooding out.

The contours of his body, the secret scents and textures of a man's skin; each and every noise he made at each and every different moment. She roamed up and around him in candid little tales, clutching sometimes for the right word, like it was a pleasure to clutch for it, to think again on what it had been like, what exact feeling, what smell, what taste.

Honey watched Moira's eyes roll back the hours. She could picture the hotel. It was down a track where lock-ups curved under the railway arches. Tin-town, they called it; there were trinket shops and pie shops and in between them ladies flashed their torches in little patterns at the men who passed. There was a house at the end of the lane, a public house with a spirits licence for the parlour. It was a poor, shabby front for a local madam who had 'rooms for soldiers'. She catered – said Wilf the cribster once, with relish – for a 'variety of tastes'.

'I mean, it's a horrid, horrid place,' Moira was saying. 'But you have no idea how much that disappears.' She was back on Reuben's skin, where he was brown, where he was pale, her words reaching up over his shoulders, in and out of his body hair, up and down the flesh on his flanks. Men who ride horses, said Moira. Men who can fire a gun. Her mouth and her head were full of him.

As she spoke Honey watched her own face in the mirror behind Moira's bed, between daubs of black mould. Her red hair was wild, sticking out like autumn beech. Her cheeks each had a dot of pink, her nose and eyes were swollen as if she had caught a cold, or might weep.

She detected a brick-by-brick wall being constructed slowly between them, Moira carving out two teams and beginning to align herself with Reuben; against whom? Honey wasn't quite sure. Then halfway through the story a different thing began to happen. Each time Moira named a part of Reuben's body, Honey would see someone else instead, some blue eyes, some narrow sinewy waist. Now when she caught sight of her face in the bloom of glass she was blushing.

Moira was entertained, by herself, by Honey. She sat back, grinning, her lids half down. 'So that's it. We've done it. Once last week, once tonight, third time lucky – tomorrow maybe. I tell you, I can't wait to be engaged. It's nicer than being married I think. It must be. We'll string it out.'

How many miles was it to Russia? A thousand? The

Nazis were pushing, taking and destroying everything. They had the west, they wanted the east. No wonder Moira looked so jealously over at her silk flower, no wonder she held on like grim death to her new lover.

Honey picked up the amber. 'Can I let you know tomorrow about the dance?'

Moira took the panels back and made a swift rubbing with an eye pencil over the tissue. 'You need a lie down, petal, and you need to stop thinking about these. He'll come crawling out of the woodwork sooner or later. Maybe he's shy.' There was something in her voice, some new confidence. Her confession seemed to have energised her. Honey remembered the brightness in her cheeks and eyes when she had first arrived. 'Maybe he'll make himself known so he can help you crack them himself. Maybe that's the point.'

'Perhaps,' Honey said, wrapping the pieces away. She stood up abruptly. The world felt as if it had closed in. Moira wouldn't believe her, she didn't believe her. She thought she was mad, paranoid. The amber in her pocket wasn't real. It was a joke, it was a fabrication. Moira had half-said as much. Moira didn't understand. Moira was only helping to humour her.

With her hand on the wood frame, she didn't know why but she paused. She could see Moira's face in the mirror.

'I wouldn't worry about it,' Moira said. 'Why would the Park single you out?' Now there was definite scorn in her voice. She raised the lipstick she'd been working on to her mouth, applied it, then rubbed her lips and turned her head to peruse her expression from different angles. After a few seconds she switched her mirror gaze onto Honey.

It was longer and more wearying, the journey back. The bundle in her pocket seemed to thump against her hip with each step she took. She found her key in her pocket. No apple tree this time, the moment had passed; the scuffs on her stockings felt wretched now. But there was one more thing she wanted to do before giving up hope.

Next door had hens in their yard. Honey had never had recourse to crime before but for what she had planned she needed a fresh egg. There was no point writing to Dickie with pen and ink. Mrs Steadman didn't allow trunk calls and neither, it seemed, did the Park, unless you asked, which wasn't going to be an option. As she had picked her way down the high street she had composed a letter in her head using their favourite code, and then torn it up again. Even the boarding school code, the silly three-level wording they used, was too dangerous. Debussy – green, a low-level call for help, if one of them had been locked in the coal cellar, or was bored in the nursery. Mendelssohn was amber. Fear or upset, a need for cover or to keep an appointment. The final code was red; Stravinsky. They had never used it yet. But pen and paper would not do. She pictured that girl, Betty Somebody, getting hauled in before Tiver. Had he shouted, or was he calm? Which was worse? And where was Betty now, in a government office in London? Logging prisoners of war or serving the wounded for punishment. Had she been forgiven?

She unlatched the gate, quiet as a cat burglar in her plimsolls, and fumbled down the path towards the stink of the coop.

With the small sliver of moonlight her eyes picked out the plumping feathers behind a wall of wire. There were foxes about in the fields. The Martins were careful with their treasure. She unlatched the coop, feeling a cloying horror at what the night was making her do. She reached into rank moisture, tamped her hand around the straw at the entrance.

She'd foraged eggs like this before, at school. It was a foul task, thieving them from under the mother, but needs must. She nudged the hot warm breast nearest to her, heard the awful cluck, and felt a startling flutter on her fingers.

The bird's terrible reptilian feet lay clutching warm smoothness. Her hand closed around it, stealing its heat. Then quickly, the booty in her palm, she darted out of the coop and prised the wire back onto its clasp before the hard peck came. A few of the hens were beginning to fuss now.

Fearful the cock might crow she hurried away, latching the garden gate quickly. There was no use taking it into Yew Tree Cottage now. She might see Steadman in the hall with his bullseye lamps. It would have to wait for the next morning, the chance to use the scullery. She hovered for a few seconds, hoping a place to hide it would present itself. There was an empty flower pot tossed beside the Yew Tree garden gate. She lifted its cool clay. No sooner had she done so, than she heard the footsteps; two sets of them. 'Sneaking into other people's gardens at nights then, are we?'

Chapter 8

'I tell you, Honey Deschamps, I never would have put you for a food thief. Eggs, of all things.'

She looked at him first, of the two. He was smiling. Cold shadows travelled up his face, drawn by the thin residue of a torch he had pointed at the ground, the beam covered over with white tissue. She saw his shoes now for the first time and all she could think of was how muddy and scuffed they were. *Scruffball indeed.* He seemed to sense her judgement and mind it, for he moved his feet backwards out of the light. But then, if a man did insist on walking his greyhound up and down the Bletchley fields in the dead of night what could he expect?

'Mr Plaidstow.'

'Felix.'

She nodded. She willed her heart to still but stubbornly it thumped on. Nijinsky's nose was working her up and down, from ankles to knees, sniffing at her stockings, tickling her with fluttering breaths. He had a crotched blanket sagging along his wiry silver back. His pupils were big black cherry stones in the torch's glare.

'Sorry to trouble you again. I hope you don't think it rude of me. But it happened again. We had another package come to the hut with your name on it. I wonder if they have a record wrong.'

He stepped forward and she caught the shape of his nose, the strong black eyelashes. His hand was extended. This parcel was bulkier, double the thickness, with something making an abrasive sound at one end of it, metal. She touched the paper with bare fingertips, and noticed in the torchlight her nails were grubby from the chicken coop. He spent a little longer than he could have looking at her hand, then nodded at her to take the parcel, and waited until she'd crammed it into the crook under her arm.

'That bloody messenger girl,' she said. 'Mind on last night's revue.'

Felix Plaidstow hung back. His face was in the dark so she couldn't see whether or not he smiled. 'Is it your birthday or something? We should make sure there's a cake.'

'Cake would be something,' Honey laughed. 'Only no icing, remember. No marzipan, no icing. But I hear there is a celebratory day coming up, happens every year so they tell me.'

At this she did see the flash of his teeth, the lips curling into a smile. 'Are you going home for Christmas?'

The package was awfully heavy, weightier than the last ones. And that metal thing in it rattled as she shifted her arm. Why did he make her think this way, in little darting thoughts that couldn't stay in one place? She thought now of her face. Could he see her properly? Was she blushing? Was it the discomfort of the night – cold, dark and shadowy – or was it him making her nervous?

'I was planning on it,' she said. 'Back on Boxing Day, mind. We're all working then, that's what you get being in a family of musicians. Nutcrackers and whatnots.'

'You must tell me about them one day.'

She waited. The greyhound shook itself out, rattling its silver collar tag, and she jumped as the flash caught the torch's beam. When it had settled, the night was so quiet she could hear it breathing, in and out. Her voice was timid. 'And you?'

Felix shook his head. 'I'm rota'd on shift. In my hut . . . I mean we can't really very well say what's what from one day until the next. You know what it's like.'

'Of course,' she shot, too quickly. The dog was beginning to tug towards the garden, smelling the chickens.

She had an urge to slice the paper with her nail and open the thing right in front of him. To watch his face. Coincidences could happen – God knew they happened all the time in war: the girl who left the shelter minutes before the direct hit; the man who accepted a place in boat thirteen to protect his superstitious colleague, and boat thirteen was the only one to make it back. Tales, so many tales of coincidence. It could happen. Three packages delivered wrongly, to the wrong hut, the same wrong hut each time. It could happen. And yet there was still something about Felix Plaidstow that made her shiver a little, the way his words seemed soft and slick, very different to his shabby clothing and his strange little dog on a ribbon, with the ballet dancer's name – ballet, another coincidence. And what was that shiver for? Was it fear? Or was it that she'd just been thinking of him when Moira told her about Reuben, about the tough flesh inside Reuben's hip-bones.

Pull yourself together. The silence had lasted longer than was comfortable. Felix was still there, his blue eyes in shadow.

'I wish I could invite you in.' As soon as the words fell out she realised how they sounded. 'I mean, you look so cold.'

He cackled gently and tugged his lapels. 'It's more efficient than it looks.'

'What is that? Boucle wool?'

'Blackout fabric.'

'Ingenious. Who made it for you?'

'I did,' he said, a little too quickly. He withdrew a step.

'Nifty with your fingers. You shall have to keep that quiet or all the ladies in your hut will want you to darn their stockings. Not to mention Katie Brewster and the dramatic club.'

She laughed. But the damage was done, and her chittering had made him retreat a step further still, pulling the dog back with him. She shifted the package and put one hand on the gate.

'Goodbye, Miss Deschamps.'

The way he said her surname pushed her heart down a little. She wished now that the dark would make her careless. She could invite him for afternoon tea, or to the Ritzy. Instead she said, 'We should go to the British Restaurant one of these days. They do reasonable meals.' Reasonable meals? Was she listening to herself? Provocative and dull, it was quite an accomplishment. Her mother would be appalled. Martha Deschamps had a way with men, strange men especially. She was silvery and shape-shifting. Honey had watched her at soirées growing up, but hadn't learned a thing.

Felix paused. He had turned towards the mouth of the street and now let out a large cold sigh. Honey scented the breath on the edge of it; bread and vinegar, no alcohol. 'I would love to, don't mistake me, Birthday Girl. One day. But this war's got me tangled round its little finger.'

Birthday Girl. He couldn't see her lips open, her eyes freeze.

'I'll drink a sherry for you though, midway through the night shift.'

'It's not my birthday, by the way.'

'Isn't it?' There was something in his voice, incurious or mocking. Was he flirting with her? Was this what flirting was for men like him? There was some note in it that said that maybe, maybe, if you were a suspicious type – like Joan Fontaine should have been – he knew that fact already. But how could he? And why would he have called her Birthday Girl if he knew it wasn't her birthday? The shiver came again. She tried to shake it off. It was the war. It was creeping into her blood, into her bones, into her thoughts.

Felix took off up the road at a long stride. She heard his hard wide footsteps; beside him the pattering of the dog, as if the dog were a snare drum ticking to his bass.

With the parcel still under her arm, she unlatched the gate.

'You've never been to an American airmen's dance, have you, Honey?'

It was all they would talk about in the Decoding Room. Sylvia, and the new girl, and a girl called Penelope who was back after three days' leave.

'I'm going to blag me some Scotch, stockings and a kiss.'

'Chocolate, if there's chocolate.'

'Why would they have chocolate? It's ices those boys have. Christ knows where they keep them cold.'

'In their hearts,' Beatrix said.

'Well, jolly good, I couldn't stand that accent a second more than I need it to get an ice.'

'They have tough skin, you know, on their faces.'

'Compared to who, Rupert Findlay?'

'It's true. I've seen one up close.'

'I heard they won't use French letters.'

'Rot. That's the sort of silly story you get when you talk to the ATS girls.'

'Don't smoke their cigarettes, they're putrid, there's my tip.'

'Don't let them grab your arse, there's mine.'

'Would you stop with this horridness?' Moira's voice rang out and they all fell silent, even Mooden at the pasting table. 'They this, they that. They're not one big lump. How would you like it if they spoke about us that way? Look at her arse, bit big but it'll do for a tumble? Would grab her tits for a bet but you'd have to stick a rag in her mouth because that accent . . . How would you feel, if they spoke like that about us?'

Mooden winced at the word 'tits'. Honey looked at her keyboard. Beatrix leaned across the desk and took Moira's wrist in her cool fingers. 'My dear, I believe they do.'

Work moved at a steady pace. The Red army and Yellow Luftwaffe keys were open before breakfast, there was no backlog. It felt to Honey as average a day as could be had in Hut 6. They typed, they cut, they pasted, they chatted in between, sometimes in tight, hysterical voices that couldn't contain the excitement. Moira had a secret calm on her face that broke into a smile when she thought no one was looking.

At half past three exactly Honey's period arrived and she cramped over in the draughty toilet hut, weathering the waves of pain, knowing that it still wouldn't stand as an excuse with Moira not to go to the dance.

Last night she had torn open the latest parcel as soon as she was back in her freezing room, with a torch, under the covers to blot the noise. This one had no wax – she had scraped it over to check – but two things about it were curious. The first was a little dip in the centre, a niche for something to stand in. It was circular, carved in steps, as if to hold some other missing piece. The second oddity was the mechanics. That metal abrasive rattle she had heard came from a small mechanical box attached to the amber with glue, about an inch behind the circular dip. A tiny little spectacles screw at the base held it fast. It was exactly like a clockwork mechanism, silver, with cogs of different sizes and shapes. But there was no way to make the cogs move. It had no quartz or battery. It was completely mechanical and needed to be powered by hand. It slotted into the base of the other three sides of the box, fitting the whole thing together like four sides of a cube, without a front or a lid.

Someone pummelled on the bathroom door.

She winced, gathered the gnawing in her guts like it was a bundle, pulled up her knickers with the rough wadding towel looped in place, and went back to work.

When the time came for the shift change, smug jibes were fired at the incoming girls, those who were scheduled for four to midnight and destined to miss the dance.

'I'll eat an ice for you.'

'I'll knock back a Scotch and soda.'

'Will you get the clap for me too?'

'Can I have some? I'm sure there's plenty to go round.'

'Have fun with your Big Band.'

'I don't know what's wrong with good old Florrie Forde myself.'

And the final, cruel instruction before the slam of the door: 'Don't be a wallflower.'

The wallflower. Piteous figure of the dance hall; Our Lady of Abandonment. The heinous sin of womanhood, to be the unasked. The warning bounced round Honey's head as she caught her corkboard heels in sinking quick-mud, clinging hold of Moira's coat. She pulled her foot free with an inelegant suck and slime splashed up onto both their legs.

'Watch it, you'll smear my lines.'

Moira twisted her head round to look at the backs of her legs. She had decided against the siren suit after all, for it would be too hot to dance. Instead she wore a patterned dress cut from one of her landlady's old cotton housecoats, printed with enormous mushrooms that looked spectral in the weak moonglow. She had trimmed a sweetheart neckline and puffed sleeves and a fishtail flare at the skirt. They had both rubbed gravy browning up their calves seconds before the army bus arrived. For Moira there was time to draw eye-pencil lines for seams. With a compact mirror on the bus she had insisted on painting Honey's mouth in bold vermilion. Finnigans brand. Colour: *Home Front Ammunition*. 'The moral effect of the possession of a superb lipstick,' said the box, 'is to a woman as essential as a shell to a gun.' Boiled with the cramps, all Honey could think about was that it looked like the colour of menstrual blood. Moira had beaded both their eyelashes with melted wax, bending carefully over a spoon and a cigarette lighter, sticking the black globs onto the ends of the lashes as best she could while the bus careered over stones in the road. Now the cold was making the stubble on Honey's legs prick in goosebumps through the gravy browning, and she felt about as ugly and unprepared for a dance as it was possible to be.

One of the weirdest facts of the blackout was that it didn't apply to sound. From anywhere and nowhere, the whine of the trumpets came reaching halfway across the airfield. The mess hall was invisible, but a couple of vehicles were parked one on each side of the door, their dipped lights shining along a concrete step. Flashes came and went as the door opened and slammed. On the field, reaching all the way back from where they had been dropped off, small torch beams scattered the ground in dainty lines. Where they shone they picked up wisps of faintly falling snow; flickering scratches on the night's celluloid surface.

Honey and Moira slipped and slid on the ice-grass until they reached the door. Men were smoking; women were clapped to their torsos under their uniform jackets. Moira's breath was already laced with gin. The soldiers held out hip-flasks as they passed.

'Hey, beauty, save the first dance for me.'

'Get him out the way and save the last for me.'

Moira groaned. The screech of a clarinet lifted in a high wash, drowning everything as the door shut behind them. 'It's "American Patrol",' she said. 'I like this one.' She was already scanning the tops of heads.

'Oh for God's sake, if he said he'd be here, he'll be here.'

They left their coats in a pile on a table by the door. Frenzy and sweat were in the air already. The floor was full; skirts and feet were kicking to the music.

The battle lines had been drawn. On one side were men in full uniform, hot under the wool, pulling handkerchiefs out from their pockets to wipe their brows. On the other side knots of women sat with arms cocked over chair backs, chatting and fiddling, talking with not much subtlety about one chap or the next. In the panting gaps between songs, some of these men would move across the floor, extend their hands and exchange a few words with a woman. If they got the magic words right, they'd end up with a dance partner. If they were lucky she'd stick with them for the whole dance. If not, they might be cut in on, and have to surrender. Sometimes you could see the relief of escape on the women's faces when this happened. Sometimes they'd look longingly back at their old partner. Either way, they didn't really get much choice. Once, Honey had seen a woman stride across the battlefloor and ask a soldier to dance. The man was so shocked he refused: her humiliation cost less to him than his own.

The Hut 6 girls had congregated round a cider barrel on a table in the corner. Whisky was being exchanged in hip-flasks underneath to spike the brew. Honey felt Moira's hand on hers, soft gin breath in her ear.

'Let's get a cider and make things fun.' As they walked to the table her anxious eyes still scanned.

And then Honey felt the hand close to her own behind. 'Well, smack me down, ladies, I feel like I've stepped straight into Hollywood.' She looked down at their mucky calves; her own patched, faded dress with flowers on it that were fashionable the previous decade. Moira's panstick shone gaudily under the dim lamplight.

Reuben had combed his hair back all the way across his head, and he smelled of the same aftershave Honey's step-father wore. He clutched carelessly at Moira's rump. When his hand dropped back it brushed against her own.

'Honey, why don't you find a nice chap to hop with?' Moira said tartly. 'I'm hot, I fancy a stroll.'

'But it's colder than the sea out there.'

'Didn't you see the stars?' Her eyes widened at Reuben. 'Hundreds of them.'

'Almost as bright as you pair.'

He was drunk; his gaze lolled on Honey, then back to Moira where it ran down her breasts and along the sweetheart neckline. There was a wilted bow at the dip she'd cut off an old powder puff and stitched on. It still had the brand name, printed very tiny. Looking at him, Honey found it hard to reconcile the man Moira had spoken about in such detail with the hard, steely staring airman, standing with a slight list to his balance. Try as she might she couldn't see him through Moira's eyes.

'Fine,' she sighed. The lovers scurried off, and she heard Moira scream with laughter.

'Want Scotch?' An airman behind the cider barrel was twinkling his eyes at her.

'No, but do you have bitter shandy?'

'What? A bitter . . .?'

A man in uniform with his cap skewed came up behind the table and grabbed a metal billy can of water. 'A Coke. She wants a Coke. We call it a Coke, sweetheart.'

'It's not a Coke, it's lemonade with—'

The man passed her a small glass bottle of cola with a red label.

'Want Scotch in that?' The first airman smiled, staring straight through her eyes.

She tossed him sixpence and scarpered, slipping a little on the wet floor.

There was a feeling in her stomach that she couldn't place, and it wasn't the cramps. As soon as they'd set foot in the hangar building she'd begun looking around. But this wasn't the sort of place where a chap could bring his greyhound. Heavens, she said to herself, the real Nijinsky would have a heart attack. Come to think of it, so would Dickie. He hated this sort of dance. When they were children she used to put on Henry Deschamps' records. Henry favoured the art deco era. He had a big appetite for nostalgia, and the twenties were his day. Deschamps Bath Soap clung doggedly to its angular design, even when Martha had taken Henry by the collar and told him it was fey, even when she sent a tea tray smashing to the floor and told him they'd make a hell of a lot more money if he'd put something on his bloody soaps that didn't resemble the wallpaper in a granny's toilet. He had records of ragtime and jazz, Fats Waller, Jelly Roll Morton. Honey liked to dance to them. Dickie had come in one day when she was teaching herself the Charleston: foot out, foot in, forward, back, kick, back. There was no malice to it. He'd simply taken the record from the turntable and replaced it with something by Debussy. Then walked out of the room.

The band were playing a furious little number. Legs were being flung, feet sliding on the mud that had flown off shoes. A woman kicked a lieutenant's shoulder and hot words were spat. The perfume of bodies, rouge and alcohol breath grew warmer and wetter. Suddenly the noise of the brass was too raucous; it hit a roaring pitch. As the final chorus screamed, the men swung the women harder. Shrieks, fairground high, carried into the air; cries of 'let's go, baby', and 'let's swing this'. Wool uniforms breathed heat through their breasts, and the silk of the skirts soared.

When it finished there was nothing but a hard, heavy panting. Honey stepped back to the sidelines where the wallflowers lurked, and clapped.

When they struck up again it was 'Moonlight Serenade', slow and swaying, and she turned to look at the girls around her. Some of them were openly staring at the floor. Others looked relieved and made their way to the cider barrel. She watched as one man chased his striding partner to the edge of the hall. 'I'm sweating, Horace, can't you see? Have to powder me bleeding nose!' Horace, left marooned in his cardigan and slacks, the only English man in the place, took off in the direction of the lavatory block.

She spied Moira and Reuben. Moira's head was tucked stiffly into his neck. She tried to feel happy for them, tried telling herself she was only jealous, only bruised and sore because Moira had dragged her out to the dance then cast her off. She wondered if she should leave, step outside and see if there was a vehicle heading back to Bletchley. She turned and wandered back to the cider table.

'Boo!' Moira's perfume came over her shoulder.

'You mean to say Honey hasn't trapped a beau? Or even a bee?' Reuben tapped the ash of his cigarette into an empty beer bottle.

'Bees aren't trapped by honey, darling, they make it. Lubricates the hive.'

'Very well. I'm off to re-lubricate,' he winked.

Honey watched him move up the queue like a fish, flirting and bantering his way to the top. It came on again, the terrible surge in her stomach that she shouldn't be there. At home lay the amber and it seemed for a swollen minute to have an urgency she was betraying by pushing it aside.

'I might go home,' she said over the music.

'Just wait till the end of this one, we can go ablute together.' Moira widened her eyes and slipped her arm through Honey's.

She looked as if she had something – many things in fact – she wanted to say but was keeping them locked away. There were so many sides to Moira, all of them alluring, all of them hard, like a piece of cut and frosted glass you could turn and turn and turn but couldn't quite see through.

But then they all had secrets. They weren't workers tonight, no one was. Who knew who had seen a death, escaped death, caused a death? Who knew just by looking at any of them, what went on in their planes or tanks or huts? And to them, what was she? Just a typist.

'You're in a funk about that silly trinket, aren't you? If you could see your face. All right, let's take a look tomorrow. I'm sure I have some notes somewhere on hand ciphers. Come on, let's go to the lavs. I need to try and smooth this frizz out of my hair. It's like a hothouse in here. You could grow tomatoes.'

The cold outside was biting brilliant, the stars in the blackout dense as crushed ice. Honey clutched Moira's clammy hand and followed her to a tent where a woman in a greatcoat checked their passes before letting them in.

The lavatories were filthy stalls with half-doors like a saloon. Faces were visible above pissing sounds. The chatter continued as they peed.

'I say, did you see the one behind the cider table? See the teeth on him?'

'That man with the three stripes. He said his name was Frank but I'm sure it was Billy last time.'

'The band leader's dreamy. Do you know if he flies a plane? I want one who actually flies a plane, not a navigator.'

They huddled and waited for stalls, peed and shucked their skirts down and reconvened where a metal mirror had been set up on top of a trestle table. Honey rinsed her hands with the cold hose and wiped them on her skirt. In the corner a girl was weeping. She'd hoped to see a black soldier she'd met at the Swan and Ferret but no one had told her about the segregation of American troops. 'They won't let them in, love. It's not that he's stood you up.'

'How am I supposed to find him?'

'If you wouldn't mind . . .' Moira peered over Honey's head into her open handbag, spying cigarettes. She shoved her hand in, nicked a couple and lit them together, watching herself and Honey in the bottom crescent of the mirror as she blew out the smoke. She passed one over.

'Has he asked you?' Honey caught Moira's eye in the mirror.

'Don't be ridiculous. They haven't played "Don't Sit Under the Apple Tree" yet and that's our tune.'

She marched out. Honey followed, letting the door slam behind. It was as she was fumbling in her pocket to check she hadn't dropped her identity card that she saw the shape of the man standing a few paces away. He was static, a black cut-out against the paler surface of the sky, smoking a cigarette. His hand rose and fell from his side. Fleecy puffs ghosted from the level of his mouth.

She stopped. Moira had melted away into darkness, into the criss-cross of torch beams.

The man flicked his fingers and a red diamond arced upwards then fell to the dirt. He began to walk away, towards the outbuildings by the gates where the Wrens' billet huts were.

She couldn't be sure. It had been easier when he had the cigarette up by his face. But the shape of his head, the shape of his shoulders was right.

She took a step towards him. He was walking faster now, still at a wander, not quite a dawdle. He turned past one of the concrete buildings. Honey looked over in the direction of the mess hall where the music roared, then turned and began to follow him. He was humming a little tune, the fast one the band had played second to last.

He rounded a grey corrugated-iron corner. Now a different sound was in the air, a noise she had heard before but one she couldn't place. It was a far cry from the music of the mess, but just as persistent. Its rumble surged louder as she drew closer. Vibrations began to filter through the grass and muck.

There was a concrete base on which the iron hut had been built, but the shadow was the same shape as those at the Park. And that was what triggered the memory. The sound was the same one that came through the walls of Hut 11.

The man was only a few paces ahead of her now. He had slowed. There was no one around and in the light from the stars she saw the murky shadow of his arm lift and his palm graze alongside the undulations of the metal. He let it scuff the wall, walking as he touched it, strumming and pattering his fingers, dragging his hand behind him so the tips went last. Honey watched the way his feet moved. She tried to fix in her mind Felix's walk, the way he had strided up the road. But it had been dark then, and it was darker now. Even if she slowed the pace of the memory down in her head she still wasn't sure she could make the two match.

When he reached the door, he hesitated on the handle. The noise was now at a clatter. There could have been a steam engine in there, or a row of knitting machines, or a clockwork menagerie.

He pulled the door and a crack of light blazed out, gold on black. The noise flared.

Honey's toe tripped on the concrete ledge and the world came flying up towards her. She cried out. In a slow, stagnant moment, she anticipated the whack, the graze, the sting. Instead she felt a searing pain in her forearm, as a hot hand shot into vision. The fingers clamped through the fabric of her dress. She swung low, missed the ground, hung, held for a few seconds. 'Careful.'

He grasped her and hoisted her back to her feet. She was so shaken that for a second she wanted to weep. Cold muck had soaked into her dress and she tried to brush it off. The gravy browning on her legs was already streaky from the moisture in the dance hall. She felt like an embarrassing mess. Timidly, she looked up, expecting his reprimand.

It wasn't Felix.

'Are you all right? Are you lost?' The man still had hold of her arm. She couldn't see his face fully, for the door had slammed shut again, muffling the noise, but the voice was completely different. He had an accent, a European one, though she would need to hear him speak again to try to place it.

'Could ask you the same question,' she said. Then, 'Thank you for catching me. Nasty stuff, that concrete.'

He didn't say anything for a second. She saw the shadow of his neck turn over his shoulder towards the hut's door. 'Were you seeking the hall?' he finally asked.

Where was he from? He sounded German to her. Was he Dutch?

'I was trying to get away from it to be honest. What's in there?'

'I'm not sure myself. I was just exploring.' He looked at his shoes.

For some reason she didn't believe him. His face was still invisible in the dark. She could see only his outline picked out by the stars. Her skirt had become twisted round her icy calves and she straightened it out. When he saw she was on flat ground he loosened his grip and took a step back.

'I haven't seen you before,' she said. 'Do you work at—'

'I work in here. In Wavendon.' He cut her off.

'Here at the airbase?'

'Just. Around here.'

She looked up and down his chest to see any reflection of stripes, epaulettes, metal badges, but only murk came back. He was wearing dark wool or linen or serge.

'Well, I suppose I'd better leave you to it. Suppose I'd better go back to the sweating throng.' She thought of Reuben and his shiny grey hair and his eyes on Moira's bosoms. She had felt so close just there, so close to having a nice time.

'Do you like the dancing?' the man asked.

'Not particularly,' she murmured. Why did she linger? Why did she feel struck to keep talking to him? The noise rattled on, but it seemed quieter now. It was easier to talk, in the dark. The dark was what had made it easy to talk to

Felix. She opened her mouth, not quite sure what was going to come out.

'There you are! Mother of God, Honey, you know how to make yourself scarce. What are you up to, creeping off around here? I thought you were behind me.' The slap of Moira's pace came seconds before the smell of her. How like animals the blackout makes us, Honey thought. That you smell a person and feel their shape before your eyes find them.

'Oh.' Moira stopped short when she saw the shadow of the man. 'Hello.'

'He helped me up. I fell.'

'Has she introduced herself yet? Probably not. For all the fame of her family she's got manners like a charwoman.'

The man put his hand gingerly forward. 'My name is Peter.'

'Peter?' Honey hesitated. It sounded such an English name.

'Peter Górecki. It's not Peter spelled the English way. PIOTR.'

'Piotr Góre . . .' Moira's voice trailed off. She took a small step away.

Honey reached for his hand. 'I'm Honey Deschamps. Also not spelled the English way. This is Moira . . . Moira?' Moira was looking over her shoulder as if someone might come tearing out of the dark. 'Moira?'

When Moira spoke again her voice was smaller. 'I need to get back to the hall. Reuben's in there.'

'Wait for me. Hold on. Sorry.' She turned her head back to Piotr. He was taking a cigarette from a case. No sooner had he sparked his lighter than she saw the shape take hold behind him. This time she did see a flash of chevrons, spiked white, followed by the strong beam of a military torch.

'Oi, what's going on here? Out of bounds, show me your identity cards, on the double.'

'Honey, run. Now.' Moira grabbed her wrist and they belted across the sliding mud back in the direction of the headlights that framed the dance mess. She turned and looked back once and saw the glow of Piotr's cigarette disappearing into the bushes. The man with the torch beat the ground with his boots but gave up after a few strides. She thought she heard a dog bark, but it could have just been his voice crying out 'stop'.

They came to a halt by the mess door. Moira held it open.

Honey yanked her back. 'Who is Piotr Górecki? You knew him.'

'I've never seen him before in my life.'

'But you knew the name.'

'It doesn't matter.' She reached for the door again. Honey pulled her away.

'Was he in the Cottage? Where do you know him from? What was he doing round the back of those buildings?'

'I've no idea, Honey. Can we just dance?'

Moira prised Honey's hand, finger by finger, away from where it clutched her sleeve, and opened the door. The hard, frosted-glass face had turned once again, out of sight, out of reach. Heat and scent spilled from the hall. Honey felt the goosebumps rise on her legs and wasn't sure it was just the cold.

Moira disappeared as soon as they were back inside.

Honey let herself be led in a waltz by a Welsh boy she knew from Bletchley, then danced swing with a couple of Americans who smelled divine but held her too stiffly for comfort. One of them tried to lindy hop but his rhythm was off and hers was distracted, and in the end he gave up and cut in with another girl instead. She wandered back among the wallflowers where she thought bitterly she must belong tonight.

As midnight approached Moira had still not surfaced. There was a core group of dancers still going at it furiously, but most people had clamped themselves to the walls, the airmen pinning in the ladies they chatted to, or had led them outside, or had gone home, or were being sick in the ablutions block. The floor was sticky with spilled cider and sweat. Only now she saw that little American and British flags had been pasted to the front of the stage. Paper streamers and Christmas decorations hung limply off the damp walls.

She thought she might finally hop onto one of the vehicles headed Bletchley way, Moira or no. There were plenty of people around. Moira would get home, if home was where she was headed. There was still the question of the egg under the flower pot too; she had not found time to deal with that yet, not with the Steadmans creeping round their cottage at every turn. The wee hours might be her best chance.

'Keep 'em Flying' played and the dance floor filled again but many couples could only manage half before they slumped off tired, rubbing their feet. The room took on the sudden sour atmosphere of the end of a party. The paper streamers sagged with moisture. A soldier with his uniform undone tripped and fell on the floor and cried out unnaturally.

'Never going to beat Jerry like that.' His colleagues yanked up his arms.

As soon as Honey pushed the door to the outside she found that the smell of the hall had sneaked into her dress. She looked back over her shoulder and caught sight of Reuben MacCrae at the cider table, pouring Scotch into a blue-rimmed enamel cup. He looked up and stared right through her until her skin grew cold. Then he raised his cup to his lips, obscuring his eyes. The band were playing the raw, sliding melancholy notes of Harry James's 'You Made Me Love You', a trombone carrying the heart of the sorrow in its lonely voice. Through the steam and the mulch of the party's aftermath Moira materialised, walking towards Honey.

They said nothing as they gathered their coats. Honey scoured the floor one final time but could see no sign of Piotr Górecki, or even Felix Plaidstow.

Outside again they made for the line of people queuing to have their passes checked onto the jeeps. She didn't dare look at Moira, whose cheeks were streaked with black lines where the wax mascara had run. Her lipstick was all but gone. *Home Front Ammunition.* The soldier checking passes whistled sharply and waved them on with a torch. Honey heaved herself up first, then Moira.

Moira waited until they were in their seats before she began to cry, heavy, uncontrollable tears, a sorrow as big and lucid as the moon. Honey touched her arm and Moira let herself fall onto her collarbone. Stormy sobs wrung out of her, she had a child's devastation that could move ships or stars. Honey looked up and wondered how many mothers, how many lovers, how many jilted and widowed and angry women were heaving their own burdens of grief to their hearthsides that night, from the cities of north Scotland to the sweating tropics.

She put her fingers lightly on Moira's hair.

'He's married.'

Honey said nothing.

'That's who's looking after his horse.' Moira's hands fell hard on her belly and her nails clawed the fabric of her dress.

Lucy Ribchester

The open wagon rolled out past the barbed wire of the airbase gates and they headed into the blackout, through the hedgerows and the dense shadowed bushes back to Bletchley, not once looking behind.

Back in her bedroom she found that rather than the peace she had been looking for, she was more disturbed than ever. Guilt tugged at her: for the stolen egg; for being preoccupied with the wretched puzzle, even as she held Moira. The night still bounced around her head, dizzying the quiet in the room, and the ciphers ran round and round like a carousel until she could no longer make sense of her own thoughts. The further she dropped towards sleep the more urgently they seemed to shout to her; *we're waiting for you*, they seemed to say. *You won't settle until you know what we stand for.*

Her ears still rang with the residue of the band. But when she fell asleep, it was not dancing that she saw. It was not the sodden Christmas flags from the mess hall, or Moira, or Reuben MacCrae, or his horse. It was not Felix Plaidstow, or Piotr Górecki, or Joan Fontaine, or even a person she thought she knew, miles away on the other side of an ocean with stolen amber stitched into his coat seams, running, hiding from the Nazis.

It was a banquet of men: candelabras on their table, antique paintings behind them, pristine shrouds covering their heads. In the dream world the smell was fatty and rich

150

The Amber Shadows

and there were no panes on the window as she walked past, no panes at all, allowing her to stop, reach in deeply with her hand, take the corner of one of the clean white sheets from under a static, faceless chin, and pull.

Chapter 9

'Moira? She's not here.' Miss Mooden went back to typing. Honey wiped her neck with her polka-dot scarf and tried to keep a handle on her hot breathing as she removed her coat. The door back into the main corridor wouldn't shut properly. She went out and gave it a good kick but the wood had warped. It would be the morning she was late.

'Need to get the coffin boys to look at that one.' Rupert Findlay was peering over her shoulder with a blotter in hand. He smelled of pencils.

'Coffin boys?'

'Yes, they get local coffin makers to build the partitions in these huts. No wonder they're so bloody cold. Not meant for the living.' He disappeared into the room opposite. She went back into the Decoding Room and gave the door a yank. It slammed, and when she turned round everyone was staring.

The Amber Shadows

'Sorry, queue at the post office.' It wasn't a lie. There had been a woman in a red hat complaining that her dog had been stolen from outside the butcher's shop last week. She'd had to wait while the cashier made jokes about being on the lookout for rabbit pie. She wasn't about to explain the reason she had been at the post office in the first place.

But she had already seen that something was different in the room. The configuration of the desks was wrong. Beatrix now had her back to the door. The packet of workstations had been spread into a horseshoe, with Mooden at the head. There were a couple of new recruits, each buddied up to one of the other girls. And Moira was missing.

Honey slipped into the remaining empty seat, keeping her eyes down.

Something had happened overnight that she was not aware of. She grabbed the nearest intercept and began to type.

That morning she had woken before dawn.

It was very important that Mrs Steadman did not see the stolen egg, for though she did not like her neighbours, she also did not like thieves. There was a hierarchy of offences in Mrs Steadman's book and being neighbourly was only minor. Honey didn't have the energy to make up a story for it being in her possession, nor did she want to have to explain why after cooking the egg she was not about to eat it.

She found the little nugget of alum rattling away at the back of her pencil case in the shiny toilet paper it had been wrapped in many years ago. It hadn't moved since she was at boarding school. With a candle in her hand she padded to the scullery in her stockings. The linoleum froze then numbed her soles. The kitchen windows let in damp and everything was icy-wet to the touch. She lit the gas stove, closed the door to muffle the hiss, then filled a kettle with a few inches of water and put the egg in the bottom. It still had specks of muck and a couple of down feathers clinging on. Tutting, she dipped her hand in the water to pick them off when a voice loomed from the corner, low and soft, 'You'll be up early. Early start.'

Mr Steadman.

He cleared his throat. He was always clearing his throat, he had a phlegm problem. She turned to see him sitting in a folding chair by the dead ashes of the fire. His bottom half was partially hidden by the Morrison shelter – a white metal cage that lay in their kitchen for the air raids, government distributed to all, but in the Steadmans' case not yet used. A pillow was puffed behind his head, and at the table by his elbow was a pat of butter, a bowl of sugar and a glass cup with a spoon sticking from it. He coughed again. 'Old girl made me sleep down here for the cough.' He caught her looking at the butter and sugar. 'Her remedy. Works.' He coughed again, weakening his argument.

The Amber Shadows

From a tear in the black sugar paper that had been pasted over the windowpanes a slate-grey strip of morning twilight washed in over the kitchen counter.

Honey realised her hand was clutching her own throat. Mr Steadman smiled. 'Make us a cup of tea too. Don't tell the wife.' And he winked as if making tea were a great secret act.

'Of course.' She found the loose-leaf tea in a counter jug. Mr Steadman was already on his feet, heading for the kettle with the egg inside.

'I'll grab that.' She took it from his hands, a little roughly, and sprinkled in the leaves in just enough time to turn the water a concealing murky brown.

'Tea leaves in the kettle. That how they make it in London? Don't let her see you doing that.'

He didn't wait for a reply but pottered back to the table. Neither of them spoke as the water took its time to boil. Eventually Steadman got up, walked to the stove top, lifted the lid then put it back. He said, 'A watched pot never boils,' and winked again, then sat back down.

When the popping sound of liquid on metal rose, he leapt to his feet. Before Honey could cross to the stove, he had seized the kettle. 'This one's my favourite.' He plonked down a cup with porcelain flowers painted on it.

She saw it in her mind very vividly; the egg plopping out of the kettle spout and into the rosebuds.

'Let me do that,' she said.

But her voice distracted him, and as he poured he missed the cup. For a second scalding water flashed onto his thumb. He lashed back his hand. The kettle slipped, then rolled on its bottom edge, then landed with a smack flat on the counter. Honey's heart seized. Another vision took shape – half-cooked egg white leaking out, congealing in the hot water. She blasted on the cold tap for Mr Steadman's thumb, but he only grunted, 'I've had worse. Once seared my whole hand to a drum of boiling oil.' She wanted to say, this from the man who took butter and sugar for a cough. But she didn't. She waited until he had taken his folding chair at the table and wiped his brow, and she brought him his tea with the tin of powdered milk.

Quick as was polite she fumbled the egg into a cup, rinsed the kettle out, gathered the other things she needed and made haste to the door.

'How on earth . . .'

Just as she reached it she turned with horror already on her face, for she knew what she would see. Mr Steadman dipped his fingers into the porcelain cup and pulled out a small white dripping feather.

Her mouth hung open for several seconds.

'The swallows, they fly in,' she said, and huddled the vinegar bottle she'd filched closer. By some miracle she managed to turn the handle of the door without dropping the lot.

As it closed she heard him say, 'Swallows? In winter?'

★　★　★

When she got to her bedroom she realised she had left her candle burning downstairs. But the gas was switched on and the room was light enough.

She heaved her chest of drawers over until it was beneath the lamp. The alum was old and crumbly and mixed easily with the vinegar. From her pencil case she removed a paint-brush with a nib as fine as a bird's tongue. She dipped it into the mix. And then she began to paint.

It had been a game of theirs, one they played every Easter time. A tree branch hung with painted and blown eggs. That year Honey's one – her gift to Dickie – was designed in swirls like the waves of the sea. Purple, green, gold and blue. She could never do straight lines. She could never do the zig-zag patterns like the lady who owned the bonbon shop and had her own tree of eggs.

She had waited for him to come in. The tree was lit with the coloured eggs, like a Christmas tree, but plumper, more fertile. Honey had always preferred Easter to Christmas.

And then Dickie handed her the egg that was her gift. It was plain, brown, still speckled, with a faint overcooked smell to it. It was heavy too, like a picnic egg. He hadn't even bothered to blow the whites. She had wanted to cry. It was a spiteful thing to do. But he'd stayed her hand as she lifted it to throw.

'Peel it,' he'd said. The anticipation seemed to steam from him. His green, animated eyes were wet with excitement to see her peel the horrid-smelling gift. Keeping her pride she had begun, slowly, chip by chip. The burn in her cheeks she could still remember. Shame and rage. What had she done to deserve this when she had painted him such lovely swirls on his egg? But as she peeled each crumb of shell away, beneath the surface was revealed the most glorious intricate world of curls, lines, dots, symbols, triangles and whorls.

They had appeared by miracle on the globular shiny white. She tore carefully at the membrane, lifting away the remnants of the cracked brown crust. In the centre, on one side, the words 'Happy Easter Honey' were scrolled elaborately, chubby and wonky.

'Ignore that bit, I couldn't get it quite right.' He pointed to the final Y, which had curled too long into the pattern below it.

Honey was too dumbstruck to speak. She turned the egg in her hands. It was like the Fabergé eggs she had tried to copy in her own designs. It was the most perfect thing she had seen.

Dickie's face was tight with the fight inside himself; to tell or not, how he had done it. He looked as if he was itching to. And yet, 'You see the priest's not the only one who can transubstantiate,' was what he said, and then cackled.

She was caught too: she knew, even at that age – she must have been seven or eight – it was a trick. Dickie was not God or magic. But she didn't yet want to know how it was done. She had kept the egg not on the hanging tree – there was no string to hang it from – but in her best Beatrix Potter eggcup, on the windowsill inside the nursery. She had kept it there for the best part of a week until it began to stink and the pattern started to fade, until one day she watched from the doorway as her nanny took it, lifted the window sash and threw it out to the birds.

She painted slowly and carefully, watching the wet slime trail of the brush, making sure the letters were thick enough to trickle through the shell. Once they'd soaked, they would vanish completely from the outside. 'IH (in haste)', she wrote. 'Bletchley Station. Please come. PS. Stravinsky. Know anything about amber?'

She had no talent for the lines. But at least if the egg was unlucky enough to be intercepted the message wasn't damning and it wasn't in cipher. She wrapped it carefully in the tissue paper from the amber, then in brown paper, then in a clean, undarned stocking, and placed it inside an old pastille tin. She addressed it to the theatre. She hoped it wouldn't be censored but if it was, there was no reason to crack into an egg – they were valuable commodities, weren't they? Worth posting. And after all, someone had once had a piano shipped to Bletchley Park.

By the time she was done, the sun was up and the air was bitten with a hard bright frost.

★   ★   ★

'SGT SHOT THROUGH JAWBONE AND NECK, PVT LURZ SHOT STOMACH. CO AND 1 PVT WOUNDED. PANZER ONE SET ON FIRE, TWO WELL PLACED CHARGES. URGENTLY REQUEST SURGEON'S ASSISTANCE. 80 CBM. TRADE WEATHER.'

They had broken both Light Blue and Vulture for the day and an inventory of Nazi boys with punctured organs was bleeding onto their tape rolls. 'PVT BRAUN MISSING. PVT LUTZ ABDOMINAL PLUG SHOT. SURGEON CONSIDERS IT URGENT THAT CO EVACUATE HIM FROM FIELD.'

'CONGRATULATIONS TO PVT SCHMIDT. HE HAS A SON.'

Honey kept her head down and typed, and tried not to translate the German in her head and tried not to wonder where Moira was. The faint noise of instructions being issued to the new girls carried beneath the tumult of the keys. A woman from the Machine Room came through to ask for a moment's peace while they worked on something.

It was nearing lunchtime but she didn't feel like eating. She took a moment's break to go over to Beatrix's desk.

'Have you seen Moira?'

Beatrix hesitated. Her eyes caught the door first, then the look of Mooden.

'I think she's in sick bay.' Beatrix went back to her typing.

The Amber Shadows

Honey felt the dance mess seeping in at her through the walls of the hut; the whine of muted trumpets soaring around the tight wood; Moira's cold hand in the wagon. She had seemed lucid when they had said goodbye. She wasn't drunk or slurring. She must have wept enough tears to wash and wring out every drop of alcohol in her stomach. 'Tea?' Honey asked.

'I think one of the boys has coffee. I just want to keep going.' Beatrix pulled her mauve cardie closer round her shoulders and picked up a fresh sheet.

Honey was about to leave for hot water when the messenger boy came in. The door had jammed again and one of the girls nearest scraped it back to let him squeeze through.

'Is there a Miss Deschamps here?'

Honey's stomach made a slow crawling movement.

She felt the final piece of the amber drawing close and it both sickened and thrilled her. But when she looked at the boy's hands, instead of a lumpy parcel he had a piece of paper. A memo. He handed it not to her but to Mooden.

'Report to Room 2 in the main house.' Mooden handed Honey the slip. It was signed with just an initial, T.

On the short walk between Hut 6 and the mansion house Honey thought her legs might collapse into spaghetti. She might as well have been walking to the firing chair. She saw the words 'ABDOMINAL PLUG SHOT' making a chain in her head, looping along and coming back at her.

It was Moira.

It was the amber.

It was Dickie? This time, could it be Dickie? Was he here? Did someone know about the egg and the cipher text?

Had Betty Somebody received a note when she was summoned before Tiver to explain her coded letters? She might as well have swum across the cold lake to the house for the wet chill she felt. Was this how Joan Fontaine had felt when Cary Grant brought her that glass of poisoned milk? Ah, but the milk hadn't been poisoned after all, had it? And Tiver, despite his threats, had not yet shot her.

Honey had not set eyes on Captain Tiver since her first day, when he had pulled out that gun and sat it on top of her freshly inked signature. The men who worked in the house dined in different places. They arrived in smoky-windowed cars. They didn't go to Hut 2 when they wanted beer.

Tiver's office was in the old conservatory, with windows spreading out to let in a fan of bright winter light. In this puddle of illumination sunlight spears picked out individual items on his desk: brown envelopes, opened letters, the red 'Most Secret' stamp. A paperweight in the shape of a brass battleship sat crushing a pile of memos; next to it rolled a fountain pen with three initials monogrammed.

He was army, but he wore no uniform, instead a dark blue blazer and a striped tie. When Honey walked in he was standing by a wooden rack of pigeon holes, stuffing his pipe with threads of tobacco.

Katie Brewster, his secretary, had knocked twice and without waiting for an answer turned the handle smartly and swung open the door. When she closed it the click brought to mind his revolver. He had been in uniform that first day, Honey was sure of it. She remembered three gold stripes, green serge, unless her mind had made that up afterwards.

'Miss Deschamps.'

He was staring. She blinked away the memory.

'Do you know why I called you in here?'

She took time to appraise his face as a tide of twined possibilities rose in her guts. Tiver had a tanned, weather-worn brow, lined and bronzed from time spent overseas somewhere hot and volatile. Across his nose, a legacy from the last war was scattered, tiny flecks of shrapnel, black pepper. His brows were overgrown and reached down towards his eyes in thin claws. His cheeks were the only sign of comfort in his military life, fleshy and threaded with a web of broken port veins.

'Have a seat, won't you?'

She shuffled into the chair opposite, untucking her skirt when it rumpled underneath her. A light sweat was taking grip on her thighs and palms, not eased by the menstrual padding.

'Smoke.' It wasn't even a question, nor did he proffer any tobacco, but she shook her head anyway. The smell of his pipe was syrup-thick and rich as he lit it and began to puff away. 'Listen, I'll make this quick as can be. It's a dirty business but I'm sure your involvement is accidental.'

He pushed a little official printed leaflet across the table-top towards her. It was government-headed, in the same typeface the Ministry of Information used for their gardening leaflets or air-raid warning packs. It had at the top 'War Cabinet'. Below it said, 'Areas Out of Bounds'.

How had he . . .? She hadn't even shown the man with the chevrons her pass. She hadn't shown anyone. He hadn't even been close enough to shine the torch beam in her face. Sickness reached up her throat.

'Come on, Miss Deschamps, let's make this simple. You tell me it was an accident, I mark your card and send you back to Hut 6. What were you doing round the back of those huts at Wavendon?'

'I thought—' She thought back. She had followed that man because she had thought he was Felix. And she had wanted to follow Felix because he was her route to the amber. And the amber was her route to . . . 'I got lost. After the lavatory hut. Who told you?'

'Things trickle down.'

'I was looking to find my way back to the dance hut.'

Tiver took a long suck of his pipe and drummed his fingers on the desk.

'Winman thinks it boosts morale to have his workers know what's going on around here. I'm not so sure it doesn't lead to mutiny. The lines get blurred between where you should and shouldn't go.'

'I wasn't trying to venture anywhere I shouldn't. There was no wire, no signs.'

'No, Miss Deschamps, we went with the more traditional doors and walls.'

She felt her cheeks colour and looked at her skirt.

'But I didn't open the door,' she said gently. She hadn't seen or heard a thing. Nothing more than she had heard every day from Hut 11.

He gave the memo a tap. 'No, *you* didn't open the door, did you? And that's the other reason you're here.'

With one hand – the one not cradling the pipe – he slid out the top drawer of his desk. She felt her skin seize, imagining the gun about to emerge, but when he pulled his hand free he only brandished another leaflet.

He pushed it across at her. A government booklet for every occasion. *Dig for Victory. Careless Talk Costs Lives. A Woman's Place Now.* 'Fraternising with Foreigners', this one said, beneath the stamp.

She looked up. 'Is this why you brought me in here?'

'This is guidance from up top. It relates to war, Miss Deschamps.'

'I thought war meant we all pulled together. The foreigners and us.'

He sighed long and wearily and took pains to light his pipe again. When he had it glowing and the sweet smoke was clouding he leaned back in his chair. 'It's not a warning, Deschamps. It's a friendly reminder of guidance. We don't circulate this to Bletchley folk in general because we didn't think we would have to.'

'Why not?' she said bullishly. 'We don't befriend foreigners?'

'I'm on your side, I wish you wouldn't take that scowling tone. Look, I know you redheads like a bit of the exotic.'

'I don't even know that boy. I've never seen him before.'

'But you can understand why being seen behind the back of a hut with him, opening the door to an out-of-bounds hut, might pose some sort of concern for us. You can see that, can't you?'

She turned her head to face the door. For a second the anger and the humiliation mixed so sharply that she forgot clean about the amber. She forgot why she had followed the man in the first place. She forgot why her stomach was now turning anxiously and she couldn't understand it. When she turned back Tiver's eyes held her. She thought about the orders he must have given in the last war, in the trenches; she wondered, looking at the brown eyes, where the tanned skin had come from, where and who had given him the shot-marked brow.

He puffed on his pipe and his nostrils flared. He took

back the paper and tucked it under the brass battleship weight, and his eyes lingered on the ship.

'Go back to work.'

Honey pushed her chair away from the desk. Tiver was looking down at the blotter pad and she thought for a second she might have embarrassed him somehow.

'One more thing,' he said before she was out of the door. Her hand snagged on the wood frame; she felt the prick of a splinter and winced. 'Something came for you in the post.' He reached down and pulled open the drawer again. The churn struck up once more, in her stomach. He left the drawer hanging open for a moment before dipping his hand in, watching her face. As Honey's horror rose, he extracted from it very slowly a parcel about the size and shape of a fist, trussed in brown paper and string.

'I told the messenger boy he could leave it with me to give to you. He was on his way to deliver it. Extremely unusual, the markings. Looks Cyrillic. Any idea what it might be?' He levered the object up and down in his hand, as if he were at a gala and might be guessing its weight to win a bag of sweets.

Honey shook her head but already her face was colouring to the shade of her hair. Tiver continued to stare. Very suddenly he extended his arm with the parcel. The movement of his hand, the way it sank and rose with the weight of the thing, gave her the impression he was passing her a grenade.

She took the creased paper in both hands. It was about the weight of a stone, maybe heavier. It surprised her and gave her wrists a sharp strain. The handwriting was the same as on the other packages. And there was a scent to this one too, stronger but similar. Sweet resin, perhaps muskier, more subtle. Distinct now in her mind as amber.

'Open it.'

She looked at him. He nodded to her. His face looked blank, expectant, as if he had wrapped it himself and couldn't wait to see her smile at the thing inside. She swallowed and her lips felt sticky. As she reached beneath the strings, she found a small tear already there, next to the glue. Tiver was still; his eyes said he knew already what she would find beneath that paper.

Her fingers had begun to tremble, sweat. Heat rose on her neck. She thought of Felix and his black belted coat, his greyhound, muscular, leggy, sniffing. Of Dickie in a theatre somewhere in central London. She thought of the things that were forbidden: Stravinsky, and *Figley's Book of Ciphers*, and the exile of a man she never knew, and of the name Korichnev. Would all these things now have to be dredged up like the wreck of a battleship, covered in slime and slapped on the table between them for Tiver to pick through? Her family secrets; Felix Plaidstow.

The paper slipped off like dead skin. It was softened by its journey, toughened by water or salt. The postmarks and censors' marks had all smeared; they had the weary look of being at the end of their road.

She knew what it was long before she saw it. She had known as soon as she saw the sides of the box, the foliage twining round the codes. There was only one thing, one piece that could complete the final picture. Something to sit inside that forest of flaming bronze, which seemed almost to glow with the lives of the trees and insects it held trapped in its sticky fossil coffins.

Underneath there was tissue. It ripped as she pulled it off. She concentrated on Tiver's pipe smoke to stop herself from fainting. The dizziness was coming. Her cheeks were hot, but her veins thrilled with ice: up and down the cold blood went as she pulled the tissue free. Just before she lifted the final sheath she looked again at Tiver. He had a plain, military blankness in his face, no hint of a question in his eyes, no suggestion of criticism or amusement. He was on alert mode, absorbing her actions, and she didn't like it.

Her thumb brushed the final sheet of tissue. She began to push it aside. But at that moment their heads were both turned by a boom and crack, followed by a terrifying cry.

The Captain looked at her. The muscles in his face gave an odd twitch then fixed into a map of ridges; each decision a line. He made his movements in succinct order. He spun to the window, put his pipe in the ashtray on his desk, and dashed out of the door. Honey followed, stuffing, as she ran, the package back into its brown paper, pocketing it in her cardigan where it weighed down the wool.

More men and women from the downstairs offices had joined the crush. There was a scuffle to get out of the front door.

'Why the bloody hell are we running towards it?' Katie Brewster was yelling. 'If there's bombs, it's the basement, the shelter in the basement—'

'It's not ruddy bombs, you idiot,' a man in naval uniform spat back. 'If it were bombs, we'd have heard the planes for starters and then—' He stopped. They all did, as they reached the outer front step of the manor.

Already a crowd had gathered from the various huts. They were a motley crew, standing out there on the lawn like some sort of roll call, each in their different chorus groups. Ships that so rarely passed one another in the working day. From the Cottage, Knox's research team – the 'fillies' – stood fussing in tweeds and patterned scarves, some still with pencils and paper in their hands. The WAAF girls from the administration hut had joined along with the FANY transportation women in khaki boiler suits. There was a scattering of men from Hut 8, one of whom was sporting a kimono, another his pyjamas, and a third a jacket so patched that one of the sleeves looked quite a different colour to the rest.

The debs or 'gels' from the secretarial units were there too, shivering in cashmere and pearls.

The Amber Shadows

But it was from the Wrens' Hut 11 that the blast had come. The door was flung back, dangling on one hinge, and a rancid plume of smoke danced and teased out, blowing black dragons on the air. A girl was crying at the centre of it, and in horror they all watched as she stood up, lifted her head and revealed a wide scarlet sticky gash across her pale cream throat.

Chapter 10

The girl with the cut throat stumbled and tripped a few steps forward. She blinked tears and dirt from both eyes. Her cheeks were scorched with dust and there were furious scratches on them from whatever had slashed her neck. But the blood had stopped flowing from the wound for now and was static and bright on her skin. Honey saw one of the other Wrens, a young woman with her uniform twisted, come forward and take the girl by the wrists, embracing her. The silence in the yard made her voice carry.

'Show me . . . come on, show me.'

As if she had broken a seal, people began suddenly to sweep forward. Honey was propelled along by them. A man came up beside the girl, supporting her weight. She pressed him back with a hand and continued to weep, shaking into the other woman's arms. The rip in her throat didn't seem to be giving her too much bother.

'I'm shocked, that's all.'

'She needs a doctor,' the man spat.

'Ambulance, man! What are you waiting for?' someone shouted from the crowd.

Honey managed to pick out Tiver, and saw with relief that she had slipped to the other end of the crowd from him. His face was back in that curious absorbed expression again, the action all stayed for now. He conferred with a couple of men in factory coats and they went into the smouldering Hut 11.

It was then that the girl noticed her throat.

She put her fingers to the sticky patch and rubbed, then pulled her hand away and looked at it. People around held their breath.

Confusion crossed her face, turning to horror. She stared at the stain. Then she laughed, cawing and raucous.

'Is that what you're all staring at? Bloody hell, I saw it come flying at me.'

The young Wren holding her tipped the girl's chin up and peered at her neck. Then she began to laugh too. 'God, they'd have had you to the cottage hospital.'

'Lipstick!' the girl cried, and she began to tell her tale. It filtered in whispers and tittle-tattle back into the thickened crowd, the story splintering into different versions even as she told it.

She had placed her metal compact mirror on the shelf of one of the machines, and taken out her lipstick. (Some said

173

she had the lipstick on the machine already). An electrical fault had tripped the thing – or perhaps with the mirror being metal it had made a battery and conducted the electricity; at any rate, the metal had melted in a flash, sparks had shot out and the lipstick had gone flying out of the girl's hand straight across her throat.

The shock had gripped the crowd tightly, and the release came hard and fast. The laughter was hysterical, the chuckling frenzied. Honey didn't know why but she was trembling and couldn't get the image of the woman's throat away from her mind. The red finger as the girl had held it up; she had laughed while the sticky gunk still shone. Honey didn't feel the escape they all did, slapping each other's backs, using the break from work as a chance to light cigarettes, 'hallo'-ing across the crowds to colleagues they hadn't seen for a while.

She looked down at her cardigan instead. It was sagging at the pocket. She scanned the lawns for Tiver but he was long gone, inside, onto another problem, for another hour.

She pulled the thing up and it dropped out of the paper solid into her hand, filling her palm. It was exactly as she knew it would be: a bright, blazing vital amber, as if it had blood and a pulse. Its wings were half-spread, like it planned on taking off, or perhaps it was extending an embrace, like it did to Prince Ivan, that first time they met in the garden of the golden apples. The choke in her throat caught her. Its eyes were perfect tiny globes. Not that the rest was rough, but there were lumps and patterns missed along the feathers, a skew on the feet. And yet the eyes were perfect, as if the best attention in the carving had been paid to them. To make them as real as possible, to make her believe the thing could see, and see her again one final time. The firebird.

The Firebird was their favourite ballet. Dickie had told her that their father knew Stravinsky while he was writing it, and had heard all his stories and gripes about the commission and the dance and the this and the that. He had explained to the seven-year-old her that ballets were made from stories, like a code. The composer took the letters of the original story and put them into a sort of machine that would blow steam and stank and would churn them round and round and out the other side would pop music, which the dancers would dance to. The dancers would know instinctively from the notes of the music what steps to take. That was how ballets were made.

He had danced while he had told her, round and round; playing the role of the firebird. When he danced at home, he was the firebird. She was never to tell this to their mother or the black-haired ballet mistress. The ballet mistress had told him that if she caught him dancing the firebird in the studio she would cut off his feet, for little boys could not play the roles meant for little girls and vice versa, and that was a very serious offence. But in secret, in the nursery or in

his bedroom, or sometimes in the parlour, he would prac-
tise the fluttering hands and the open kicks of the firebird;
he preferred it to being the base partner, Prince Ivan. Later,
when he began to dance professionally, he forgot all this;
Ivan became one of his favourite roles. Maybe it was the
name Ivan. Dickie said he had seen a glorious performance
of their father conducting *The Firebird* just before he left for
Russia.

Honey remembered Dickie's descriptions of their father's
hands – it was as if he was a conjurer, Dickie said, and could
make the music lift from the squiggles into something real.
He would take nonsense and he would make something
beautiful and understandable and real from it, and that made
him a wizard or an alchemist, or a codebreaker. And Honey
had felt proud.

His alchemic hands, in exile; creating these hard amber
images, bringing the memories to life. She felt certain, as she
stood there, one hand on the imperfect rivulets of the firebird's feathers, that he knew she understood the gift. He had
carved for her this firebird. He had smuggled it past the
censors. He was true. He was real. He was alive. And his
gifts, his coded, enciphered gifts, had brought her here, to
Bletchley. They said it was her stepfather's connections. But
it wasn't. It was the gift for codes and ciphers and secrets
that her real father had passed to her.

The reverie snapped. She lifted her eyes and saw Felix
Plaidstow.

The Amber Shadows

He was standing a little apart from Hut 3, looking towards the mansion. His clothes appeared dirty and unkempt as if he had been bent long over a messy desk. His blond hair stuck out in little feathers at the crown, and at the sides above his ears. His shirtsleeves were rolled up and he wore a knitted tank top but he didn't look cold. His cheeks shone red. Staring at him she saw where sweat had pushed the tails of his fringe away from his brow.

He turned his head in that instant. His eyes switched to her and she felt, for a second, as if she had been shot. She looked everywhere and anywhere; at the gravel stones, wheat-crunchy and fine, at the tennis courts where two old men were bashing out a match in greatcoats with cigarettes hanging from their mouths. She looked at the smoking door of Hut 11 where the loud, unpredictable machines still rumbled on. But eventually she could not help it and she looked back at him.

He was still staring. If she didn't already know his face it would have appeared to her very stony. But Honey was not foolish. She had seen that look in a man's eyes before.

She didn't want to break the gaze. She thought she could see the green-blue streaks in his irises from where she stood. He was icy and yet he burned. His hands were loose by his sides, as if he had forgotten he had them. She could have kept staring, and staring, if she hadn't remembered Fitzgerald's line: 'He looked at her the way all women want to be looked at.'

It was a spear in her throat. Stubbornly she turned, because she did not want to be looked at. Not even by Felix. She felt filthy, a repository for his filthy thoughts. But when she turned back he had raised his hand in an avuncular wave, and was smiling. And she blushed then for a fool. It was strange how some moments seemed real only in the seconds for which they existed. They passed, and you didn't know whether you had actually felt something, or imagined a ghost. The firebird was still in her palm, hoarding its secrets. And Felix was waving at her as if she were a new friend; someone he didn't know very well. She heard a cheeping sound behind, turned and saw a robin on a tree branch, its blood breast swollen, and wondered if, for that moment, Felix hadn't been staring at her at all; if in fact he had been staring at the robin, and was a little myopic.

He turned and went back into Hut 3.

'Where in God's name did you get to?' Beatrix's voice came at her like a cannon. She felt a mauve-cardiganed arm pinch round her shoulders. 'Didn't you say something about fetching tea? Come on.'

But Honey didn't feel like tea. She felt instead the weight of the firebird pulling down her pocket.

At lunch she took her cheese and piccalilli sandwiches from her plate, and buried them in a napkin.

The manor hallway was busy and smelled of brewing vegetables from the cafeteria. She moved quickly past the door to Tiver's office, watching it as if it might burst open any second and drown her in seawater or snakes. The sick bay was at the very rear of the building, past the cafeteria kitchens. The smell grew stronger, then became tempered with an ethanol bite. Immediately she thought of red splashes on hospital cotton and felt queasy. Whoever had fond memories of a hospital? Her own were limited to a broken collarbone and her brother's ear abscess. She had always felt ashamed of her nausea at other people's blood. Nursing was something young women were supposed to be good at.

She knocked on the shiny wood and waited. The door was opened by the matron, thin but solid in a white slab of headpiece and flat cork shoes. She looked Honey very swiftly up and down – a quick, hard assessment of her state of health – then breathed out, satisfied. Honey had never had cause to see the matron, but people said she could smell both lies and pregnancy.

'I'm looking for Moira Draper. I heard she was sent here this morning.'

'She was.' The words had a conclusive ring.

'Is she still here? Can I see her?'

'No to both.' The matron's spidery hand crawled in slow steps up the doorframe, blocking the view. Honey had the fancy that even if she were to slam the door right now, the matron's iron fingers would deflect the blow. Her body filled the remaining gap.

'Has she been sent home? I'm only asking because I'm worried.'

Her tone must have softened the woman a little, because she glanced behind her then let her arm relax. 'She'll be all right. Just had a bit of a turn. All you girls are tired the morning after those airbase parties. I can't imagine there's a link.' It seemed to Honey that making a joke was such an excruciating effort for the woman that it put her even less at ease. She scrutinised the matron's face for signs of a twinkle but could find none.

Honey sighed. 'I suppose I can call at her billet.'

The matron opened her mouth briefly, then whatever she had been about to say was tucked neatly back in. 'Yes, try that.' She closed the door and the sick-person scent dulled.

Honey stepped outside. Despite the cold she could not face eating in the cafeteria. She could not face the small talk, the little conversations about Christmas and books and whoever was home on army leave and whichever weddings were happening this week. She tucked her skirt and coat underneath her bottom, and took a seat on the frosted lawn beside the lake. She pulled out the sorry-looking sandwiches from their damp napkin and looked across to the thicket of bushes. The spot was close to where she and Moira had first met.

It had been very late spring or early summer, in what must have been 1941, because Honey had only just arrived.

The Amber Shadows

The warnings from her induction interview were still popping off at odd moments in her head, making her jump and flinch at noises. Things the Captain had said as he passed her that heavy pen to sign the Official Secrets Act had moulded together. Hanging, treason, firing squad. 'And if I had my way you'd get your head chopped off.' Had he actually said that, or was it one of the young guards at the gate, messing about with her afterwards?

When she heard the scrabbling in the hedges behind the lake that day, her lungs had leapt. War made one jumpy enough anyway. *But it must be pigeons*, she told herself. *There are pigeons at the Park. There are pigeons bloody everywhere.* The cracking of the branches came again, too loud for birds. It was a heavy tread, a weighty animal stamping the earth. Human feet, red and shiny at the toes, flared into vision. And a curse. 'Fuck.'

It was a woman's voice. 'Look, you out there, can you help me? I seem to have snapped my heel.'

Honey paused, then began prising back the blackthorn branches, raining fresh blossoms down into the mud. She saw at eye level the side of a curtain of chestnut hair. Strands had threaded upwards into the branches, and become caught on the thorns.

'It's all going to pot. My hair's tangled, my feet are stuck. Who'd be a bloody woman. Hold these, will you?'

She shoved a bunch of bluebells into Honey's hand, and it was then that her voice struck Honey as incongruous. She looked, Honey thought, like one of the stars of the silent screen. Dark hollows ringed her eyes – but rather attractively, as if she were feeling sleepy or had drunk a little too much. Her lips were shiny, their bud shape like small fruit. She looked well-fed and taut and sallow-skinned; slightly exotic. And yet she spoke like a woman who worked in a tea-room or pub.

'What on earth are you doing?' Honey asked.

'What does it look like? Carpeting the cat.'

'Are we allowed to pick the flowers here?'

The girl threw back her head and guffawed. 'You think they're going to shoot me on sight. Not likely to get taken for a German parachutist. They favour the nun's costumes, don't have the legs for stockings. Come on, grab me.'

Without thinking Honey had reached out her hand. The woman's palm was cool and slightly moist. Her heel creaked off clean as Honey yanked her onto the path, and yet she had insisted on turning back around, squatting down and scrabbling in the muck to retrieve it. They stumbled out of the briars onto the gravel. The sun was scorching the lake, blinding harlequin blue and gold diamonds on the surface.

The woman patted down her hair. The mats and tangles made flat lace against the rest of her lacquered wave.

Honey said, 'You do go to extraordinary lengths to make your billet room nice. I mean mine is horrid but—'

The woman cut her off. 'I'm Moira.'

'Honey.'

They shook clumsily as Honey handed back the flowers. 'I was just thinking I might fancy myself some—'

'They're not for me.' She was brushing herself briskly down. Crumbs of dead foliage were sticking to her wool skirt. The way she said it was like the end of the conversation. But it made Honey keener to press. 'Lucky boy. Does he like bluebells?'

'I'll find out, won't I?'

She saw Moira again and again that week, tangled in the bushes, picking up flowers – azure, mauve and white – and when the bluebell patch was bald she took to the hedgerows outside Bletchley station to cut down armfuls of blossoming green twigs.

Honey couldn't remember how she found out, but on some canal of slow-moving BP gossip it came to light that Moira was gathering wildflowers for the Park chef. They had brought him up from the Savoy Grill in London, but he had taken ill with the strain of cooking for codebreakers with fussy appetites and was on sick leave. No one was sure whether Moira's interest in him came before or during that leave, but she brought him flowers every day, until he tried to hang himself and was taken back to London.

After that Moira had changed her style for a little time. Honey noticed her, for she was hard to miss, striding into the Research Cottage, round the back of the manor house in flat men's shoes and cornflower slacks. The lipstick vanished; it was as if the chef and the bluebells had never existed.

After weekend leave in autumn of that same year Honey had come back to find Moira working in Hut 6. No one made mention of it; it was as if she had always been there, like the coke stove in the corner, only no one had noticed her until now. The clothing ration had just come in and the chatter from her was nothing but rayon and ribbon and raiding grannies' wardrobes at garden fetes for the most elaborate Edwardian hats.

There were lots of rumours about Moira: about her work, about her personal life, about how she had won a scholarship to Oxford, about how she had to beat the dons away from trying to seduce her, about her fragile mathematical mind. But she had an air about her like an unexploded bomb that stopped you from asking. Even in their most private picnics, even when they talked about corns, sanitary towels, how to notify a man politely that he was sticking his fingers too hard into your intimate parts, how awkward it was to have to go to the toilet in a tiny outdoor hut when you didn't know who was waiting outside the door – even then you could not ask Moira about the chef. You could not ask about what had happened to bring her from the Research Cottage to being a typist in plain old Hut 6 Decoding Room. She was candid, she was intelligent and she was vulgar, but she alone decided what secrets she told.

At four the shift change arrived. Mooden murmured instructions for takeover to the new Head of Room while the women picked up their cigarettes, shoved stray magazines into handbags and gathered their belongings.

'Honey, you've dropped something.' Beatrix bent down, then stuck out her hand. In it was a scrap of brown paper, torn around the edges, raggedy. Honey took it without thinking. It was only when it was in her palm that she saw the Cyrillic writing stamped on the brown paper, and in the centre the little picture punctuated by frilly marks round its edges, beneath the postmark.

'Must have fallen from your pocket. Can I look at that?'

Her heart jumped and a wash of horror rinsed her from head to toe. Beatrix straightened out the brown pulpy wrap, then frowned at the stamp. It had a picture of a carriage on it, pulled by black horses. It was faded and cracked. Honey waited for the question to come at her: *What is this? Where did you get it from?* Instead Beatrix broke out a curious smile. 'Very cute,' she said, taking her hand away, and shoved her bag further up her shoulder and moved towards the door.

Honey listened to Beatrix's footsteps cracking over the wood in the corridor and then the rush of cold smoked air and the silence as the outer door slammed shut. She waited for a few seconds before making her own way towards the door. Miss Mooden caught her arm. 'Honey.'

She jumped out of her skin.

'Gosh, are you all right? I didn't mean to frighten you.'

Her nerves were in tatters; her heart drummed. 'I'm fine. I just need a little rest perhaps after last night, the dance . . .'

Mooden interrupted. 'I was going to ask if you wouldn't mind awfully swapping with Sylvia? She's on the rota to switch to night shift tomorrow, but we're a girl down. I know you usually go day, back, night, but we're in a bit of a fix.'

Honey breathed out. 'Is that all? Of course. No problem, I'd love to help.' The words came out of her mouth before she realised the weight of them. Agreeing to flick straight to night shift without warming up on back shift wasn't a good idea for an unquiet mind.

At this time of evening the other Bletchley workers were clocking off shifts and the streets were busy. Shoulder bumps and trips in the dusk were followed by jollity. 'Gosh, I'm sorry'; 'Never thought the war would bring you this close to your neighbours': 'Good job it's a blackout and not a soundout, if Jerry was using his ears he'd hear this town seven miles away.'

There was good nature in the frosty air. Christmas was coming and folk were making the best of it. You could orient yourself on the high street by the smells: the oily blood of the butcher's, the vanilla yeast of the baker's, the motor grease of the mechanic's. But even now it felt so temporary, a game of blind man's buff, after which the lights would be switched back on and the world could breathe out again. Honey couldn't quite believe, didn't want to believe, that this was now their reality; this blacked-out life was the foreseeable future, this was the present and could go on for ever.

Outside the newsagent's she heard two people talking about the headlines: 'Struggle in Stalingrad'. The borders of that country were bleeding. She had thought that the worst horrors that could ever have been reported had happened in the last war, and now she didn't want to look at the stories. She'd heard it on the wireless. Bread running out. Fields frozen to a crumb. Nothing came of the last harvest. People were melting down lipsticks to spread on bread. Little girls in red sashes were leading the charges. Hunger was spreading as the Nazis bombed grain mills, and meat plants, and sugar and tea warehouses. They'd starve them out. When London's sugar wharves were torched the streets around them had run with rivers of treacle. When the food was gone it was gone. One journalist had said at the time they'd make cannibals of Blighty before they'd invade, and then we'd submit to them for shame.

And in Russia, he was there, somewhere, running, hiding, a speck in her imagination. But she could see him, as if she was flying high above a blackout and he was the blue flame of a cigarette lighter.

You didn't have to have met someone to know them. You didn't have to have held their hand or held their gaze to feel what kind of person they were. Objects and stories and artefacts were as much the building blocks of a person as what they told you about themselves when they stood in front of you. Honey knew that. She knew her father, though she had never met him. Sometimes she felt that through Dickie's stories she knew him better than either of them knew their mother.

Moira's landlady was slow to the door. Honey could hear the baby inside the front room, crying, a one-note dirge. When she did finally pull open the door, she did what the matron had done and cautiously placed her arm in the frame as if she had no intention of letting anyone in. Her face was pricked with blotches of red and she had coal dust on her brow beneath a patterned band. Strands of her hair poked free, and the lumpy outline of rollers made her head look huge and misshapen. She kept looking back over her shoulder in the direction of the crying.

'I'm sorry, it's just . . .'

'Is Moira all right? She was sent to the sick bay, and then the matron said she'd gone home. We were together at the dance.'

The landlady looked uncertain. Her forehead puckered. From over her shoulder there was a milk-pudding smell.

'Is she here?'

'Yes, but—'

Honey's patience slipped. 'I've come all this way in the blackout. I mean, I haven't got anything to bring her, but – what's wrong with her? No one will tell me.' As she heard the words detach from her mouth they took on a shrill quality she hadn't intended.

The woman's brow furrowed even further, then Honey watched in slow vivid strokes as piece by piece it crumpled. Her cheeks burned violently. 'I can't,' she said. 'I can't – with all of this, and that . . .' She widened the door and pointed a hard finger at the wailing parlour.

She put her hands to her headscarf, clutching the rollers, pressing them into her head. She pushed as if they were stoppers that could keep the madness in or the grief out, or whatever pain she was feeling she could transform into a simple physical sensation that was easier than the confusion of mental pain; nothing but a sharp scratching on the head. Her arms fell.

Honey reached across the threshold and touched the fabric of her sleeve. Her own hand felt awkward and cold on the hot, damp nylon. Her voice when it came was woefully small. 'Cup of tea?'

'There's none.'

'All right, brandy. Where's your brandy?'

She took Moira's landlady by the sleeve and guided her into her own little parlour where the neat furniture sat in a strange orange light behind blackout curtains. For a brief second the woman looked around her as though she had never seen such a place before in her life. She just stood in the middle of the room, on the middle of a round soft pile rug, gazing at her knick-knacks and her framed photographs, all the things she had acquired and built into the picture of a life. Honey closed and latched the front door.

The baby was still howling in a wooden cot in the corner of the room. She didn't know how to pick babies up, but under the arms seemed like the best way. She hauled it over to the woman.

The landlady looked at her child with the same vacancy for a couple of seconds. Then instinct swam up in her and she lifted its head and began to rock it against her shoulder.

'It's just that I get no word from him for weeks,' she sniffed. 'Have to go on good faith from the British Army, but would you trust them with your loved one's life? He's in Africa somewhere, in a desert. I can't remember the name. And now her.' She gestured with her chin upstairs. Honey was scooting around the parlour sideboard, pulling the best crockery and stacked knitting patterns out of the way.

'There was a song his daddy used to sing to him. I wish I knew the words, I wish I could remember it.' She burbled a little tune, wordless, nonsense words, up and down, then gave up. 'It was the only thing could get him to sleep.' She looked up and saw Honey scrabbling in the sideboard. 'It's in the medicine box, in the kitchen.'

The brown bottle was easy to find behind the breadbin on the kitchen counter top but there was only a finger left. Honey stood in the parlour doorway. The landlady waved it away. 'Go on, take it to her if you like.' She had wiped her tears on the baby's burp flannel; there were splodges of wet on it and now she was sitting on the couch bouncing the child on her knees, her focus absorbed. He was still noisy but the crying had slipped into a more ambiguous scream now, happy on the high notes, uncertain on the low.

Backing away from the room, the last thing Honey saw was the woman smothering the infant with kisses, from its pink and white cheeks to its feathery head. Her smile was restored as if nothing had happened.

The depleted brandy bottle still in her hand, Honey crept up the stairs. Moira's door was ajar.

She knocked softly. There was no response so she pushed it open a fraction more. Inside, there was a peculiar smell, half-chemical, half-perfumed, all in a fug of unwashed cotton and hair. In the slice of room that came into view she could see the head of Moira's bed, and the bedside table spread with stitching patterns, elastic and thread. Moira's chestnut hair was spread out tangled over the pillow, her face obscured by the strands. She was lying on her side, facing the door. One arm dangled above the covers, the fingers fish-white and floppy.

On the floor beneath the head of the bed someone had placed a zinc bucket. A glass of water and a brown bottle of little round pills sat closest to her on the table. She was snoring softly.

'Mo,' Honey whispered. 'Mo, are you awake?'

There was no response. Honey pushed the door a little further. Before she crossed into the room she hesitated.

That panic downstairs when she had spoken shrilly to the landlady, the shiver in her spine; it had come rising up the staircase with her. Was she invading? What had Moira done to end up like this? She wondered why she had come. At the back of her mind she knew it was partly because she wanted to tell Moira about the firebird, and she felt a tingle of guilt.

Looking at her friend now, Honey was pulled sharply back into reality. The room felt low and wet with sadness. It was cold despite a whimpering gas heater. The thick curtains fluttered in a draught. Moira's hair looked damp with fever sweat and congealed tears.

Honey pulled across the rug, moved the bucket out of the way and knelt down. She touched Moira's cheek. Her skin was very hot but the touch didn't wake her. The cotton pillow was clogged with wet breath beside her mouth.

'Oh Moira.' She looked at the little prescription bottle. Bromide. A doctor perhaps, or the matron at the sick bay?

Moira's eyes pinged open. The hazel colour in the mess of her hair was startling. 'It's you,' she said to the pillow.

Honey's tongue jammed. Everything that came into her head seemed trite.

'They're going to take me away, aren't they?'

'They'll let you go home.'

'I don't know why I did it, Honey. I was just so sad. This morning when I arrived at the hut. Sad and tired and I don't know what else. I can't even organise my thoughts—' She broke off and sighed into the pillow, but the sigh shook her head.

'What happened?'

'You know what happened,' she said to the pillow.

'You seemed all right last night.' As soon as Honey said it she knew it sounded stupid; accusing. 'You could have talked to me more.'

Moira turned away, pressing her mouth and nose deep into the sheets. 'You can't talk about anything to anyone. It's like acid, the secrets, all tainting you inside. I want to tell my mum what a shit he is, but then I'd have to explain what I was doing stepping out with an American – where did I meet an American? What are Americans doing in my office? Why are there Americans at the FO? You can't say anything about the Park without opening a can of fucking worms.'

She twisted her face and the words spat towards Honey. The muscles of her eyes were tight, pressed open; the eyes shone for a second.

'Did you see a doctor?'

Moira nodded.

'Did he give you something to calm you?'

'He was nice. He didn't ask what was wrong. I think he thinks it's work nerves. I don't know what's happening to my body. It's as if my brain . . . but then it's my body, not my brain going wrong . . . I don't know why I did it,' she said again.

Honey paused. She wanted to know what Moira had done.

'Shall I put the wireless on, or read to you?'

The hair wriggled back and forth. Honey's eyes strayed along the table and she saw among the dressmaking patterns and pots of kohl two slices of tissue paper, each with blue eyeliner rubbings brushed daintily over their surface. The carvings had come through sharp. Next to them, on two separate scraps of white paper Moira had scribbled equations, tables and blocks of letters.

Moira stirred all of a sudden and Honey jumped.

'Tell me something that happened today,' she said sleepily.

With her gaze still on the fluttering, incriminating papers, Honey began to witter; nonsense about Beatrix and the new girl and how she'd asked a question about what went on inside Hut 11 and they'd all gone quiet with shock and had to explain to her you don't do that. Miss Mooden's face. All Decoding Room stories ended with Mooden's face. She didn't mention the explosion or the girl with the lipstick throat. It wasn't Moira, but something in her own unease about that event that kept coming back. She wanted to whitewash it from her day. It had been horrible. She had believed in that moment she was looking at a person about to fall on their knees and die. And she had hated it with a terror she had never thought possible. Christ, how it must be for the boys in the battlefield, where blown limbs and cut throats would never turn out to be lipstick. How could a soldier ever erase that from his mind? There were the dead she had seen lined up on the pavements in the London Blitz, the bloodied chorus girls at the bombed theatre; the memory made her shiver. But to see a person die, to see the blood turn from purple to livid . . . *abdominal plug shot* . . .

After a while she heard Moira's breathing slow. Loose snores came in soft bursts. She touched her brow. The forehead was wet, as if she had been running in her sleep.

Two nights ago love had swelled her beau to enormous importance. Everything about Moira had been different then; her silky movements, her quickness. She had ballooned with Reuben, spilled with words about him. Now he was removed, there was only a collapsed shell. The silk flower was nowhere to be seen.

Honey stood up. Her legs felt sore and stiff from the pressure of kneeling. She pulled the rug back to the middle of the room. Gently, in small short movements, she began to move the tissue slices with the rubbings and the little sheets of scribbled paper towards her. The first one slid like water over the mountain stack of make-up cases on the table. But the second snagged on a perfume bottle. Moira's eyes stirred.

'Shhh,' Honey whispered. 'It's all right.'

'I tried. Really I did. I didn't forget them.'

'It's all right, it doesn't matter.'

'It's a Vigenère.'

Honey stopped.

'Your cipher. It's . . . I haven't managed to crack it yet. But I think it's a Vigenère square. An old hand cipher. Leave the papers and I'll . . .'

Honey's hand loosened on them. What were these, if not her own silk flower, her own trinket to cling on to that stood in for someone who wasn't there? She let the tissue rubbings fall back onto the table. The two little pieces of paper dropped from her hand to the floor. She bent to pick them up, then Moira sighed and it seemed she was a little more content, and Honey let her hand fall again and let the papers rest where they were. She stood back up, then left quietly, without saying goodbye to the landlady.

Chapter 11

As soon as she hit cool air she felt the tears come quickly. It was a hurried sobbing that rose and just as swiftly vanished, the same feeling as being sick after holding it in. Afterwards her face felt washed, her mind cleaner.

She took the same path she had taken back from the revue a few nights ago. The roads had cleared. Families were inside and grilling smells filtered through chimneys, under doorframes.

It was hard to picture in the sparks of frost that shone now through the shadows of trees, this time two years ago. Christmas 1940 she had been at home in London when the barrage balloons rose, great bloated sheep into the sky. The aeroplanes had come ripping through the clouds, dropping fire, blasting whole neighbourhoods, turning rubble molten red, while all she could do was peep through the blackout blinds at her mother's house.

'Safe in Kensington,' her stepfather had said. But then, 'Safe in the theatre,' he had said too. And the Empire had taken a direct hit when her mother was on stage, and forty people in the stalls had died. Their limbs were buried with painted stars and cloth woodland and bits of gilt plaster from the boxes. The chorus girls, the show's baritone, they had died onstage. It had made Martha Deschamps more determined than ever to sing.

'But what else,' she said every time to Honey, 'could I do for this war?' There was a part of Honey's mother that truly, wholeheartedly believed the role of an opera singer during wartime was a political one, as essential as a nurse or ambulance driver. And sometimes when Honey saw the men in uniform crowding the back of the Bletchley Ritzy or sitting in the front rows of the ENSA concerts where they sang Purcell and Bizet – anything that wasn't German – she would wonder for a second if there was something in what her mother said.

She turned past the church and onto the lane where that large thatched building squatted next to the road, where the blackout blind had fallen and she had seen the shrouded men. Curiosity couldn't stop her looking sidelong as she walked, as if it might happen again. She stared hard at the ghost outline of the whitewashed stone and then at the window frame. She imagined if she stared hard enough she could bore through those heavy black wool curtains and see again those figures draped in white.

And then, she reasoned, she would probably see that they were not in fact people round a dinner table at all, but furniture draped in rags. She would see that the candelabras on the table were just for a caretaker to lift as he checked the room, as he checked the loose blinds. And she began to wonder what the house was at all. It didn't look like a dwelling. It had the feel of a village hall, a meeting house. It had an old-world spirit that made her uneasy.

Of course, she reasoned, she was only lingering over it because it stopped her from confronting the other things, like Moira and like the lump of amber that sat now in her pocket, still making her cardie hang on one side. She would be home soon. Then she would have to fit the firebird into its slot, look at the damned thing goading her with carved letters and curling vines, and try not to dream of it when she went to sleep.

She remembered with a jolt the shift change she had agreed to tomorrow. Time to double-up on sleep. It was the custom to slip onto back shift for a week after days so she had never gone straight to nights before. Night shifts were a terrible place. The brain tangled easily; sleep came only in distorted clouds during the day and then the brain was cloyed even more by the next nightfall, until reality felt unreal. After some time you would reach such a state of disconnection that phrases from the Typex machines would begin to drum and repeat in your head. Last time 'KEINE BESONDEREN VORKOMMNISSE – nothing to report' had stuck, and the waltz from *The Merry Widow*, lilting round and round as if it would spin her mad.

She had just passed the house when the rain came on. At first it was only a spattering. Then very quickly a powerful downpour began, slanting on the wind, hitting window-panes and turning the ground to sludge. It hadn't rained so hard since November. Apart from afternoon drizzle or flurries of snow the weather these past weeks had been cold and bright, good air fighting weather with strong moons. Now the sky took its revenge.

She was into the wooded thicket that ran between the building and the entrance to her own lane by the time it properly set in. She huddled for a few moments, stranded, heavy drips shooting down either side from the branches. From her shelter she could make out the side door of the thatched house. Then suddenly from nowhere a man was there, running across the lawn, his arms at full stretch by the size of whatever he was carrying. He looked huge, roguishly huge behind a flat rectangular slab, and he glanced around him as he went – which was probably what made him slip on the lawn. He didn't fall, but the thing he was lugging, wide and unwieldy, skidded from his grip and bashed its corner in the muck.

'Christ,' she heard him curse.

'Mr Plaidstow!' It flew out of her mouth, and before she knew it she was running towards him in the rain; him, in his blackout material coat with the belt pulled tight round his skinny waist. He had no hat. The rain had pushed his hair down flat to his brow and it splashed off his nose as he turned to her.

'Can you take that corner?' He gestured to the bottom of the slab. It was sheathed in an oilcloth, running channels of rain down to pools where the folds lay. Her fingers were already icy from the walk. They slipped a little on the cloth and the piece shot back down into the mud. She caught it just as it cracked the ground.

'Oh, blast it.' Felix craned over, pulled up the oilcloth and examined a small crack. Virgin wood had appeared in a straight fissure, beneath gold paint. It looked like a flesh-wound. 'Thank God it wasn't the painting itself. What are you doing running around in the blackout?' He fidgeted with the oilcloth while the rain continued to fall. The wood frame slipped from his palm, and Honey saw one of the upper corners of the cloth fall away, revealing a crackled canvas, the topmost quarter of a beautiful intricate web of flowers, spectral in the moonlight, shining under a spidery varnish glaze.

'Could ask you the same question, Mr Plaidstow.'

He caught her eyes on the painting. 'I'm waiting for someone. Come here. Let's haul it in here. I was trying to get under the eaves. Blasted fellow's late. Said he'd meet me down by the kerb but I can't wait there. It's far too wet.'

'Where are you taking it?'

'It's heading to . . .' He broke off, peering towards the house. When he glanced back down at Honey's expectant face he relaxed into a grin. Bracing the bottom of the frame with one arm he lifted the top edge of the cloth. 'Stunning, isn't it? It's a van Dael, you know? Do you know who he was?'

The prickle for some reason stung deeper this time than it usually did when a man assumed she was stupid.

She looked down at the part he'd exposed. The finish was so luminous it looked almost greasy. She could make out the frothy bloom of a crimson carnation. After a couple of seconds she looked back up. Felix was staring at her. 'What do you think?' The way he asked, the frisson in his voice, it was almost as if he had painted it himself and was waiting for her judgement.

'It's . . . I'd need to see the whole thing, but yes, he's a lovely painter. Where is it from? What are you doing with it?'

'Oh, taking it to hang up somewhere. Someone's country digs.'

She snorted and the cold rainwater sprayed through her nose, making her cough. He laughed at her, then the hand that had unsheathed the oilcloth reached around and rubbed gently the part of her back between the shoulderblades. He patted her until she stopped coughing. 'You should be more careful when you laugh.'

'I'm sorry but it's just the sort of thing you Hut 3 fellows would do.' There was so much that was strange and beautiful about Felix she thought it would not have surprised her if he had produced a Fabergé egg from underneath one of the church chickens and given it to her with a wink. She imagined him lugging priceless family paintings into his Bletchley digs on the grounds that it might 'help him to think better'. But then, why at night, and why in the rain? She remembered the sight she'd caught of him a second ago, against the backdrop of the thatched building, the rain lashing at his coat and his face. Had there not been something monstrous, something furtive in the way he lugged the thing? Who moved paintings around the country, at night, just before Christmas?

But he had a slick answer. 'He's holding it for a fellow in London who's worried about the Blitz. Shipped the whole set of family crockery up to the country. You know how these things work.' She didn't. But she nodded.

Something about his nonchalance rang oddly, but she wasn't quite sure why. There were limited nefarious things you could do with paintings. She told herself she'd been watching too much Hitchcock.

'They're shipping out paintings from various museums too. In case of invasion. Going to a sort of hoarding station, caves, you know. It's been a project for a while, but . . . hallo—' He broke off and gave a small double whistle.

A whistle returned from the road. She hadn't heard the approach, but now she looked back there was a car with its headlights switched on very dimly. A blue glow cast Felix's features into strange shadows.

'Give us a hand, old girl?'

The rain was still hammering sidelong in sharp needles and hit their faces hard as they scurried, two hands on each side of the frame.

The man driving the motor car got out and rushed to help. He had on a thin mackintosh that sopped already at the collar and shoulders. They made a little pantomime of English gents, calling each other 'old chap' and shaking hands while they talked about the cold.

'Out on the razzle tonight, then?' the man in the wet mac asked. Who on earth said 'razzle'? Perhaps, she thought, Cary Grant might, at his most villainous.

Felix hefted the painting into the rear seat of the car, stood back and tapped the roof twice. The man heaved himself back in and the car crawled very slowly away from the kerb. As it picked up pace, sputtering the dirt, the gloom took them both again. Felix removed from his pocket a heavy and elaborate cigarette lighter. He twisted it in his palms for a second, then dropped it back.

'No use bothering about that in this weather.' He looked at the door of the house and Honey had the impression that he might be considering if it was possible to ask her inside. She was considering how she could decline, when she felt his hand on her wrist, very gently.

'Come on, the dog's inside. I'll fetch him and we can go for a walk.'

'In this?' She gestured around her, to what, she wasn't sure. The cold? The rain? The war?

'Greyhounds don't stop needing to walk because it's raining. Wait here.' Being close to him, in those few minutes her senses had sharpened, the way senses do in the wet, and as he passed her his scent drew her in; musk, leather and something like turpentine. She felt like an idiot for her suspicions.

He opened the door of the squat building, letting a buttermilk warmth slide out into the night. 'In there?' she said. 'You live in there?'

'Wait under the eaves, will you,' he said. 'You'll soak. I'll bring you an umbrella.'

Mindful of the ARP wardens who would fine you for even a chink of light, she pulled the door until the glow faded into amber shadows. Down on the road she could hear the beginnings of laughter and singing in choral harmony. A concert must have just come out, or a rehearsal. Cold breath was fa-la-la-la-ing Christmas carols, and snippets of Handel's *Messiah*. It had only been three nights since the revue, when Moira had taken her by the arm and asked her about sweethearts. How swiftly things could change.

She thought then of how many things there were a person needed to keep in her head all at once: people who were far away, people she was only just acquainted with. How was it that she was able to walk a dog and talk to a man when Moira was in bed half-conscious and fearful of the future? How was it that a building that had given her the terrors three nights ago could be the billet of a man she knew? She felt suddenly uneasy about Felix again and had the urge to run, when the door opened and a thin silver muzzle with a wet black nose blew breath onto the back of her fingers.

'Nijinsky.' She felt his silk brow. How the touch of a dog could make a person feel normal again. She took one of his ears between two of her fingers and slicked them along it. The rain had begun to ease off the worst of its assault but Felix handed her an umbrella anyway and propped up the collar of his coat. Nijinsky shook his hindquarters as soon as he was free of the front door. He was wearing a slip of the same oilcloth as the painting, with a cut-out hole for his head, tied round his absurd little waist with a piece of string.

'You made him a coat.'

'He's only a runty thing.'

'It's not as good as the one you made yourself.'

He laughed. 'Shall we go this way, or do you want to cut through the churchyard?'

'I don't mind the churchyard.'

'You're not afraid of the coffins?' He grinned.

It struck her as odd that he didn't say 'ghosts' or 'bodies', but she smiled anyway. 'They're no more spooky than stage scenery banged together,' she said, and took the arm he offered.

The dog bounced, ears alert, sniffing the air and the ground in quick succession and struggling to walk at heel. The umbrella he had given her wouldn't open.

'Here, give me that.' He wrestled with it for a few seconds, shaking out the spokes, then gave up and leaned it against a tree. 'That's that then.' She caught his sidelong glance, the hand on the belt of his coat, as if he was about to loosen the knot and offer it. Then he dropped the hand again; the offer, if it was ever there, was put back. The rain had begun to turn into spittle anyway.

'You're on days at the moment?' he asked.

'Switching to nights.'

'When?'

She hesitated.

'I'm not about to ask what you do. I'm not so much of a dolt. Here, shall we take this path? I'll walk you all the way to your front door.' Dead winter branches reached out from between the headstones, along with soft yew and other evergreens. She tried to keep an eye on her feet for the mud and slippery leaves. The air was frigid with a cold humidity left hanging after the rain, and her hair clung in threads to her face and neck. There was a small amount of moon; the clouds had cleared.

They passed a thriving cluster of bushes and Felix said, 'Thankfully they haven't turned the graveyards into vegetable patches. Yet.'

'Quite.'

'You're quiet, aren't you? I don't believe in the few times we've chatted you've given away much about yourself at all. Except that you like dogs. I know that much.'

'Why did you want to know about my working hours?' She raised her glance to him but his face was obscured by shadow. She could only see the sharp tip of his nose.

She was ready this time for his response. 'Because I wanted to ask if you would consider coming to the cinema with me one night? If we could tie our shifts together.' He stopped walking. As she gathered her bearings she realised they were beside the church door. It was slightly ajar. The stained glass had been blocked with blackout blinds but there was a thin red glow coming from inside; someone burning candles, incense, rearranging the flowers or prayer books. She looked to her other side and saw moss-bitten headstones.

'You do pick the strangest place to ask a girl out.'

'I'm not the one who suggested the British Restaurant for its reasonable meals.'

'What do you want to see?' She felt colour in her cheeks. She tried to look casually at him but he had that firm stare he'd worn in the Park grounds earlier in the day. Mr de Winter. It popped into her head all of a sudden. Then just as swiftly she remembered what Mr de Winter had done to his first wife.

He broke the gaze and shrugged. 'Anything you like. A musical?'

'I don't like musicals.'

'Just as well, neither do I.'

She gathered courage to smile. Her heart was beating unfathomably fast.

208

The Amber Shadows

'Look, we don't have to go and see a film. It's just I thought you liked—' He began to walk slowly again. 'It doesn't have to be a film. We could go to one of the Christmas concerts. In the town, not at the Park. See enough of that place.'

Honey considered him for a second. She tried to remember whether she had ever mentioned cinema to him before. How would he know . . .? That night, the first night they met, she'd been at the flicks. Perhaps she'd said something about it . . . 'There's a new Hitchcock coming,' she said. '*Shadow of a Doubt*. It's a crime story. Want to see that?'

'You don't get enough horror in your day-to-day life, is that it? Is Mr Hitchcock required to supplement your nerves with fear?'

'No, it's . . .' She hadn't thought until then about why she might like watching frightening movies, alone in the dark. Sometimes twice in a row.

Why had she watched *Suspicion* twice that night? It was to make sure of Cary Grant's innocence, because she didn't believe him. She hadn't wanted to step outside the cinema thinking a woman would be murdered inside it the moment the film finished. She needed to know it was safe to leave her alone with him. Or was it just because it was late and it was something to do? Or was she so afraid of the film that she thought by stepping outside the cinema *she* would be murdered? That perhaps in the blackout, and the cold and the wartime crumbling laws, perhaps there would be a young man waiting for her, just as handsome, just as charming . . .

'I like to be frightened,' she said.

'That's a strange thing, isn't it?'

'Why do so many people read detective novels? They can't all be looking for inspiration to plot the perfect murder.'

'Is that why you think people read detective novels?' Felix laughed as he held open the graveyard gate that led to the main road. 'Curious. On the contrary I think people want to see the world restored to safety. There are always clues in a crime novel. The villain always makes a slip. You always know they'll be caught. Red herrings too, of course, but it's the amount of information rather than the lack of it you get. Most detectives I shouldn't think have that luxury. Most detectives suffer from a lack of information.'

'Bosh,' said Honey. 'Most murders are extremely dull and easily solved. It's much harder in a detective novel. That's what makes it fun. So elaborate there's barely a logical trace to anyone who did it.'

'But there's only ever one solution, isn't there? And it's all very neatly wrapped up. You see that's where real crimes are different. There are usually a number of possibilities, often you'll never truly know. Beyond reasonable doubt, that's what they say to a jury, isn't it? Because in real crime there are no definites, no flashbacks. It's that maddening fact that drives you lot to your Christies and your Hitchcocks. You want reassurance, not thrills.'

'You lot,' Honey muttered. The moon had dipped behind a cloud, casting them into darkness again. She had taken his arm earlier as the ground dipped and she hadn't yet let go. His coat felt rough. Day-old soap came in warm drifts from under his collar, but she couldn't see him.

'What do you mean, you lot?' she pressed. 'Don't you like a good murder?'

'I prefer opera,' he said, and though she still couldn't see his face she had the impression from the direction of his breath on her cold cheeks that he had turned to look at her. The thought of her mother squirmed between them for a second and she felt an unexpected panic, something that made her step a little quicker. Her cork heels slid precariously on the wet pavement. *He has my arm*, she thought. *I'm safe if I fall.*

'Steady now. I know Puccini's not for everyone.' He laughed and then quickly said, 'If you read detective novels you must know how to plan the perfect murder. What would you do? Ice pick through the heart? Melts and there's no weapon left. Isn't that the classic? Or would it be better to hire a hit man with a secret identical twin? That way your man would have an alibi.'

'Oh, I don't know,' said Honey. 'I think anything strange like that, anything that draws attention to the murder means you're less likely to get away with it. Make it commonplace,

I say. A brawl in a public house. Shot in plain sight. Brazenly dump the body where it will be found.'

'Or double-bury it? Hide it in an existing grave? Bribe a coffin maker to make an extra layer for the latest corpse.'

'Oh, ridiculous,' she laughed.

'You say that but actually in a brazen brawl in plain sight you are more likely to be spotted. In real life it's one in a million who actually gets away with it and they are the ones who go to extraordinary lengths. The ones like Crippen—'

'Ones like Crippen we hear about precisely because they go to extraordinary lengths. Murder is very tawdry really, and more common than you think.' Her voice dropped. 'I think people get away with it all the time.'

Felix was quiet for a couple of seconds while they turned past the brickworkers' cottages onto Honey's street. They were approaching from a different route to the one she usually took. She could see the thatch of the Steadmans' in the distance. Fine grey smoke puffed out of the chimney. She thought about what was lying under her bed there; in her pocket now.

Felix took in a breath. 'And how do you think people get away with murder? If not through ingenuity.'

'They change the laws, don't they? Make it fine to kill people you don't like, that's the way people get away with murder, isn't it?' She knew then that without wanting to she had altered the atmosphere between them and she wasn't sure why. Why was it all right for her to watch Hitchcock films to forget the war but not all right to talk about it with him? She felt their conversation was nasty, and yet she didn't want to talk about opera or music either. Those were parts of her family that belonged to her.

The silence hung for a moment. 'I'm sorry I brought it up,' he said. And then, with a quiver in his voice, 'I thought you might be the sort of girl who liked murder.'

She sensed the smile on his lips. He was playing with her, the way he had played with her when he knew it wasn't her birthday.

'Have you received any more birthday gifts?' he asked.

The shock rang up her in a little wave. Could he read her mind? Or was it the approach to the street that had reminded him? Nijinsky was pulling ahead now, tugging on the ribbon. He could smell the rabbits in the Steadmans' garden.

'No more,' she lied. 'It was a parcel from my brother. Emergency chocolate. Heaven knows how it passed the censor. I suppose because he put it in a jewellery box along with some things I really did need, like old jewellery.' It was rather easy to lie once you got going, embellishing the details. Felix said nothing. While they continued to walk, he reached down and straightened the oilcloth on the dog's rear.

'What have you missed most since rationing came in?' she asked.

'Theatre.'

Honey frowned 'But you get plenty of that.'

'Yes, yes, I know. The army stuff and am-dram. What I meant was that I'm too much at work these days. I don't hardly get to catch any of it. I try to make it up to London but it's so damned expensive and with the trains being foul and taking four times as long as you expect them to. Then . . . well, so many extra shifts.'

'What was the last thing you saw?'

She still couldn't see his face but she heard him hesitate. 'Probably that awful revue at the recreation club. Did you see it?'

'Yes. It was very strange seeing the man from the billeting hut dressed as a squander bug.' She paused. They had reached the garden gate. 'I didn't see you there. You must have come on a different night.'

'I was helping out with sets. Saw some of the rehearsals.' He reached inside his coat, took out a cigarette and tried to light it, concealing the flame and holding the dog lead aloft. There was a breeze up and the flame danced.

'Let me help you.' Honey reached up to shield the lighter and their fingers touched. His skin was cold and uneven, and very coarse. So much coarser than she had thought it would be. She could feel his creases and gristled knuckles, the calluses and wrinkles of hard labour, not chess and mathematics. She held her hands still. She couldn't be sure, but she thought she felt the movement of his thumb deliberately and ever so slowly along the soft part of her index finger, stroking towards the palm.

The cigarette flared amber. He cupped it and sliced the light off quickly. 'Doubt Jerry could see a flame from all the way up there but still. Can't be too careful with these ARPs. Fine you a shilling or whatnot. Shall I give this one to you?'

'I don't want one.'

She watched him in the tiny halo of light the cigarette gave off. It only really clarified his mouth, the dense pinpricks of dark round his neat, rather girlish lips.

'So you make stage sets as well. Busy, aren't you? Surprised you have time to ask a girl to the cinema.'

He waved the cigarette. 'I help out.' The dog started to whine. 'Shush, Nijinsky.'

She couldn't help but snort. The name.

'All right. You don't want murder. How about I take you to a music concert, then? How about something Christmassy, something Russian?'

The word stuck a pin into her. She felt herself lurch, her warning hackles throwing themselves up underneath her coat, just as they had outside the squat building, while she waited for him to come out with the dog. Say it, she dared him inside her head. Say what I think you're about to say. It was a sort of masochism. In that moment, by naming the name on her tongue, by saying the word 'Stravinsky', he'd have the power to destroy the illusion of their walk, to make manifest every suspicion, every doubt she'd had about him since she set eyes on that very first parcel. He had the power to then and there snatch back like the gauze in a theatre the picture of the little girl who wanted to believe her father was alive and speaking to her. He was from the Park. It was a test after all, she knew it. Or something worse.

He bent his head. 'I don't know, someone has to be doing *The Nutcracker* suite, don't they? Can't promise you Vaslav Nijinsky but I'm sure one of the Christ Church boys looks all right in a pair of tights. That Turing fellow or the one in the navy blazer.'

'Or the Captain?' Honey laughed, her chest suddenly thawing. The adrenaline faded. She was paranoid. She was Joan Fontaine again. He passed her his cigarette and she took a draw, warming up her lungs. 'I'd love to come to a concert with you.'

'Well, that's jolly lovely news for me . . . I'm glad I ran into you.'

'Goodnight.' She bent down and stroked the dog's forehead. He sniffed her breath in twitches.

'He's got such eyes,' she said. 'You'd think they could see through anything. They'll always tell the truth.'

'That's the thing I like most about dogs,' said Felix, beginning to walk back up the path. 'They always tell the truth. Quite incapable of lying.'

'Quite incapable of speaking, you mean,' Honey called after him. But he was already halfway up the street, trotting in step with the dog. Nijinsky looked up and barked once, sharp and playful. There was a dancing quality to Felix's step that hadn't been there before. He looked lighter and more fun than the brooding amused man she had just walked with. It was only when the dog barked a second time, she remembered the bark she'd heard at the base at Wavendon, and she realised she hadn't thought to ask Captain Tiver exactly who it was that had passed the information to the Park about her unexpected meeting with Piotr Górecki.

Chapter 12

Securely pressed behind her bedroom door she took off her coat and brought from under the bed the other pieces of amber. She pulled the rug from the warm spot again and sat down on the wood. Mrs Steadman was listening to a thundering Gilbert and Sullivan on the wireless below.

Carefully she slotted the amber box together, trying not to grate too much dust as the joins ground. Once assembled she removed the firebird from her cardigan and slotted it into the hole at the front of the base.

It didn't quite fit.

The base of the bird went into the dip but it wobbled about and wouldn't stand straight. She tried again from various angles but couldn't make it work. It seemed childish, the disappointment she felt. Of course it couldn't be perfect, if he was smuggling out fragments, if he was sending them one by one from exile. God knew where he was and what he was using to carve them. She turned over the panels and looked again. There must be something she was missing, some instruction hidden. She wished Dickie would telegram or telephone or simply turn up.

The sound of the national anthem on the wireless drifted up through the floorboards. Honey heard creaks as Mrs Steadman moved across the parlour and then the sharp severing of the sound. Across the hall Rebecca's bedroom door opened and closed, and a smell of soap-steam came filtering in. Honey had never seen Rebecca. They passed only as noises in the billet; they always seemed to be on different schedules at the Park. They communicated in notes under bedroom doors, knocks on the bathroom. She had come across her name once; she worked in the main house's Index Room. Everything was logged in shoeboxes up there, rather like the Hut 6 index. Any time a new word came up – for example, an officer's name – they would create a reference for it and keep all the notes together, to try to build a pattern of who that officer was. They kept everything, so that they would know everything.

She wished she had a log now, of back references to her own past. She thought about trying to find a telephone box to place a trunk call to London but didn't know whether Dickie would be at home or in the theatre and besides Mrs Steadman would want to know why she was going out again, and without a scrambler on both ends of the line you couldn't be sure who was listening. How horrid it was to be living surrounded by lies, so that you yourself were forced to lie too.

She put the pieces away, went downstairs and washed her face and throat miserably in tepid water from the bathroom tap, then burrowed into bed. Her finger still shivered with the residue of Felix's touch. She hadn't imagined it, that movement towards her palm. He had touched her with his thumb. But then the image of Moira's tangled hair crept into view, and as she began to drift off her sleepiness was tainted with a sickly feeling.

The next day, she thought to herself; tomorrow. I don't begin work until midnight. She would heap the pieces into a bag, and take them to Moira's. Moira was the one with the brain that worked. Of the two of them it was Moira who had been plucked from top of the mathematics pile, Moira who had spent time in Dilly Knox's Research Cottage. Moira was the codebreaker.

'What do you mean, gone?'

'She's gone. Been taken away. This morning. They had official papers, I didn't know what to do.'

Moira's landlady had the baby braced against her hip. It watched them calmly, batting its eyes from face to face with an infant's sixth sense. With a mother's sense the woman spoke quietly, and watched the baby back with half an eye, as if she were clutching a bomb.

'Was it to her home? Where were they taking her?'

'I don't know. Hospital? They had an ambulance.'

'But she's not ill. How can they spare a hospital bed with all the bombing going on? This is absurd.'

In the crisp morning light Honey could see that veins had popped across the woman's nose. Beneath her skin her bones were visible, sharp. She looked like a survivor, like a woman Honey had seen once in London crawling through the shards of a burnt-out house with her toddler clutched to her.

'I was talking to her last night. She was on bromide but she seemed . . .' A dread feeling began to thread round her. It started at her shoulders, very cold, and worked down into a hot lava in her belly. 'When you say official . . . were they from the Park?'

The baby threw back its head and let rip a piercing shriek.

The woman looked at Honey cold and hard. Honey saw her again in that moment the night before, her head bent, seated on the couch. She had regained her strength now; it had doubled, tripled. She was in charge of her house and Honey was an intruder.

Through this though, another vision persisted; two sheets of thin tissue, scrawled in blue, the rubbings of the cipher standing out. Next to them two scraps of white paper covered in equations. Slowly she said, 'Did she leave anything in her room?'

The landlady sighed. 'Whatever she left the men will have taken. One of them was definitely a doctor. The other looked like an orderly. He wore overalls. But the Park must know because they sent the billeting officer round hot on their heels. I'm to have a new girl by this afternoon.' She shifted the baby on her hip. For a second the wailing sank to a gurgle. Honey heard the woman's next words perfectly. 'Sweetheart, she's not coming back.'

It was only when she had reached the gate that the landlady called out to her again. 'Actually, wait a second. Is your name Honey?'

Honey turned. The landlady's hand was stuffed into her pinny pocket, scrabbling. She cast her eyes sideways at the hedges. 'I didn't know what she meant when she first said it, "for Honey". Before she left she said "for Honey". I thought . . . I thought perhaps she'd lost her marbles, she was meaning honey for toast or . . . I don't know what I thought she meant but she gave me these. Mean anything to you?'

Honey met the woman's eye, for she already knew what was in her hand. When she did look down, the two pieces of tissue-thin paper were folded, containing the two other small papers. She could make out notes and diagrams on the outer edges and her stomach tripped. She pulled her mind back from straying too far onto what would have happened had the Park men found cryptanalytic equations in a billet.

The papers crackled with static charge as Honey stuffed them into her pocket, and they continued to rustle, loud, incriminating, even as she began to walk. She didn't dare look back at the woman; she took the path at a clip in the direction of the Park. But in a bramble thicket she pulled the papers out, separating them from the tissue rubbings.

When she pulled them out, it was the opposite side to Moira's lurching bold hand that was face up, and as she unfolded them, the typing printed on the back of each slip caught her off guard – the paper Moira had chosen for her scribblings.

I don't know why I did it.

As Honey gazed in growing horror she began to realise just what Moira had discovered, and why it might have been so important those Park men get rid of her as quickly as they could.

She banged her knuckles into the panel of Tiver's door, sending the impact of the wood right back into her bones. Katie Brewster looked up. 'Deschamps, what the devil are you . . .?' Honey knocked again, twice.

The door snapped open. Tiver took a couple of slow breaths. His eyes travelled down from her burnt cheeks to her scuffed shoes.

'You'd better not just stand there, you hot-headed little wretch. Come inside and mind how you talk to me.'

She took the leather seat opposite the Captain's desk again, biting her tongue as he pulled a small green bottle from his top drawer and poured himself a sherry. In the silence that followed she noticed more of the details of his office: the rivets holding the leather to the wood frame of his chair, a curlicue swivel chair, a Captain's chair. On his desk he had sheaves of paper stamped in Cabinet red. The battleship seemed to have swelled upwards under a wave of new documents and memos.

His voice was more measured than before. 'You're supposed to be adept at keeping secrets. But it seems over the past day or so you've been party to more than your fair share.'

Honey tried to keep her face level. She was still stinging from being called a 'hot-headed little wretch'. Flame-temper, that was what the teachers at school said. Had she been blonde or mousy they never would have.

'I'm only telling you this because I hear you've been making a fuss in the village and you know as well as I do, Deschamps, that simply doesn't do here.'

'There are a lot of things that don't do here.'

Tiver didn't flinch, but neither did he try to conceal a flutter of confusion that came onto his brow. 'You're worried about your friend. I understand. But we have more reason than you to worry about her.'

There were things she wanted to say. She phrased and recast them in her head. But at the final barrier of her mouth, each time, they dissolved and she couldn't. Eventually she said, 'It isn't fair what you did, taking her away, for that.' She kept her voice soft to stop it cracking as she felt the tide rising.

'Miss Draper needs a rest. The work is too taxing for her, personal matters were playing on her nerves and she disobeyed a boundary. You know as well as I discretion is not just a standard we aim for here, it is of mortal necessity.'

'But you haven't sent her for a rest, have you? You sent her away because she found you out.' *I don't know why I did it.* She had stolen those pieces of paper, one of them at least. She had chosen to write on them for a reason, and she had passed that reason on to Honey; another code.

Tiver's face was furrowed into lines. He was not a man who enjoyed being on the cloudy side of a conversation. 'I beg your pardon,' he said.

She had the impression she was being invited to tell him he had misheard. But 'hot-headed'; she couldn't get away from that. It was nagging at her, and she wouldn't let a friend be dragged away without kicking up a fuss.

'I found them in her room. The two payslips.'

Now Tiver let his confusion show. 'Sorry, what do you mean?'

Her hand paused on the crackle of her pocket. The pieces of paper Moira had scribbled on. Playing with equations, cipher-breaking, making notes for her amber messages. Betty Somebody had been disciplined for writing to her boyfriend in code. Honey moved her hand back onto her lap. 'She showed me two payslips with very different wages.'

The Captain deflected his eyes, the way he had done when he passed her the 'Fraternising with Foreigners' memo.

'You haven't sent her home,' Honey said. 'You sent her away because she found out that the junior men in Hut 6 earn more than twice as much as the women working at the top level in the Research Cottage. Isn't that true?'

One of Tiver's eyebrows floated into an arch. 'Miss Draper is not well.'

'She was well enough to collect the evidence when she saw it.'

'Where is this evidence?'

Honey blushed. She looked at Tiver's desk, a barricade between them. 'I don't have them. She showed me them last night.'

'Whose payslips?'

'I won't say.'

She wasn't ready for his crimson face barrelling across the desk, swelling vengefully close to her own, incendiary and quivering. His hands braced him up. 'You'll say all right. You'll say because I won't be bullied by one typist any more than I'll stand for the histrionics of another.'

'Rupert Findlay. Rupert Findlay, Hut 6. The one they call Poo,' Honey blurted.

The words had an instant effect on Tiver. It was as if he had woken to his rage, as if someone else had thrown it over his head like a rag, startling him, and now he had managed to get a clutch on it, pull it back off. He blinked and sat back down.

Honey went on. 'He's a junior in the crib room. He's a Cambridge boy but only twenty if that. And yet Moira found out his wage slip is £6 2s a week. When she worked at the Cottage, as well you know she earned £3. Like me. Like all of us. They're talking about this in parliament, this difference between the women's and the men's wages and you know as well as I it just isn't fair.'

Tiver raised his hand to his brow and tamped on each of his weak, papery eyelids in turn. While Honey waited he shook his head and took a sip of sherry. 'Miss Deschamps, whether or not you lot are vulgar enough to swap confidential money matters with each other, I won't discuss it with you. Whatever gripes Draper had with her pay she never brought them to me. This is the first I've heard of any of it. You ladies do get some funny notions, but it's one thing I'll say for that girl; she wasn't the sort to come in the middle of a war and demand more money. You work for your country, and your country rewards you with what it thinks you're worth, and what it thinks you need.'

'Who decides that?'

Tiver sighed. His eyes fell on his pipe and Honey could tell immediately that now they were no longer talking at cross purposes, he wanted rid of her. 'You came to me about Draper, didn't you?'

'Who sets the tariffs?'

But Tiver just reached into his desk drawer again and retrieved a piece of paper torn from a magazine. Honey recognised the half-shine of the page; *Country Lady* or some other weekly, one of the type Moira liked. On the back was a pattern for turning old lace curtains into a wedding veil. He unfolded it and smoothed it onto the leather blotter. The headline was about a parlour maid who had spilled the beans on an affair with Baron Glenkinchie. There was a picture of him on one of his polo ponies outside some castle. In the inset was a grainy photograph of a voluptuous young woman in her Sunday best, a cloche hat and suit. Further down was a picture of the Baron and his wife at a fete. 'Downfall of a Lord: the Other Woman Speaks.'

'This was left on Lieutenant MacCrae's desk.' He paused. 'Miss Draper went into Hut 3 and left it on his desk.'

Honey looked down at the picture, imagined Moira tearing it carefully, sneaking past the forbidden boundary into the hut, her vengeance bigger and harder than any of the rules that were set at the Park.

'You see, Miss Deschamps, we all speak in codes, all the time, when it boils down.'

Honey took a second to swallow. Her mouth felt tight and hot. She remembered Moira's dribbles into the pillow. *I don't know why I did it. I was just so sad.* Such sadness as Honey couldn't conjure in her imagination, not in her wildest attempts. She had never been in love. She had never placed in another person so much trust, to be so wretchedly betrayed. Of course it could not be as simple, as cold as money. She had misread the notes. Of course there was more to it. But . . .

'I don't understand. You can't take away a woman because of an affair. You can't whisk her away. When will she . . . when can I . . . where have you taken her?'

'She walked into a hut that wasn't her own, and we *won't* have scandal at the Park.' The pitch of his voice cut through Honey. The silence that followed it was hostile. She sensed in that outburst all of his impatience; she saw herself for what she must be – a nuisance to him. Moira, nothing but a nuisance too, a nuisance to Lieutenant MacCrae, to be removed. The silence seemed to reach past and around her like a smothering pillow and she saw it travel right through the wood of the door, into the lobby, into the other offices, strangling, smothering sound, gagging everyone it touched on its way. Silence was the only thing that mattered here, and if you broke it, it would be forced back on you.

When Tiver spoke again his voice was quiet, and the black marks in his face from the last war seemed to shine. 'There are men whose lives depend on your ability to keep your mouths shut and bloody well get on with it. And that's exactly what your friend couldn't do.'

'She wouldn't have said a word about the affair.'

'We can't take that risk.'

'Where is she?'

'It doesn't matter where your friend is now. But she's safe. Remember, Deschamps, you signed the Official Secrets Act. I said then that if you broke the terms I'd take you out and shoot you myself.' He held her gaze. 'That still stands.'

The lady at the cafeteria counter made jovial chatter about marmalade and predicted the war would be finished up in less than three months. She was unhappy about bacon rationing, found rabbit too flavourful to entertain cooking with, and there were never any of the soup brands she liked left at the grocer's. Honey took the black tea with the floating dead leaves and chose a table.

She had no sooner sat down than a familiar cloud of perfume plumped down opposite.

'You've heard about Moira?'

She looked across. Beatrix's eyes were kind but wary. She seemed to be broadcasting a small warning, or perhaps she was worried that already she had said too much.

Honey sipped her bitter tea.

'We're all very sorry for her,' said Beatrix, 'But it's for the best.'

Honey thought for a second about pulling out the payslips. Her guts had flipped when she thought about that headline, left on the lieutenant's desk. Surely Moira wouldn't have . . . but it was possible. Anything was possible when passions flamed.

'Did you know that Poo is paid more than twice us? More than twice what Moira took home when she worked in the Cottage?'

The Amber Shadows

Beatrix tilted her head. 'What? Of course the chaps earn more, that's just the way it is. You didn't . . . you didn't think that was why she's . . . Honey, what has Moira been saying to you?'

Honey shook her head and looked down at her skirt. It had crumbs of foliage on it from the dash to the Park; it made her think of Moira, wading through the bluebells on her quest to cheer up the suicidal chef.

'The thing is,' Beatrix was saying, sipping her own black tea. 'The thing is, you didn't know about Rachel Mason, did you? I think she came and went before your time.'

'I don't know the name.'

'No,' Beatrix said. 'No one tends to mention it.' She readjusted her cardigan – a green one today – and gave a proud little toss of her set curls. 'Well, you see the Head of Room back then was Lily Blackthorn. She's gone to Hut 8 now. She was maths, Cambridge. So I don't quite know the ins and outs of it. But you couldn't help but gather the gist. There was no way of keeping it quiet. Think of it. Bletchley Park. We're guarding the safety of the nation in secret and yet no one can quite disguise it when something that cruel happens on one's doorstep.' Beatrix sipped her tea again. Honey wondered about her, where her good sense had come from. Had it been drilled into her by a governess or boarding school? Or had she been born with the bossy blood, always so self-assured about what she was doing and saying? The pearls in her earrings rattled as she talked.

'Christ knows how no one knew. But she was pregnant. Not, it seems, to one of the boys from the Park. I think an airman. An RAF man, who perhaps left her or perhaps he died. And who knows, maybe he would have married her. But when the baby was born, she hid it in a drawer. It was only discovered when the landlady's cat—'

'Please, don't.' Honey thought she might vomit into her tea.

Beatrix reached across the table and seized her hand. 'Don't faint, dear. I'm only telling you because I want you to know that whatever happened to Moira – and I don't know where she is, I only know what Mooden's been told, she's in hospital somewhere – wherever she is, it's the safest place for her. Oh God, you're so clammy, please don't faint.'

Honey found from somewhere the strength to croak a reply. 'I'm all right.' But she wasn't. Moira had been so convinced. He would marry her. If there was a baby he would marry her.

Beatrix clutched her knuckles and Honey became aware of the pressure of the ring on her pinky. She concentrated on the cutting sensation, fixed hold of it. Because the alternative was a drawer opening . . .

'When one looks the way Moira does,' Beatrix said slowly, 'one has to be careful around chaps. It's as simple as that.'

'But it's hardly her—'

'Keeping your head,' Beatrix interrupted, 'in a place like this is the only thing that matters. Whatever happens.' She loosened her grip but kept hold of Honey's hand. 'When I think of what the alternative could be. Stitching boys with blown-open faces, standing by during amputations, driving ambulances. I really am grateful to be doing something. Like this.' She stroked Honey's fingers thoughtfully, one at a time. 'No matter what happens, no matter what secrets you have to carry, keep your head.' She downed the dregs of her tea and stood up.

Honey watched the path of Beatrix's footsteps back to the counter and heard the scatter of bright conversation she had with the woman behind the till. And she thought for the first time in her life how wretched it was to be a woman. War was ferocious to men. But when it was over the ones left would go back to their lives. For a woman, there would always be pillaged wages, affairs broken off, promises unfulfilled, family shame, babies to be hidden in unmarked graves, in wooden drawers.

Chapter 13

She thought that the walk to town to collect the household ration herself might steady her. Mrs Steadman was suspicious but counted off the coupons for butter, sugar, milk, soap, tea, margarine into her palm.

Beatrix was right. She had to keep her head. There was no use falling apart. And perhaps it was true Moira was in the best place. Honey pictured serene lady doctors in white coats with their hair pinned up – lady doctors who had not been sent to the front line. Ambulance drivers in blue slacks with kind faces. A bed and morphine and rest, good food, unrationed food, to patch her mind back together.

Still she felt shivers in her torso as she passed the Home Guard, marching in their slack uniforms. She felt queasy as she saw an ambulance parked up idle beside the doctor's surgery in town, and even sicker when she caught sight of a motor hearse pulling away from the church. Everything seemed to be a sign to her, everything, even the trees waving their winter talons seemed to scream that something was wrong.

She passed the postwoman, and her stomach dipped. 'Has the second post come?' she asked. On hearing it had, she hurried back to the Steadmans'. But there was nothing, no reply from Dickie. The post, Mrs Steadman said, was slow. 'It would be easier to send a pigeon,' she went on. 'You should tie your letters to the collar of a hare, that's what you should do. Then set a greyhound after it and send it in the direction you want the message to go, for all the good the bloody Royal Mail does.'

Honey climbed the stairs to her bedroom feeling lead in each step.

Her room felt like a prison, the air suffocating with secrets. In the pallid grey light she took out the pieces of amber. They didn't glow like they had done in the bronze of her gaslamps. Now, in the cool day, they stole the light and reflected nothing back, a network of ugly bubbles and thread veins, the thousand-year-old tree's blood no more special than cracked and scratched Bakelite. They seemed to take the warmth right out of her palms. All except the fire-bird. When she picked it up, its eyes still caught a glow, its wings were still poised half-open, half-embracing, as if they might take off.

She lay down on her bed and stared at the hard drips of plaster in the ceiling, watching as the pattern probed textured claws towards her, then suddenly popped inwards when she stared at it for too long. She sat up and switched the wireless on, crackling between stations to see if she could find some music that suited her mood. But there was only the one o'clock news. Air raids on the south coast. She knew already. The intercepted Luftwaffe signals had come through the day before. It was like seeing the headlines before they happened. Sometimes there was time to do something about it. Sometimes there wasn't. Sometimes Churchill wanted to act, and sometimes he didn't. That was the problem with secrets. You had to be careful with them. You had to know what to do with them.

Sitting up she reached across her bedside table to the bureau and scraped open the drawer. Inside was a stack of biros. She pulled one out along with a notebook and began to look at Moira's notes and the carvings.

But it was beyond her. It was something only Dickie would know. He had told her the story after all, he must have known the full extent of it. It was Dickie who showed her the code book, Dickie who knew about Stravinsky. Dickie with his ballet legs and his ambition. Nothing her mother had ever said . . .

Exhausted from doodling, eventually she fell asleep, still clutching the amber firebird.

When she woke up her room had the strange static tinge that said someone had been in. She looked across at the bureau and saw a tea tray, gold-edged and patterned with gaudy flowers. Some fruit scones and a smear of jam and marge lay on the side of the plate. A glass of water and a cup of tea with real milk, stewed to gunmetal, sat cold beside it. Honey looked at her bedside clock. Ten past five.

Outside the sun had sunk and she felt goosebumps of cold on her arms. Her fingers were frozen. She looked down and saw that in them she still had the amber.

Groggy and feeling as if the day had been a dream, she ate a few bites then crept down the stairs. There was a pile of evening post in the hallway. She riffled through it and found a short postcard from her mother. She was performing for naval troops in Hastings for the Christmas season. Honey was welcome to come, and the winter sea breeze was fine and on and on it went in tiny, messy handwriting. The card was dated two weeks ago.

The house was curiously quiet, and unsettling because of it. She could hear a distant scrabbling in the garden and a small squealing sound, and she knew with a sickness she had never got used to that it was rabbit for supper. She retreated up the stairs as the back door banged open into the scullery.

From the glass on the tray she splashed her eyes with cold water, and the shock made her feel more alive. Still seven hours until her shift. She remembered there was a Hitch-cock at the Ritzy tonight and thought it might help to keep her awake.

She considered for a moment, then stuffed the carved amber and her sketchings into a hatbox and placed it, not under the bed this time, but in the bottom drawer of the bureau. It was only as she was returning the drawer on its runners that she remembered Beatrix's story.

She straightened the creases out of her skirt, chose a hat from the wardrobe and her electric torch, and headed out.

Alfred Hitchcock had made a film of Daphne du Maurier's *Rebecca*. And there was Joan Fontaine again with another murderous man. But Honey disliked the film. Mrs Danvers wasn't skull-like enough. Her face was too human. For a cinema in wartime she wanted her villains drawn in black and white lines, visible. She was fed up of the hidden ones. She went to the cinema to see evil outlined, easy to spot.

Although she had missed the beginning she made up her mind not to stay for a second round. Before the final chord sounded she had climbed to her feet, and was picking a path through the cigarette smoke. The silver light from the projector cast a haze, and she felt for a second like Mrs de Winter herself, scrabbling through a Mánderley sea mist. Her foot collided with something on the ground, a metal claw from the base of one of the cinema rows. The trip sent a shock up her spine. But when she steadied herself, clutching the hard velvet of the chair back, she noticed it was not cold metal at all that had made her trip but something warm. A peppermint-sugar and cigarette scent drifted up in front, and she felt the hard edge of a brogue on the instep of her cork shoes.

'I've got you.'

'Felix.' Her elbow was compressed into a man's grip and she laughed uneasily. 'Are you following me?'

The shadowy figure took so long to answer that Honey thought she might have made a mistake. Was it him?

'You said you were going to wait and come to the next Hitchcock with me.'

She breathed out. 'I said *Shadow of a Doubt*. That's next week.'

'What do you think of Mrs de Winter?'

'Which one, the first or second?' She hesitated. 'Come to think of it, I don't think I'd like to be either.' She smiled hard as she spoke, to make lightness creep into her voice, to take the shake out of it. For some reason she did not want Felix to know she was bothered, or shocked, or afraid, or whatever it was she was feeling at the sight of him. But the more buoyant she tried to be, the harder the day pushed in on her. They moved into the foyer where blue electric bulbs had replaced the regular golden ones. The insides of the glass doors out to the street were tacked with sheets of black sugar paper, and half-covered in a thick moth-eaten velvet curtain.

The light gave Felix's face an odd hard tinge. He seemed stiffer than the night before. She thought about the three W's of conversation: war, weather and work, then looking at the blacked-out doors said impulsively, 'Don't you long for the golden light again? I love a cinema foyer. But the thrill isn't the same in this strange blue. Makes me feel like we're part of the movie. It's unsettling.'

He had paused next to the kiosk; he leaned his arm on the empty counter top. It smelled faintly of butter, scents ingrained into the fabric and metal before rationing.

'I just long for the winter to be over,' he said. 'All those Monte Carlo drives and Manderley walks. Makes me want to have a picnic. Did you say you were on the night shift?'

'Starting midnight.' She caught herself beginning to yawn and raised her hand to her mouth. Then she remembered something, a fact she had once come across about giving someone your yawn. She had read somewhere it was a sign of empathy, being able to catch a person's yawn, and she thought it might be funny to try to make Felix catch hers. She let her mouth fall right back and her hand drop. He continued to stare, but he didn't yawn.

'You look tired. Do you want me to take you for supper?'

'That's a fine way to ask. You make it sound like a chore.'

'Well, it wouldn't be.'

For a second she felt that she was the callow Mrs de Winter and he the passionless Laurence Olivier. Then he leaned over and, as casually as if he was picking up a dropped pen, he took a strand of her hair from nearest her ear and tucked it into the deep red fringe that hung curling on her left side. It was impulsive; as soon as he'd done it he dropped his hand.

'Eight Bells?' she asked, quickly to stave off embarrassment, on whose part she didn't know. 'Mind, it would almost be dancing girls time. I mean, I have a cold supper waiting at home, which I shouldn't waste. And we're fed at the canteen on night shift.' The thought of Spam sandwiches in the middle of the night made her want to retch. 'But . . . fish and chips? Only you have to bring your own newspaper to the place on the high street and I haven't got any, have you?'

'I thought perhaps . . .' He was smiling slyly. 'I thought we could each do with a reasonable meal.'

'Suet pudding, canned sprouts and perhaps chipped potatoes. Come on, then.'

He extended his arm. Looking sidelong at him in the blue light, she caught the asymmetry of his face; from this angle his cheekbone seemed almost askew, his eyeline harder. Every time she looked at him there was something a little bit different that she noticed, and she couldn't store all of these bits in her head at once, try as she might. He glanced suddenly down at her. His eyes had taken on a very beautiful gleaming grey. She took his arm and as she did so she felt his body soften a little, as if he might almost be relieved.

God only knew how they found so many things to talk about. Later when she tried to recall it she could barely remember a sentence. But the conversation was easy. Felix talked about where he had been when the war broke out; in a theatre in London, watching a dress rehearsal for a Noel Coward play. The stage manager had interrupted it to break the news and the actors had worked harder at their jokes afterwards. He talked about his favourite paintings. The Nazis, he said, were looting art by the truckful. Huge altarpieces, Catholic statues. All gone to their German castles and underground vaults and who knew if they would see the light of day ever again. It was on the tip of her tongue to say 'the Amber Room too' but she bit it. She told him instead about Dickie, about his ballet dancing. She didn't say that he had been a Conscientious Objector and spent five weeks up in Wakefield, only that he now did firewatching and worked for ENSA.

He caught her looking at her watch.

'I'm sorry. But you see, I sort of have the impression he might come to visit me, and maybe it will be tonight.'

An odd, quizzical frown was on his face. He stared at her and tilted his head. 'You have the impression?'

'It's just that I invited him. But I don't know if he'll have got the letter yet and . . . oh, it's probably too late anyhow.'

Half past eleven crept up swiftly and they realised they were the only ones left in the restaurant alongside a bonneted, rather old-fashioned woman behind the counter, a man in a greatcoat who seemed to want somewhere to bed down for the night, and an anxious-looking woman in silver monkey fur. The fur woman kept rushing to the bar to ask questions, then retreating to her seat into endless cups of tea.

The proprietress began to mop the floor with hot disinfectant and the anxious lady rose again. This time Honey and Felix were close enough to hear. 'You say it still hasn't come in? The eight twenty-four from London. I mean, are you really very sure? I did go to the lavatory about an hour ago, and it would be awfully late if it hasn't.'

'Duckie,' the woman said with some effort. 'You'd have seen it, I'd have seen it, they'd bleedin' well have seen it and he certainly would.' She nodded at the tramp. 'Whoever he is, he'll be here. The trains have been late for two years now. If this is the first – and the worst – you've had of it you're doing well for the war, my girl.'

The anxious woman pulled back her large monkey fur and looked at a wristwatch. She seemed like a little frightened animal in that coat, with her tiny pinched face. 'You're really sure?'

'As sure as powdered eggs are not really eggs,' the proprietress muttered. 'Station master said he had one in at three last week. Seven hours delayed but they get filled up with the Tommies. No station signs so sometimes they get the track changes wrong. Don't panic.' This seemed to give the woman some comfort and she sat back again with her empty cup and nursed the porcelain to her lips. 'Hope he's bloody worth it.'

Felix held the door open and Honey passed through, dipping under his warm arm. 'I'll walk you to the Park, shall I?'

In the distance they heard the sound of grinding on the tracks. The smell of coal lifted towards them in a faint cloud.

'At least she's going to get to see him after all.' Honey nodded in the direction of the train. They mounted the station bridge together.

Out in the open air the moon was blinding. The sky was a mauve velvet. On the horizon, where it met hill or field, traces of amber burned the edges, almost like a very pale sunrise.

They heard, then saw, in the distance planes taking off, heading for the south coast that would lead them across France to Münster, Lübeck, Cologne, where they would drop their incendiaries on steeples, factories, houses. Tiny blinking black moths, so small and far away they could have been dark shooting stars. They watched for a few seconds, not saying anything.

Then Felix murmured, 'Moon's a blinder.'

'It's beautiful. Like a jewel.'

'You can see where the name moonstone comes from.'

'I was just thinking.' She looked at him, though she could see only light and shadow, not the features of his face. 'I was just thinking that on a night like this, you realise how very little you want to die.'

'Honey.' He spoke very quietly.

She placed her fingers on the knot of his coat belt, moving delicately into the hard scratchy felt. She had a compulsion to clutch it in her hand, to have something firmly attached to someone, and know exactly who was on the end of it. No ducking into shadows, no games. The knot of his blackout coat fitted her palm exactly. It led her straight to him. His heart was thumping. She could feel it through the layers of wool.

But they had walked too close to the Park. A torchlight shone, roaming for their faces, and she felt for a frightening second as if they had been caught naked in its glare.

'Night shift, love?' The Military Policeman held his hand out for her card. In the spillage of light from his torch, she became aware of footsteps coming and going all around them, soft as insects in the night's foliage. They had stumbled into the ecosystem of the Bletchley midnight changeover and there were no places to hide, no places to kiss.

She found her identity card in her pocket, and handed it over. The man took it, shone his torch on it then up to her face, then waved her through.

'You're not coming in at this time of night, are you?' he said, shining his light on Felix.

Felix laughed; a hollow, curious sound. 'No, no, not tonight.'

'Hmmm,' the Military Policeman said. 'Wouldn't have thought so. Bit late for you.'

In the checkpoint hut beyond, the policeman's colleague was stamping his feet. Clouds of white diamond dust sprang from them. Felix waved to Honey and in the torchlight that shone still from the MP she caught his face, and it had that avuncular expression again, the one he had given her in the grounds, right after the stare. She waved back, then for some reason embarrassment took her and she dropped her eyes and couldn't bring herself to look again as she walked away.

There was a somnambulant queerness that filtered through the Park at the midnight shift change. It had none of the chatter or bustle of the day change; it was as if nocturnal creatures had crept from their burrows. Scurrying came from the bushes and you couldn't immediately tell whether it was human, bird or rodent. Here and there a dipped electric torch, its lens covered over with white tissue, would make a low slate-tinted portion of the ground show up, and sometimes a scream from another part would tell you that people were still buoyant, still playing on the rounders lawn, or the tennis courts, or arguing as they skated on the lake.

But she could have orientated herself to Hut 6 even if it had been pitch black. She visited the freezing privy outside first, to avoid having to venture back out once in the hut, then she pushed open the door.

Even from the door end of the hut she could tell when the Typex machines were in swing. But tonight the noise was riotous. Rupert Findlay dashed from one room and into another. 'Light Blue,' came the cry through the walls. 'Can we have some Typexes for this one from Decoding?' He flew back out of the room and into another. Doubling back, he clung to the doorframe, bracing the weight of his body. 'Deschamps. You starting?'

'Yes.' Honey was struggling to shrug off her coat. She saw her breath cloud, thought better of it and buttoned it back up again.

'They're in there.' He gestured with his head to the left.

'The Decoding Room's been moved?'

'Supposed to happen yesterday but the duffer from maintenance said he got the day wrong.'

'Oh.' She pushed the door to her left. It was a nasty feeling, being confronted with these sudden changes of rooms, especially on night shift. Night shift was bad enough but the sight of familiar equipment in an unfamiliar order and setting, with a different team, made her feel dizzy. This wasn't the first time it had happened. They frequently moved rooms around in order to accommodate the shifting of staff.

She took a bundle of Light Blue raw intercepts from the pile by the door and set up station. She only knew a couple of the girls on this watch. Switching shift patterns had put her out of sync with her usual lot. The night shift Head of Room was a timid, spiny woman named Roache who kept an unsettling silence most of the time, but if riled she would spit. She was always cold and kept the coke stove at full poisonous pelt.

As Honey sat down the women on the back shift end of changeover couldn't pick up their coats or cigarettes quickly enough. The midnight crew settled, idle chatter died away and Honey began pounding through the Light Blues, spewing out German. She was out of Russia now, back into France.

Lists of names, repetitious weather reports, slips that said 'KEINE BESONDEREN VORKOMMNISSE' – nothing to report – again and again came pouring through the traffic. At night her technique was to focus intently on each letter, as if the letters themselves were nothing more than pictures, shapes like hieroglyphs for her to recognise, input and recreate. She took note too of the shapes of the German on the other end, identifiable as words at a glance. But she took no notice of what they said, only that they made sense.

As the night wore on it seemed to clasp her more and more tightly, until she felt as if she had been sucked down into a half-conscious underworld, where nothing mattered but the shape of the letters, sharp-cut and black and crowding around her. Above this underworld Moira walked breezily; she danced high up in dresses cut from parachute fabric with bluebell sleeves. Her father was reaching towards her with hands made of amber, his fingers conducting batons, stretching across a salt lake that became the sea the further he stretched, until ships rocked and rose on it. The ships turned into battleships and mastered the ice-tips of the waves for a time, but soon the sky began to sink and black clouds puffed lower and lower and began to gather in and swallow them. Flying fire came ducking out from under the clouds, turning into the shape of crows with wings flaring furnace-bronze, roaring as they swooped, and swooped closer to the front of the ships, their flame-wings opened in a half-embrace, and that was when Honey brought her mind back to the letters and their shapes, the letters and their shapes. Always, on the night shift, it had to be about the letters and their shapes. A song began to strike in her head, a nonsense song like a nursery rhyme, keeping her sedate and awake. The letters and their shapes, the letters and their shapes . . .

She didn't know how much time had passed before she rose to roll up the decrypts she had worked through, stuff them into their tube and load them into the pulley for Hut 3. She remembered later that she was still standing up when the door flung back.

The noise of the machines was so loud she didn't hear it at first. It was only the gust of cold that cut through the coke smoke and reached around her shoulders that made her turn.

'Deschamps.' It was the boy Findlay again. 'Someone's here for you.'

Afterwards it seemed to her that the moment had spread itself out into broad splodges – Picasso strokes – like the waking dream about her father and the sea. She turned. There was a man standing in the doorway, in Military

Police uniform. Her first thought was for her identity card – it was habit when she saw one of them. Her hand went for the pocket of her coat, and found the corners of the card. She couldn't read the man's expression. He had a moustache and eyebrows that were just as thick and he looked for all the world as if he were exceedingly cross. But about what?

'Would you come with me to the house?'

'What's it about?'

'My instructions are to bring you to the house.'

Honey let go of the card corners in her pocket and let him lead her from the hut.

For the third time in the past two days she trudged the dirt gravel that skirted the lake, bypassing the lawn. The MP insisted on going without a torch. He held her elbow and she still didn't know whether she was being arrested or protected. The light had shifted. The sun was far from rising but there was a telltale violet glow that said it was on its way. When they were inside the mansion hallway she looked at the clock. It was six thirty in the morning.

Dread balled in her stomach as they steered towards Tiver's office. But the MP turned off at the cafeteria instead, and took her to a table in the furthest corner. There was a man in a double-breasted grey suit already waiting. The café was surprisingly lively for the time of day. Men were playing chess over piles of cooked offal and glossy gravy. The smell of burnt toast and bacon was sharp.

'Cup of tea?' The man in the double-breasted suit stood. He did introduce himself but she forgot his name instantly. He was a detective from the local CID. He dismissed the MP with a murmured word, and Honey muttered thanks, though she didn't know yet for what.

'I'm not sure if I'd like a cup of tea. Can you tell me why you're here first?' The image of the drawer closing in her bedroom sprang up in her mind. That evening before she left for the Ritzy . . . the sheets of Moira's tissue rubbings, she had pushed them in, along with fragments of amber and those scratchings: letters and shapes, letters and shapes . . .

'Do you have a brother?'

'You can find that out from my administrative record. Captain Tiver keeps details—'

'Miss Deschamps.' He reached out across the table as if he might take her hand. She flinched back. 'I'm not here to challenge you. I know you're Martha Deschamps' girl. Aren't you?'

'Yes. What are you here for?'

'Is your brother Whittington Deschamps?'

'Dickie. Why, what's he done?'

'Have you any reason to believe he might have been coming to visit you tonight?'

Her spine cried out. It was all she could do to stop the cracking note from escaping her mouth, to keep it trapped inside her skeleton. She coughed and swallowed. 'Yes. I wrote him a letter, yesterday. But he hasn't replied yet.'

The detective shrugged. 'It can take days from London at the moment. Telegrams are as bad.'

'What's he done?' she repeated. In a strange trick of fate or time, the way the universe shifts a notch when déjà vu occurs, Honey knew exactly what he had done the second before the detective opened his mouth.

At the moment he told her, a cry went up from the far corner. A man's fist hammered the table, sending the chess pieces and a blue-rimmed cup of coffee flying. Steaming drips splashed up and flecked back down. 'By Jove, you're a rogue. You belong to the Jerries!' The sound of the cup striking the floor split the air, rendering the detective's words inaudible. But Honey read the shape of them on his moving lips.

'Miss Deschamps, sit steady. We believe Dickie may have been murdered.'

Chapter 14

The cup's crash on the floor seemed to knock the wind from her. For a second she was back in her lucid dream, swimming under the purple shadow of a battleship. She found it hard to focus on the detective in front of her; her eyes seemed cloudy; the world was spinning at a nauseating rate.

It had happened at last. They had come, they had come, and this time it really was about Dickie.

But oh Dickie, what a *coup de théâtre*.

They got her to the police motor car, two men, one on each arm. Her knees were wrapped under a freezing itchy blanket, and the car stank of the pipe tobacco coming off the large officer sitting next to her. She thought of Dickie as they drove: Dickie the dancer, Dickie the pacifist. Dickie who had objected to the sign-up because he believed, like Martha, that ballet was a salve to morale, that music could one day save the world. Dickie who danced to Tchaikovsky and Stravinsky and Prokofiev in tights and his little leather shoes that creaked on the polished parlour floor. He had grazed his knee in the garden once as a child and howled so hard a family of starlings had flushed out of a tree. Dickie with his cipher books and his puzzles who never finished the crossword because he didn't have the attention span to keep still for long enough, and Dickie who chewed his lip so hard when he was thinking that he had a wart-like growth on the side of his mouth that would flare when he was under pressure and he chewed it too much. Dickie never picked up his caramel wrappers – he left a little trail of them wherever he went – and complained they gave him indigestion when he danced after eating too many. Dickie hated cigarette smoke and he hated his birth name, Whittington. Dickie was a vegetarian. How could he be dead when she felt his force so alive inside her?

She felt rageful, burning with nerves beneath cold flesh, and she felt entitled to her rage. Her brother's death was huger and more tragic than any other death, surely. It was bloodier, it was more brutal, it hurt more – surely no one, no wife, no cousin, no mother could hurt this much. Surely the country could not be filled with people who felt this way, or how could it function? She hoped bitterly that it was someone else's brother or someone else's son murdered and lying in the cold morgue. Then she would not care. She would feel sorry, but she would not sting like this. The car moved slowly and swerved to avoid a scurrying creature on a country lane. Silvery moonlit flecks moved like fish past the window. Once the driver let out a curse – then, 'Sorry. Sorry, ma'am. Nearly there.'

After they reached the hospital, the events became tangled and muddied in her mind. She couldn't remember whether it was before she saw the beaten body or afterwards that they told her where it had been found.

'There's a coffin maker's behind the railway line,' the man who had spoken to her in the café said – his name, she knew now, was Detective Inspector Cole. They were standing in the lobby of the hospital and it smelled powerfully of ethanol and rot. 'The proprietor is Edwin James. You might know him up at the Park as he has the contract to work on the huts. He started work at five this morning. He said the wagon horse was crying over something or other. He found the body in the back of the stable, underneath the cortège carriage. Local roughs, brickworkers perhaps. Everything in his wallet was gone.'

'How did the police know it was him?' She saw Dickie's face floating in her mind. The conversation must have been after she saw the body because Dickie's face seemed to her blue and livid on one side, perfect on the other.

'He had this buried down inside his clothes.'

The officer had taken her aside, and sat her on a leatherette bench. Now he pulled from his coat a book. Honey's hands began to tremble as she reached forward for the green leather binding. It was softened now to scraps, frayed at the edges. *Figley's Book of Ciphers*. So it did exist. She hadn't dreamt it, she hadn't conjured it in memory. And he had brought it. Dickie had come to help and he had brought *Figley's Book of Ciphers*.

She had last seen it when she was seven or eight, just old enough to understand, not old enough to do anything about it. It was much smaller than she remembered. The detective held it lightly by its corners with a handkerchief. She flattened her hand to touch it and he pulled it back. 'Use this, and only touch the edges.' She opened the cover. The pages were old and creaked like doors as she turned them. The smell she knew, sweet vanilla paper, cut straight through the hospital scent.

'Whittington Deschamps,' had been written at the very top in a child's spidering hand, then scored out with a different-coloured pen. In the same hand, smoother, 'Whittington Korichnev' was written below, and below that, also in the same hand – Dickie's hand, there was no mistaking it now – the inscription: 'To Dickie, Love from Papa.' Further below still was an elaborate, artful squiggle, code for a signature.

She had seen it before many times, but only now did she see Dickie's hand in the whole thing: the message, the signature, the care taken in the flourishes, mimicking the quick hand of someone debonair and creative. She had believed with everything in her soul that the book was a gift from their father. Why had he done that? Had Dickie stolen the book, before their father left? Was it a relic he was never able to give to Dickie? Snatched by the child just before their father was exiled to Russia? Had he perhaps sneaked a secret message to Dickie later that Dickie had copied into the book? These were the things she wanted to believe. She had no reason to doubt what Dickie said. That was the story and that was what she believed. Because what else was there to believe? It wasn't as if she had a selection of lies from which to choose.

She turned the first page. Inside the title page, in the top corner, the same hand had scrawled, 'This book belongs to Dick, and if it you nick, you'll get a kick.'

The swing doors of the mortuary flapped, letting out the pathologist in his stiff white coat. From his breast pocket several metal instruments poked, and a pen, and the sight of them raised with grisly force the face she had seen: his broken collarbone, his vulnerable ballet dancer's soft skin, the blinding starched sheet that had only one rogue smirch of brown blood on it.

'Miss Deschamps.' The officer had been repeating her name. His yellow-stained fingers landed on her arm. She looked down, then up at him, startled. 'Did you know your brother was coming to visit you?'

Honey shook her head, and realised she had not yet cried.

'He didn't give you any word?'

'No.' She cleared her throat. She thought back to the British Restaurant at the station. The train had been late in.

The girl in the silver monkey fur had been waiting for her sweetheart. She wondered if the sweetheart had arrived on the same train.

'When was the last time you had contact with Dickie?'

'I told you, I wrote to him with—' She broke off, swallowing back down the story of the painted egg. It seemed absurd now, a childhood game turned sinister and sour. So many games of late had turned sour, not just for her but for so many little boys, playing soldiers with colanders on their heads. She didn't know why that image came to her now, but thinking about other people felt steadying. Her upper body swayed. 'I wrote him a letter. He didn't reply.'

The detective pulled his hand over his face and rubbed his lips. 'Damned post. All right, miss. Where's your billet? We'll take you home.'

He helped her up by the elbow and she felt resentful and repelled by his hand. The cold corridor air swam on her neck and ears, and she felt her senses of textures and temperatures had heightened, the way they did after a faint. She heard Beatrix's voice inside: 'Keep your head.' It jigged round and up and down like a carousel. 'Keep your head. Keep your head.'

It was half past eight by the time she closed the cottage door behind her and spied Dickie's handwriting on an envelope on the hall table. She leaned on the wall. Blood rushed to her gut. She imagined his cornflower blue dead shoulders rising from the steel table; his bloodied eyes snapping open, winking once, taking the pen and saying, 'Don't worry, gel, I've got it,' and then penning that affected curvature of her name straight from the grave.

She snatched it. She sniffed the paper, feeling reckless, masochistic, wanting to be repulsed. But it smelled only of ink. Not the sweet vanilla of the cipher book nor the surgical rot of the mortuary. She tore up the stairs, slammed the door behind her, ripped open the envelope. And it was only then she began to cry hard, howling childlike sobs.

The amber was spread out in front of her on the floor. She stared at it, as if she could melt the pieces. If it had been him, if he had some reason to taunt her, then this would all stop now.

His letter was still in her hand. Tears had smudged some of the ink but the message was plain, in characteristic pompous Dickie style:

'I receive your communiqué dear sister with interest. Stravinsky is a very exciting composer, I'll own, but I can't fathom his appeal in such a context. In truth, it is all a most peculiar choice for this type of concert. But you can tell me more when we meet. I'll be on the eight o'clock train from Euston. If you don't meet me at the station, I'll be staying in the Eight Bells.'

He signed with the flourish she recognised now from the book. Light strokes breaking free on the up and downward tails of the letters. But more assured, practised: a hand accustomed to signing silk souvenir programmes and stage postcards.

She dug out her notes on Moira's sketchings.

She thought about what Moira had told her about traffic analysis and building up a picture of how a cipher was used. How it would be impossible to crack an individual message so short, but that enemy ciphers were designed not to be broken by interceptors. In the case of these messages, by the nature of them being sent directly to her, she was expected to know the key.

Her mind moved now with a desperate intensity. Someone was trying to relate to her. Someone had killed Dickie, and if it was not a robber there were only two options.

Someone at the Park was testing her, and the test was so great that Dickie had to be killed before he could get in the way, before he could expose to her what they were doing. And the second, more potent option: Dickie knew the truth, and someone didn't like it.

She put a record on to disguise the noise of her scribbling and discourage Mrs Steadman from entering, and set to work. She worked solidly for the rest of the morning, trying to pick over the patterns, lining up various alphabets set at intervals along the letters, so A became D, B became E and so on. It didn't work. Then she remembered that Moira had said something, a name she'd used, for a type of hand cipher. But she hadn't written it down.

The Amber Shadows

It was useless. She was useless. She was not a cryptanalyst, she was not a codebreaker. She was a typist, nothing more. A hollowness crept through her as she threw down her pen and pushed the papers aside. The record came to an end and all she could hear was the hissing gaslamp, a horrid whispering, like half a dozen people hushing and gossiping in a room close by, too quiet to overhear. She listened to it for a few seconds until she felt it would turn her mad, then wrenched the switch and the room fell into grey gloom.

Tonight she would return to the Park where she could be of some use to someone. She would work harder than she had ever worked. She would race through the decrypts, she would type until her fingers numbed. If everyone who lost a relative in the war, everyone who grieved, took a day away from work, the casualties would rise. And work was a constant.

She took the amber pieces and threw them in the waste paper basket where they hit the bottom with a crack. She left the Steadmans' and walked along the lane to the end of the road until she found a telephone box. With her heart hanging heavy she dialled seven for trunks and asked the operator for her mother's hotel in Hastings.

The line carried an irritating buzz, and her mother's voice was distant, brittle. 'I know, dear. But what do you want me to say? At least he didn't lose his legs in a bomb attack, can you even think what would have happened . . . that would have been worse.'

She was relieved when eventually the pips sounded to tell her she was out of coins, and she threw down the telephone. She flung the red-panelled door of the box back so hard it hit the wall next to it. An old man in a peaked cap with a crate of milk bottles in his arms stopped and turned to look, and his scrutiny, his judgement was too much. She covered her cold wet cheeks with her hands and ran, as far as she could, towards the edge of the village.

For most of the afternoon Honey walked in the crisp winter light. Dead things were all around her and she couldn't help but notice them, as if their death was more potent and intrusive now, demanding she see how ugly and horrifying they were; spindles on blackthorn bushes, rotten slush grass at the sides of roads. The brickworks nearby was in full motion. A baked clay scent was drifting in clouds, and sometimes she came across a bush that had caught a mist of red dust on the twigs. A cold wind bit her face. She passed a pair of birds squabbling in a tree and remembered an argument she'd had with Dickie as a child, about *The Firebird*. There were two versions of the story that she knew, one she'd read in a fairytale book and the one by Stravinsky. But Dickie had grown angry. He had grown violently cross and danced in a rage around the room, screaming her down that there was only ever one story, to everything; there was only ever one version of events.

★　　★　　★

She arrived two hours early at the Park. The MPs waved her through and she picked her way with her torch beam low, shining over the spokes of bicycle wheels and scuffed brogues. She headed for the cafeteria and stood still for a moment, looking around at the room where she had been told the news, to see if it had changed at all. But it was the same. There were still half-played chess games and tea and the smells of burnt toast and cheese pie in the air.

Earlier Mrs Steadman had had a hard-hearted stab at sympathy. 'It's a damned shame these young men dropping, it is. I remember when my brother didn't come home after the first war. My mother didn't change his sheets for weeks. I was still finding bits of his underwear when we had the clean-out before my wedding.' She'd had the grace to leave the tea tray on the floor outside Honey's room and disappear just after knocking.

Honey couldn't face anything to eat but took a cup of tea. She was staring at the black bubbles breaking on its surface when the other side of the table jolted. Beatrix sat down opposite.

'What are you doing here? The news is all over the Park. Go home.' She got up again and dashed the length of the table to take the chair next to Honey. She smelled of lavender and something sweet and resinous as she clutched Honey's shoulder. Honey wanted to say something but her throat clogged. She held the tears in there, mute, because if they broke she would never be able to stop them. 'Beatrix,' she managed. 'What are you doing here?'

'Tea break. They've got me on back shift. Honestly, they'll find the brute. Word is already going about that they've got a man from the brickworks. You know what thugs the townies are. The Eight Bells lot.'

Beatrix's eyes were fixed on Honey's. She had a pucker in her brow. 'A hot bath is what you need.'

'I can't very well sit in a hot bath all day and all night.' She thought of the oily water in the Steadmans' bathroom; the amber slipping from her hands, its wax coat dissolving and the letters appearing . . . well, that would never happen again now. The amber was where it would stay, in with the refuse, toenail clippings and yesterday's newspaper. She was finished with it.

'Have you telephoned your family? They'll have to know to expect you?'

She nodded.

'You have to go to them, Honey. It's London, isn't it? I can lend you the Rolls, I can have someone drive you in fact. I'll have our chauffeur come down on the train and he can take you back. Don't worry about the petrol rationing, he knows a man. Can you wait until tomorrow morning, or would you rather I called him tonight? In fact I'm going off duty in a couple of hours, I can drive you myself.' Her words came quickly but they hit Honey and slid off, like her flesh was made of duck feathers. She couldn't hold them in her head for long enough to understand their sense. She had become very aware of the muscles on her face. They felt brittle, like they might be on their way to collapse if she moved them. She managed a smile but the only thing she could think to say was, 'I hope Moira's all right.'

'Dash it, Honey, you're in shock. You should be in bed. I can't believe those policemen didn't take you to a doctor.'

'I'm all right. For goodness' sake, how many other girls here have lost someone since we arrived? Ten, fifty? Fathers, brothers, a sweetheart?' She stopped herself, seeing Beatrix's silk map scarf tucked almost out of view between her collarbone and mustard pullover. Beatrix stopped her too, by taking her raised flailing hand. Very carefully she pressed it down onto the tabletop. Grains of saccharine had spilled out onto the Formica and Honey felt them cut an itchy rash into her palm as it was flattened under the pressure of Beatrix's.

'Honey, listen to me. War is not a competition. You are entitled to your grief.' Her mouth stayed straight and very level. Honey felt afraid to contradict her, scared in that moment to do anything against what she said. 'I'm taking you straight to the Captain. Leave is what you need.'

'No.'

'No ifs or buts. Let me deal with Mooden and that nasty little Roache. And if they won't let you go then I'll drive you myself and they'll have two renegades to deal with.'

She gripped Honey's hand as she spoke, beating it down towards the table on each word. She reminded Honey of all the teachers, all the governesses she had known. People who were able to control themselves, take control of a situation. What good would she, Honey, be in any situation? She couldn't even solve the mess of her amber and now she had led Dickie down into a fatal trap. Blame suddenly swamped her. It was all her doing. If she hadn't summoned him, if she had thrown the trinkets away without thinking . . .

She let Beatrix lead her towards the Captain's office.

'He's just left,' she heard his night secretary say. Then, 'Hold on. Rogers.' She called to a man in plain tweeds with a newspaper under his arm. 'Did the Captain leave?'

'The engine's running in his car.' The man pointed with his pipe.

'Can it wait?' The woman looked expectantly at Honey and then at the clock. It was half past ten.

Honey hesitated. The letters of the cipher travelled through her mind. If there was one way to put a stop to this – perhaps this was what had been expected of her all along. She found her tongue. 'No, it can't,' she said and raced down the stairs, ripping her hand from Beatrix's, sliding on the herringbone parquet and tripping the single stone step. The gravel sprayed into her shoes as she ran to Tiver's car. The driver's side door was open. The headlights had been painted black on the top halves and made shining oblong slicks on the dirt.

'Captain, wait.' She waved her arms. The Captain was half-bent towards the open car door but he rose again, turned his face to the noise and widened his eyes.

'If your aim is to wake the whole of Bletchley town then I'm sure you've succeeded. This had better be an air raid or nothing.'

The cold made her short of breath. Her lungs pricked as she tried to gather her words. 'Please can I talk to you, in your office?'

His face took on a scandalised expression and he looked ready to open his mouth and rebuke her when suddenly a memory caught hold of him. It was only afterwards that Honey thought he must have forgotten about her brother until that moment. 'Do you need leave to go home, Deschamps? I can grant it. I'm sorry for your loss.'

'No, no, it's not that at all. It's just, I think I know why Dickie was killed.'

'Then you'd better tell the police but I'm afraid it's not something I can do anything about. I'm very sorry to hear it and we'll look after you well like we look after—'

She cut him off. 'But it might concern you. Would it concern you if someone somewhere was sending me things?'

Now Tiver stood to face her. He snapped closed the car door. The engine was still running, pumping out chemical smoke. 'That parcel you got the other day?'

Honey looked around. The night was pitch black but footsteps crackled far away in distant knots and patches, in different parts of the Park. From somewhere across the lake came a shriek of glee and a thump. Someone had fallen over on the ice.

'There are more of them. They're coming from Russia and I know who's sending them.'

The Captain paused, looked very calmly and discreetly down, first at his shoes, then at Honey's. Then he opened the car door, switched off the engine, and strode up the single step back into the building.

'I know you're grieving, but this had better be worth my while,' he said, and while his words were soft, they carried hard as hail on the night breeze.

Chapter 15

'The first one came last Monday.'

She was settled in the chair opposite Tiver's desk. The wood and the upholstery felt more comfortable this time. Or perhaps it was the weight of relief lifting from her, the lightness of the confession she was about to make. Honey had always wondered about Catholic confession and where its comfort came from. Now, with the dark wood and the velvet curtains drawn inside the office windows, with the gas fire giving off its eerie blue-gold light in the corner of the room, thawing the air chunk by chunk, and with Tiver's pipe smoke curling like incense from his hands, she thought perhaps she understood a little.

To carry one less secret. It was solace.

'I'd been at the cinema when one of the boys from Hut 3 dropped it off.'

Tiver frowned. 'Which one?'

She hesitated. There was nothing for it. It would have to come out. She braced herself to hear something she didn't want to know. 'Felix Plaidstow.'

The Captain frowned and foraged in his pipe with the end of a biro. After a couple of seconds recognition released the springs on his brow. 'Ah, Felix. The chess boy. Magdalene, Cambridge. Went up in '37.'

'That's the one.' Honey felt a peculiar uncoiling of relief to hear his name in another person's mouth. 'He said it had been delivered to their hut by mistake.'

'Every chance,' Tiver muttered. 'That boy brings the canteen post in here sometimes.'

'I took it upstairs and I opened it. It had stamps on it, just like the one I opened in here.' Her voice caught suddenly as she opened her mouth. The words stuck. Her throat jammed a valve. It was hard, so hard sometimes to tell the truth. The truth could shock you with its strangeness once the words became real. Once they had sounded there was no putting them back.

'All the packages,' she said. 'They all had the same stamps on them. Russian censors—'

Tiver interrupted. 'All the packages? How many were there?'

She counted backwards. The two panels, the backdrop, the base with the mechanism. The firebird.

'Five.'

Tiver leaned forward in his chair. She felt the benediction of his pipe smoke filling the space between them. But his eyes were keen and small and in the dim light the shot marks across his nose burned in tiny black shadows.

Honey didn't dare move. She wanted to look away but thought that somehow that might give the impression she was lying. All the things she had learned about liars – that their palms sweated, that their eyes flickered, that the saliva dried in their mouths as they lied – all those things now happened to her.

She took a breath and retreated a step in her mind. 'They all had the same stamps. Russian censors' stamps and British censors, the crown—'

'I know what the British censor's stamp looks like, but I'm afraid you are mistaken about the Russian. Leningrad is invaded. It's impossible—'

'But what if someone got away before the invasion was complete? What if they took something to Murmansk or Stalingrad, or Vladivostok? What if they posted it before the Nazi stranglehold?'

Tiver was shaking his head. Honey couldn't tell but she thought she saw pity in his eyes.

She went on. 'What if there was a man who was in charge, or knew someone in charge, of the Pushkin Palace museum, of the Amber Room, and he took some pieces with him when he escaped? Isn't it possible that he would be able to post them overseas, to keep them safe?'

'You said you think you know who is sending them.'

'I do. I can fetch them. I can show you. Three panels, a mechanism, like a clock. And one carved like a bird.'

'The bird.' The Captain took a deep breath. So he had opened it. He fiddled with his pipe, tapping it out and filling it again. He smoothed his wrinkled hands over the blotter on the desk, found a speck of ink and picked it away.

'My father . . .' Her voice cracked. 'Was Russian. A few months before I was born he fled the country, into Hungary we heard first, where he had a great-aunt, then Russia. He was a composer. He was experimenting with codes, using mathematical patterns in his music. He left my brother a cipher book. He worked in Leningrad after the revolution, he played, he conducted. And his favourite piece was always *The Firebird*. Dickie saw him conduct it when he was a child. It's his earliest memory, at the opera house. We didn't know where he'd gone at first, but Dickie used to keep an eye out in the newspapers, and sometimes he'd see something with our father's name in it.'

Captain Tiver didn't meet her eye. 'And what was that name?'

'Korichnev. After he gave up music he worked as a curator at the Detskoye Selo – the Pushkin Palace, the old Catherine Palace. He was the guardian of the Amber Room. You know about the Amber Room being taken by the Nazis to Konigsberg? It came through on the intercepts last year.'

Tiver looked away. 'Five thousand signals pass through this estate every day. I did not know about the Amber Room being looted.'

'But you think it's possible? That my father smuggled out pieces of amber from it before the room was pillaged? You think it's possible that he's sending me messages, not because he knows I'm here – the packages came via London 222, via the Foreign Office – but because he wants us to connect? And that after all is why I'm here. I'm not here because my stepfather knew someone at a club. I'm here because I know how to work with codes. I understand codes. I have an instinct for the machines and I can learn languages and the only reason I know how to do any of this is because my own father, my blood father—'

Tiver looked into her eyes very suddenly and said, 'No, Honey. You're here because your stepfather knew someone in a club.'

The words slammed a guillotine between them.

Honey stopped short, shocked by the cut thread of her thought. Her emotions tangled together in a ball. Slowly she let them all separate out from each other; what she thought of herself, what brought her to where she sat now; how she had spent the past week reconstructing, evaluating the different bits of herself and where they might have come from. What she was left with after the thoughts had divided up was shame, anger and humiliation.

She wanted Dickie, only Dickie, and yet she felt his pull leading her down into an underworld of gloom. But he was the only one who would understand. And now he could never defend her.

Tiver watched her expression change. She felt like one of his wounded battlefield soldiers being appraised for duty. His brow creased.

'You're very tired and you're grieving, and it's very late at night,' he said. 'Go home.'

'But my father, my real father—'

'Your real father as far as we are concerned is Henry Deschamps. That's good enough for us.'

'No.'

'Honey.' He made a shifting motion in his chair. He watched the blue glow of the gas fire flame for a second, looked at his pipe, then thought better of refilling it. 'We are at war. And at war you cannot dwell on what is past. You can only look forward. Ask your friend Beatrix. Ask anyone who has lost someone. It does not do to seek blame. It does not do to dig up things that might be best left alone. Recrimination comes later. Right now we only have the present and the future.'

'You know the truth about him, don't you?'

Tiver shook his head. 'For our purposes your father was Henry Deschamps.'

Honey said softly, 'But it's your job to know everything. You said that, you said it on my first day. "We know every-thing about your past. Don't try to pull the wool . . . you'll be shot, beheaded," you said it.'

'I didn't say beheaded.'

'Shot then. Captain, tell me the truth. If no one will, I must be able to trust you. You are my commander.' Her voice came out shrill and quiet, a trapped wail. She found herself, without warning, wanting Felix's arms, right then, his strange little eyes, his beaten hands.

Tiver looked across the table and kept his gaze steady on her. His wrinkles were picked out deeply in the light. It did not flatter; it made him glow orange and monstrous. When she coughed he broke the gaze, and looked again at the fire instead. He kept looking at it as he spoke.

'We talk about truth as if it always has some kind of special dignity. Your real father was a man called Ian Kurtz. He lived in London and he was a cocktail pianist in a number of hotels. You're right, I know everything. That's how I also know that those forged censors' stamps were made with British ink. Do you know why I know this? Because it's my job to know secrets. You're right. I do know everything about every single person we employ here at the Park, and I judge who to tell what and when. And if I get it wrong, then a boy on a ship may die a very cold and very watery death. Or a family in Coventry may wind up with their house razed to ashes. Your brother Dickie was considered as a recruit for the Park but we deemed him mentally unfit. He is a fantasist and a storyteller.'

Honey clutched the wooden arms of the seat. She felt as if she were the one on a ship. The ground kept swelling. She had never wanted so much to leave the skin she was in and run from it, lie dormant for a while under the ground until it was safe to come out.

'Your father was a drunk and a bully and he died . . . in a brawl outside a public house in Smithfield one evening late in the first war. He never conducted *The Firebird* at the Royal Opera House. He wasn't Russian, he was half-Scottish, half-German. And he was never exiled to Hungary or to Russia; he died in Britain. We have his death record. The Park doesn't employ people with foreign parentage except under special circumstances. Since you never met the man, and were brought up as a Deschamps, you were deemed safe.' Tiver softened. 'He may have had a cipher book that he gave to Dickie; a child's gift.'

'But Dickie was certain about *The Firebird*. It was his first memory.'

'Miss Deschamps.'

'That was never my name. Korichnev—'

'Deschamps. Yes it is. You wanted to learn the truth. I'm sorry if it's disappointing. I respect my staff here but you must respect me in return.' He spoke quietly and calmly and Honey realised that perhaps that was what she had wanted. In time the truth would settle on her like skin after a scar. But right now she only wanted the old comfort she knew. She wanted to take back the old story. Tiver was right, it did not do to dredge up the past, she wanted to put back his words, to burn them in the fire until they were nothing but grey ash.

'I don't know why Dickie sent you those things. But he did. The little bird ornament we checked went through a post office just north of London.'

The last part hit her the hardest. There was no Russia. The hoax felt crueller than a noose.

'Go home, Honey.' Tiver looked at the clock. 'It's almost midnight.'

'My shift's about to start.'

'I don't think that's a good idea. The other girls will draft someone in.'

The thought of someone filling in for her, while all she was left to do was go home and contemplate her own idiocy, surrounded by the trinkets that had never passed through the hands of her father, her dead father who didn't exist, whose *Firebird* was only ever a fantasy – it was too horrible to contemplate. Her skin felt hot and cold and as if it wasn't hers but a snake's, and she must now shrug it off for it was shedding-time, time for renewal, a new body, new skin.

She wanted to take Dickie and shake him by his livid blue shoulders. He was a wretch. He was a fool. What had he meant? Did he even believe his own story? There was only ever one story, that was what Dickie said. She thought of how viciously he had pressed the story of *The Firebird* at her: Stravinsky's version, not the one she had found in the Russian fairytale book. Hers had been wrong, his had been right. His version of the truth dominated. But why? Dickie, why? For his own ego. That was Dickie all over. Dickie Deschamps the dancer; with a secret genius in his past. Dickie who deserved to be on the stage because it was in his blood, the blood that was wronged by his father's exile.

But how did she know Tiver was telling the truth? He might know everything, but knowledge and lies were different things. Tiver had not grown up with her. Tiver had not danced the *Firebird* prince with a passion that could not have been made from lies. She had never seen Tiver cut his knee and cry for his father to come home from Russia. Even now she felt Dickie's version of the story slipping its iron fingers up from the grave and wrapping itself around Tiver's.

Dickie's voice kept creeping in on her. It cut through Tiver's story with its stony persuasion, so that now, in the grey icy smoke of the office confessional, she thought that it could be Tiver who was the liar.

He had opened the door into the hallway. This time there were no warnings about the Official Secrets Act. No stern decrees. There was only sorrow and sympathy for a silly girl who had believed in a silly story. He must think her just like Joan Fontaine, the first time Cary Grant dupes her over the chairs he has gambled away, her father's chairs. She felt the itchy wool pulled over her eyes, the tricking of a wolf somewhere. But which wolf, and why?

As she left the room Beatrix stood, her arms outstretched. Honey sank into them, relieving herself of her own weight, and nurtured the only silver lining she had left. She had not told Tiver about the wax-covered codes.

Chapter 16

Beatrix smothered her with perfumed cashmere. Honey
knew then that she would remember the scent for years to
come and associate it with hollow sadness. Her body was
shutting down, each switch tripping off like lights in a house
about to be left abandoned. A numbness swept her up and
she found she couldn't cry or connect to the sense of everything she had just lost.

It was not uncommon, she thought, for a girl to lose both her
brother and her father in wartime. She was commonplace. Her
grief was no bigger or heavier than anyone else's. But it seemed
to her more shameful somehow, to lose a father not because he
had died in glory, with shot across his nose like Captain Tiver,
but because he had never existed in the first place.

'Are you still in there?'

Beatrix's voice came down through the frizzy channels of
her ruined wave. Honey nodded slowly, and felt it odd that

her movements could be so slow and sad when her mind was racing.

'I'll take you home.'

'Will she be all right? I can call in Matron.'

Tiver's night secretary's voice and Beatrix's drifted in soft murmurs over her head, dulled by the embrace. Her ear was pressed against the shoulder of Beatrix's cardigan. What was that scent? Dior. And pearls. Did pearls have a scent? Or was she wearing amber? The voices drifted the way they did through the nursery floorboards when her mother had been giving a dinner party.

Her mother. Her mother who had married Henry Deschamps, the soap man – 'the man who keeps me in lavender' she would gaily laugh again and again when anyone asked. Always the same joke. Sometimes the flowers would be different: 'the man who keeps me in roses'. Her mother who threw extravagant parties because Henry Deschamps' wealth was as big as the Palace Theatre. Her mother who sang at the Royal Opera House, great warbling arias that Dickie hated. 'Verdi and Puccini are vulgar. All Italian composers are vulgar. Wagner was a fascist.' Dickie only danced Russian ballet to Russian scores. Dickie only listened to his Russian ballet mistress.

Her mother must know the truth.

'You must make sure someone keeps an eye on her.'

'She's in a billet with a couple. The woman doesn't work.'

'Call this telephone number if you need the Park doctor.'

'She'll be fine. The body repairs itself, it's clever that way.'

The secretary hesitated. Beatrix squeezed Honey's shoulder, which was the cue for her to lift her head in a dignified manner, like she had seen the tragic heroines do on the great silver screen time and time again, affect a smile, take a look back over her shoulder at the closing door of Tiver's office, try to meet the eye of the man who didn't return her stare, and follow Beatrix out into the chill night.

From over on the lake came jubilant screams. A wild scraping sound, like metal being dragged across glass, was carrying on a breeze. 'You can't use a trestle as a bloody sled, you'll—' The crack cut them off and then a shriller scream from a woman came with shrieks of laughter.

'Midnight dip,' Beatrix murmured. 'Takes all sorts to work here. Come on. I'll drive you home. Let me deal with Roache.' They walked in step towards the small parking area round by the Research Cottage. Every time Honey went to open her mouth she could only think of trite observations, empty things to say for the sake of saying something. She imagined herself saying to Beatrix, 'This grass is so frosty. The darkness is so grim. This cold is so brutal.' In the end she couldn't bring herself to open her mouth at all.

Beatrix snapped the car door open and shut her in. The leather seats were freezing, and in the small amount of time it took Beatrix to walk round to the driver's side the silence and darkness in the car seemed to Honey like the inside of a tomb. She wondered what her father had seen in his last moments. Did it feel cold to lie there on the ground? Was a doctor sent for? Was he taken to hospital?

But what if he hadn't had those last moments yet? What if he wasn't in a tomb, wasn't even in a grave? He was in a hideout, hoarding secrets to keep them safe from Nazis.

Suddenly the car became not a tomb but a dark shed, a bleak underground workshop somewhere close to a border town. There was a soldier – a guerrilla fighter, a woman in a red sash – who came to him and smuggled the parcels through the military post. Her father's mind worked overtime, crafting ways in which he could reach her, without letting the British know it was him for fear of capture. He had escaped them once. He wasn't to trust them again.

The driver's door opened and clicked shut and as Beatrix choked the engine to life a powerful petrol smell drifted in through gaps in the steelwork. 'Right, let's get her going first. I've got half an hour. They're not doing anything in there anyway. No one's broken a thing today. They're all panicking in case the design's been modified. That's the rumour going about. It happened once before when they started rotating from five Enigma wheels instead of just three.'

Beatrix crackled the car over the gravel. Passing the Military Police she wound down her window.

'I'm taking her home. Sick bay orders.'

The guard waved them past.

'Can tell them anything you like on the way out,' Beatrix muttered, churning the glass back up. 'Still, suppose it's harder getting in. Even the hairdressers have to have passes. There was a girl last week forgot hers – she'd left it inside and managed to slip out for some shampoo. They wouldn't let her back in, not even when her boss vouched for her. Had to call in Tiver or something. I don't think he was best pleased.' Honey felt Beatrix's gaze flash on her quickly, then back to the road. 'I hope he treated you well.'

'Fine,' she murmured.

They turned past the station, then bent up round the Eight Bells. The slats on the headlights made the road look like a piece of sliced toast. Egg with soldiers, Honey thought. It seemed ages since she had been in a motor car, but then she remembered she had been in one that morning with the police. They passed the phone box where she had telephoned her mother, and the house where she had seen Felix with the painting. Smoke was pouring out of the chimney again. Beatrix turned past the red row of Edwardian villas at the top of Church Green Road and pulled the car to a halt. The handbrake squeaked.

She reached into the pocket of her cardigan and pulled out a broken cigarette and a piece of ribbon. She grunted and placed them both on the dashboard then went fishing again. This time she retrieved a piece of crumpled paper. She snapped the cigarette in two, picked the stuffings of tobacco from the break and placed half in her mouth, then passed the other half to Honey. 'Can you have a rummage in there, and see if there are matches?'

Honey unclipped the glove compartment. Maps and bonbon wrappers spilled out.

'Oops. God, if I was caught with maps they'd fry me.'

'Here.' Honey handed across a rattling box.

'Give me your cig.' Beatrix lit them both.

She tossed the matches back then bent forward and smoothed the piece of paper flat.

Honey took the cigarette from her mouth. 'What is that?' Her stomach knotted. She felt as if she were in that mortuary again, with the sheet being peeled back. 'Is it a decrypt?'

'Heavens, no.' Beatrix coughed. 'Stealing decrypts? I've not got a death wish.'

It was almost pitch black outside but the 'Secret' stamp stood out crimson, a level down from 'Most Secret'. She picked it up and held it close to her eyes. The glow of the cigarette bounced off the paper and she let out a small cry.

'I thought you'd need it,' Beatrix said. 'You were in there so long that when she turned her back to fetch a cup of tea – well, it was poking its nose out of the file. Burn it, once you've been, won't you? I'm afraid I can't take you. I told Head of Room I'd only be half an hour.'

It was a carbon copy of a memo signed by Tiver. The top line told her all she needed to know. 'Removal of Moira Draper to Bexworth Insane Asylum. Action immediately.'

★　★　★

Later, in the cooling water of the clean bath, Honey lit another cigarette and looked over the memo again. Mrs Steadman had begrudgingly prepared her the bath. 'Special circumstances,' she muttered as she sloshed in the half-warm water from the stove. She had taken a thick indelible-ink pen and drawn a line five inches up the tub. 'Keep it so I can wash the clothes after,' she had said. The stolen paper – a flimsy shining carbon-copy tissue – was wilting in the steam.

'In the opinion of Dr Langley she should be removed immediately from duties and placed in a secure environment. Miss Draper's knowledge of the operations in Hut 6 is of a nature that if leaked could prove extremely damaging. She has been signed off for nerve disturbance before and subsequently had her duties reduced accordingly. But Cpt Tiver on the recommendation of Hut 3's Lt Swann believes this is of a different nature. We would recommend having her certified, and kept in a secure solitary environment for the duration of the war, or until further notice that she be deemed to no longer pose a risk to security.'

In a secure solitary environment for the duration of the war. She read the words over and over again. They chilled her. How strange and awful it was that such men could decide one's future, one's present.

She pulled on her cigarette and read it again: 'a secure solitary environment'. Moira, who had done nothing but love a man, whose brain had tipped and had torn a spiteful message from a ladies' magazine, sneaked into a hut she shouldn't have. That such flighty, spontaneous, rageful actions could not be undone made Honey's guts churn.

The water rippled as she moved and she saw it as the waves beneath the cliffs at the end of *Suspicion*, when the door of the car had flung open on Joan Fontaine's side as they drove. Cary Grant could so easily have pushed her out. He could have sent her spiralling and tumbling with only a few scrapes on the rocks to show. But he didn't. He had reached over and closed the door. Because the picture needed a happy ending. Or perhaps because after the picture finished he wanted to give her a crueller and more calculated death. Sometimes stories were only told in part. They didn't finish just because the picture stopped rolling.

Tiver could have been wrong. If her father had died in a brawl how would the Park know? How could they? How could they have traced back that name to that man – a common enough name, Kurtz. *And yet my birth certificate says something different. It says . . . Kitts, doesn't it?* How could they be sure they had the right man? And why wouldn't I have been told before?

Something didn't add up. She measured up the two options and knew that the sensible thing would be to take Beatrix's offer and go directly to her mother. But the piece of memo paper sat damp and wrinkled in her hand. And the amber still lurked at the bottom of her waste paper basket.

The Amber Shadows

A little more than twenty-four hours ago Dickie breathed.

The amber could have been his doing, but she wouldn't know unless she decrypted the cipher. The police would never let her have the book, and there was only one person she could trust.

She memorised the name of the asylum, then set fire to the paper. The flame took. The edges turned black with a gold edge, like very fine iron in a blacksmith's forge. Turning to ash they dropped into the bathwater. She stirred them around until they made the water grey. A couple of shards clung to her as she rose, stuck to her towel as she wiped them off her skin.

She woke up in pitch black to the sound of the gate clicking closed in the garden – Mr Steadman on his way to work. She switched on the electric lamp and looked at the clock beside her bed. Six thirty in the morning. Mrs Steadman was already up and clattering pans in the kitchen. Across the landing Rebecca was snoring.

She opened the wardrobe, letting out the smell of clothes and dust. On the top shelf were hats, boxes of unsuitable shoes her mother had given her and folded blankets. She scrabbled until she found the object she was looking for. She hadn't used it for over a year – despite the threat of fines, people didn't carry them in Bletchley any more. She pulled the little box out, dangling it from its leather strap, and unclipped the latch.

The gas mask was still inside, pristine, shocking in its ugliness and stinking of rubber. She had only worn it twice; once in London in a raid and the other time at a London party where they had all taken photographs of themselves kissing under the mistletoe in masks.

Hesitating for a second, she took it by its thick bands and placed it back underneath her hanging clothes. The silk dresses swayed and the eyes of the mask looked back at her, with their blank warning stare.

Before going to bed she had fished the amber pieces out of the waste paper basket and wrapped them in the same fur she'd used to take them to Moira's. She loaded them now into the gas mask box, packing down the hairs on the fur where they stuck out.

She picked up a road map she had brought with her when she first made the trip to Bletchley, then, thinking of Beatrix's words, stuffed it underneath the furs, at the bottom of the box.

She crept back up onto her tiptoes and felt around on the top shelf of the wardrobe again, then pulled out a hat she never wore – except to weddings – and a light summer mackintosh in navy blue, which she had never worn at the Park. Down under the furs she stuffed spare knickers and a pair of darned stockings.

At the last minute she found herself unable to form the words to Mrs Steadman, so she scribbled on a piece of notepaper on the hall table: 'Away today and on night shift tonight. Feeling a bit better, please use my ration for dinner.'

She took her latchkey and escaped into the rising mist of dawn.

The roads were quiet and murky. A few bicycles rattled past, but the shift change at the Park was not for another hour and most of the brickworkers and railway workers had already begun their day.

The frost was brittle and prickly on the grass ledges, slippery on the pavements. It was only when she walked past the baker's and saw fruitcakes advertised she realised how close it was to Christmas. Less than a week to go. The thought was like a thorn, and on the end of its stem she saw a vision of the empty place at the dinner table.

She hesitated outside the house where she had met Felix that night in the rain. The curtains were drawn back, but in the twilit gloom and with the ancient panes divided into tiny leaded squares it was hard to sneak a look in. But she did notice for the first time the inscription above the door: Rectory Cottages.

On the fenced grassy patch beside the building lay a small allotment with the shape of an empty chicken coop, and beyond it the block shadow of a wooden hut on stilts, about the size of an elevated rabbit hutch. As she passed, trying not to think of Mrs Steadman's pies, a small irregular cheeping sound made her blink and take a step back. She hesitated, waiting. It was an odd noise, distinctive. It came once more – three sort of trilling top notes and two sad little low ones answering, like an echo. She had not imagined it. She waited again. But then perhaps she had imagined it, because although she listened hard now there was nothing but the sound of the roads and ordinary birds fussing in trees.

She moved on, making careful progress towards the station. The platform was crowded. Soldiers were in high spirits, carrying garlands of holly, brown parcels tied to the tops of their khaki duffel cases. Through scratched high gothic windows she saw the bonneted woman who ran the British Restaurant dripping out cups of tea from an urn.

Without signposts and in the dark of the morning it was difficult to remember which platform to choose for which direction. She bought a ticket and asked an army man who directed her across the bridge. The first train approached and she clutched the gas mask case close.

On an ordinary day reaching the small village of Bexworth should only have taken twenty minutes, a peaceful jaunt between two nearby towns. But the train was already full and it stood at Bletchley platform for what seemed an age as more soldiers appeared from another train and piled aboard. She had bought a second-class ticket and chose a compartment that was half full. She ended up opposite a couple of soldiers passing around a bottle of wine. One of them had a single chevron on his shoulder, the other's uniform was blank.

'It's fucking French,' the blank one said, pushing the bottle under Honey's nose. Sharp sherry wafts came out – whatever it was, was the very opposite of French wine – curdling her empty stomach. She smiled and the boy took it away and passed it down the bench.

More and more boys filed in and she became aware after a few moments of a youth opposite staring at her with bloodshot eyes. His gaze lurched but stayed on her, as if he could see under her skin. A song struck up: 'The Washing on the Siegfried Line.' They banged their feet and slammed the side of the train carriage louder and louder with each beat of the rhythm; the noise seemed as if it would shatter the walls. Honey felt it rooting through her eardrums, into her skull, so loud it made tears prick at her eyes. One of the soldiers pointed. 'Hey it's all right, miss, we're home now.'

Attention turned to her – the only woman in the carriage – and she was bombarded with shoulder shakes, pats on the back, cries of, 'for king and country'.

'I was there at Dunkirk when the boats came.'

'Were you, my arse. He worked in the mess. He was a kitchen porter. I was in Palestine, miss. We had to sleep in the desert.'

They were children. They couldn't have been more than nineteen. Their shining red scalps showed through their downy hair.

The door of the compartment opened and a couple of

young ATS girls squealed in. One held her fingers to her nose. 'Pooh, doesn't half whiff of boy in here.'

''Cos it's full of soldiers. Come here, sit on my knee.'

'You want a swig of wine? It's French.'

The girls looked at each other. The blonde one held out her hand then sniffed the neck of the bottle and tossed her head away. 'French somethingorother but it's not wine.'

The brunette took off her hat and plumped up her hair.

The train was still stationary and Honey felt panic rising as the girls squeezed into two seats made vacant by two of the youngest boys who got down and perched on the floor on top of their duffel bags. She wondered how long it would be before the train began to move. On the platform, the guard was in conversation with the station master. Neither man looked in a hurry. The engine had lulled and the coal smell for a few moments was tempered by the dry stink from the brickworks, coming via the open doors.

'Where's this place again? Bletchley.'

They began saying Bletchley in different accents. Then one said, 'Shhhhhhh, yer not supposed to . . . how do you know she's not a Jerry spy?'

One of the men poked Honey on the arm. 'You're a good girl, aren't you? Brought your gas mask? Have you ever had to use it?'

'Once,' she muttered. 'A raid in London.'

'You'd look a doll in a siren suit, I'll bet ya.'

'What do you do for the war effort, miss?' another man asked.

Honey flinched then felt the blush rising as she said, 'I'm a typist.'

'Typist, eh? My sister's a typist. Here, aren't you lot lucky, you've got brave men like us out fighting to protect you? Do you have a brother?'

She frowned as the panic swelled. She nodded then shook her head. 'I did.'

The mood changed immediately. One of the lads took off his hat and stared.

She opened her mouth to correct him, but at the last second couldn't bring herself to do it. The only respectable death in wartime was a wartime one. The bottle was passed round again and the back slaps stopped. The ATS girls were whispering to each other. Honey found her panic replaced by a terrible bloom of guilt that grew inside her, threatening to burst.

Finally she smelled burning coal and the wheels began to strain the tracks. And then the noise of the whistle drowned out the cackle of the blonde ATS girl who had thrown back her head laughing and was showing a mouthful of filled metal teeth to the soldier she sat beside.

They had only gone a hundred yards when the compartment door shunted open and made her poke her head up. Out of habit she searched for the card corners of the ticket in her pocket. But when she looked up her eyes fell not on the uniformed shape of the ticket conductor but on another familiar form she recognised.

'Miss Deschamps? I thought it was you. Even in that pretty hat you're very distinctive. There's space in my compartment, I thought . . . I thought perhaps you'd like to join me?'

The rush as she saw Felix leaning casually into the carriage nearly brought fresh tears. She had the urge to stand up and charge at him with an embrace, launch her arms about his shoulders. He looked freshly washed, with his suit and blackout coat neatly pressed and an old school tie with fat purple and thinner white and pink stripes. He pushed the brim of his hat from his eyes and Honey saw traces in there of the look she had caught from him across the Park.

She fumbled with her gas mask box and hat, and found her coat was ungracefully caught under the bottom of the soldier next to her. But she managed to stammer up at him, 'Ever so kind. What a surprise.'

A couple of the boys adjusted their buttons and sat up straighter. They watched Felix with suspicion, looking up and down his clothing with a mixture of deference and disgust. The soldier next to where Honey had sat slapped the vacant seat hard and pointed at one of the ATS girls, as the carriage door slid shut.

Honey followed Felix a few paces down the narrow corridor, bracing against the hand rail as the train pitched like a ship round a corner. They entered a tunnel and the windows blacked out. She saw their reflections; her summer hat and coat beside his sharp silhouette. They looked for a second like two figures on a silver screen, two figures who might be about to turn towards one another and fall in love.

'I was lying, I'm afraid.' Felix touched the sleeve of her mackintosh. 'There is no other compartment and no room.' He gestured behind him where the corridor was packed with soldiers sitting on the long fat columns of their duffel bags, and women perched on box suitcases. One older lady had commandeered a young man's case and was making herself comfortable with a skein of wool, knitting at lightning speed.

'But I didn't think you were having so much fun in there,' he said.

When he spoke, she felt a strange mix of discomfort, the desire to run away, and the pull of a magnet to stay staring at him. His soap from last time came to her in a memory and she wanted to draw close to him now and breathe it again.

'Where are you going?' she asked, fiddling with her hairpins under the small lacy hat.

'Oxford. My alma mater. There's a professor I'm going to have lunch with. That is if we ever get there. You?'

Something struck her then but she couldn't work out what it was with her sluggish brain so she shook it off. She tried to think quickly of an excuse for her own travels but it was no good. Sighing, she gazed at their feet. His shoes, in contrast to the rest of him, were still mucky.

'It's no good. I can't lie,' she said. 'I'm going to try and see a friend.'

'Sounds like rather a reasonable thing to do. It is your day off, isn't it?'

'I . . .' She shook her head. They were on a train, sharing breathing space with at least two dozen other people. Felix leaned closer. She saw for a moment a shine in his waiting eyes, and wanted to take it all back, that opener to the truth, and talk instead about the weather or Christmas or detective films again. She wanted murder to be a tawdry thing, an imaginary thing that happened to other people, like she had always thought it would. But it was too late. Her mind was saturated and she had no other diversions or lies left to grasp for. She felt the pressing of the secret on her lips.

'How far is it to Bexworth? Is it the next station? Please say it is.'

He took a step towards her and now she could smell his soap again, as well as fresh coffee on his breath. 'This person must be very special for you to be so keen.'

'Something's happening to me, Felix. I don't know what, but I'm afraid.'

As soon as she had said his Christian name she felt strange. It was relief but also panic. He didn't flinch though or even seem to notice.

'Is that why you've got your gas mask box? What are you afraid of? There's nothing to be frightened of. Is it . . .' He took a step further in until their coats were touching, the Bakelite buttons, the fabric of their wide, open collars grazing at the threads. The closer he grew the more she felt the strangeness rise, a desperation to reach out to him, even though she knew him no more than the station master, no more than any other Tom, Dick or Harry or Hut 3 man at the Park. 'Is it work?' he said. 'You know we mustn't talk about it here, but you can tell me anything you like. You can trust me.'

Her right hand rested on the clasp of the gas mask box. It was pressed into the side of the carriage, jamming between them. With her left she reached for his collar and pulled the wool down towards her. She whispered in his ear. 'Someone is trying to reach me.'

She waited, and let her fingers relax. His head stayed where she had brought it. He was silent for a few seconds and she thought perhaps she had drawn him too close. But then she felt his arm slip behind her back at the waist. His lips opened and paused.

A tap came on her shoulder. 'Leave it for the honeymoon, miss. And can I trouble you for your ticket while you're on?'

The conductor, ashy-faced, stood next to them smoking a cigarette.

Feeling her cheeks scorch Honey reached into her pocket

and poked about, but the ticket was gone. She searched again, then the other pocket, and the inner ones inside the coat's lining. She was about to unclip the latch on the gas mask box but the conductor was standing close enough to see inside and she worried about her spare knickers falling out. She thought back to the moment when Felix had opened the compartment door. She had felt the thick card edges of the ticket then, in the right-hand pocket of her coat. And she hadn't opened the box since it was closed this morning.

'I'm so sorry.' While she fuddled, feeling her face burn as scarlet as her hair, Felix lifted his ticket from his breast pocket. The conductor clipped it and handed it back. He took another drag of his cigarette and coughed smoke in their direction.

'I just . . . I don't know where . . . one of those soldier boys must have . . .' She gestured towards the compartment.

The conductor leaned against the rattling wall. 'Forces get special discount, there's no reason they would. If you've dropped it you've dropped it but I'm afraid you'll have to buy another.'

'Will you let me?' Felix had reached into his own coat and withdrawn a shining leather wallet. It looked brand new, the leather giving off warmth from his chest.

'Well, I'd be very embarrassed to but I—' She reached for her own purse.

'It would be my pleasure. You wouldn't let me pay for

you at the restaurant the other night. Now you're in a fix it's the least I can do.'

The guard took the money from him without looking at her. When he wedged past them his belt purse nudged Honey's hips closer to Felix. 'Wait, excuse me. When do we reach Bexworth?'

The man shrugged without turning. 'How long is a piece of string? Second stop.'

She reached to her brow. She felt light-headed, aware she hadn't eaten any breakfast.

'I should find you a seat.'

'Thank you for the ticket. That was very . . . I don't know what happened. I swear those boys were up to trickery.'

'No harm done.' He was looking at her. 'I say, there are an awful lot of them.'

She caught his eye. 'Are you staying at the Park for Christmas?'

He looked down for a second, then pushed the brim of his hat back. It made his brow look boyish, showing more of his blue eyes. Such exotic eyes, she thought, with their gem shape, gleaming and focused in the irises; lapis lazuli, cobalt, hard precious stones. 'Yes, I think I will,' he said.

'What do your family think of that?'

He shook his head lightly. 'My whole family were killed in an air raid last year in London. Wiped out, the lot of them. In one go.' He made a gesture with his hands, palms down, slicing the air. 'I was on a train home when their shelter took a direct hit. The train was delayed.'

She thought she must look away but couldn't help staring. He pulled at his collar behind the knot. 'It's awfully hot in here, isn't it?'

'I'm sorry.' She looked down. She had a desperate urge to tell him straight away what had happened to Dickie, to share, but she remembered Beatrix's words: 'War isn't a competition.' *We are all entitled to our grief.*

Felix's face had changed. He looked pale and stricken. He peered around as if he might be seeking an escape route. An awful shine had come upon his top lip, the rest of his face had drained. She felt as if she had caused it.

Her fingers reached very slowly out to his; his huge rough husk of a hand leaning on the window rail, which contrasted so sharply with the skin on his face. What had he done at Cambridge to make his hands so rough? Punting? Sculpture? Or was it Oxford he had said? But she was certain Tiver had said Cambridge.

She closed in on his skin. It was cool; a thick protectant around the blood and muscle. She stroked until she felt a hard line and looked down. His index finger had a welt around it, almost a perfect circle like a ring. 'What's this?' She traced it with her own finger.

His gaze, which had been flicking round the train, anchored back on her. They both looked at their touching hands. He hesitated. 'I had my finger blown off by an incendiary. I was trying to reach my mother. The doctor stitched it back on. He says I should still be able to feel, but . . .' He shook his head lightly. He took in a huge breath and let it out as a sigh.

They felt the pull of the engine brakes and a slowing as they entered another unnamed station with its signage blacked out. Staring across at her was a brick building and on its wall a poster, the letters blue and white capitals. 'CARELESS TALK COSTS LIVES'. It was impossible to know what to say to a stranger. There were so many mine-fields to tread, no matter the conversation. Secrets, faux pas, dredged-up memories of horrors no one wanted to talk about. Every blown limb, every pile of rubble, they all led a path to someone in the end. It was all veins and blood and beating hearts, connected, or searching to connect.

'I'm sorry,' was all she could manage again.

Carriage doors were cranking open and snapping. Gay laughter and shrieks flew through windows, and in other corners, knotted embraces and tears.

Suddenly Felix leaned towards her and rested his fore-head on the brim of her hat. 'I have thought often about where I might kiss you first, but never was it on a heaving train.'

She tilted her chin up. Her right hand still rested on the clasp of the gas mask box. The secrets in it felt suddenly lighter. As the whistle blew and the choke of the steam rose hot and mineral into the bright freezing winter air, as the train began to crawl again, their lips met, and for a blinding blissful moment she was not on a train, not in a war, not in a tangle of deceit and trickery in which she did not quite yet know her part.

Chapter 17

They hurried up the station path and found themselves at the edge of a village green, flanked on all sides by red-brick houses and a collection of pubs. The absence of street signs was disorientating, but Felix went into the Old Ostrich to ask for the address.

He had abandoned Oxford. He had done it for her, and that made her heart beat hard. 'I'll make a telephone call from the station,' he had said. There was no telephone at the station. But he had rushed into the post office and sent a telegram while Honey waited, stamping her feet on the platform. 'Hang it if it doesn't reach him in time. Plans are going awry left, right and centre in this war. For all he'll know the train was sent to Reading instead.'

He emerged from the Old Ostrich now with a piece of paper and a map drawn in pencil on the back of a beer mat, leading them out of the village towards a farm lane. When they rounded the bend and saw the gate sign they both stopped short.

'Are you sure this is the hospital your friend is in?'

The building was not what she had expected.

'The name's right.'

It was no bigger than a farmhouse, about the same size as a vicarage, with a decent sculpted garden, like a garden in a child's picture book, and a pond at the end of a silver pebble lane. Though it was cold the sun was out. Some men were wheeling barrows of dead foliage to a compost or bonfire pile beyond a shed in the corner nearest the lane. There were ancient apple and plum trees crowded at the perimeter, and a short red wall marked the boundaries of a small kitchen garden where trunks of Brussels sprouts came knobbling free from the ground. In the pond stood a man in waders, lugging heavy stones from one end to the other. In turn he picked each up and replaced it down onto a different spot without aim or direction. Just outside the front door of the house a woman sat bundled into a wheelchair and furs, swaddled, with a violet felt hat draping the top of her face, so that every bit of her except the nose and cheeks was invisible. She was reading a book in gloved hands. She looked up as they passed but they couldn't see her eyes. The air had a scent like pigs, and somewhere from round the back of the house a cockerel crowed.

As soon as they crossed the threshold the telltale signs were there though. The smell was replaced by Caporal and the underlying tang of vomit. Each inner door was braced by heavy fire prevention bars. There was a metal rod pinned to the wall at the bottom of the staircase that could be stretched and clipped across if needed, while a set of regulation sand buckets were placed at intervals in the hall. Gas masks hung on hooks behind a solid reception bench, where a woman in slacks and a tweed jacket sat. She wore curled around her ears a pair of tight and very fine wire spectacles, so tight they looked ready to grow into her head.

'Can I help?' She spoke while still looking at her ledger, then halfway through the question her gaze snapped up onto Honey. Her eyes were huge and brown, magnified by the circles of the spectacles.

Honey cleared her throat. 'Miss Draper. I'm looking to see Miss Draper, a patient.'

'There's no one of that name here.'

'You didn't check.'

'I didn't have to. There's no one of that name here.'

'No, but I think she must be. At least I've been told she must be.'

'Are you family?'

Honey hesitated. She looked at Felix. 'Sort of. I'm a good friend.'

The woman smiled and put down her pencil. 'In that case I hope you find your good friend. Sorry not to be of any help.' She went back to her ledger. A door at the bottom of the stairs opened and a woman in a crisp tweed skirt suit and white coat with a clipboard emerged. She too wore spectacles, horn-rimmed. Her hair was pinned haphazardly to her head.

'Miss Draper.' Honey tried again with the receptionist, watching the doctor from the corner of her eye as she said the name. 'The name is Miss Draper.' She spoke loudly. 'Moira Draper. Check your records. I'm certain it's here she came. It's really very urgent.'

The woman with the clipboard crept towards them until Honey found herself startled at her proximity. 'There are set visiting procedures, Miss—'

'Deschamps.'

The doctor frowned then continued. 'Patients here are on strict recovery programmes. Even if your . . . very good friend were here it would be unlikely you could speak to her without an appointment.'

'We telegrammed ahead,' Felix cut in. 'Did you not receive it? The telegrams have been terrible. And I think my fiancé wrote a letter too, didn't you, Miss Deschamps?'

Honey took up the tale. 'The post has been terrible. It really has. I can't fathom why you wouldn't have—' She broke off, her nerve failing as the lie embroidered itself.

'We haven't received any communications,' the receptionist said.

'We did send ahead.'

The two women exchanged a glance.

'It's no good. You'll have to go,' the doctor with the clipboard said.

'But she is here.'

'Miss Deschamps, I'm afraid I didn't introduce myself. Dr Steerpen.' The doctor smiled and her eyes flashed wide through her thick horn glasses. 'As you'll appreciate we're a small hospital and I do know all my patients. And your friend isn't one of them. I'm very sorry, have you had far to travel?'

Honey looked closely at the doctor's face but her expression was as blank as a queen on a coin. It was funny how easily some people lied while to others the task was like climbing a mountain. She stared and stared and still the doctor wouldn't break her cool smile.

'Just from . . . London. Not far. Sorry about the mistake.' Felix tugged her sleeve and they moved back outside into the garden.

Once in the open air she pulled him towards the lawn. 'That was a nice way to propose. I never thought it would happen inside an asylum. My mother will be pleased. I've made you blush, I'm sorry. I know it was a joke.'

'I just thought—'

'I know. Thank you.' She looked around.

Beyond the apple and plum trees the house was enclosed on all sides by a high wooden fence cut at the tops of the slats into spikes. It was a square building, Georgian probably, with large sash windows. She counted along the sides.

Nine in total. 'We'll have to be very stealthy.' She lowered her voice.

'What are you – you're not thinking . . .?'

'I have to see her. There's no getting around it.'

'But the doctor said—'

'She's lying. Did you see that smile?'

'Honey, you have to tell me what's happening. What are you involved in? I thought you wanted to see your friend.'

'I do.'

'She's not here.'

'She's here all right. They don't lie on Secret memos.'

She saw Felix reel. He turned away down the path.

'All right, I stole a memo. Leave if you like. I won't hold it against you. But I can't.' She pulled on the back of his coat. 'Someone . . .' One of the garden men looked up and she dropped her voice. 'Someone killed my brother. Two nights ago. Someone murdered him in Bletchley.' She waited and watched Felix's face but he only shook his head slightly then began to reach both hands tenderly towards her. For some reason she found herself batting them away. 'The police tell me it was thugs but I know it wasn't. It wasn't a coincidence. Someone is trying to contact me, and it . . . it was either them, or someone else.'

'Them, who are they?'

'I don't know. But you see Moira might be able to find out. Moira used to . . .' She stopped herself. He was Hut 3, he would know anyway, there would be no harm in mentioning the bones of it. 'She used to work in a different part of the Park. She's the only person I trust to help me.'

'Except me,' he said quietly. 'You can trust me.'

She looked up at him, searching his eyes. He was staring deep into her. She could see the variation of colours, changing in the light like the sides of a sapphire. The breeze carried across from the pond; the man in the waders was singing softly, a wartime tune, a soldiers' ditty, up and down, up and down.

'I . . .' She hesitated. 'I don't trust you. Wait here.'

'Honey.' He hissed her name but she had disappeared round the far side of the house.

She searched each of the nine windows that looked out over the back lawns. In one corner was a poplar tree but it had been cut back so that there was at least six feet between its branches and the window opposite, and the drop should she fall was more like twenty. She walked the length of the house, staying close to the wall. The fields beyond the fence skated flat all the way to the horizon, chopped up and marked out like a patchwork quilt; green, brown and amber. At the bottom near the fence was a barn, but it was silent now. There were no sounds but the tramp and slap of the gardeners out front and the fluttering of a bird on the poplar's branch.

She looked at each window in turn. White-painted bars were braced across some of them, not all. Her eye ran right along to the building's far side and she saw a plain wooden divide at the end of it, and beyond it an annexe that had been erected off one of the house's back corners. The masonry was duller and more modern than the rest of the building, concrete and roughcast, grey compared to the stately red brick of the main house. It was only one storey tall and had chubbier bars cross-slatting each of its tiny windows. Its discreet plainness had a forbidding quality. No sounds came from it and the only access seemed to be via the main house.

She looked back along the downstairs row of windows of the main building. The blinds were still drawn in four of them but in the fifth she found herself looking into a neat parlour. A chintz sofa was covered in patched cushions and throws next to an upright piano scattered in music scores. She was about to test the window sash when a hand clutched her shoulder.

'Are you out of your mind? If they catch you, Honey, the Park will . . . I mean it will go to the Commander . . . really.'

'I'm afraid it's too late for warnings.' Another voice sounded beyond the annexe. A door opened in the wooden divide and the spindle of a winter morning shadow emerged first, then the shape of a clipboard, sticking from a hand. Finally the tight tweed jacket, crisp white coat and stock-inged legs of the doctor appeared.

'Did you say you were a friend of Miss Draper's, or a colleague?'

Honey looked at Felix and then at Dr Steerpen.

'It's not a tricky question.' She had a calm expression that seemed to Honey fraudulently open, maliciously serene.

'Friend,' she said firmly.

'Can I see your 1250? Your identity card.'

Honey reached into the pocket of her jacket then stopped. The story about the girl who had shown her papers to the RAF man swam like a pike in her mind. 'I'd rather not. I don't know what authority you're under.'

'A higher one than you.' The doctor took one hand from the clipboard and extended it. There was a creeping calmness in her movements. Honey felt at that moment a piercing fear, as if someone might be about to reach a pair of bare muscled hands about her throat and strangle her. Her breathing tightened. The doctor waggled her fingers in the air, waiting.

'It's no use, Miss Deschamps.' Honey flinched at her name. 'Captain Tiver knows you're here. I just spoke to him.'

Honey turned sharply to look at Felix, then back to the doctor. She dipped her hand into her pocket, pulled out her identification card, and passed it across.

The doctor didn't look at it. She kept her gaze on Honey, but as her fingers touched the paper Honey knew what she was about to say. 'And the Bletchley Park papers too.'

'I don't know what you're talking about. I'm a Foreign Office typist.'

The doctor looked at her, indifference behind her spec-
tacled eyes, then down at the ID card. She thrust it back.
'Come with me.' Her white coat flared a little as she turned
and began striding along the gravel path that ran through
the garden back to the front of the house. Honey was still in
the shadow of the façade.

'Well, come on, look smart about it. He can stay outside.'
She pointed to Felix.

'No, I won't come with you.'

'Sorry, but you don't have much choice.'

'Felix, telephone the police. Go on, find a kiosk in the
town, do it.'

'I'm afraid he won't,' said the doctor.

'But I can't—'

'Go with her,' whispered Felix. 'I'm here, I'm outside.
You'll be all right.'

Honey looked at Felix, searching his face again for
something; she didn't know what. But he was as unreadable as the doctor. His hard, gristled cheeks gave nothing
away. There was no grimness, no amusement. She felt as
if she might be walking towards a guillotine, towards a
block.

They tied one to the bedframe in such places, that much
she knew. They tied your arms in cotton so thick that a pair
of scissors couldn't even cut you free. And metal restraints,
manacles. She tried not to think of these things. She tried
not to think of a long corridor and a line of iron doors, each

one thicker and colder than the last. She tried instead to see what was in front of her for what it was. Serenity: gardens in winter time. A robin. She tried not to look at his blood-red breast, which became to her a stab wound as she rounded the corner, his fluttering little cry, an anxious territorial scream.

The doctor took twenty-three paces to reach the front door of the house. Honey counted as they went. As she turned the corner she looked back over her shoulder at Felix and felt a twist of betrayal. What if this was it? What if he had been part of it? He had served his purpose, used the puzzles to lead her where they wanted her. They had incarcerated Moira, now they had come for her.

She took one last look back at the gardens as she stepped once again into the dark of the lobby. The woman in the wheelchair raised her head again. Her eyes smiled above the scarf that covered her mouth.

In the lobby the doctor turned the brass handle of a door at the bottom of the stairs and gestured for her to pass. It was at that moment the adrenaline rose to an unbearable swell and she felt the urge to spin around, tear down the front path, past the village green, hide in the back barn of the Old Ostrich, secrete herself in the postal carriage of the next train. Bletchley was out of the question. London. She could disappear in London – forge papers, find herself a space in an old bomb shelter. She would live like a tramp for as long as it took for the war to end. She would find refugees and fetch soup for them and nurse the wounded and help the war effort, but she would not, she could not be incarcerated. She could not be manacled. Like Moira.

The doctor gestured for her to sit. She lowered her clipboard onto a large dark wood desk; it hit the blotter with a slap. Honey noticed how clean the desk was compared to Tiver's. There were no pens, no paperclips, no pairs of scissors. Even the plastic flowers were in a Bakelite cup. Grimly she realised why. Soft edges.

'Can I see your Bletchley Park papers?' the doctor asked again.

Her tone had changed from childlike calm. It seemed to speak of an authority that Honey must obey. And yet she found herself hesitating. The gas mask box sat on her lap. She felt her hands slide protectively about its clasp.

'I don't know what park you're talking about. I told you I'm a typist for the Foreign Office. I live in London. Can I ask why you've brought me in here?'

The doctor looked around, and it seemed to Honey a glimmer came into her eyes. 'You've had a bereavement recently, haven't you?'

She shook her head.

The doctor sighed. 'Very well. Let's keep it this way, shall we. I don't know what you FO lot are up to down there, but I've spoken to Tiver on the telephone and he's agreed to let you see her. For five minutes. I'll let him deal with you when you get back there.'

Honey's heart seized. She felt herself start forward, then consciously leaned back very slowly until her spine made contact with the ribs of wood on the back of the chair. 'Is this a trick?'

'No, Miss Deschamps. It's a rest clinic for people who have severe nerve strain. I'm afraid for the benefit of your friend and others we've been instructed to keep her in isolation until further notice, because of the nature of her work. Don't mistake me, we don't know what it is you do, but it's really no more sinister than that. As your own paranoia demonstrates, there is a lot of tension in the air about careless talk.'

Sweat that she hadn't been aware of until now began pooling cold between her shoulderblades, dampening her blouse. She looked around the room. In that sudden moment its terrifying austerity softened. She saw the windows for what they were, lungs to let in fresh air. The flowers were not plastic at all but cheerful winter blooms, fresh-picked, with that hard plaque look that Christmas foliage always had. The desk was clean and ordered, not ominously hazardless. Most importantly the doctor was not about to look inside her gas mask case, find the amber, and demand an explanation.

The doctor saw her looking and went on. 'Tiver's not a monster, you know, Miss Deschamps. And Miss Draper is being looked after, I promise. She's by herself. She can't be with others for reasons you know. But she's getting better. Let me take you to the parlour.'

As they passed the reception desk the doctor made a gesture with her hand to the woman behind the counter and she began to follow too. She sandwiched Honey, bringing up the rear, and Honey felt her blood draw a wash of cold fear again. The gas mask box bumped against her thighs as she squeezed through the narrow doorway into the parlour. It was the same room she had peeped into from the outside. Ludo boards lay abandoned on tables, along with several days' newspapers, some of which were propped on the piano stand. As Honey looked closer she saw several of the headlines had been cut out. There was the sound of a gentle wireless playing, and from somewhere further away, a water sound, like a fountain, or a tap that had been left running.

The doctor left via another door on the opposite wall. As Honey made a move to follow she raised her arm as a bar. 'Just wait here, will you?'

Honey looked to the receptionist, who raised her hand and pointed to a sofa. She still felt too agitated to sit, so instead moved towards the window. Outside she could see Felix strolling the perimeter with a cigarette hanging at an angle from his mouth. He had both hands in his pockets and sometimes looked towards the windows when he plucked the cigarette from his lips, letting the smoke out in a thin track.

'Have a seat,' the woman said.

'I'd rather not.'

'Suit yourself.' The receptionist idled by the piano, tidying and straightening the loose-leaf music and newspapers. From the corner of her eye Honey spied a Tchaikovsky suite arrangement and shuddered. Gradually she became aware the woman was not going to leave, and her hand fell back to the gas mask case. It was impossible. It would be impossible to show Moira the carvings again if she stayed.

The door on the opposite side of the room opened. Honey didn't know what she had expected to see but it wasn't the Moira she got. She looked almost like herself, but very slightly different, as if another spirit had crept inside her body, replacing certain parts of her. She was cheerful and a little hazy. As she looked around the room her gaze would latch onto something and then blink away. She didn't say anything but stretched out her arms in front of her, and Honey took the offered hands, squeezing them as tightly as she could, then awkwardly moved into an embrace. The different wools of their cardigans and the silks of their blouses flared alive with static as they pulled apart.

There was a puffiness to Moira's face. She had been crying not too long ago. But for now her tears were boxed away, and she looked up with a detached happiness, the kind a distant aunt might bring to dinner.

'Hello, old girl. I bet you didn't expect to find me here.' She tucked a strand of hair behind her ear. Her pristine chestnut wave had sagged. She had put on make-up – rouge and mascara – but it had all been done in haste and the mascara globbed on the ends of her lashes, giving her a clotted, showgirl look.

'Shall we sit?' She pointed at the sofa. Honey heard the door click closed, looked up and saw the receptionist leaning against it.

'I'm allowed five minutes, they say. But I just wanted to . . . Oh Moira, look at you. You're here but you're all right, aren't you? They're taking care of you?'

Moira flashed a glance at the woman beside the door. 'Of course.'

'And your family. They know you're here?'

'I . . . I think so.'

'What do you mean, think? They haven't had a letter from them?'

Moira smiled, a tight, friendly expression. 'Of course not. They can't trust me not to talk, you see. I'm not allowed to write to anyone. The doctors think it best.'

'The doctors.'

She dropped her voice. 'Honey . . .' The woman took a noisy step closer and began arranging a vase of mistletoe and firs on a dresser beside the door. 'You know why I'm being kept solitary. Shall we have some tea?' She pointed to a table beside the piano where an urn stood next to a stack of cups. When Honey came closer she saw that the cups were pink Bakelite, the saucers too. Moira's hand trembled as she drew two cups from the urn. The tea was stewed and floating, weaker than the stuff at the Park, and tepid, almost cold. They stirred in powdered milk from an earthenware pot with a spoon attached to it by a chain.

'I know why you're here.' Moira looked into her teacup. Her hand twitched on her knee. It was distracting, the soft scratch of skin on wool.

'I have to know what's written on them.'

'Does it really matter?'

Honey thought carefully whether to tell Moira about Dickie, and in the end couldn't bear to turn it into words. 'Yes, it really matters,' she said. 'Those workings you did, the notes on the back of the payslips—'

'You got them?'

'I thought you'd stolen the wage slips, that was why they took you away.'

Moira's head shook tightly. She had a film of water over her eyes that she was keeping static, like two small thin ponds. No tears were flowing yet, but they were on the alert, ready.

'What were you doing with Rupert's wage slip?'

Moira shook her head. 'I don't know. He must have dropped it. I sometimes pick up bits and pieces of paper in the hut and maybe I meant to give it back to him but put it in my pocket instead. I don't know what I did the scribbles on, it was so late and I was thinking about . . .' Her hand shook the teacup, and waves of liquid rose, overspilling the lip; little pasty gold rivers landing in splashes on the saucer and on her skirt. 'Oh God, look what I've done.'

Honey stood and looked around for a napkin. The woman at the door produced a handkerchief from her skirt pocket and silently held it out.

Honey gave it to Moira and watched for a second as she dabbed at her skirt. She sat back down and unclipped the latch on the gas mask box. *Please*, she tried to say with her eyes, catching Moira's. *Please help me, and I'll do anything I can to get you out.*

'It's no good, Honey. I don't think they want me back at Bletchley. Three strikes and I'm out – isn't that what they say in America?'

'I just need to know. It's driving me . . .' She stopped short.

She pulled out the first set of panels, still wrapped in fur. Moira's hand stopped her as she began to unfurl them, and she shook her head gently.

'You said . . .' Honey dropped her voice. 'You said a name. Something beginning with V. A type of . . . you know what.'

'Listen carefully.' Moira's voice cracked. She spoke loudly so there could be no mistake about secrecy, no impression they were trying to hide anything. 'These games these Park boys play are damned silly. If you ask me, sending a girl creepy trinkets when you're trying to woo her in the middle of a war is foolish. It's the sort of thing one of those RAF men we met at the dance would do.' The cup on her knee jigged again, her eye went to it, blinked, then flicked over to the woman by the door. 'I mean, the boys that we met at that RAF dance, at Wavendon. Those sorts of boys. They're the foolish-minded kind of boys, the kind of boys who might think it's romantic. The way they think it's romantic to go wandering off around the backs of huts. That sort of a boy.'

Honey couldn't follow the code of what she was trying to say, but her own body language wasn't up to conveying this to Moira. She shook her head mildly then followed Moira's gaze down to the shaking teacup. She put her hand on Moira's arm and the shaking briefly stopped.

'Amber comes from the Baltic,' Moira said very quickly. 'If I were you, I'd ask that boy from the dance if he's your secret Valentine.'

'But how could he know about my . . .' The penny dropped. Moira had worked in the Cottage. The boy behind the huts, the one who had opened the hut door, that was how she had known his name – from the Cottage. The boy might not have anything to do with the amber. But he must know how to break a cipher.

She squeezed Moira's hand and the teacup lurched, slipping from Moira's grasp. It tumbled to the floor, bouncing off the sofa sides, spilling khaki brown onto the rose chinz, turning blue flowers to green, and then onto Moira's ankle, dripping down into her shoe. Moira yelped and put both hands to her mouth.

'I can't help it,' she said. 'Sometimes my hands shake so much I think the only way to stop them is to throw something. And then it just slips my fingers, like my body doesn't want to risk me throwing it.'

'It's all right, sit back down.'

Honey grabbed the cup and fumbled it back empty onto Moira's knee.

'I think you've probably had enough,' the woman by the door said. Honey grabbed the wet handkerchief and began to mop at the spot where the tea had landed, but the cloth grew sopping quickly. She looked up at the receptionist. The woman let the breath hiss between her teeth and left the room, leaving the door wide open.

Moira seized Honey's wrist. 'His name is—'

'I know. Piotr. How do you know him?'

'I don't. I only know his name. I heard of him. The Cottage. The . . .' She broke off. 'There isn't time, but Honey, find him. They're in Wavendon, the Polish code-breakers. They don't work at the Park, they're not allowed. But I swear to you he's the best. He gave blueprints to the Cottage – those machines they built, for Hut 11 . . . he invented an early version of them. Everyone knows his name in there. The Station Inn is where the temporary billets are, I think.'

'And what if—'

Moira hissed at her to hush.

'Honey, there's something else.' Her eyes flicked up to the open door. Footsteps echoed far away on the corridor. Honey slid her foot around slowly in the shining patch of tea on the floor; she watched the puddle slip about under her cork toe. She looked back up but Moira wouldn't meet her eye. 'I don't know what they're going to do to me. Did you see that building, to the side of the house? They call it the sick bay. It's for the worst cases. That's where I live now. There's bars on the door, I don't have any . . .' She swallowed. 'I don't have any privacy.' Her shaking had slowed but her voice trembled. 'They'll tell you it's nice in here. They'll show you this part but . . .' She pulled her skirt a little lower over her legs; just an inch. 'In America they cut out part of your brain, the part that makes you mad. Only sometimes they slip and take more than they need. And you don't quite know what you're going to be left with until the job's done. They're talking about electricity here. Giving shocks to soldiers. I know it. A man sent back from Africa, the man who throws stones around the pond, he's had it.'

Honey looked to the open door. It was a blank, gaping dangerous maw. The footsteps were still far away.

Moira wiped the corner of her mouth with the sleeve of her cardigan. 'The thing is, if they take my mind, I don't know what will be left of me. If they do something with my brain, and I can't get it back, will you keep the secret, that I saved that ship once? Will you keep it safe for me? Tell no one. I trust you. Oh, but Honey, maybe one day you'll be allowed to say.'

Honey felt the strap of the gas mask box trapped under her knee, pressing into her thigh. She could see out of the corner of her eye Felix through the window, sitting down on a bench by the pond. 'No more secrets,' she began to say, but Moira's face was so brutal, so afraid, she could only nod.

'It was a silly old thing. I made a breakthrough with a message. There were no T's in it. So odd, I thought, not to see a single letter scrambled into a T in the whole message. I realised then that it was because the operator was testing the Enigma machine, testing the day's settings. He had his finger down on the T button. You see you can't scramble another Enigma letter as itself. Did you know that?'

Honey shook her head.

'There you go. I broke into the key that day. We got the lot. And I can't even write down what I did. All I'll have is the memory of it. And if they take that memory away, if they take my mind . . . Silly to be so proud, but that's that. That's what I did. And even this . . . this now, whatever I've done to deserve being here . . . well, that day, no one can take that from me. As long as someone knows the story. Will you keep it safe? I'll keep your secret safe in return.'

The woman walked back into the room, brandishing a mop and a bucket of foul-smelling hot liquid.

Moira stood. Honey took her left hand but she couldn't bear to embrace her. She would fall to pieces, she would fall to the ground, she knew it.

'Thank you,' was all Moira said.

Chapter 18

'I'm all out of Player's, I'm afraid.'

Felix was standing on the front path, a small distance from the woman in the wheelchair, when Honey emerged. The sun had dipped behind a cloud and the light had turned cold and grey. 'I suppose a picnic is out of the question?'

Honey walked past him. She gathered her summer coat more closely around her. Stupid, stupid, to think she could disguise herself with a hat and thin blue coat. And for what? 'I have to go to Wavendon,' she said.

He held her gaze. 'Very well.'

'You should go on to Cambridge. You should catch the next train.'

'Oxford.'

'Sorry, that's what I meant.'

'Well, I'll be late for the luncheon now for certain, and the truth is I'd rather stay with you.'

'Well, you can't.' She moved ahead of him towards the end of the pebbled lane.

'Honey, wait. What did she tell you?'

Honey shook her head tightly. They had reached the little road that led back into the village. The track was muddy with the melting of the dawn frost. Honey's shoes stuck crisply with each step.

'For God's sake, Honey, I work at the Park too.'

'Then you know the rules.'

'But this isn't about the Park. This is about your brother.'

She turned and looked at him keenly, searching his face. His brow had furrowed and he looked confused. 'How do you know,' she said, 'my brother didn't work at the Park too? And I didn't tell you.'

He held her gaze until she looked down at the mud and her shoes. 'You're paranoid. They've got to you. With their posters and their warnings. Fifth columnists, spies hiding in every bushel of hay. Why, talking like this in the fields and the open air we could be eavesdropped on by any number of German parachutists, just plonked down to target you – just you, out of the millions of others they're slaughtering.'

'Stop it.'

'You watch too many of those films, and read too many of those bloody novels.'

'Felix, stop it.' He heard the knife in her voice and ceased his step.

He looked at his shoes, their scuffed surface capped now with icy mud, and wandered over to a stile and began beating his toes against the wood.

'This morning, I was so pleased to see you,' she said. 'And now . . .'

He didn't turn to look at her. 'I can't help you, Honey, unless I know what it is you're doing. This isn't one of your Hitchcocks. We can't just escape together, magically knowing we're on the same side.'

'They're not always on the same side, are they?'

He spun. 'Dammit, Honey, if you don't trust me say so. What did she say to you in there?'

'I can't tell you.'

'Well then, I'd better find the platform for Oxford.'

He began to walk away. She noticed the dip in his neck, the slope of his shoulders. He looked younger, a lot younger, from behind. She thought of what he had said on the train about his family, about finding his mother and searing off his finger with the incendiary and she felt a surge of something towards him – not guilt, not love, but some cloud of feeling, some need to be at his side, that made her pick up her step.

'Felix.'

He stopped walking.

She picked through the dirt until she had almost caught him. She took a great sigh, in and out, and reached forward to the back of his coat where his shoulderblades rose. She touched the fabric lightly. 'You said you worked in Hut 3. So you know Reuben MacCrae?'

He nodded and turned but didn't meet her eye. 'Yes. And Steve Trindle and Robin Hass and the rest. Do you want me to name them all?'

'No,' she cried out. 'No, don't name a single one of them. Don't trust me, Felix. We can't . . . we can't trust anyone.' Her hands came to her face but she found the tears wouldn't flow.

He stood watching her for a second, and though her hands remained in front of her face, she felt she imagined a certain coldness from him. She imagined he was looking at her the way she had looked at Moira, back at the hospital. But when she took her palms down she saw nothing but fondness.

'When everyone is keeping secrets, all the time, all around you,' she said, her voice shaking, 'how do you know what's a safe secret and what is a dangerous secret?'

'Sometimes, Honey, you are left with nothing but your own wits.' He took a breath. 'You can trust me.'

'It's – I can't, Felix.'

'Whatever is happening won't go away until you tell someone. I can help you. Honey, look at me. I can help you.' He took both her hands in his, but held her at arm's length. She was shivering now, despite her coat, despite the mid-morning sun peeping out from behind the clouds, and she felt the same sense of release and relief pushing at her that had pushed at her inside Tiver's study. It was comforting to tell. It would be comforting to tell him everything, to take half the burden away. She would see the secrets, like little puffs on the tails of clouds, drifting away from her mouth, all the way into the sky, very high up into the world where they would detach from her and take on a life of their own and she wouldn't have all the responsibility for them any more.

Very quietly she said, 'Have you heard of *The Firebird*?'

'The ballet?'

They were in there, the words. She had all of them gathered in a tumult, in a swirl behind her lips and they wanted to come out. It was beyond her will to stop them now. She would tell him everything. She would do it now, quickly, before she changed her mind. 'Do you think that every story has a truth, a definite version that is right?'

Felix continued to look steadily at her. He was waiting for her to talk. She turned her face away and felt his hand slowly brushing the sleeve of her coat.

'Oh, my brother,' she said, covering her eyes. She took her hands down again and he was still staring.

She gave a great sigh. 'Once, I found a book of Russian fairytales in the school library. It was an old book, I remember finding it stuffed in beside lots of mystery novels. I've always liked old things, they seem more important than new ones, don't they?'

Felix was patient. Honey took a leafless branch from a nearby shrub and began to rub its length between her fingers.

'The story of the firebird was the first one I read. When Dickie began to dance, I realised then that I'd heard it before. Prince Ivan goes on a quest to find the firebird who has been thieving his father's golden apples. He saddles his horse and heads into the woods and he meets a wolf who tells him where to find the bird, but he also tells him that he must not touch its golden cage, or else the Tsar who owns it will awake and catch him in the theft. Of course Ivan, being just like Dickie, ignores this, he's so in love with the glint of the cage, he wants that too.'

Felix's brow was creased but he was listening.

'Sure enough the Tsar wakes and captures him, and as punishment he sends him on a quest to steal a golden horse. Again, the wolf warns him, this time not to touch the golden horse's golden bridle, but again he can't help himself. That in turn wakes up the next Tsar, who, as punishment, sends him on a final quest . . . to steal a princess. But the prince falls in love with the princess and doesn't care to give her up to the second Tsar. And at this part I get muddled and I can't remember how he gets out of the pickle. I think he fakes his own death.'

Felix nodded. 'You have a good memory for tales. But I can't see what this has to do with—'

She interrupted him. 'When I told that story to Dickie, he was angry. Not confused, but spitting hot with rage. Oh, he was just a boy, I know, but it was frightening. "What a stupid thing to say. Everyone knows the story of the firebird is the way Stravinsky tells it." He played me the record. He made me sit in the nursery while he played it on the gramophone, and I just remember wanting to cry, because I felt trapped. But he insisted. He insisted. "This is the story. This is the right version. This is the only version." I don't know why I'd forgotten about that day, but I had, until yesterday.

'In Dickie's version – Stravinsky's version – the prince comes upon the firebird in his father's garden. "Listen," he said. "This is the part when the prince dances round the garden. Listen, hear, the instruments each represent magic. Listen." And I thought I was stupid because I could hear orchestra, nothing but a tangle of orchestra. But I wanted to please him because he was older, he must know better, mustn't he? He must know the truth.

'So the prince catches the firebird in the garden. And he steals her feather as a pledge that if he is ever in trouble, she will come to help him. When he finds himself in an enchanted castle, surrounded by imprisoned maidens, captured by an evil Tsar, he has to summon the firebird to save them all. She comes to rescue them and she makes all the evil spirits dance until they fall dead.' Honey sighed.

Felix was frowning. 'You think that you are the firebird, that someone is summoning you . . . or Dickie faked his death . . . I don't understand.'

331

'No, it's nothing like that at all. It's just . . .' She closed her eyes. 'He was so excited to correct me, he was so certain of the truth. He danced the steps himself, hysterical little flourishes he'd learned in his ballet classes.

'"Stop it," I said. I can see myself, looking away, afraid of him, afraid of the energy he had. But he didn't stop. He was manic. He danced as if he would explode. He had a child's determination. "Ivan steals the egg that has the soul of the sorcerer. And the sorcerer drops dead." And he fell then. I remember watching him fall, and listening to him crack his shins on the ground. He believed in the fairytale so much, it exhausted him; he was living it through as he told it. That's how much power a story had over him.'

She opened her eyes. Felix had pulled her closer; her head was resting on his clavicle, her cheek against the knot of his tie. 'What made you think of *The Firebird* now?' he whispered.

'I . . .' She clutched the thorny branch in her hands. The words were still there, they were all still in there, the secret waiting to come out. She steadied her breathing.

But at the last second she couldn't say it. 'I just want to know: if you believe a story, does that mean it's true?'

'Honey, I can't help you unless I know what you're talking about.'

'What if . . . what if the truth is somewhere in between two stories?' She looked up and saw his expression. He was staring ahead. He had lost patience. She had lost him. 'Felix,

I can't tell you. I can't. You have to trust me. Felix, someone is sending me things, strange things, and I don't know why, or who.'

He reached both of his arms around her and wrapped her close to his chest. She rested her head and felt his heart beat through the light shirt, through the stripes of the old school tie.

There were no trains back to Bletchley for over two hours, so they caught a lift in a farmer's wagon, bumping along beside crates of apples and cabbages in a bitter wind. Honey whistled to the driver to let her out as they passed Wavendon. She took Felix's grubby hand to help her down, and watched him pull his coat in around him against the wind as the wagon left. When they were in the distance she saw him bend and slyly steal an apple from a crate. The truck rattled out of sight and the lightness she had felt beside him washed away. She felt leaden as she turned towards the high street.

She found the Station Inn Moira had named and savoured the warmth inside the thick doors. Her eyes adapted to the dark as she approached the counter. A short woman with hair bound tightly in a turban was wiping beer taps.

'I'm looking for someone who lives here.'

'No one lives here, love, they're all passing through.' She slapped her cloth on the bar and began rinsing through the taps.

'Is there a Polish boy?'

'Can't help you with nationalities.'

'Piotr . . . something.'

'Can't help you with first names.'

'I'd know him if I saw him.'

The woman leaned her arms on the counter. 'Are you on official business?'

Honey was wrong-footed by the coolness of the woman's gaze. Her eyes were large and assessing. She roved them up and down Honey's clothes as she began to place beer mats at sparing intervals along the counter.

Honey shook her head. 'No, I met him at a dance.'

This brought a smile. 'Listen, I don't want any nonsense around here. I don't want any funny business on my property. You know what I mean. War or not, it's not right. And especially when you got people to keep an eye on . . . foreigners.' She said the word slowly. 'You have to be careful to keep yourself clean when folk are suspicious of you already.' She finished with the beer mats and leaned on the counter again. 'Look, love, if you wait here he's sure to be down later.'

'What, just wait here?' Honey caught the panic in her voice as she looked around the small saloon. The place was dark, heavy-beamed, with a loveless atmosphere. Although the walls were bunker-thick, they made the air close rather than welcoming warm. Their paint was old and chipped and they were coated in horse brasses and farming tools all pinned at odd angles. It was not a place that whispered *cosy inn*.

The woman sighed. 'I'll put a note under his door. Who shall I say?'

'He won't remember my name.'

'I'm trying to help you.'

Honey sighed. 'I'll write it.' She accepted the torn sheet from the ledger book the landlady passed her. With the pen in her hand, however, her mind went blank, and the absurdity of the situation rose before her. In haste she scribbled, 'Hello, it's Honey Deschamps, friend of Moira Draper's. I wondered if you wouldn't mind ...' She scored it out. 'Dear Piotr, we met at the airmen's dance at Wavendon a few nights ago. Moira Draper introduced us.' She asked for another piece of paper. Why was it so hard to navigate the social codes of introduction?

Formalities, indirect requests: we are all cipher clerks and cryptanalysts, she thought, as she wrote in a fierce, determined hand: 'Piotr, sorry to use your first name but it's urgent. Will you meet me in the bar downstairs? I'll be waiting. Honey Deschamps – from the airmen's dance.'

She looked up and the woman was watching her, amused. She folded the paper once and handed it over. The woman disappeared and Honey heard the tramp of footsteps on the stairs behind the bar. She sat down at one of the heavy tables and picked at the edges of a tile on the wall, a brown one with a pastoral scene painted on it.

When the landlady came back down there were two sets of footsteps. The face of the boy Honey had seen the other evening materialised from the gloom. In the dark, with his hair hastily combed and his jumper on back to front, he looked terribly young. They were all so young, these children that had left their homes, their countries.

She stood and stuck her hand forward. He looked at it warily. 'How did you know where to find me?'

'Moira Draper.'

He gave a single nod, then looked down at his wristwatch.

'Can I buy you a sherry?' she asked.

He crossed the small space of flagstones between them and shook her hand softly. There was still caution in his eyes.

'You see, the thing is, I didn't say thank you to you properly for helping me when I tripped.'

He almost snorted. Then bit by bit his smile evened out. 'I think I'd like to have a walk, you know. It's a sunny day, I saw from the window. It's nice of you to come by.'

The landlady watched as he took his coat from a hook at the bottom of the stairs. Honey opened the door for them both, and the woman went back to wiping the tables and didn't ask anything more.

'They came to visit me the night after the dance.'

They were on the edge of a village green. The wind pricked and both their eyes had watered over. Honey wiped hers with the back of her hand. 'Who came?'

He shrugged. 'Park men. Secret service men. I don't know. But they told me it's best not to talk to you girls. Best if I stick to my own work at Wavendon.' As soon as he'd spoken he looked away as if the mention of work at all was already too much.

'I'm not going to talk about work.'

'You said it was urgent.'

'Is there a spot we can go to?' Honey was shivering in her patched summer coat. He looked impatiently down the high street for a few seconds, then said, 'Come on, this is the best place for quiet.'

He led her into the yard of the nearby church and they sat under a yew tree. She didn't ask and he didn't volunteer what made him choose the spot. She wondered if he prayed there. He wore a cross at his throat. It wasn't a Catholic church, but then it was wartime. How many people had he left behind and did he know what had happened to them? These were the questions that burned the edges of Honey's mouth but she could not ask them.

She unclipped the gas mask box. He started, then frowned.

Hastily she pulled out the scraps of paper where Moira had made the rubbings of the codes, and the scribbles of equations. He took one look at the pencil scrapings and his eyes widened.

'It's not what you think.'

He stood up.

She leapt to her feet. 'These aren't from the Park. I haven't stolen them. It's not the work there. It's just . . . Moira said because you were a mathematician. She didn't tell me what you did, just that you might be able to help.'

He shook his head. 'I . . . those men. If I am to continue here, I don't want to . . . I've seen what happens to people. There is a prison they put them into in London and I'm claustrophobic and . . . you shouldn't be here.'

'They're not from the Park. They're not Enigma.'

He thrust his finger to his lips and hissed at her. 'You don't say that word out loud. Not here, not anywhere. If you care about your country—'

'I care about my father.' He was still standing but the flare in his cheeks, the animated sting in his eyes, diluted a little. 'I don't know who is sending me these, but I think my father might be trapped in another country. I think . . . these are from him.'

'I don't follow.'

She took a breath and sighed. And then the lie came pouring out. Or the truth, or the halfway in between, or whatever the story was that she had believed. Had. She didn't tell him about Dickie. She didn't tell him about *Figley's Book of Ciphers* or Captain Tiver or her other suspicion that the whole thing could still be a trick. She only told him about her father and the exile, Stravinsky and the compositions, the wild, unfathomable compositions, and how they had led him to the palaces, to guard Russia's treasures. And somehow telling the story made a little burnished spark in her chest and she felt as if she had brought Dickie back to life just a little, for those few moments. Even so as she spoke the details seemed to disconnect a notch and she saw the gaps between the facts; facts Dickie had told her that had sparked across those divides with his enthusiasm when they came from his lips. She felt herself slipping back to the tale Tiver had told; it was a betrayal of Dickie, and yet she couldn't help it. Only the ciphers and the amber would tell the truth.

Piotr listened quietly. He didn't say anything but when she finished, he took the papers out of her hands. 'You must burn these as soon as you're finished. You don't play around with cryptanalysis. Even talking about it is dangerous.'

'I know.' She thought of the girl, Betty Somebody, disciplined for coding letters to her sweetheart.

Piotr kept the papers close to his body. The tops of them flapped in the breeze. She noticed a small scar on the side of his neck below his ear, a tiny little scar, the classic kind, like a winding sailor's rope with ladder bars across it, that could have been there for years, or months, or just weeks. Why was she asking a boy she had never really met to help her crack ciphers she couldn't even tell to her friends? But what choice did she have other than to trust Moira? People's lives now were won and lost on trust, and it was something that couldn't be quantified by the amount of time you had known someone; it couldn't be unravelled, or deciphered, or made plain. There was no code of confidence to crack inside every person, no Enigma machine that scrambled integrity, which could be unpicked by knowing the right key. Trust lay in the murky ponds out of reach of anything but animal instinct.

He pointed to the middle section of the crease. The wind carried his soft words away and Honey strained to hear. 'The first thing you have to think about is why the piece was enciphered in the first place. The person obviously wants you to know what it says, which is why . . .' He couldn't say it aloud '. . . machine enciphering is unlikely. Why would you need something that complicated, and how would they know you could access it?' He paused for breath. 'So. Was there ever a special language you used together?'

'I never knew him.'

'Ah.' Piótr looked contrite for the first time. He blinked and glanced in the direction of the church. There was a weathervane in the shape of a moon. It looked oddly pagan on top of the square steeple and punched battlements. 'So what makes you think . . .?'

'There was a book. A cipher book. It was an old thing. A bit like the ones you see for children. I think he'd bought it before the first war, and my brother said he was working on this . . . piece of music with it when he left.' She sighed. 'I'm telling you more than I wanted to.'

'I'm helping you more than I want to.'

'All right. His name was Korichnev. He escaped to Russia because he was worried about being exposed as a Bolshevik or . . . I'm not sure what.'

Piotr gave a small, bitter snort but didn't say anything.

'He made music using codes. That's what my brother said.'

'And where is your brother now?'

She paused. 'Dead. He was murdered two nights ago in Bletchley.'

Piotr stood up. 'I can't help you.'

Her hand shot out as he moved to leave and she grasped the hem of his jumper. He looked down at her fingers clutching the wool; gradually she released the knitted threads.

'Miss Deschamps, I don't know who you are but I can't get tangled up in anything involving police, or murder, or Bletchley. You don't know how hard it is. How hard they watch us.' He flicked his eyes around frantically as if there might be spies in among the headstones.

'No, no, no.' Honey strained to correct herself and keep her voice quiet. 'I have to tell you more.'

He sat down again and rubbed his fingers back through his hair, flattening it. 'I don't like this at all. I'm here on your king's business, and I tell you they execute people like me if they even think we talk. I've heard of what your government does. Do you know about the London cage?'

She shook her head.

'It's a place where they torture prisoners of war. Foreigners. Native traitors they simply shoot. Us?' She watched his eyes grow fearful with whatever images he was conjuring in his head.

'Trust me,' she urged him. 'Please. I'm trusting you.'

Whether it was the word 'trust' or a note in her voice, he rubbed his hand over his chin and held the paper close to his face again.

'Dickie, my brother,' she whispered, 'had the cipher book on him when he was found. The police have it. It was the only thing he had left on him at the time. He'd tucked it into his trousers. The rest of his papers and money and things had been stolen. Them, they, those people you speak of, the authorities, they know about the amber pieces. They know someone is sending me them. But they don't know about these.' She pointed at the piece of paper with the cipher rubbings. 'Please. I need to know. I need to know what they say.'

His head twitched impatiently. He slapped the paper. 'I need time. I can't just look at this and break a code like that.' He snapped his fingers. 'Have you tried anything? Letter frequency analysis? An alphabet shift?'

'I'm not a codebreaker. I—'

'Do you know anything about the most basic tenets of cryptanalysis? It's not all magical shape-shifting of numbers and letters. Most of it is counting, and has nothing to do with that . . . that . . . machine you mentioned. Before you have even read a word of the first message, you count the number of messages on a particular frequency, you count the number with the same callsign, count the number from the same battalion, the same distance . . .' He rubbed his lips together and pointed at one of the headstones. 'Go on over there and count the number of T's on that.' He saw her pause. 'Go on.'

'Letter frequency analysis. Traffic analysis. Moira explained all that.'

'She did, did she? Hmmm.' He went back to scribbling on the page. 'Then you'll know it's very difficult to crack an individual message. Almost impossible to intercept it if you don't know anything at all about the sender or recipient.' He looked at her.

'She mentioned something. A word, beginning with V. A common cipher. Not a common one but a known one, a classical one.'

He smoothed the papers out on the bench between them. On the backs of the payslips Moira had copied only the letters, not the curls or the drawings of the branches, and they looked plain and ugly in the raw capitals of her handwriting.

'All right. All right, I'm thinking. Something beginning with V. Your father was a musician? You said he was inter- ested in art, a renaissance man.'

'Well, I don't know but—'

'We go on assumptions for now, because this starts with trial and error. Classical ciphers. Assuming he's not a professional cryptanalyst, which, I understand, he is not—'

'That's right.'

'Then he's relying on ciphers commonly known to people who look for them. He's probably using an old-fashioned one. There's no dominant letter frequency here.' He saw the confusion on her face and breathed out impatiently. 'If you have a single letter substitution cipher – for instance one letter is always used to replace another, the same letter – then you should have the same letter frequency as you get in plain text. E is the most common letter in English – you know that, don't you? So whatever is the predominant letter in the enciphered text is likely to represent E.'

'Simple,' Honey said bitterly.

'Well, there is no predominance here. That suggests multiple enciphered letters are being used to represent the same plain text letter. In a single alphabet transfer the frequency of each letter in the normal alphabet will correspond to their frequency in the enciphered one. That . . . machine . . . uses multiple alphabets – a different random one for each new plain text letter, decided upon by the scramblers. There are millions and millions of options, literally. It makes it more difficult to tell.'

'All right.'

'Didn't you read the cipher book your brother had?'

'He never let me have it, that was the problem. He was a very selfish child.'

'Anyway, I don't see any letter occurring more frequently than another. That suggests to me multi-alphabet. And the most – well, let's say – flourishing of those hand ciphers is the Vigenère square; something that would appeal to a man in love with art.'

'Vigenère. That was the word Moira used. That's it.'

'But.' He hushed her with a finger. 'You need a keyword.'

'Oh, bloody brilliant,' she sighed.

'You need to make a square of alphabets and you need a keyword that runs along the top of that square and determines which of the multiple alphabets you will use to encipher each letter. Without the keyword, I'm afraid there's no way round it. Well, there is, but it would take – not as long as . . . the machine—'

'Oh, for God's sake just say Enigma. You know it and I know it too.'

The colour in his face rose.

She lit on it. 'Stravinsky. Try Stravinsky.'

She watched as he scribbled out a rough grid then wrote StravinskyStravinskyStravinskyStrav across it.

'Aren't you going to finish it?'

'Be patient,' he hissed. 'I had to hide in a well for eight hours to escape Nazi troops, you can wait a little longer for your code.'

She saw him scribble out beneath the row of Stravinskys the enciphered text from the panels. 'What is this letter?' He pointed.

'I don't know, let me check.' She reached into the gas mask box and pulled out the fur-wrapped slabs. As she uncurled the pelt from around the surface of the first one, a few of the threads stuck. She brushed them out. Over her shoulder his eyes burned. 'Is that the amber?'

'Yes.'

'Where did it come from?'

'I don't know,' she lied.

'Did he steal it?'

'Please can we—'

'All right, all right,' he muttered. 'It's an H. Your H's are strange.'

'Not mine, Moira's.' She liked watching him work his way down the code, scribbling out the squares. His gaunt, childish face took on concentration. He drew a grid and then twenty-six alphabets, one after the next, each one shifting down a letter, so the first row started ABC, the second BBC, the third CCD and so on. Then he counted down and drew a long oblong round several sets of alphabets. 'The keyword determines which alphabet you will use to crack each letter.'

'Is this what they're doing in the crib room?'

He smiled at her. 'There are thousands of possible combinations for the Vigenère cipher. The French called it *le chiffre indéchiffrable.* For Enigma there are more than 150 million million million. What they're doing in the crib room is part of what we've done here – guesswork. But on a much larger scale. Is it a supplies report? Maybe the name of a General or the words Heil Hitler come up at the end of the message. Maybe the coder at the other end used the word "*Scheisse*" or "*Fotze*" as the start of their ring settings for the day. You learn a lot about German swear words working on Enigma.'

'What are you doing now?'

'With the keyword Stravinsky, you have ten alphabets in play in the message as a whole. If you look along each of the letters of the keyword and where they correspond to the enciphered text, that tells you which alphabet you use and where.'

He saw confusion cross her face.

'This is not . . . quantum physics. This is – I mean, you could get this from a textbook on ciphers you'd buy in a bookshop. No army is going to use it. But it's a good cipher for people interested in trying their luck. Now, let's see. The letter S at the start would mean we use the first alphabet along. This would encrypt it as F. If we try the next one, we're looking for the letter that corresponds to the T alphabet. This makes D.' He continued at a pace, cracking through each letter until he had a pile of new letters in a third row beneath the keyword.

FDLWULJLHSRZVZAYGVHSRGEIKMMPFBD

He turned his head to look at her and she saw the wry amusement on his face. 'Mean anything to you?'

She frowned and snatched the paper from him. 'It's not right.'

'Then it's probably the wrong keyword. Or the wrong cipher. Or someone is making it up. Do the letters themselves mean anything?'

'No, but . . .' She cursed her stupidity. 'The bird. It's not Stravinsky at all. It – I mean it must be *The Firebird*. It's only *The Firebird* that means anything to us. Try firebird.'

Piotr took another of his slow breaths and removed the paper from her hands again. He worked down the pattern. The letters that came out though were still nonsense.

SOLSOLFAMISOLREDOFAMIREFAMIDORE

He looked sour. 'Perhaps it's a double encryption.'

Honey frowned, then looked more closely and let out a small cry. 'It's them. It is a double cipher, but how could I . . .? What is one of the most common forms of encryption?'

'I'm not in the mood for riddles.'

'Musical notation. Music. You see that pattern. Sol sol fa mi-sol re do fa-mi-re-fa-mi-do re.' She sung it gently, then dropped her voice. 'It's *The Firebird*. It's the theme. It makes perfect sense.'

She surprised herself as the emotion caught in her throat. Through a choke she saw the amber come to life, the fire in it glowing gold as the music burned through her head. She closed her eyes and saw Dickie dancing. But she saw it with new meaning now. He had loved *The Firebird* because it belonged to him. Every time he danced it, he danced because in some way it was part of his blood. It belonged to a performance he had seen their father create, a performance that was locked in him, every time he moved his feet. She imagined him, imagining the man he'd seen conduct at the Opera House. And as she did so something else rose in her. She opened her eyes and looked at the carved gold.

The Firebird had belonged to Dickie because he danced it. Now, fossilised in its enciphered form, it belonged to her too. For a second she loved not ghosts from the past but that they had made her who she was.

'Thank you,' she murmured to Piotr.

He unwedged something from between his teeth and spat it gently onto the ground. He nodded at her lap where both slices of amber sat, half-peeping from their fur shrouds. 'That's only the first. What about the second?'

Using the same keyword they worked through the second slab in the same way. This time the text was plain, the message clear, in English, and it snatched away her daydreams.

In Piotr's looping hand was written, 'To get mixed up in politics is ruination for art.'

'It's not quite got the same romance,' he muttered.

Honey went over the words to herself but they gave her no recall. She hadn't heard them before. 'It is the sort of thing Dickie would say,' she said quietly.

Piotr was shaking his head. His hand had dropped to his side and he played with a little scrape of lichen embedded on the bench.

'Is it a famous saying?' she asked.

'I don't know.'

'What's the matter with you?'

'Was this what your father believed?'

He looked up. Honey was taken aback by his face. She struggled for words. 'Why are you angry?'

He hesitated. Another secret flared behind his skin and he opened his mouth briefly, then closed it again.

'Ruination for art, is it? Politics.'

'I didn't write it.'

'And yet you . . . you want to know the person who did? Only an idiot in a war could say a—' He hesitated again. His mouth had soured and he was glaring across at the church wall, not really looking at it, clutched in some horror. Whatever he was holding was on the verge of sinking back down into a pit inside. His expression shifted. He went from looking worried to resigned; the resignation brought relief to his brow. He kept his mouth sealed for a few further seconds. Then he rose and said suddenly, 'I'll be late.'

'For what?'

'Work.'

The Amber Shadows

'What work do you do?'

He spun and his eyes were aflame. 'How dare you ask me that? My government, my people, we reach out to help you, and all you do is ask, ask, ask. I come here for help, and do they let me do the work I was trained to do? The work I passed on to them? No, they keep my machines to themselves, they develop them and won't let us see the finished ones. They took our plans, they took our name for the machines, and then they shove me into this horrid little industry of theirs and they keep my research to themselves.'

He began to move off in the direction of the church path but stopped beside a huge ancient tomb. Above it rose a colossal angel, smothered in ivy and moss, suspended green tears draping to its toes.

Her fingers stumbled to gather the amber and stuff it back into the gas mask box.

'Wait. That was what you were doing that night at Wavendon? Behind the huts? Looking into the hut the Wrens use, where the noise was coming from?'

He didn't turn but spoke as if he was talking to the stone. 'We developed plans for those machines back in Poland. We called them "*bomba*" after an ice cream. We passed on the plans to the British. I believe your people call them only "*bombe*". Perhaps the French is easier to say, I don't know. It seems they work well. You have the Professor Turing in your midst.' He turned and his face was hollow and sad. 'If you can see further it is by standing on the shoulders of giants, isn't that right? But even standing on a regular person . . . he would not be able to see anything at all were it not for that person. We gave away the idea for the *bombes* but they don't trust us enough to work with you at . . . that place you work. They shove us in another building, another camp, to do different work. See, that word again, trust.'

'I'm not sure I quite understand.'

Piotr smiled. 'It's all right.' He put his hand on the angel and pulled off some of the moss, then crumbled it to the ground. 'I like that you trusted me. That's all. With your amber.' He was gazing into her eyes now and there was a penetrating sorrow in his, a look that was almost childlike. He was so far from Dickie and his fiery moods, and yet somehow he reminded her of him. 'I can't help you any more. I hope you find your father.'

The word tore at her, and Tiver's story loomed too large in her head. And on some level she knew that even though in her wildest dreams she might not find what she was looking for, she was going to seek it anyway. As she reached the edge of the cemetery she turned at the same time Piotr did, and saw two more words on his lips. 'Be careful.'

Chapter 19

There was no time left for pause. The stories were fizzing in her; Stravinsky, Leningrad, the palace, the amber, the censors' stamps. She wanted to know what was real and what was not, and she knew where she had to go to find it. It had been there all along but the terror of confronting it was too great, for wasn't it enough that houses, streets, towns, families were being blasted away without the shaking to pieces of one's own past?

Heaving her heart from where it had sunk to the dirt and moss she left Piotr at the stone angel and caught a bus back to Bletchley. She was racking her brains to think where she could borrow a car from. Perhaps Felix had one. Beatrix's was no good if she was on back shift. She would need it again too soon. The trains weren't reliable enough to get back in time for midnight.

In the village she hurried up Church Green Road towards

the Rectory Cottages in the hope of catching Felix. He had said three o'clock, but that wouldn't be soon enough. She turned the handle of the gate, keeping half an eye on the gardens, and she saw a shadow move, on the vegetable patch.

A man was slinking towards the raised wooden hutch at the rear of the patch, a hatless man in a brown overall coat like a factory worker, with white hair oiled to his head and a small sack in one hand. Horror is a magnet, Honey thought, as she watched him unlatch the little hutch, dip his hand in and take one of whatever creatures were inside. The melancholy sound she had heard that morning came again, three notes high, two low. And then it stopped, and a thin scream chilled her. He did it again, and again, and again. The sound was like the mice fighting behind the Steadmans' skirting boards, the panicked rabbits at catching time in the back garden. You could not un-see or un-hear anything, and yet she wanted to look, the way she had wanted to look at the sheet being pulled back over Dickie's blue and white shoulders.

The man turned, saw her and stopped. He greeted her with a crooked smile, yellow and courteous. 'Afternoon, miss.'

'Afternoon.' The small sack moved in his palm. They could not have been bigger than swallows, the little creatures, and they cheeped hysterically. But swallows didn't stay in England over winter.

'What are they?' She gestured to the wooden structure. Now the odd little song inside it had resumed.

'Oh, these?' He looked down at his sack. 'Swallows. For the pot.' He winked.

'Eat all sorts during the war.'

'That's right, miss.'

'Is Felix here? Felix Plaidstow? I've come looking for him. I've seen him here before and I thought this might be his billet.'

The man's face puckered. He had something slow-thinking, slow-moving about him. The bag made a sudden lurch and he looked as if he wanted to be getting it to the kitchen. 'There's a lot of men come in and out here. I'm only employed to help cook and garden, miss.'

'He has the dog. The greyhound. Nijinsky.'

'Oh, him.' The old gardener's face stayed blank. 'Well, I'd better . . .' He gestured to the door.

'Is he in there?'

'No. They don't come for lunch. Don't come till later.'

'What do you mean, come?'

'You ask a lot of questions for someone who ought to know better. If I asked as many questions as you, I'd, well, I'd . . .' He let the words hang and before Honey could press him further he had slouched with his struggling little bag towards the open back door.

Something about his unkemptness haunted her. She looked again at the sign. Rectory Cottages. But there was nothing ecclesiastical about anything she had seen there. Except perhaps that first evening, hoods on heads. It floated in her vision, at the corners, like something a medium in a tent might conjure up for you in their glass ball, that you couldn't quite see fully; the men at the tablecloth, bolt upright, the white cloths probed by the shapes of their noses, their brows.

She took a step closer to the wooden hutch. The things inside it were scratching. And then a different scratching sound came much closer behind. A cold wetness wriggled into the cup of her hand. She jumped out of her skin.

'Nijinsky.' She breathed out. The dog jerked his muzzle along the length of her arm. His nose was chilly but the breath that came out was hot. A drip congealed on the back of her knuckles.

'There's no teaching him.'

Felix stood at the ribbon's length. She detected some kind of distance in him. He seemed to look cautiously at her, his head tilted sideways, eyes pinched. 'Did you find what you were looking for?'

Her hand dropped to the dog and she stroked its grey ears. 'I need to borrow a car. Will you come with me?'

He almost spluttered with laughter. 'Are you out of your mind? Where are you off to now, Hercule Poirot?'

She felt heat in her face and eyes and he saw that laughter wasn't what she had hoped for. 'Do you have a car?'

He shook his head. 'No.'

'But what about . . . the people you know, in there?' A woman was approaching from along the road; her shabby coat chimed recognition in Honey but she didn't know immediately why. She racked her brains to think where she might have seen her and realised it was the woman in the post office, the one who had complained about her stolen dog.

Felix took Honey by the elbow and guided her away from the cottage's garden fence round to the back of the allotment. 'Honey, I don't think it's likely that the Ministry for the Protection of the Arts will grant you loan of a car. I told you what they do in there; they shift paintings, artefacts. It's important work.'

They stayed tucked close to the cottage walls until the woman had passed.

Honey looked down at Nijinsky. Felix had clamped his hand around the dog's muzzle. Its silvery tail was wagging, thumping the wall. A strangled whine escaped its nose. He caught her eye. 'I'm sorry,' he said. He let his hand drop. Immediately Nijinsky shook himself out. 'Sorry I pulled you sharply. It's just that I can't be seen wandering about the Ministry.' There was a flush in his cheeks that could have been anger or guilt, or anything. Again, fresh coffee was on his breath. It only then occurred to Honey what a strange scent it was, one she didn't smell often, because of rationing. There had been excitement in the hut when Beatrix received coffee. He must have a contact in the Ministry of the Protection of Arts or whatever he had called it, someone who could get coffee. He peered around the corner of the building, then seemed to follow the path of her thought to the ministry garden, where the wooden hutch stood.

'They keep birds, you know, for suppers.' He gestured and Nijinsky began to whine. 'Hush, hush. He gets excited.' Felix held her gaze.

'Is this where you live?'

'Golly, no. I only help out some of the time.'

'I see.' She looked over his shoulder back towards the road. The streets were quiet and a fragile breeze blew and it seemed for a second as if Bletchley were the calmest, safest town in the whole of England.

Felix took a step forward, placing his fingertip on the exposed skin at the base of her throat. He pushed the blouse collar aside to where the bone was warm. His finger was cold. The dog was wriggling about their legs, at the hems of their coats.

'It's rare to find someone in such a small place,' he said, 'that you feel kinship with so soon.'

The timbre of his voice had dropped. The tendons inside her neck, where his breath now brushed, seemed to swell and then slowly melt. Her hand fell onto the dog's head. 'Or maybe you believe,' he said, 'it was only a matter of time before our paths crossed. Tell me what's happening to you, Honey, tell me and we can make sense of it together.'

The urge was in her hands again, the same urge she'd had after the restaurant, when she had wanted to take his coat belt knot. Now she wanted the woollen lapels of his blackout-cloth coat braced tightly between her fingers. But instead she pushed her palms flat on his chest. 'I need to find a car.'

Felix took a step back. His blue eyes dropped. He pulled the ribbon of the dog closer. It stopped whining for a second and looked up, appealing. His hand fell to its bony brow and massaged a small circle, the dead finger hanging aloft.

'That girl you know. The aristocratic one. She has a car.'

'Beatrix? She won't lend it to me. She's working back shift and anyway I don't know where she's billeted.'

'Where do you need to go?'

'Hastings.'

He frowned. 'Hastings? It's miles away. Why—'

'Never mind why, I just need to go.'

'We can go by train.'

Honey shook her head. 'I don't trust them. They're unreliable.'

'But . . .' He looked around him, as if an excuse might present itself on the fence. 'What about the petrol ration?'

'Beatrix knows a man. My stepfather will be able to—'

'Is that who you want to go and see?'

'No.' She breathed deeply. The air carried the faint tang of cookery now from beyond the cottage's back door. 'My mother.'

'Honey, I can't – I can't come with you. I want to, but . . . I have a shift. I should leave now, in fact. I don't think they can spare me.'

'I thought you were on nights. We can make it back.'

'Where are you going to find a car?' She couldn't understand his sudden belligerence. This morning he had been the picture of help. She watched him inch his back towards the house. He had pressed himself against the wall, against the white harl. Nijinsky watched her with globular eyes, blinking. Then Felix moved forward again, sweeping her with a sudden compulsive clutch into an embrace. 'All right,' he said. 'I think I might know someone who can help.'

He called her attention with a tuneless blast of the horn, and it was the last thing she expected to see outside the window of Yew Tree Cottage: a truck, filthy with brick and wood dust, a pickup truck with a scorched and worn logo on it, rusting at the corners.

'Where on earth did you find this?'

'Just . . . I know a few people. Drivers for the Park and whatnot.'

Nijinsky sat perk-eared in the middle of a cracked leather bench. Foam bled from between the stitching. She minded her skirt as she sat, for the leather looked hardened enough to snag. 'Sort of thing a builder would use. Sorry, I didn't mean to sound ungrateful. Just – it's extraordinary. Have you seen this?'

From the dashboard she picked up a tiny wooden Madonna and child, pink, white and blue. There was a scattering of them, crosses and tiny little metal-carved prayer books and miniature charms of golden urns clustered into one corner beneath the grimy windscreen.

With a swift hand Felix scooped the lot up and tossed them into the glove compartment. She opened her mouth, but by then he had put the key in the ignition and the sound covered up her words. The truck was noisy and between the engine growls and the greyhound whining it was difficult to talk. Once or twice she caught Felix looking at her; at her stockinged ankles or the curve of her cheek. The journey took over three hours including stops for fuel, and despite the bleakness of the mission and her rising nerves at its outcome Honey found that as they neared the coast, and the sea smell began to permeate the cab of the truck, she couldn't help but feel lifted.

The light was beginning to dim into late afternoon but it was still bright enough to make out the froth tips on the waves below. The rocks and sprouts of sandy grass at the side of the road were so dry and alien compared to Bletchley's dense hedges and fields. Instead of cloying railway coal and baked brick smoke there was iodine and sea brine in the air, and although ominous concrete barricades lurked in the shallow waters not far from the cliffs, their presence didn't spoil the ocean's freedom.

The seafront had been sandbagged. Battlements, coloured slush by the tide, sagged in piles, some crusted over with seaweed in tiny ragged lines. As the truck rounded a bend in the road the fragile white stucco of the seafront houses came into view, like brittle icing on a wedding cake; a cake that couldn't exist any more now rationing had put paid to sugar. The road was winding and high, and the wind shook through fissures in the wagon's frame, making it sway. Honey felt vertigo, thinking of the coastal drives Joan Fontaine had taken with Cary Grant and Laurence Olivier.

Felix swerved to avoid a creature at the side of the road. Nijinksy wriggled round in his seat to look and began to bark. It was a stoat, or perhaps a tiny thin hare, galloping to safety. They veered dangerously close to the edge and in her mind she saw the door swing open – the passenger door; she saw herself dangling over the cliff, clinging hold of Felix for her life and then . . .

He righted the truck and soon they began their descent towards the promenade.

'I'll find somewhere to park and take him for a walk.' At that word the dog perked up and began to stamp on the seat with his haunches, struggling into song.

'Won't you come up for something to drink or eat?'

'I can find something on the front. I don't want to intrude.'

'Really it wouldn't be—'

'You want to explain to your mother what you are doing taking lifts from men in rusty trucks, with whining greyhounds?'

The Amber Shadows

Honey looked down. 'My mother did more outrageous things in the last war.' He didn't see the funny side. He looked embarrassed and began threading the ribbon through the dog's collar. Why don't you get him a proper leash, she wanted to ask, but she didn't. Instead she stepped out of the cab, minding her shoes in the sand that had leached from the seafront.

The wind pinched; still, it felt milder than at Bletchley. There wasn't the biting frost, only a cold, salty moisture.

She found the hotel she wanted. The Pavilion, right next to the Alhambra, one of the stucco white-cake buildings on the seafront. Up close they needed a clean.

There were day-trippers and Christmas holidaying troops, women skipping and two little boys firing guns made of sticks and cockleshell bullets at each other on either side of a sandbag bank. A gash in the landscape, like a missing tooth, showed where a building had been blitzed to rubble. It was two doors down from the theatre where her mother was performing, and it sent a jolt of memory shocking through her: two years ago, Christmas in London, when the Empire came down and the dancers had to be carried out on their backs, blood trailing down pink stockings. There was something so horrifying about their spoiled beauty. Fairytales and plays had brought Honey up to believe fragile dead women were somehow beautiful: Snow White, Aurora, Ophelia. But there was nothing somnambulant or sensual about the bruised dancers, or their screams or the dirt and the rubble crushed into their clothing and skin.

She turned away from the theatre into the hotel lobby. It was a crumbling thing, more boarding house than seafront palace, but they had made an effort, with gilded tassels on cheap drapes and factory-produced furniture polished to a shine. The lobby was sparse and stained patches on the wallpaper showed where furniture had been removed. A sign hung in black ink on white paper: 'The Government has commandeered our furniture and other equipment, distributing it to war purpose buildings all over the country.'

A porter intercepted her and asked if she was looking for anyone. She dropped her voice but when she said her mother's name – as she knew it would – the fuss began. He snapped his fingers, and a sorry-looking girl in boy's livery appeared with her hands held out for Honey's coat. Protectively Honey clung on to her lapels. The porter mouthed the name elaborately to the concierge, who placed his pen down and ferried her to the reception desk. The receptionist made a telephone call – 'She's not in her room. She's at the theatre. No, she's in her room. She's answering' – and ushered Honey into a lift, meeting her eye with an offer of tea being sent up 'or anything, anything you wish for'.

Honey felt her heart sink a little. She didn't like it, this nasty little pantomime. It always made her feel horrid. She hated her mother's reputation marching before the family, like a gaudy trumpeter with a pompous flag. She realised then that perhaps at Bletchley, one good thing had come of her place in the war: she was nothing special there, she was only a typist.

The lift operator had been given a look by the concierge. Now he passed the look on to the waiter he met in the corridor, who leapt aside and stuck his arm out as she passed as if to protect her derrière from the horror of touching something as filthy as a wall. Honey dipped her head. They passed two women with arms full of wrapped Christmas gifts and she felt a stab of shame that she had not even thought to buy anything for anyone yet. At the end of the corridor a plaque labelling The Lilac Suite had been recently screwed to freshly painted white wood. She knocked and waited.

'Come in.' At those two words she knew that her mother wouldn't bother to get up off the chaise.

Martha Isolde Deschamps was sprawled at an angle facing the door, one leg tucked beneath her on the chaise and the other splayed in a straight white cubist line towards the floor. The crisp slope of the chaise back shot her waist skywards; the image was topped by her round porcelain face and blurred black hair. She was wetting her lips delicately with a teacup.

When she saw Honey she leaned forward and chinked it onto its saucer, on a spindle-legged table beside her. Everything in the room was bone-thin: the carved legs of the couch, its narrow upholstered cushions, Martha's long, straight legs and her muscular fingers. She was a woman who carried her power in her muscles, and carried not an inch more of anything to impede it. Her black hair was dyed, very thick, brushed, oiled and set until it shone like hot wax. Her mouth was thin and wide. Lips that had once been sensuously big took up the better part of her jaw, now toned and tamed into an even pair of lines that she painted a dangerous red, always, whether on stage or off.

Her personality too was carefully cultivated. Not extravagant, not Victorian, not chic, nor flippant, nor flapperish, nor kind, but designed to instil curiosity in the beholder. She was warm, and yet the coolness of her voice always made one feel – even Honey, but certainly maids, and most definitely gentlemen – that there was something she wasn't telling you, either out of politeness or otherwise.

She was wearing huge white silk trousers that clung to her bony hips and flared at the base, concealing most of her freakishly long feet, which ended in bending acrobatic toes, the nails painted to match her lips. Often Honey had brought a friend back from school, university or somewhere else, and they pulled her aside late in the evening to whisper, 'Your mother is nothing like what I expected.'

'Have a cake, dear.' She pointed at a tray of fancies, iced in pastel shades with white-line patterns glooped on the surface. 'I don't know whether they're edible, I haven't tried one.'

This was always the first battle. Food. Her mother had wanted her to take up ballet when she was a girl, but as if to challenge her to its discipline she would also always present her with sugared things after every class, twirled and iced like precious gems. She herself would never touch anything of the sort. She picked at meat and never ate bread or fruit. She lived off eggs, poached, scrambled, boiled, coddled. Honey lost the challenge every time, but then she had never wanted to be a ballet dancer anyway.

'I'm sorry you couldn't come sooner. Wretched FO, keeping you there, heartless I say, but there you go.' There was a single worry-line on her mother's brow. She didn't extend her arms or lean her face forward for a hug or kiss. Honey went to her anyway and her mother accepted the hug and put her thin fingers into Honey's wild hair. The gesture made her feel young and weak. She looked for somewhere to sit.

It was then that she saw her stepfather was in the room too. Henry Deschamps, ever in the shadows, always discreet, sat on the bed beyond a set of open double parlour doors. The outlines of his face were blended into a mist of cigar smoke. Honey couldn't be certain but she thought there was a dark look on his brow. He hadn't yet stood to greet her, although he did now.

'How did you get here?' His bulky body clasped her behind layers of suit and waistcoat fabric and watch chains, and he smelled the way he always did, of a myriad of different types of soap, one for the ears, one for shaving, one for the face, one for the body. 'If a factory man,' he used to say, 'won't trial his own products, what faith can he expect merchants to put in him?' This was Henry; practical and good as his word. Up close, Honey saw the blood threads in his wet eyes, as she had noticed her mother's marble-dry face.

'It was bound to happen,' said Martha from the couch. Honey's ears were still muffled by her stepfather's arms but she heard. 'I'm sorry if you think I'm callous but I can't even cry. That boy went about recklessly, saying things, doing things, not caring—'

Honey pulled away from Henry. 'How are you, 'on?' That was what he called her, 'Hon', but without the H, as if she was French. He had been born in Dijon and there were still little affectations he liked to play with. And it was, after all, just a different diminutive of her real name. 'You're not just some little Honey,' he used to say to her when she was at school, and then at university. 'Remember your real name.'

'I don't know how I am,' she said. 'I don't know.'

Over on the chaise her mother threw her head back and swallowed heavily.

'I've cancelled her concerts,' Henry said.

'I am here. I can hear you.' Her mother sounded very far away, like she was in the corner of the room instead of just in front of them. It took a while for Honey to notice that faint music was playing on a wiry gramophone; a scratched and worn record, a tiny baroque voice, Monteverdi or Bach.

'I keep trying to tell myself that there are other mothers. Mrs Harvey, you know, that woman who charred for next door, who sometimes helped cook at our parties, she lost a son. Bunty Niven, she's volunteering as an Air Raid Warden, do you remember Bunty, she used to give you tangerines at Christmas? She lost one of hers last year, the middle one I think, Percy. Percy the Pilot, he had terrible acne, like a seed cake he was, we all said he'd never get a girlfriend, and then once the uniform was on he was peeling them off like leeches.' She paused and looked at her muscled hands. 'But it's not the same, is it? And then sometimes it is.'

She looked up again and her gaze roamed idly about the room. Sometimes she studied Honey, but not her face: just her clothing and her cork shoes. 'You know, you're very lucky being a girl. The number of girls who will die in this war—'

There was a silence; the last vestiges of niceties died away.

'Shall I ring for some tea?' Henry asked.

Honey unclipped the latch of the gas mask box. 'The thing is,' she said, then stopped cowardly as she saw them watching her. 'The thing is, there's something I have to ask you.'

'Not now, please, my girl, not now.'

'Yes, now.' She met her mother's eyes and there was an understanding there – that the air was liable to turn unpleasant.

'How did you get here?' Martha said.

'A friend drove.'

'Your feet look filthy. Did they make you pedal the car yourself?'

Honey shook her head, not as an answer, just at the criticism. She thought of Felix's finger, that he said had blown off touching an incendiary, climbing across rubble to reach his mother. A grasping for something she wanted to feel but didn't clawed deep in her. She got up and looked out of the window at the brown sea with its wet sandbags and concrete barricades. She felt Henry's eyes on her back.

'You have to tell me,' she said to her mother. 'You have to tell me about Ivan Korichnev.'

There was a pause. Then her mother laughed – just briefly, a roguish, uncharacteristic tinkling. 'I beg your pardon.'

Honey turned suddenly and the anger in her flashed. 'Every time, every time I asked, until I grew ashamed of asking. But you could never stop Dickie telling me the truth. You can never stop the truth from growing and spreading because it will always be there, waiting to get free.'

'And so will a lie.' Martha used the full power of her mezzo-soprano voice. The fork on the cake stand trembled. Silence spun out between them; in the time it took Honey to speak a spider could have crawled along a thread from one to the other.

'You always denied it. But he's alive and he wants to know us. Dickie knew it. Dickie *knew* he would come looking. And now . . . so do I.'

'I think . . .' Henry stood up, pulling at the knees of his trousers '. . . I should like to go for a walk.'

'Oh, for God's sake, where?' sang Martha. 'Along the fine promenade of the seafront? Up where the soldiers take their mistresses? Or where the Home Guard are doing rifle practices? Good luck and—'

Henry cut her off. 'Don't lose both your children in one week.'

Martha glared at him until her eyes boiled. 'Go.'

Honey waited until Henry had finished tucking himself into his waxed coat and collecting various things to put in his pockets, until he had very quietly clicked closed the door, before she retreated from the window to the couch on the other side of her mother's coffee table. With a shaking hand Martha reached for her cigarettes and her lighter, picked one out and sparked it up. She took a long dignified draw. 'Dickie told all sorts of stories when he was young. We never paid him much attention. Children say things. Little girls pretend they're abandoned princesses. Little boys . . .'

'Pretend they have a father. Stories come from somewhere.'

'Books, fairytales, operas. Ballet.' Martha sat up fully, pulling a paisley cashmere shawl from the arm of the couch and draping it about her as if she were suddenly cold or shy. 'Secrets are given to children on a need-to-know basis.' She smoked her cigarette.

With her own hand trembling, Honey unclipped the gas mask box and prised open the lid. She took from it the bitten fur, the bound loot.

'What are those?'

'I'll tell you in a minute. But first, what happened to Ivan Korichnev?'

'Honey, you know what happened, I've never lied to you. He never existed.'

'He must have done.'

'It's a fairy story.'

'So I'm a fairy story, am I? Dickie, your son, is a fairy story?'

'Dickie wanted to believe he was Russian because he was in love with Russia. Obsessed with the damned country. He was just like those fools, those fools who think that communism will save their souls. It was that ballet mistress of his, filling his head with nonsense, making him . . . Boys develop crushes in strange ways. Dickie's wasn't with a woman or a man. It was with a country. It was a child's story, Honey.'

'Dickie said,' began Honey, 'that Ivan fled to Russia, that he joined the revolution. He was a composer and later he became custodian at one of the palaces.' Her voice cracked. 'He showed me newspaper clippings. With his name in them.'

'And how would he have fled to Russia? You tell me. You think the Bolsheviks let anyone in? You know nothing. Did you know that Stravinsky – Dickie's beloved Stravinsky – hasn't even returned to Russia? He's in America. Your father never knew him, by the way.'

Martha took a moment to swallow. She leaned back in her chair, far enough to see through the window. 'Your father was half-German, half-Scottish. He died of the Spanish influenza just before you were born.'

'Lies!'

'I'm not lying,' she said coldly.

'Cap—' She stopped herself. 'I heard, I heard from someone at the Foreign Office, someone who does our security checks, that he died in a brawl. Dickie said he escaped to Russia. You tell me he died of the flu – who am I to believe?'

'Why do you care, Honey? You have a father. You have Henry. What has he ever done for you that hasn't been good enough?'

Martha leaned suddenly forward and grabbed her daughter's hand with three punishing fingers. Honey could feel the pressure of the rings her mother wore, cold on her pulse. The world had not stopped swimming for two days and nights, since the hour the policemen had found her, but now the waves were high. She was on a fairground horse, a runaway carousel, and she felt sick.

'I need to know who I am because I need to know what I am fighting for.'

Martha's hand snapped back. 'You are fighting because you believe in good. You are fighting to end torture and murder. You are not your blood, Honey. You are not your country. You are you.'

'Then where is the harm in telling me the truth?'

Martha waited. Honey, her head bent, heard the breath rise and fall in her mother's lungs. 'Look at me,' Martha said. 'I am telling you the truth.'

Honey lifted her head.

'He was called Ian, not Ivan. Ian Kurtz. Ivan was an affectation. It was what I called him. You know the way I sometimes say "Honora" or "Deechie", it was just a silly nickname because I didn't like his name. But I suppose Dickie's story has to have its roots somewhere.'

'What about Korichnev?'

'Madame Korichnev? The ballet mistress, don't you remember? With her hair scraped back and her red lipstick and cane?'

'Is he dead?'

'Yes. He died just before you were born. It was the tail end of the Great War. We'd been back from France for a year but it took some time for them to catch up to him.'

'Who are they? What do you mean, catch up?' The echoes of Dickie's story rang in her mind. He had been on the run from someone. Two men, he'd said. She waited. Her mother paused.

'I'm not really surprised the FO didn't want you to know this.'

'Who are they?' Honey felt her voice growing tight. She looked into her mother's eyes and saw a flash of panic. She could taste the truth now, she could smell it coming.

Martha's voice was quick and level. 'Look, the government was rounding up anyone with a German name, they had been since the start of the war. They called them Enemy Aliens. They sent them to internment camps.'

Honey felt her hand, as if it wasn't hers, rising to her mouth in horror.

Martha went on. 'He did die of Spanish flu or pneumonia, I don't know which and the inquest wouldn't say. There was nothing I or anyone could have done for him.'

'Camps?'

'Internment camps, they called them. They're doing it again, this time around.'

'Yes, I know. The Germans, the Italians.' There had been a ship, a couple of years back, a ship that had been torpedoed and sunk, carrying, what had they called them? Yes, 'Enemy Aliens', they had called them. 'Internees.' The newspapers said they were all the same – dangerous, fifth columnists, people feeding information back to their families in other countries, spies. Hundreds had drowned being deported across the sea to Canada. It was for British safety, the government had said. 'Collar the lot!' Churchill had cried, before they set sail. She couldn't remember the name of the ship.

'He was a spy?' she said quietly.

'Good God,' her mother said, and for a second there was laughter in her voice. But when she saw Honey's eyes her own turned with sorrow. 'Spies no, these men aren't spies, they are ordinary men. Ordinary men, born where they were born, now living in Britain with the wrong name. Even second-generation Germans were rounded up, people who didn't know they had German ancestry until the knock on the door came, rounded up, taken away to be incarcerated for the war's duration. Spies . . . No, Honey, your father was not a spy. He was a pianist. A hotel pianist with a German father.'

A hotel pianist. Just like Tiver had said.

'But why didn't you tell me? Why did it take me to want to hurl myself from a window until you'd tell me something, anything, about my father? Why am I twenty-four years old and only hearing this now?'

Martha mashed her cigarette in a nearby cup, so hard it rattled the table. 'You don't talk about the death of your first husband. You don't talk about your first husband getting arrested and bundled into an Enemy Alien camp because he had the wrong nationality. You don't talk about him catching pneumonia and dying a cold little death in a filthy prison. The shame they bring on men, the shame. There, you want to know who your father was? The lover of Martha Deschamps, the opera singer? He died a shivering, wronged man a month before his daughter was born.'

The Amber Shadows

When Honey looked up, Martha was sitting with her hands clasped in her lap. She looked a little like the Madonna from the truck, the blue and white paisley shawl slumped over her shoulders, a caricature of piety. She had been worried about the shame then, had she? And yet at that moment it was not her father of whom Honey felt ashamed. To lie to your children, to abandon a person not for what they had done, but for what had been done to them . . .

'On my birth certificate, it doesn't say the name Kurtz, it says Kitts, doesn't it?'

Martha nodded. 'We were still at war. Having a German name was enough to be made a pariah. Those camps? Dickie, wanting to be what he is, growing up with . . .? Look what's happening now, again. I didn't want you – I didn't want us – to have a German name. I destroyed that part of you.'

Her mother opened her mouth, took a small suck of air in, and, as if the sigh had been interrupted, let it out. She shook her head lightly. 'You don't understand this country. Look around and see how some people treat the refugees now . . . They put the refugees in camps too, it didn't matter. Neighbour, migrant, if you had German ancestry that was that. You were looked on with suspicion. The war might have ended, but the feeling dragged on. It dragged on, Honey, and I did what I did to protect you. Do you think you'd be working for the Foreign Office with that name? Do you think you'd be treated the same? Dickie, he'd have been incarcerated, he could have been put on one of those sinking ships.' She shook her head.

Honey picked up one edge of the black fur and lifted it. The amber panels tumbled out. With shaking hands she grasped the main panel with the metal mechanism. Finally she removed from the case the tiny muffled shape of the firebird, and peeled it from its furry skin. 'Then explain these.'

She shifted the cake plate with her arm, dropped the furs onto the floor and placed the amber pieces out on the table. Next to the yellow and blue icing of the stale fancies the resin looked gothic and rich; its carvings, its bubbles, its scars, veins and its peculiar smell.

'What are they?' Martha reached forward and picked up one of the panels. She held it up to the light, wincing as if it pained her to focus. 'They're carved.'

Honey found herself fighting disappointment. She didn't know what she had hoped for; rage perhaps, rage would have ignited her hope that everything Martha had just told her was a lie. But there was none. Martha turned the piece around, staring at it from different angles.

'Do you remember the code book Dickie had?'

She looked at Honey sharply and her eyes shot wide. 'You think Dickie made these?'

'I don't know.' She thought she had said it with intention but her mother looked blank. Honey asked, 'Where did Dickie get that book, that book of ciphers?'

'Oh, *Figley's* . . . whatever it was. I think he found it somewhere, in a Barnardo's bazaar or a church fete. Yes, it was a Barnardo's bazaar because – well, I don't remember. But it was.' After a moment she brought the amber piece close to her nose. 'What do these smell of? They smell of something.'

'Amber.'

'Amber base notes, but they're too sweet for pure amber. Soir de Paris, that's it. Golly, whichever boy made these for you has it bad.'

Honey's voice was quiet. 'You think they were made by a boy.' It had been Moira's first reaction too, even before she knew what was inside the parcels; that little smile of hers in the hut. Only boys send extravagant gifts, only frivolous boys, not long-lost family.

'I thought . . . I thought Ivan was sending them to me from Russia. He'd smuggled them out from the Amber Room, and was sending them. They came in packages postmarked Leningrad. I thought he was there, in Russia, now, smuggling them to me. If it's not him, who else can they be from?'

Her mother looked at her for the first time with pity, her mouth straight and even, her eyes downturned, the same pity she had shown Honey that time when she locked herself in the bathroom. Was pity what it took to bore through Martha Deschamps' ice? She was not capable of affection, but her love sneaked through in extravagant gestures, in songs she sang on stage, and in pity.

'The carvings on the side come from an old hand cipher, one that I think was in Dickie's book.'

The walls of Honey's belief – a belief constructed from snippets of information she had gleaned through her childhood and built into the secure walls of a room – began to dissolve. She saw empty black craters beyond them. And then it dawned on her. Everything she knew about herself, about her father, she had learned from Dickie. Everything went back to Dickie.

She was shaking her head. Trembling so violently that her mother reached across and grabbed her. She could never return to the Park. Surely, surely they would know. Tiver knew about the Enemy Alien camp and he had deceived her. Now, she knew, he had deceived her to keep her obedience. It was an insult, to think that she would take vengeance on innocent people, punish the government for the sake of a man she had never met. But was it so foolish? For those brief moments when the amber had come from him, his presence had been so vivid to her that had he reached out, like the wings, like the feather of the firebird, she could have followed him across Europe to his exile, just to stand and face him, and try to see who he was.

Her mother waited until she locked eyes with her. 'There is a reason we gave you the name we did. Not the short version, Honey, but the real one. And it's who you are.'

Honey waited until she felt she could breathe again. Her eyes closed in a long blink. The tears, the worry, it was exhausting.

'He's not out there.'

Martha shook her head sadly. 'Honey. He died in the British prison camp.'

'How do you know they didn't make a mistake?' Her voice grew thin – as if it was coming from inside the tinny gramophone.

'They didn't make a mistake.'

'How did they know how to find him? If he had changed his name to Kitts?'

At this Martha took hold of her daughter's hand again, but tenderly this time like the stems of a bouquet of flowers in her long-fingered grasp. The other hand she put through her slick hair. She sighed, but this time it wasn't theatrical. 'The reason he was taken was that he wouldn't change his name. He was dogged about that. He didn't think it right that he had to. I changed yours because I couldn't have children growing up in this country with a foreign name.'

'But . . .' Honey stammered, disbelieving. 'Henry? Henri Deschamps. He has as foreign a name as can be.'

'Yes, my darling, but the right sort of foreign.'

Chapter 20

Martha stood up and went over to a silver tray, where a bottle of something bronze stood next to a trio of glasses. She pointed the neck towards Honey but Honey shook her head.

'If only you'd told me what happened to him,' said Honey quietly, watching her mother pour herself a drink, and then the path of the short glass travelling to her large red mouth. 'I think I had a picture of him in dribs and drabs and—'

'Because no one ever says what they mean in Britain. How many children – how many people at the Park do you think know the real story of their parents? Oh, you might think you have an idea. An idea is enough, sometimes.'

Honey watched her mother. For the first time, she thought she could see beyond the glamour and the drama.

The Amber Shadows

Martha had made herself in the image the world wanted to
see: silk fabrics and a bellowing, haunting voice. And she
stuck rigidly to her persona. There was no place in it for Ian
Kurtz. But she had learned from the operas she sang too.
She knew how to take the path of least pain.

Martha picked up a side panel. 'I don't think this is real
amber. The smell is too strong for starters, and . . .' She
grabbed the firebird. 'This, on the other hand. This is . . .
Look.' She breezed into the bedroom. As she passed Honey,
her trousers braced the air like ship's sails. Honey heard
fiddling sounds coming from the dressing table, a drawer
being opened. Martha returned holding a velvet box.

'Now this is amber. You can see the way the veins and
bubbles work. They're all different sizes.' She held up a
huge brooch set in grubby pewter. 'It needs a clean of
course, I never wear the damned thing, it belonged to an
aunt of Henry's. But do you see? There's intricacy there,
the way the resin has settled.' She sat down next to Honey.
'I know these panels are carved so you can't see properly
but . . .' She picked up the bird again to compare. 'This bird
I think is real amber. But it's as if whoever made it couldn't
afford, or didn't have the materials, to make a whole whatever it is, clock, music box . . .'

'Music box?' Honey's head snapped to her mother's gaze.
She grabbed the pieces and assembled them into their shape,
slotting the side panels into their tracks, balancing the bird
in front of the mechanics. But with the final piece missing

it was impossible to turn the cogs. She looked at the piece of paper Piotr had written on, and read aloud the quote. '"To get mixed up in politics is ruination for art." Who said that?'

Martha's head flicked up and though she composed herself almost instantly, Honey caught the dark quick lines on her face, before they vanished.

'Who gave you these pieces?'

'They came in the post.'

'It's impossible. Impossible.'

Smudges of the things Dickie had told her, the wall of memories she had built around herself, that had dissolved a few minutes ago; she saw again little flecks of colour coming back into view.

'That was what Ian said when they came for him. I still remember the bang, bang on the door. He said it to the agents who took him away. And then Dickie, at his tribunal . . . He said it at his CO tribunal when they asked why he was objecting. And I thought he said it deliberately, to spite me, to make me think of . . . It's a quote by—'

They said it together: 'Stravinsky.'

'Of course,' murmured Honey.

Dickie said, Dickie said . . . Dickie was a child. He always had been.

Martha sat back on the chaise and began picking at the edges of the shawl, pulling one little thread free so the others bunched up around it. 'Do you know it was me who met Stravinsky, not Ivan, Ian. Can you imagine that? It was in Paris, a couple of times actually. I didn't like him very much, but then you know how I feel about composers. Of course it's not enough, though, is it, to have your mother give you your identity, your talent, your heritage. Your mother can't even give you your name, can she? It all has to come from the father, otherwise it's not valid.' The line of her mouth was bitter. 'Stravinsky would have hated your father, you know, hated him to bits. Not because Ivan composed terrible music – though he did, he was one of those men who confuse nonsense with profundity. But because Stravinsky is a raging xenophobe – he hates Germans, isn't that a bit ironic for you? He would have hated Dickie and you.'

'Do you think Dickie sent these?' Honey asked tentatively.

'No,' Martha said straight away.

'But how can you tell? Who else . . .? He's the only one who knows that story.' Honey sat down on the hard wood of the floor. For the first time the amber slices looked malevolent, burnt, orange and false. It all came back to those three possibilities, now the first, the one she wanted to believe, had been shattered. So someone at Bletchley was trying to test her then, to see if she was trustworthy, and would disclose the secret of the gifts. If that were so she was balancing on a knife edge for she had told Tiver about the amber but not the ciphers.

Or the third option. Now she began to picture in her mind Dickie; Dickie and his fairytales about the firebird and the prince and the shape-shifting wolves, sitting with the mirth barely contained in his body as he moulded, shaped and carved the amber and smeared on the wax. Perhaps it was true; perhaps it was a horrible coincidence that night; he had been murdered by thieves after all, his body dumped. What was the alternative?

She saw the ritual of the patterned Easter eggs, their childhood ritual of making things for one another.

She stood up and went over to the window. The light was gloomy but she could make out the barricaded beach below. The tide was far out. In the distance, a speck was moving at lightning pace, charging to and from the water. It took her a few seconds to realise it was an airborne dog. He ran so fast all four of his legs left the ground, splayed long in each fresh gallop, then tucked together under him. She saw the other speck then too, standing by, throwing a stone every now and then. The dog ran furiously. He doesn't have a care in the world, she thought. He doesn't know there is a war on. He doesn't have to change his name if he fathers offspring. No one will put him in a locked box for having the wrong name.

The song on the gramophone stopped. After a beat of two seconds, it began again. Martha had a record player that jumped back to the start of the record when a song ended. Dickie had loved to hear things again and again too. She listened to a few seconds of the warble, up and down, then pulled the needle off abruptly.

'Shall we walk on the beach?' she said.

'The beach? What beach? You mean venture beyond the sandbags? I don't think so, it's not very safe.'

'The promenade then.'

In their coats, with the wind on their faces, Honey felt a wakefulness that seemed to shift things into perspective. They could see the hulking forms of ships on the horizon, huge liners. The *Arandora Star*, that was what it had been called, the ship that had sunk into the sea two years ago, carrying 'Enemy Aliens' into exile. They were headed for prison camps in Canada. Italians too, this time round, were being taken away. Pianists, café owners, doctors. '*Collar the lot.*' It was rumoured that when the ship started to sink, the British soldiers shot holes in the lifeboats.

They talked in small loaded bursts as they walked. They spoke about the funeral for Dickie, of the songs that would be played, of the importance of choosing the right casket because he had a fondness for elm, of the amount of work coffin makers must be landed with because of the war, of the gratitude that she, Martha, felt for at least having her son's bones, and of his death being no less pointless than any other death at sea or on land. Martha was not angry. There was a quietness to her misery instead.

They passed a photographer with a heavy flash lamp

offering cut-price Christmas snaps for young couples. They passed the posters that had 'Martha Deschamps' crossed out. There was a baker's shop with a 'guess-the-weight' competition for the Christmas cake in the window, advertised as 'made with real eggs and marzipan' and it made Honey think of the egg she had stolen for Dickie, and whether he had eaten it, and the cobnut saccharine experiment the Wrens had given her in the beer hut the day after she received the first amber.

And where was the missing piece? The firebird still wouldn't sit in its hole because of a piece that she now might never have.

She looked up to see Felix on the other side of the sandbags. They watched him pick up a stone, throw it for the dog, and begin to run at a clip, clumsy in his town shoes on the mucky shale.

'Felix,' Honey called. The wind must have carried her voice away for he didn't turn. In fact he sped up, bolting along with the dog. Nijinsky leapt at him, spraying sea mud onto his coat. 'Felix,' she called again, louder.

'Do you know that man?'

'He works alongside me,' she said. 'Sort of, in another department. Felix!' She turned back to her mother. 'He drove me down in a borrowed truck with the dog.' She stopped herself before saying, 'He was the one who first gave me the amber,' though she didn't quite know why. 'Hold on.' Honey grabbed a fistful of her skirt and clambered over the sandbags, hearing her mother's howls of disapproval.

She lurched on her feet as she tried to find purchase on the stones, then, settling into a rhythm, jogged towards Felix. When he was close enough that there was no doubt he could hear her she called again. 'Felix!'

He stopped at once and brushed down his coat before he turned. He was panting. Salt wind had pushed the hair on his brow backwards and set a glimmer going in his eyes.

'Were you shouting me for long?' he called across the twilight, labouring his breaths. The dog still thought it was a game and leapt at him but now he pushed its muzzle away and began to walk towards Honey.

'I'll just go back to the truck and wait, shall I?' he asked.

'Come over and say hello to her at least.'

'I don't think it's right.'

'What on earth—'

'It's not appropriate, I mean.'

But Martha Deschamps, having forgotten already her chastisements of her daughter, had rolled up the legs of her billowing trousers and was reconnecting with the tough mettle that had once seen her take a train to Paris with nothing but a suitcase. She climbed the sandbag wall and began to take the shale in huge strides.

'Look, she's coming over. I just want you to say hello.'

Martha's arm was outstretched when she was still five

paces away, with that confidence she always had that the person she was greeting would want to touch her hand. She pasted on a large smile and jigged Felix's palm tightly.

'You drove my daughter down. Very kind of you.'

Felix muttered an apology for the loss.

Martha's head was cocked to one side. 'Do you know the way you walk, it's so very like a boy I remember. One who used to do the stage sets at the Royal Opera House. Do you remember, Honey, Freddie Mox. God knows what age he'd be now. Same as Dickie I suppose, poor boy.'

'His name is Plaidstow,' Honey said.

Felix and her mother were staring at one another, both frozen in curiosity.

'Isn't it, Felix?' said Honey.

He hesitated. 'Plaidstow,' he said. 'That's right. I don't know anyone called Mox. I haven't a brother either. Or a cousin of that name, for that matter.'

'Yes, of course, it's a funny thing when you think you recognise someone, especially now. This fellow, I remember him because he was a tremendous carpenter. He was only a boy, a few years older than Honey. Honey, you must remember Freddie Mox.'

'I don't remember ever visiting you at the theatre,' Honey said.

'Oh, you did. Not as much as Dickie. He was in the junior ballet. Golly, I suppose this war is so unsettling you start thinking you're seeing people you know everywhere.

390

Do you ever find that? You think you see someone you know. Or you see someone you think you know.'

Felix was smiling. 'I can't say I know the feeling. I . . . I was at Cambridge when the war broke out.'

The air seemed to have staled. Felix was looking over towards the horizon. 'We both have shifts at midnight. I know it's a terrible thing to have to drag you away from your mother, Honey, but . . .'

Martha broke her gaze off him then and looked at her daughter.

She reached across, ran her hand down the strap of the gas mask box and patted the surface. 'Forget about all . . . this,' she said, tapping the box with a red nail. 'There are more important things. You are flesh and blood, Honey. You are not made of stories.'

When they hugged, her mother smelled of the same perfume, unchanged since the day she was born.

Chapter 21

The sun had disappeared by the time the truck wove up into the heights of the cliff tops, climbing from the khaki sea until they were close to the clouds. A three-quarter moon was in the sky and the temperature had plummeted to a biting chill. Honey pulled the dozing greyhound's head across her knee, feeling the warmth spread into her legs, and stroked its ears.

They had said little since they had left Hastings. Honey sensed not only politeness in Felix's reserve but something else. He had not been hostile to her mother, but there had been something in the way he had deflected her. She remembered herself how little she liked to be mistaken for someone she was not. 'You were the girl in the choir. You were the girl in the ballet, weren't you? You were in the hut with Dilly Knox? You were the one who won the mathematics prize at Durham?'

The Amber Shadows

But then Martha's memory was sharp. It was how she kept all those warbling operas safe in her head.

Felix began slowing the truck. They were swaying higher across the crumbling earth, flanked by rabbit dugouts, that barely made a road. On the side away from the sea the trees had petered out and bushes turned to scrub, almost moorland. They were approaching the single-lane bend, the one that on the way there Honey felt she might lean out and fall from. This time the drop was on the driver's side. She looked across at Felix.

His face, in profile, was more angular. He had neat features, perfect and keen, always smaller than she expected them to be when she looked at him afresh. He was dainty, the way he took care of himself; everything well-scrubbed, his lips soft, his nose and eye sockets hard. For a second she thought she might kiss him, just lightly, along the line of his jaw.

He dropped a gear and the truck began to crawl round the edge of the cliff. Honey peered past his ears towards the sea, tucked beneath a thousand-foot drop, stretching beyond the coast's grottoes and nooks to infinity; a blank space on a map. Looking at it spread out into nothing made her mind spin. The dizziness and the heaviness of the day pushed her thoughts upside down. How much could one brain take? And her mother, her mother had not accused him of being someone else, no, she had not done that, but he, on the other hand, had not wanted to say hello to her.

The thought floated like a little ribbon, trailing just north of her eyeline. Who was Freddie Mox? What if the amber was some sinister hoax? And what, if that were the case, would she do about it? All along she had thought that whatever was happening she was Joan Fontaine in this mystery, fighting to protect herself from danger. But how far would that protection have to go? How far could suspicion take you? What if destiny had driven her here, lifted her high, circling into the clouds, with only the gulls as witnesses, to take her chance and fight before danger unmasked itself; what if this was the Park's challenge? What if it were not the Park, but the war itself challenging her? Would she be able to do it?

She had thought that Cary Grant must have murdered Joan Fontaine after all – after the film ended. But perhaps there was a third kind of ending. Perhaps after the credits had flashed on screen, after Cary Grant and Fontaine had driven back down the cliff-top road, it would be *Fontaine* who would put the poison in *his* coffee, *she* who would open the car door, to protect herself; and in trying to protect herself it would be *she* who would turn murderess. Honey could feel it; possibility seemed everywhere – it was frightening how close the horror of possibility could loom when the air was turned by a single thought. Everywhere, on land and at sea, boys who had dreamt of being train drivers and clerks facing off against mirrors of themselves with guns. And the thing that was more terrifying even than becoming the victim was that you could end up being the villain instead.

Felix inched the car closer to the cliff edge. His door creaked in the wind and a draught shot through. He creased his brow, concentrating on the broken camber of the road. He had brought her two of those packages directly, himself; one of them had come through the hut pulley. The gusts were coming up thickly from the sea swell below, rattling the glass and iron of the truck's structure. Then there were the remarks about Russia and her birthday. He had wanted to know, today, he had wanted her to tell him so badly what was happening. He had asked and asked. She could see white shards far away on the tops of the waves, moonlit, sharp as shark's fins. She could do it, and maybe it would all be over, the suspicion.

They rounded the bend and the car hit a loose stone. It threw her. She jolted into Felix and he caught her hand. And there was nothing but softness in the tops of his fingers, warmth in his grasp. She felt suddenly ashamed of her thoughts and was glad of the dusk that hid the blush blotching her neck. She reached up, placed her fingers round the back of his ear and this time she did kiss the line of his jaw.

He slowed the car and veered off towards a patch of scrub.

They sat in silence for a second.

'Not a nice day.'

'Not a bit.'

He shifted in his seat, then half-turned so he could look at her in the dimness. With his fingertip – the damaged one – he brushed along the silk of her eyebrow. The dog whined between them. Outside the wind rustled dead brush.

'Nijinsky, hop down.' He shifted places awkwardly, the greyhound's long legs and muscled haunches getting in the way of his arms as he strained to shift it into the driver's seat. Nijinsky grumbled and groaned, and stepped his ungainly limbs one at a time down onto the floor of the cabin. He curled into a ball underneath the steering wheel. They sat next to each other now. Their hips were touching.

'You taste like honey. Not like sugar, but a flavour that's summery, almost wild.'

Half a minute ago she had been thinking about killing him to save herself. Now she trembled with a different sensation. The gas mask box tipped down onto the floor. She heard something crack inside it. Her fingers slid softly up into the cream in his hair.

The bench of the truck was wide and smooth; she slipped along it easily, crooking her knees. Briefly three images flashed across her mind: Moira; her mother; Joan Fontaine. But this was different. She would not be caught out. There would be no baby in a drawer, no children whose father was hidden in the shadows.

The stitching of the leather scratched on her calf – she wasn't wearing stockings. His wool coat gave off heat and scent as he untucked his arms, and despite the chill his fine-knit pullover was a little damp across his chest.

Various phrases came crawling into her mind. 'Is this right? Aren't we in danger of being spotted by the Home Guard? Shall we not wait until tomorrow? Do you have a French letter?' But she didn't like to say any of them, for it was pleasurable, the kissing and his dry, hot palms and the comfort both of those brought. Sometimes he was clumsy, and she had to wriggle away from him until she was comfortable again. He wasn't boorish, but he was persistent, and the curious ways he touched her sometimes, she couldn't help but think – even in those slow moments, she couldn't help the doubt coming into her mind – that perhaps he might have learned them that way from prostitutes or men he talked to at university or the Park; he was so oddly assured.

When he'd had his climax, not long after they had begun, it was quiet with a low sigh. He was very clean. He leaned across to the driver's window and tossed his handkerchief into a bush, and only at that did the dog look up.

On the way back to Bletchley, she leaned her head on his shoulder, and although the bone made it uncomfortable she stayed there because the feel of the wool and his pulse were too comforting not to be right next to, and though he did nothing but watch the road, for the blackout gave the country lanes lined by trees a darkness that was thick as treacle, she felt the jaw muscles tighten, the smile on his face.

★   ★   ★

He said he would be back for her before half past eleven. He'd call by the billet on foot to walk her to her shift. He wasn't in fact on duty, he said, but he might be tempted to pop into the Park as there was a Christmas masquerade at the recreation club. She had forgotten it was happening.

'I'll come with you to drop the truck off,' she said. But he waved his hand.

'No need, why put yourself out of comfort.'

She didn't say, 'So that I can be with you for half an hour longer.'

In her bedroom she turned the wireless dial to the frequency for the BBC news, but instead it was a ballet, Prokofiev's *Romeo and Juliet*. She listened to it for a few minutes before it began to chill her and she switched it off. She felt as if it was Dickie, calling to her from the grave. It still played on her mind that the final piece of the puzzle – the music box, her mother had said – was missing. But she was fizzing too much in her limbs and her chest to think much about it. Felix's touch had imprinted itself on so much of her skin; she felt him there like stakes in the ground, flag-posts and waymarkers, the way Moira's words had stuck on and claimed parts of Reuben's body, that night.

She was lying on her bed, on top of a cold pile of furs, when she heard a sharp rap on the front door directly beneath her. Mrs Steadman made a noise like a crow; Honey heard her muttering to herself, crossing the hall and winching open the ancient wood.

The Amber Shadows

'Oh. Are you for Rebecca or Deschamps?' Mrs Steadman had never liked her first name – either the real or the diminutive – so used it as little as possible.

Honey strained her ears but she couldn't make out the reply. She sat up and threw the frayed fur from the amber round her shoulders. Slowly she crept towards the top of the stairs. At the bottom, floating on the hatstand where the shadows were darkest, Mrs Steadman's luminous bird glowed like a beacon. It took Honey a few seconds to adjust her eyes. She saw turquoise wool cross the threshold; the clip of a brown polished shoe; a hat with pheasant feathers ruched in neat waves across it.

'Yes, I'll just wait here, shall I?'

'Beatrix,' she called from the top of the stairs. 'How did you know where I lived?'

Mrs Steadman looked as if the ghost of cottage owners past had just materialised. After waggling her arms in fright she tutted at Honey and went back into her parlour, muttering something about a glass of water and powdered egg.

'I drove you home last night, have you forgotten already?'

'Sorry, I'm a little tired. Will you come upstairs?'

Beatrix hesitated, looking around the hall. Then, 'Very quickly,' she said. 'I have to get home for Christmas. They let me go a bit early.'

'You're driving home in the blackout?'

Beatrix shrugged. 'I miss my family.' She realised what she had said and her hand flew to her mouth. 'I didn't mean – I'm sorry.'

Honey led the way to the bedroom and opened the door, silently hoping she had left it tidy enough – she never thought of these things until there were visitors. Beatrix looked about and seemed to approve of the austerity. Honey had no pictures on the wall; she hadn't really bothered to settle in at all. There was only the crowded flower-patterned wallpaper of the Steadmans, her wardrobe, the chest of drawers, the bedside table with the electric lamp and a wire-less-cum-gramophone. Honey made space for them both on top of the furs. They scrabbled for small talk: 'How nice to see boys home for Christmas, how awful the headlines, what memories of Christmases past were clutched in war and would it ever be the same again?' Honey wondered whether to mention her visit to Moira but thought it best not.

When Beatrix reached into her pocket and withdrew a tiny envelope – a memo envelope with the name crossed out – Honey couldn't conceal her surprise.

'It's a gift.' She pushed it forward. 'Take it.'

Wary of anything in packaging, Honey took the envelope tentatively. Beatrix was poised on the edge of delight as she watched Honey ease open the flap. Down at the bottom of the envelope's crease were a few flecks of paper with the edges torn. It crossed Honey's heart for a sudden second that Beatrix held the key to the amber, that this was it. But when she took the scraps out she saw they had the heads of men and women on them. One was riding a horse. 'Stamps,' she said.

Beatrix shrugged and dipped her head. Rolling her eyes to the ceiling, in the gaslight she looked sheepish. 'Merry Christmas,' she said softly. 'I know it's not much but I wanted to give you something and . . .'

There were too many feelings that came swooping down: gratitude, sorrow, the comfort of a small act of kindness. But above them all hung confusion. 'Why stamps?'

'You collect them, don't you? These are from my own collection. I collect them too, you know. I couldn't very well get you rouge or fragrance and sugar seems too shallow a gift. Why are you frowning?'

Honey straightened her brow. 'I just don't know what made you think I collect—'

'The other day in the hut, you dropped one. A rare one. In fact, it was only a couple of days ago now I think of it, but it seems like a lifetime. You had an old heritage Russian stamp.'

Honey felt very cold in the tips of her toes. She opened her mouth slowly. 'What do you mean, heritage?'

'You know, one from before the revolution. A collectors' item. It's the Tsar's Cavalcade, that one. Do you still . . .' She cast her eye around the room. Honey paused for a moment, then reached across to the bottom drawer of her chest and dragged it open. She rummaged at the back. The parcel wrappers were screwed into a ball but all still there, as intact as they had been after she first tore into them.

She pulled them out. In the shadow of the lamp she tugged away the piece that had wrapped the firebird. 'That's it,' Beatrix said. 'Worth a fortune, I'd say. Can I touch it? Actually, hold on a second.' She peered more closely at the image. 'No, that's not right. The original has black horses and these are white. Hold on. Where did you get this? Did you buy it from a collector?'

'Someone posted it to me. The London 222 box.'

'Who?'

Honey closed her eyes for slightly longer than a blink. Her muscles were beginning to feel strained after being stretched out and pulled, after the positions she had cramped herself into in the truck. 'I don't know,' she whispered. When she opened her eyes Beatrix was staring at her.

'Honey, this stamp is a fake; a forgery. It's a very good one, but see, it's been hand-drawn, not printed. There are little blobs.' She pulled it over to the gaslight. 'It's absolutely minute, the detail is astonishing. Now who would do such a thing?'

The whole saga ebbed at Honey's mouth like the tide but it made her feel weary; she sent it spinning back.

'You have to be careful with the boys at Bletchley. And the girls, for that matter. Eccentric doesn't even cut it sometimes. Mooden says she saw you with one of the coffin makers who does the fit-ups.'

'I don't know any coffin makers,' Honey said, and though she laughed, she shivered. She stood up from the bed and moved to the window, checking for a draught. In her mind came the image of that extraordinarily large and shabby truck, the religious icons, dirty and piled in a corner; and the face of a man whose clothes were covered in sawdust, staring, staring at her across the quadrangle from Hut 3.

Beatrix was still talking. 'They've been doing an extensive one in Hut 3. Look, you mustn't say anything because Mooden's not spying on you, but . . .' She sighed. 'Everyone's a little jumpy because of Moira and no one's saying *you're* a fifth columnist, or that you're stupid enough to talk to people who might be. It's just that she asked me to check in on you since someone had seen you hanging around with him and someone else had seen you . . .' she dropped her voice as if the walls might judge '. . . *kissing* him. On a train of all places. And I said Honey Deschamps is not the sort of girl who goes around kissing men on trains, least of all coffin makers, but there it is. I know it's been a rough ride the past few days.'

'Where would I meet a coffin maker?'

'I told you, they hire them to do the fit-outs in the huts. When they want walls shifted and suchlike. There were some working in ours too. You know when you come in one shift and the rooms have all changed sizes and partitions have been thrown up and the pulley system no longer works or needs a good shove.'

'But why coffin makers?' She heard her voice very echoey in her head.

'I don't know. I suppose there's a surplus of them while the carpenters have been sent away with the troops. Apparently one of them's a real genius – some stage designer who can't find work right now because of the rationing and can't be sent away as he has some nerve problems up top. Don't we all? Anyway, about this forgery. It really is very curious.'

Honey was rubbing her head.

'Are you all right?'

All she could see was the wagon, the leather seats, Felix's hard, bright ultramarine eyes. A trailer that transported wood to the dead.

'Do you want me to fetch you a brandy, or some aspirin? You look positively green. It isn't me warning you, is it? It's not a warning, no one's told Tiver or anything. It's just you know what they are like about us and the local boys. Local boys are far less mad than any of the Cambridge boys inside the huts, I should say. But there it is.'

That was it, a Cambridge boy. Tiver had told her. Felix Plaidstow from Hut 3 went to Cambridge. There had been a mistake.

'Do you know . . .?' She could hardly get the words out. 'Do you know a boy called Felix Plaidstow in Hut 3? Went to Cambridge?'

'I know a Plaidstow at the Park. There can't be more than one with that name. Small, plump little boy. Yes, I think he did go to Cambridge.'

They said it together. 'Magdalene.'

'He plays in the chess club,' Beatrix went on. 'He knew—' She was about to say the name of her sweetheart, her RAF man, but she couldn't get the word together. 'He's quite fat. Black hair, round glasses. Honey, where are you going?'

She was throwing on her coat.

'What have I said?'

Honey grabbed the gas mask box and pushed the amber pieces back into it.

'What are you doing?'

'Drive me somewhere.' Beatrix looked startled at the instruction. She glanced over at the clock. 'But you start shift in a couple of hours.'

'Now. Please.'

Outside the Rectory Cottages it was dark as hell. Shadows cast by the clouded moon moved like oil slicks; murky, impossible to pin down. Honey carried her torch but dared not switch it on.

She had insisted Beatrix leave to begin her drive home, for if they were both caught in whatever trap was lying there, it would be plain Honey had spoken to her. She implored Beatrix and told her to telephone Mooden the next morning to see if she had made her shift and to alert Tiver if not.

She breathed deeply. Fear slid its tentacles around her ankles and throat but she fought it back with anger. She had made love to him in the seat of a truck, that afternoon. And maybe his lies were innocent lies or maybe they were as poisonous as the embalmer's touch.

She had the gas mask box across her shoulder and a stone in her hand. She pushed the box so it balanced against the small of her back while she clutched the delicate wood fence, and placed one foot on the first slat. The wood squeaked but bore her weight. Beyond it, in the dark of the vegetable patch, whatever creatures were confined in that little hut chirped and cried.

She had both legs wedged over the top and was balanced on the middle slat when something furry brushed her foot. She looked down, but it was too dark to see. Then out of the quiet came a hollow meow. Two clawed paws and a butting head breached into view.

'Shh, puss.' Honey waited for her heart to stop thumping.

She dropped down into the garden. She could feel the proximity of stone a few feet away; the ancient cold white walls pressing towards her with their thick harl. Up above, hot sweet chimney smoke danced into the night.

The cat brushed her ankle again, this time more slowly, softer. Trembling, she reached down to pet its tiny skull, working backwards from the twitching nose to the thick, hard brow bone, plush with a dry fluffy pelt. She reached her fingers behind the kitten hair at its ears, and tickled them, feeling her breath calm a little, and that was when the leathered fingers clasped her throat.

A chemical smell came from nowhere, surgical and burning, toxic on her lips. The inside of her nose seared. An arm wrapped tightly around her waist.

And she fell into an even darker pitch than the blackout.

She was on her back when she woke.

Her shoulderblades came to first, pressed into something slowly smashing a pattern into her skin. She saw white wire from the corner of her eye, shifted, and felt new cold on the fresh patch. She wriggled back and there was the warmth she had left.

Metal, she must be on top of metal; nothing else absorbed or gave back heat so quickly. She was lying on her back and she felt very peaceful, like the first moments coming round after a faint. Perhaps she was in the sick bay, that would account for the white and the bars. Honey had fainted the night the Empire fell and when she came to then, there had been a moment of blank peace and delirious exhaustion, the feeling of having been asleep for a very long time. Then she had opened her eyes to blood and chaos.

She felt now that first awareness, emerging slowly and beautifully from some hidden place out of reach. First her fingers tingled, then her ears sang, then a slow horror and confusion replaced awareness as the sleep faded, and she realised in a blinding shot of panic that she had been captured and stuffed inside a Morrison shelter, with the door banged shut and locked.

The room the shelter was in seemed small but ahead of her a door was pinched ajar, and while the open side was away from her, the crack it left at the back gave just enough space for her to see the thing that had terrified her the first time she passed the Rectory Cottages.

A thin candelabra burned on a tablecloth beside flowers and the shapes of bodies. The blackout drapes and the bronze light slid shadows over their shoulders. On the table, sliced into vision by the doorframe, was a feast of meats and fruits and condiments. Bottles of wine were open, mixing with metallic smells of gravy – a gravy prepared with offal and port, smells such as Honey hadn't breathed in two years since the start of rationing. In front of each man sat a tiny covered pot. And on the head of each was placed a thick white shroud.

She could see full-form only the figure to the left of the table's head; but scanning her eyes down beneath the table she was certain she knew his shoes, and those trousers had trodden a familiar flimsy wooden corridor time and time again. But how and why, by God, could he be part of this hellish pageant?

She was confused, and understood nothing but the need to open her mouth and cry. But now there was another figure in the room, a fast foot firing across her vision, kicking the door shut. She tried to sit up and choked. Her mouth gagged on bitter silk. She saw two calves in woollen slacks, and very mucky shoes. Fingers reached forward and opened the top of the shelter. A hand cradled her to sit up. 'There we go. Don't mind them. They're gluttons, nothing more.'

Honey bent over onto herself, partly to still her nausea – for her head throbbed – and partly because she did not want to look at the owner of the voice. She did not want to see his face. She did not want to know it was him, and not know him at all.

But he wanted to look at her.

Felix took her chin in his hand and pulled her face until they were staring at one another square. 'You talk in your sleep, you know. That's not very good for a Park employee.'

'What are they doing?'

'Them?' Felix gave a short laugh and hesitated. She saw him turn his head and look over his shoulder. The prison room was bigger than she had thought; it was long, with a lamplit desk beneath a tiny window, stapled over by a square of blackout fabric. Beside it a bench was strewn with tools and bottles, and the air smelled strongly of sawdust and another, sweeter scent. Felix turned back to her. 'They're eating, I'd say. Feasting. Like the big-bellied bastards they are. They don't let me dine with them. That's the lot of a contractor, I'm afraid.'

She rotated her neck in both directions. It ached and she wondered how long she had been compressed inside the shelter. As her eyes adjusted she saw across the desk sheets of draughtsman's paper, curled at the edges, along with pots of implements – dentist's tools, scalpels and picks, paints and varnishes. On the bench, lying on its side, spine-out, was a book: *The Origin of Amber.*

'Can you keep your mouth shut and not panic?'

Her eyes grew wide. Felix, though he smelled the same, was different. His touch was different. His voice was over-familiar, as if he was talking to someone he knew far better than he knew her; as if he thought he knew her better than he did.

Her eyes moved towards the closed door.

'Is it them you're frightened of?'

She wanted to laugh. She wanted to say, 'No, fool, I'm frightened because the man who made love to me, who kissed me on a train, has drugged me and dragged me to his lair, and . . . is that my hands tied behind my back, and is that smell in the air the same as my carved amber? The like of which has been goading me for almost a week, that might have killed my brother?'

But she didn't dare mock him. Now she was afraid. Right now, afraid of everything. She felt tiny as a child, and though she fought against it, to breathe through her nose, take stock of what was happening, find an escape route, it was futile and she was afraid.

The Amber Shadows

She nudged her shoulder to her face. Felix craned closer. 'What are they . . .' she tried to say through the silk bar. It was rammed right back into her wisdom teeth, gnawing at the sides of her lips. 'Him . . . him – why?' She had, in her shock, forgotten the name of the man she had recognised.

'Shhhhh,' Felix soothed. 'Silly and pretty. You are a catch. It's just Christmas dinner, fool. The . . .' He waved his hand across his face, demonstrating a shroud. 'Ortolans. They smuggle them in from France. I don't see the appeal myself. All those feathers and bones. But it's Christmas, says the chief, him at the head. Is that who you mean? You won't see his face. He's careful of that.' Felix stroked the top of her spine where it bent away from the shelter wire and she shuddered at his touch.

'It's a silly ritual,' he said softly. 'They hide their faces while they're eating the ortolans so God can't see them doing it. It has something to do with the shame of it.' He sighed. She heard him place something metal from his hand down on the floor. 'It's rather disgusting. The birds are drowned live in hot flaming brandy. Then they eat them whole. It's tradition to hide your face from God. But it's . . . it's just a silly thing. They like it, because of the rationing and . . . well, perhaps because of the cruelty. There's a link between wealth and cruelty, Honey, I think. They're not folk like you and I.' He stroked her again and where his hand fell it left a chill path on her flesh. There had been

411

more at that table – more pâtés and sherries and fruits – than she had seen in two years.

'Where . . .?' she said. She felt spittle dribbling down the side of her chin. Felix reached a finger forward and dabbed it up then looked around for somewhere to wipe it, settling on his trousers.

'Where do they get them? My, you are curious for someone who's just been chloroformed. Smugglers. Bandits, black market. You can get anything if you know the right person.' He shrugged. 'But listen, Honey, we don't have much time. If you'd just let me take care of you, you could have been spared all of this. Instead you have to come snooping, bursting in on the whole operation. I didn't have a choice but to tie you. If they'd seen you you'd have been shot. It's important you keep your mouth tight shut. You hear me? Once you're in on it—'

'In on what?'

'Keep your voice down, you shrill little ape. What did I just say? They shoot people for far less round here.'

She swivelled on her bottom so she could get a better look at him. Her upper arms had cramped to an ache. She tilted her head to look at the rope that was binding her and saw that it wasn't rope at all but silk stockings. He had got hold of silk stockings. He saw her looking.

'They were supposed to be a Christmas present.'

'Untie me,' she said through the gag.

'I can't trust you.'

'You can't trust me? *You* can't trust *me*?' She felt her voice rise then dropped it to a hiss as he shot up and pinned his back against the door.

'You're not listening to me, Honey. You're a prisoner now. They can do what they want with you. They have power and they don't want scandal. Look what happened to your friend. You were treading on razor wire going to Captain Bloody Do-Good Tiver to fight your battles. You had to tell him about your amber, didn't you? No one likes a squealer though, Honey. Not them, not us and certainly not Bletchley Park, so I'd be careful what you say if I were you. And quiet.'

Felix leaned back on the door panels. He looked down at her, and whether through genuine pity or a worry about the stockings snagging and spoiling he bent down and took the gag from her mouth, then untied her wrists. He glared and she felt his eyes chiselling into her, those little hard gems she had loved to see in her dreams.

'What is this place?' she whispered. 'I don't understand.'

'It's just, you know, a bit of smuggling, a bit of forgery.'

'Forgery?'

Felix rubbed at his eyes and sighed. 'Look, you know the Nazis are pillaging art all over Europe. Looting. You know that because you get the intercepts through at the Park. Sometimes they itemise what they've stolen. Sometimes it's reported in a newspaper. If it's itemised, so much the better. We get in first before the story gets out, make a fake, flog it to whichever unscrupulous art dealer will have it, and then

413

the news reports of the art being looted make our fake more genuine. Those folk out there have the contacts, me and a couple of others have the skills.'

'A forgery ring? You're forging the Nazi art thefts to sell on to the black market?'

'They call themselves the Magpies.' He leaned down and perched at an angle on the lip of the shelter, then lifted her chin again. For a second there was pride in his eyes. 'Look.' He pulled her up. She tweaked her hand out of his grasp and clutched the rim of the shelter as she stood. Minding her skirt she stepped high over the edge.

He led her to the desk where he had spread out a sketch. On the draughtsman's sheet were diagrams of a triptych, an altarpiece. Next to them were handwritten recipes for anti- quated pigments, and a tiny piece of curled, browned paper with the word 'Provenance' and a half-finished paragraph beneath it.

'War piracy,' she said. 'Pillaging.'

'No,' he said. 'Just profiteering. You wait and see. You wait and see who has money left after this war. There will be winners, Honey, and it won't be the good folk with guns on their backs dressed in khaki. And if you're an art dealer cruel enough to want to purchase stolen Nazi art, taken from churches, palaces, the homes of Jews . . . well, you deserve to waste your money on a fake. I only make the frames for them. The painting is done by another man, that man you saw with the car.'

'Oh, proper Robin Hood,' she whispered and there was a needle in her voice. She spotted the open gas mask box at her feet and bent down to it. Felix clutched her arm.

'You cracked one of the panels,' he said. 'I took an age over those.'

With a small vain flourish he moved aside a pot of paintbrushes, then flicked back his hair with the other hand. A tawny object glowed beneath the gaslamp. He had mended the panel. There was a scar that ran diagonally across the carvings, but it had been brushed, glued and sealed so that the whole thing stood. He had assembled it so that it formed a box. And the missing piece had been added so the bird stood perfectly.

It stood within a gold wire cage.

'Here.' He pointed to a lever at the top of the cage. 'Turn it.'

Slow in her terror, she crawled on her knees and rose until she was at eye level with the gift. She turned the handle.

Out tinkled the melody of *The Firebird*, but it was a hollow, creeping, tinny sound, the mighty orchestra reduced to the tawdry pings of a trinket. She felt tears surge up to her eyes to hear the tune humiliated. But Felix's gaze lit up. 'Go the other way,' he said.

With a scratching, hating heart she turned the cage handle anticlockwise. The melody struck up again but this time the bird turned too.

'It's brilliant, isn't it?' His mouth hung open. He stared at her in genuine wonder at his own accomplishment. 'I mean, they say that man Turing is a genius, but I . . . I made this for you.'

She felt the tears now. They came hot and raw. Her past, a past that didn't even belong to her but that she had believed in so faithfully, had been made into a toy. 'Why?' she sobbed. She stared at the sorry little firebird inside its cage, a phoenix that could turn and cheep and glow with flames but never ever dance. 'You made a forgery of my life. You dredged up things I never should have thought.'

'It's not all forgery. Some of it is real.' He poked at the bird's beak. 'This is real amber. The rest . . . well, you'll forgive me a little pride but it's a solution I made myself. Bakelite, melted from airshields, coloured with honey – I hope you like that – and scented with—'

'Soir de Paris,' she whispered. And now she saw it, there on his desk, the blue bottle, with the Arabian-shaped stopper. Sometimes her mother was right.

'That's right,' he whispered back. Honey watched his face change in the shadows. His eyes were reaching out to her. He took a step away from the desk, and looked at his feet. In the next room music had begun. The sound of dishes being cleared away came clanging through the closed door, hearty laughter, relief after ritual abated.

Felix leaned towards her. 'Now listen to me, fool, I'm not an idiot. I know that all over Europe the cities are rallying to hoard their art, they want to protect it from looting. They're doing it in England – half the National Gallery's gone to some cave in Portsmouth.'

'What?' she spat.

'Keep your voice down.' He rammed his flat hand hard across her airways. 'I'm sorry, I'm sorry, I'm sorry.' His cheeks were flushed and his eyes looked watery. 'I never meant to hurt you, Honey, ever. But by God, you have to do as I say.'

'What is it you want?' she whispered.

'Your father.'

'My . . .' Her throat closed. She looked him hard in his eyes, then cast her gaze back to the trinket box. The little firebird was sitting off kilter. Its open embrace was tilted, it looked drunk. For the first time she felt the tickle of a smile. 'You want my father. You did all this for my . . . You're out of luck, old boy. He died in 1918.'

'Not true,' Felix growled. 'He's curator of the Pushkin Palace in Leningrad. I know these things. I know all about you, little miss music. Your father knows where the Leningrad art is hidden. And you are going to lead me to him.'

'You know all about me, do you?' The man whose overcoat she had clung to on the train; the man who had implored her to tell him her secrets. He was a child, he was no more a man than Dickie had ever been.

Felix gripped her wrist. 'I lost my family over a year ago now. What I told you on the train, it was true. Every word.

All of them, gone. And that night will be in my dreams forever. My finger, see? I was telling the truth. I did come home that night. I did lose it, and the doctor said I should be able to feel, but the nerves are gone, Honey, they're gone.

'On my way home, I had heard the story of your father. While they dropped bombs on my house I heard that story. And I knew then it was a sign. God was giving me a chance. For both of us to start new lives, to rise . . .' His gaslit eyes looked mad '. . . like firebirds from this damned war. What do we have left if we don't take chances? I know you, Honey. I know you. I used to watch you in the theatre when your mother was rehearsing, fiddling with your red hair, biting your nails. I worked there with my own father. You see, I did see Nijinsky with the Ballets Russes. I was a toddler at the time and my father worked in the theatre. She was right, your mother. She did know me. She's a smart gel. But how could I – scenery boy – talk to the daughter of the star? When I saw him that night, it was not coincidence, it was fate. Fate, there you have it, you'd been brought back into my life. Now there's something that can help us both. If you lead me to your real father I can help him and you smuggle out the art – these men have passages all set up, it will make us rich.'

'My real . . . what are you talking about?'

'Honey, I know you know how to reach him. You're his daughter, there will be a way. We follow the trail together.

The Amber Shadows

We can do it. Follow the trail all the way to the palace art. Forget the Amber Room, it's gone, but there's trainloads of it, I know it and you know it. And the Nazis know it too. I'm sick of all of this forgery. I know I'm damned well not good enough for anything, and this war's done for my hand. But just think . . . to control a stash of brilliance that large. Imagine . . .'

It began to dawn on her. *When I saw him . . .* 'Dickie told you . . .'

'Dickie told me everything. He told me about your father escaping to Russia, he told me about *The Firebird*. How your family knows Stravinsky. How he became custodian of the Mariinsky theatre for a time, and then curator of the greatest collection of art in the world. Baroque paintings of Tsars, bronze statues, amber. He knows where it's been taken.'

Honey felt the blood drain from her head. 'Where did you meet him?'

But even as she asked she saw it. She saw it like it was a cinema reel, Felix and Dickie – Dickie, stuck on a train with nothing to do, enthusiastically regaling this nervy stranger with his lies, for his own entertainment.

'It was the end of May last year and we were stopped at . . . God knows where. Spent the night in a siding. You know how you get chatting to strangers on trains. This war . . . well, I recognised him, from the days when I did carpentry for the theatre. Anyway we chatted, and he talked and he talked. Your brother loved to talk. He showed me his cipher book.'

'Why did you have to beat him?'

Felix lowered his gaze. 'He was trying to keep me from you. The other night, when he came off the train, he tried to take it all back, the story he'd told me, he tried to tell me it was lies, but I know he was only jealous to let a man like me near his precious sister. I'd gone too far to let that drop.'

'You waited for him at the station. I told you. God, I told you he was coming.'

'You don't need him, Honey. I have no family, don't forget. Clean start. We'll track down your father, find the loot, build our own stories. The chance to have control of something real and material and worth money, real money. We can build our lives on riches. Love, Honey, is created from acts like this.'

'You thought that the three of us – you, me and my ficti-tious father – would live happily ever after in invaded Soviet Russia? Have you read the newspapers, Felix? People are dying by the thousand, starving to death, melting the fat from lipsticks to spread on bread, to eat.'

'I thought . . .'

'In God's name . . . the ciphers, the Vigenère . . .?'

'"To get mixed up in politics is ruination for art." Stravin-sky. It's true, Honey. This war, we don't have to be part of it. We are people of art, not politics.'

The Amber Shadows

'This war is not politics – it is families, neighbours, torture, murder.'

'Keep your voice down, imbecile! It was supposed to be a puzzle. Nothing but a beautiful puzzle.'

'You carved the codes? You cut up the box, you made it into a game, you were just waiting for me to need your help, lurking—'

'If you didn't have something to solve, how would I have been able to get close to you?'

His hand was resting back on the draughtsman's sheets on the desk, and she saw it then, the diagram just above his spread palm. It was an altarpiece, with the carvings sketched out, a Madonna in a heavy draping gown, holding a child. Beneath her hood, in the shadow of the fabric's folds, she could see the beginnings of the cheeks, lips and eyes, pencil-drawn out, to be scored and gouged into the wood. And they were unmistakably the echoes of her own face. He had built her a firebird in a cage, and now he was carving her face into an altar.

Paralysis cloyed with a feverish need to escape. He was a madman. Never had she thought in all this war that the greatest danger to her would be found not in the clutches of a German soldier, not in the lair of a Russian spy ring, but in the cave of a madman. Like the wolf in the story he had come to her in disguise, clothed in the safety of her family . . . She glanced around her. The only window was behind his head, on the other side of the desk, patched over with blackout fabric. The door led onto the dining room.

Her voice wavered. 'How do you know about the looting, and the hoarding? Did you steal the decrypts from the Park? Do you really work in Hut 3?'

'I work in Hut 3,' he said quietly. 'But not as you know it.'

'I think I do,' she whispered.

His head snapped up. He looked at her and for the first time there was contrition in his blue eyes. The ardour and the chivalry had drained. He was nothing but a boy, a boy like Dickie playing with stories, pretending to be someone he wasn't.

'Are they Park men out there?'

They both heard the click of the door handle and Honey's neck flung round. The base scraped slowly against the floorboards. At first she could only see the figure's shoes, but it was enough. They were the same. He was who she thought he was. 'No, not Park men,' he said. 'I'm the only one.'

'You?' she said.

'Yes, Honey, me.'

He took a step closer and she let her eyes travel up his trousers. If she could have named the one person in the war untouched by the horrors, the one person uncorrupted, unhardened, the one person kept pure and hopeful and unscarred by its corrosion, it would have been him.

'Rupert.'

'Do you think they know she's here?' Felix asked over his shoulder.

The Amber Shadows

'Magpie thinks she was shooed off trying to steal vegetables from the garden. But if she saw anyone we might have no choice but to shoot her.'

'She says she didn't see any of their faces. Do they know she's from the Park?'

He nodded. 'But we should all get out as soon as we can. You have the truck, enough petrol?'

Honey stammered. 'You . . . you stole the decrypts . . . you passed the art lists to those men . . . you were part of . . . this?'

'Honey, be sensible.' Rupert Findlay passed his hand through his hair, gluing back the long hank of greased golden fringe. 'We're none of us going to come out of this war any better than we went in. You loot what you can; the sooner you wise up to that the better.'

'But . . . where did you meet them?'

'Them out there?' He grinned. 'Hotchpotch. Cambridge, Oxford, London. Where else? Honey, there isn't much time left, for Freddie and I. We're relying on you. We've promised them a good haul of Russian gold. Now come on, you must have names. Did your father mention anyone else working at the palace? Anyone we can track down?'

'You're as mad as Felix.'

'I know the Russians have that art stashed. I broke into that message key myself over a year ago, you idiot.' His teeth clenched; he leered close. 'They took it away on a train just before the siege. Now stop lying to us. Who did he work with at the palace? Come on, or I'll break your jaw.'

'Steady on, old boy.'

'Poo,' Honey gasped.

'Don't call me that fucking stupid nickname! Would you call a man like him Poo?' She watched as Rupert Findlay's pokey little eyes, so often friendly and excitable beneath his high forehead, shifted across to Felix. And then the absurdity of the jealousy hit her. Each wanting to be a little bit of the other. Rupert – darling Poo – ran his eyes up Felix's strong frame, his spiny, strange, exotic, indefinable face. While Felix gazed at the weave in Rupert's trousers, the starch on his non-utility, high-thread cotton collar, the smoothness of his little pale educated hands, hands kept for the mathematics and the chess; little hands that could have painted any picture they wanted to and had it exhibited in a gallery, peopled by the friends of his family, purchased for sale to hang on their walls, if that had been what he had wanted. War was a leveller: on the field they might have fought side by side, they might have shared a billy can of water or helped the other limp. Here, stuffed together in their bleak little underworld of black-market forgeries, scrabbling for spoils, the envy flared out of each of them until it rubbed raw, one against the other.

Honey's voice dropped. 'I don't know quite what I'd call Felix.' She looked again at the sordid amber box, then at the altarpiece sketches. The music ran in tinny patterns in her head, she couldn't escape it. She squeezed her eyes and pictured the gleam in his. *It's brilliant, isn't it?*

'Come on, Honey, when did the old pop last contact you? Was it last Christmas? Where did he holiday? Did he ever mention any names to you?'

Felix had relaxed his grip now. The pair of them stood next to one another, peering down at her, their elaborate catch, braced against the top of the Morrison shelter.

'You idiots.' She took a breath then leapt towards the table, stretching her arms to reach the window. She knocked over pots and crashed bowls of chemicals to the floor. Wet seeped onto her bare kneecaps but she kept going, scrambling. She felt Felix's arms on her calves. He had a wiry strength, disguised through his tweeds and his pullovers, the strength of a man who hefted wood and sawed and hammered coffins. She saw his fists making the blue weals on Dickie's face. And for what? For his horrid mawkish tricks, for his foolhardiness, his obsession and his greed. She kicked. She caught him on the mouth; she could feel it – a hard slice to her skin, his teeth biting down and wet saliva on her heel.

She beat with her legs again. This time she caught a jaw. She heard the breath knocked out of Rupert, and felt a crack on her ankle. But Felix's other arm was quick and tough. She reached for the blackout curtain stapled to the window frame. As she tore it down, sending it smashing into the desk, her horror doubled for a second. There was a face on the other side of the window.

Chapter 22

It was only after a few frozen seconds that she made out the hat and the armband. The tin brim cleared into view, half a perfect green metal globe, and she saw beneath it the woman's features, her brick-red lipstick beaconing out. *Beauty is your Duty.*

She was an ARP warden with a Women's Voluntary Service ribbon wrapped round her sleeve. She knocked sharply on the windowpane. Honey, still kneeling on top of the table, felt Felix slide out of view beneath the desk. Rupert's shadow receded beside the door. Crouched on the table, through the warped glass, she held the warden's gaze for a moment. Could she pass her a message? What code was there for danger that could not be broken too quickly by the enemy standing by?

With tentative hands she reached for where the blackout blind had fallen. The woman tapped the glass again and Honey's head shot up.

The Amber Shadows

The warden made a rising gesture with her hands, flicking them. Her voice was muffled by the pane. Honey reached for the blind and began to lift it but the woman shook her head and tapped again. She shouted something Honey couldn't make out. At the back of the room she could hear the two men breathing.

She slowly pulled up the sash and let the cold air rinse the atmosphere. Her skin felt hot and clammy. The breeze gripped her forearms and blasted through the neck of her dress.

'What's that you say?' she stammered.

'You'll have to put the curtain back up. But I'm afraid I have to fine you anyway. Come out and I'll do the ticket.'

Honey looked hesitantly behind her. She could see one set of eyes in the dark, low down, Felix's; the shine on them caught by the gaslight. He was still panting from the struggle. Rupert had squatted low beside the Morrison shelter, his round freckled face damp in panic. Honey wriggled across the desk to the open window and squeezed her legs through.

'By Jove, I didn't mean through the window. What's wrong with the front door? Now what's your name?'

Honey leaned back, strained her fingers across the desk to where her coat was lying, pulled sharply, then hopped down onto the grass, weathering the thump that rang through her ankle.

'Can I see your identity card?'

Honey looked the girl square in the eye. 'Thank you,' she said, squeezing her arm, beneath the band. And then she ran.

She ran hard over the muddy frost and frozen grass. She ran over the cracking dirt and onto the path that led to the Park. She kept running, ignoring the Air Raid Warden's cries, ignoring the stings in her soles and her ankles. She ran up to the gates. A figure stepped in front of her blocking the light from the military hut.

'It's Honey Deschamps, Hut 6,' she stammered.

'Papers,' he called. And then again when she didn't slow. 'Papers. Stop there, calm down and get your papers out now.' He fumbled at his waist and raised his revolver.

Her hands felt as if they were slipping through water. No matter where she touched she couldn't get purchase on her coat. The fabric seemed to tear and shiver away from her. At length her hand found her pocket and plunged.

The papers weren't there.

The Military Policeman shifted the gun from one hand to the other and stepped closer.

She tried the other pocket. Nothing. Then the inside ones.

'Miss, calm down. I recognise you but I need to see your papers. I can't let you in without.'

She heard a scuffling of the dirt behind her. 'You dropped them. Goodness me, you're a terror to keep up with.'

The beam of the Military Policeman's torch struck the figure behind her and Honey turned, nursing dread, her hands at her stomach as though they would somehow protect her.

Felix's face was washed with sweat and he was working hard to control his breathing. In his hand he held up a small packet of papers and bounced them against the air, twice. 'Don't worry,' he said. 'I haven't opened them.'

'I know you,' the guard said. 'What are you doing here this time of night? Your lot don't work nights.'

'Actually we do,' said Felix smoothly. 'But not for another half hour. I was returning the papers to the lady. She dropped them at the cinema. Very careless, you might say.'

The Military Policeman extended his arm and took the documents from Felix. He kept the torch beam high on his face. Felix held up his other hand as if surrendering. He shot a sidelong glance at Honey. Her stomach curdled.

The neck she had kissed and held, the ears, the dip in his chin, the hard line of his jaw; they were all monstrous. His jugular pulsed where before it had been tender. She wanted to lunge forward with her teeth bared, push him to the dirt. Instead she had to watch while he retrieved, hot and creased from his trouser pocket, his own papers, and passed them for inspection.

In the time it took for him to do so the pasty face of Rupert Findlay had appeared at the fringe of the torch beam, clammy as a wheel of cheese.

The policeman waved them all through. As Honey went to slip her identity card back into her coat she felt Felix's hand deftly intercept her and his voice in her ear. 'I think I'll take care of those for now, thank you. And before you scream or do anything that will make us all into traitors think on the consequences, idiot. What you did, with me in that truck this afternoon. I could have it broadcast on the wireless stations. I could have it printed on flyers. I could spread it like wildfire round this Park. They hire good girls here, you know. That's what I heard. And the ones who aren't good . . . well, you know where they bundled your friend Moira.'

The words stunned her. She was only distracted from the horror of his face when the clock on top of the stable chimed half past eleven. Half an hour until her shift began.

Rupert pulled Felix's sleeve. 'How are we going to get her out of here?' He cast his eyes in the direction they had walked from. The red caps of the Military Police had now faded into a torchlight blur.

Felix gripped Honey by the elbow and opened his mouth.

Suddenly voices sprang out of the trees. A man holding a banjo and a girl with two sprigs of holly in her hands skipped forward, laughing. Both were wearing carnival masks. Felix twisted his grip so that his arm was about Honey's waist and laughed heartily to the couple. The man pinched the woman's shoulder – she was a Wren by her uniform underneath – and they veered off towards the house.

'Fun in the recreation club tonight. Christmas masquerade.'

The Amber Shadows

Honey slithered from his grasp and ran for the house. But she hadn't gone two steps when Rupert's leg shot out to trip her up. Felix grabbed her forearm as she fell.

'Don't be an idiot, Honey,' Felix said slowly. 'Don't be a fool. I'm not sure I quite meant to be so spiteful. I . . . I'm in shock, to be truthful. Honey, you have to trust me. If you find us a lead to contact him, we'll find a way to get that stuff smuggled into Britain. And your father too. What's safer for him? Out there on the battlefields of Russia? And the art, I mean, God only knows if wood and paint that old can survive without being properly looked after. We're doing this not just for ourselves; but for you, for him, for the art.'

She looked at Rupert Findlay. He was pursing his lips, scowling, the way he always scowled thoughtfully when he asked about her mother.

'You're a child,' she whispered to him. 'How can you care about paintings, how can it matter, the fate of an old chair? If I knew where the Pushkin Palace art was I'd tell the world, so the people in the fields outside Leningrad could chop it up for firewood. By God, what does it matter what art there is, if we haven't a world left?'

'You don't mean that, Honey,' Felix muttered. 'What world is left if we destroy what reminds us we are beautiful?'

'Come on.' Rupert's tweed arm pulled her to his weedy body. 'Just come to the Eight Bells with us. We could have your father on the road to Britain by midnight. I know commies, spies, people who can help.'

'You're not listening. He doesn't exist.'

She looked around her for an escape route and her eyes fell on the bench that ran along the front of the lake. It was frosty and the sparkles of ice on the wooden seat caught prickles of moonlight. Further up at the mansion, shouts were coming from the windows of the recreation club and Christmas carols were pouring out. Over on the other side of the lake Hut 11 was rumbling, picking over the ciphers of the night.

She looked at the lake and imagined a tiny paper boat upon it, and in that paper boat, tiny fragile paper sailors, all listless, all giving their fate up to the stars; all sinkable when saturated, drowned. She wished, just for a second, that she could know what it was to be at sea, to fight a war with her body and not her mind.

Her mouth opened to scream but Rupert was quick as a weasel and had his tweed sleeve across her throat. 'Come on,' he said, beginning to haul her towards the feathers of ice at the lake edge.

'What are you doing?' said Felix.

Honey rammed her heel down onto Rupert's toe but he dodged in a quickstep.

'She'll fall – you'll slip. Come back.'

'She'll do as she's bloody told.' Rupert continued dragging her but he was reedy and weak and she slipped her arms free.

'Felix, you won't let him . . . you said . . .'

'Cooperate, Honey. It's your last chance.'

'But I can't cooperate. None of it was true, why won't you listen to me?'

Felix took a step towards her and she closed her eyes. Rupert had steadied himself and had her arms pinned to her waist again.

She screamed.

There was silence as the noise sliced into the blackout. Then, on the other side of the park a scream answered, followed by a loud guffaw. Snow was beginning to fall.

'Get that away from my blouse!' came a cry from the lawn in front of the house.

'Help!' Honey yelled.

'Help *me*!' the voice came back. 'They're going to bloody freeze me to death.' The laughing rose.

'They killed Dickie,' she cried out.

'Keep your voice down,' Rupert shot. 'Or you'll wind up before the firing squad. We've got enough on you to put you before a tribunal for treason. Stealing decrypts, discussing codes.'

'But I didn't—'

'And who are they going to trust more? A Cambridge boy, or a bloody woman typist?'

'Felix.'

'I'm sorry, Honey. It's gone too far. We can't be found out.'

Rupert was still grasping her, Felix ahead. Her only escape was the ice. She plunged down to the dirt, slipping Rupert's arms, and ran for the lake. The glassy plate spread out, its frayed edges seeping into lace along the bank. The centre looked solid, but appearances could be deceptive. Its surface was battle-scratched from skates and sleds. She heard scrabbling behind, felt fingertips clutch for her coat and took the first step, her eyes closed.

She expected it to crack, but it held. She took another step. Her foot slid to the side and her arms flashed out to steady her.

'Come back. Honey, it's not safe.' Felix's voice came behind her, yards away.

She took another step, slipping again – the whole thing seemed made of oil – and carefully turned, but she couldn't see their faces in the dark. Her strides had been big; she had gone further than she thought, and still she stood. But her weight was slight and she was only in cork shoes.

On the banks the black shadows of tree branches criss-crossed the grey surface of the night. Her arms became a balancing pole. She tried to think back to how Dickie held his arms when he did a grand jeté. Once she had learned to do a grand jeté too. That was something that was real. These were the things that had happened. There were things that were real from her childhood. He had not taken it all away, erased it all in forged amber.

She heard brush crack. 'Honey, this isn't funny. Come

back and we'll . . . there's been a misunderstanding. Come back and we'll . . .'

She felt Felix step onto the ice, the extra weight. She slid a shaky step further to the centre.

The black shadow branches danced, slow and lethargic. Felix took another step.

Sirens were sea women who led men from their ships to watery graves. In some myths they would sing. In other myths they were mermaids, and would comb their red-gold hair until the sailors were mesmerised, reached out to touch that hair, and only then they would be pulled down to the depths where bladderwrack grew and crabs lived in shells.

She took a step further into the centre of the lake. There were boys in the Atlantic tonight, in colder air, with harder, keener enemies. They were the ones Hut 8 worked to save. Even their typists – even their lowly woman typists – did their bit to protect them.

Felix's arm was stretching towards her out of the dark-ness; his fingers caught the moonlight, fading backwards to the shadowed head and face. He took another step forward. Another inch of his sleeve came into view.

And then the ice could no longer bear his weight. It yawned and cracked in a great plate, rose up from the lake and like a see-saw pushed him down. She had to be quick. She found her own island of broken ice, but in leaping to it she tripped.

Her feet slid, and instead of hard ice rising up there came

a flat black hole. Her face hit freezing water and she plunged. The cold seared into her lungs. She opened her eyes but the dirt stung. Her hands numbed so quickly it felt as if they had already disappeared below the elbows; all else was stumps.

She spun a roll, thrashed to the surface and stole a breath. In the bleary moonlight she saw on the surface of the water a breaking wave, looming forward, a spitting mouth, an arm beaconing the air.

'Honey!' Felix shouted her name. He was breathing – hard, rasping breaths. The water closed over her head again and for a second all was silent. Now her upper arms had ceased to feel. Delirium took away her neck, she thought she might be moving her limbs but couldn't be sure, and then all of a sudden she was black in unconsciousness, dreaming, plunging down to frozen depths where she became a spoon in an ice she had eaten as a child; an ice made of nothing but water and sweet lemon, and there she was diving right to the bottom of the thick crystal that cupped the iced sweet lemon and . . . She felt a weight on top of her, pushing her lower. Above the surface, hollow cries, the spluttering of water. In her mind she saw Felix's blue Fabergé eyes sinking on top of her, the water sealing them both in tight. And the panic was enough to send her breaching up.

Reaching out high above her head her hand hit something solid; mud and root. She pulled and grasped, feeling her wet fingers slipping, frozen, numb, fumbling for purchase. She heaved her stomach onto the mudbank and yanked her leg high. When she hauled herself out she saw she had come a small distance from where Felix was extending a sodden arm, Rupert pulling him free.

She squeezed the water from her skirt and ran.

'There she goes.'

It was Felix. Footsteps and the slop of water closed on her over the mud. She kept running. Her feet had swollen in the cold, stuck fast inside her corkboard shoes which poured with every step. Still she ran. She ran as if she were running from fire. She discarded her wet coat as she struggled out of the bushes and onto the path that led towards the gate. The Military Police were her beacons but they were not her friends. She knew if she were to tell them what she knew, there would be questions: the amber, the ciphers, the wax, why had she not spoken sooner. No, she could not stop for the MPs.

She tore past them. 'Sorry I forgot my—'

'Slow down, miss, you'll do yourself a mischief in those heels.'

'Did you see her, she looked wet,' she heard the other say as she flew past, spraying drips. Thank God for the blackout. Thank God they could not see her blue skin, her terror.

She came out onto Wilton Avenue, tearing past the construction site for the new cafeteria. Her feet slipped on gravel. But she heard heavier feet – two sets behind – and kept running.

A cloud had descended over the moon, blocking its glow.

The end of the road seemed a void. She could no longer feel what was around her. She stopped and turned a circle, panting, searching for the right direction. But as soon as her bearings were abandoned, she couldn't get them back. The blackout was too thick. She was lost.

From her right came sounds of traffic, a vehicle roaring close then receding, then another. She was near the main road. She took a step towards it then stopped.

A gravel stone had slid very close behind her. A foot was correcting itself on dry turf. She heard the heavy slow drip of cold water falling from fabric; raw, hard breathing.

She chose a direction and hurled herself forward, hoping for the main road into town.

A machinery shriek ripped into her left ear. Wheels displaced gravel; an engine fired to life, a vehicle came searing round the bend, travelling at breakneck speed. The slatted blue dip of headlights appeared with just enough time to see Felix and Rupert Findlay standing frozen in the middle of the road, caught in twin beams. The glow threw light onto their legs. They raised their arms to block the blow.

The last thing Honey saw before diving to the gravel was a pair of solid silver angel wings, shining in a halo of white on the car's bumper. There was a terrifying crack and thump, then rubber stank as the vehicle skidded to a halt. For a few seconds there was only the sound of her own panting.

Then the car door clicked open.

The Amber Shadows

Petrified and stunned, Honey tilted her face up from where she was pressed prone to the road. She had an unsavoury throbbing in her mouth; she had bitten her tongue. The blue light from the headlamps streaked a diagonal line in front of her, so that when two high-heeled feet slipped out of the vehicle and down onto the gravel she could for a moment see nothing above the stockinged legs, nothing until they came further towards her, into the light. As they hurried forward, the centre of the glare began to pick out the full figure, and she saw a hand clasping a hat to its owner's head. A single feather fell down into the road; peacock blue, pheasant gold.

'Dear God, what have they done to you? You're soaked.'

As the woman leaned close the familiar lines of her face blurred into recognition. Beatrix. 'What were you . . .?'

'You didn't think I'd drop you off at a dark house after that panic you put up, and bugger off home for Christmas, did you? I got as far as the edge of Bletchley and then I felt guilty, so I came back, ate my powdered egg sandwiches – rotten things – and when I saw you running for your life towards the Park I drove round the corner. I was about to head in and check you were all right when you came running out again, with them. God, it's Rupert Findlay. I'll fetch a doctor.'

'How did you see me running? You didn't have your headlights on.'

She saw Beatrix shrug. 'Carrots, I suppose? You can tell

me later what happened. Hang on, I've got a blanket in the car.'

She crunched back off over the gravel and returned brandishing a thick Scottish woollen rug, which she wrapped around Honey. Almost at once Honey felt the water on her skin begin to warm. She shivered to her senses and struggled to her knees. She crawled over to where the two bodies lay.

Felix was still gurgling but Rupert was silent.

Beatrix placed her hand on Rupert's chest. 'Still breathing. He might make it. I'll telephone for an ambulance. Wait here.' She took off towards the Park gates, her legs melting away out of the silvery beam.

Honey looked down and saw Felix's eyes flick open. He rolled his head from side to side. She stayed kneeling at a safe distance.

'You would have killed me.'

'It wasn't my choice.'

'But you would have. Just like Dickie.'

'You can't . . . my temper . . . You can't understand what it would mean, if those men thought I'd betrayed them . . .' He craned himself up onto one elbow. 'I say, you couldn't roll me a cig, could you?'

Honey looked up at the stars; so many stars at Bletchley, all over Britain, a side effect of the blackout. In another life they could have been star-crossed lovers. But he had taken it on himself to direct their path. He had murdered her brother out of greed, out of idiocy.

440

The Amber Shadows

She reached forward into his pocket, took back her wet identity papers and made to stand up. She wanted his face to fade away from her, back into the dirt, back into the shadows of the street from where he had come that first night after the film at the Ritzy. But he reached out and grabbed her leg.

'Honey . . . you said that wasn't your real name. What is your real name?'

She hesitated. Did he deserve to know? Then she said it plainly, and as the word fell from her mouth she realised it meant as little to her as 'Honey' or 'Kurtz' or 'Deschamps' or 'Kitts' ever did. 'It's Honor,' she said. Honor. *You're not just some little Honey.*

She stood up fully. Her own feet were still numb to the ankles; beyond them her wet calves had started to thaw. She walked a few paces then looked back over her shoulder. Felix was sitting up, hugging his knees. She kept walking until she reached the gates. She held up her wet pass for inspection.

Beatrix was busy harrying two uniformed men down from the mansion house. Honey caught her eye, and she stopped running. Slowly her hand raised; she called across, 'Go to your shift. They'll take care of this.' She had a blind trust, Beatrix. She didn't need to break into any codes of behaviour to know what was the right thing to do.

Honey walked carefully over the gravel path, minding each foot until she had reached her hut. Her hair had almost frozen dry. Outside the door she towelled it on the blanket and rearranged the pins so it was tighter on her head. She clenched her puffy fingers just enough that they melted to be able to turn the hut's handle.

In the nauseous light of the corridor she shook the cold out. She went straight to the Decoding Room and held her hands above the stinking grate of the coke stove.

Winman, Head of Hut, caught sight of her through the open door and stopped. 'Dear God, is it sleeting out there? With the bloody blackout curtains up you've no idea what's going on in the outside world. Get warmed up, you could have caught your death.'

The voice of the night shift's Head of Room, Miss Roache, came laconically out of the dark corner, without stopping the slap and paste of her brush. Fresh decrypted messages were being prepared for the pulley; she was rolling them up into the tube to be sent to Hut 3 where they would be actioned for the lives of any number of chosen young men, the lucky ones.

'You're early, duck. But that's just as well. Those bloody eager beavers in the Machine Room have broken the Red already. Something about wanting to be home by Christmas and wanting their homes intact this time round. So you'd better get to work.'

Epilogue

She doesn't feel the sun rise inside the hut. It comes with a shift in the pace of work, a feeling of light at the end of a very long and very dark tunnel, a rising from a sea bed.

It's only when the morning shift arrives and the paper pile is depleted that she knows the work is done. The coded intercepts, handwritten in red pencil, cut and stuck in strips on pages, motorcycled in from the listening stations, have now been passed through her channel of the Park: through the cribsters, the menu-makers, the *bombe* machines in Hut 11, through the Typex operators. Now they sit snug in their red leather tube to be pushed into the pulley and taken to the intelligence agents. There they will be logged by the indexers, and the secretaries who register each callsign, every unfamiliar word, every name. The burden they all carry; the names of the dead, the names of the killers, every typist, every secretary will carry them with her to her own grave.

At some point during the night talk had turned to the flicks. *Suspicion* was coming back to the Ritzy. 'Did you know,' said one of the American Machine Room men, leaning in the door, 'did you know that the studio made them change the ending of that film? Apparently Cary Grant *was* the killer after all. But the studio thought that the good people of Blighty and Uncle Sam wouldn't stand for it. They thought a story about a neurotic suspicious woman and an innocent man was more plausible. Sorry, did I just spoil the ending for anyone?' He laughed and left.

'Done.' Roache, Head of Room, dusts her hands and holds them open. They've finished the pile just in time to hear the cry of 'Broken the Light Blue,' from the crib room. But that is for the morning shift to deal with.

Outside the hut the sun is frightening. The Military Police shift has changed and the men who stopped her at the gates the night before have gone.

There is no evidence of the night before. The whole world feels like a murky dream. The ice has re-formed in the night. Maybe one day, she thinks, maybe one day the lake will be drained and they will find a shoe, something from the men's pockets, and their story will come out.

On the dirt path just down from the lake lies a single red velvet mask, edged with gold. Its ribbon is torn. The eyes are black holes. In the daylight it's plain to see that the ribbon was made from old knicker elastic, dyed and streaky.

At the site of the car smash there is nothing but some

disturbed gravel and broken branches. Soon the news will come filtering back and she will have to hear it; Rupert Findlay is injured, or gone, a terrible accident, one of two hundred blackout road accidents this year, another terrible waste, and Beatrix, one more young person to bear the burden of killing or maiming another.

She has to pass the House of the Ortolans on her way to Church Green Road, and at first she thinks she might be too afraid to look. But then she does, just sidelong, a single glance. And no monsters rise up, no sea-serpents come tumbling from the windows to swaddle her. And she looks again, more carefully this time, and the sun is shining on their winter cabbage patch and she wonders what has become of Felix, whether he made it out of the hospital.

It doesn't take long for her question to be answered. On the doorstep of Yew Tree Cottage there is a package. At first she thinks it might be a basket of eggs.

But it is too heavy for eggs. She doesn't hesitate before tearing the old newspaper away.

In sunlight the completed thing is tawdry – laughable – and she realises she has not looked at it in pure sunlight before. Its panel surfaces are far too shiny; they look greasy. She sees it now, the streaks, the staining. Later on, much later, after she has napped and listened to the wireless, she puts it back in its basket and heads to the forest.

★   ★   ★

There are patches of scrub that line the routes in and out of Bletchley. Perhaps it's here that the great Professor Turing from Hut 8 has buried the silver treasure Moira told her about. Or perhaps that is inside the Park walls, she can't remember. One day someone – a child – will dig it up, she is sure. And then people will speculate and guess what it is, what it means; pirates, plundering, a dead drop for a secret lover, a lost father leaving treasure for his children to find.

She takes the music box and puts it in a nest of brush while she scrapes a little hole in the dirt with her hands.

In the view of the town that waves in and out of the moving trees, she can see the chimney stacks of the brickworks, the steam of the station. But now there is something new that she hadn't noticed before. A small factory building, set apart down a lane, near the funeral parlour with its black horses; the place where they found Dickie. Smoke is rising gently from the chimney and the whole building is shrouded in pale dust. That's it, she thinks, the coffin works. And where would we be without them in the middle of the war?

She thinks about burying the music box, but it won't do.

Instead she takes matches from her pocket and strikes several, dropping one at each corner, one in the middle. It doesn't take long for the Bakelite to catch. Bitter chemical ribbons rise and stench the air, and the plastic liquefies. It melts in rivers and waves, lava channels that cave in on themselves and bring fire to the insides. Even the gold of the little cage eventually bends and buckles and tumbles.

The Amber Shadows

But the firebird stays. The firebird is curious in the face of the flames. Instead of melting, it waits until the heat surrounds it like a blue blanket. It sizzles as its sugars burst, and it sends out the sweetest scent, one that knocks the burnt Soir de Paris fumes of the plastic away. This real, true perfume does not erode as it burns; it is brought to life by fire.

She watches the amber burn, and thinks of the plundering Nazis inside the Amber Room in Leningrad, ripping panel by panel, thieving the ancient resin. And though it is not her father who is stealing shards from them to preserve and send to her, she hopes that somewhere, someone else's mother or father is.

She stays until the face of the firebird is unrecognisable. She doesn't wait to see it vanish.

On the way back to her billet she has to cross Church Green Road. It's only because the traffic is heavy with military vehicles that she has to stop. And that's when the familiar eyes blink at her from across the street. Like wet pebbles – that was what she had thought the first time, but in daylight his eyes are hazel brown. She follows the line of his collar up, up the small ribbon to the hand of the woman she'd seen in the post office. And then it all becomes clear.

Felix stole him.

He was part of the lie. He was the reason she had trusted Felix in the first place. Nijinsky, the ballet name, no coincidence. And her grandfather did use to race them.

That's the thing I like about dogs. They're quite incapable of lying. Quite incapable of telling the truth.

'Nijinsky,' she cries. And hearing her voice, a familiar voice – like anyone in the war hearing someone they know – he steps out into the road, takes a pace towards her, wagging his long tail. The woman yanks him back just before an army vehicle comes blasting past, and as he trips back onto the pavement it enters her mind how like Dickie he moves, how perfectly like a ballet dancer.

She waits for the army vehicle to drive off – a tall rattling lorry full of soldiers clinging to the canvas – then crosses the road. The woman pushes her red hat back to better catch a look at this strange young debutante running towards her dog. 'What did you call him? His name's Scamp. Scamp the miracle dog. Took himself off on an adventure last week, and only just came back.'

Scamp.

But it is him. Honey knows it is still Nijinsky, and that no matter what name he answers to, no matter who he belongs to now, under his fur, through his thin silken skin, the same heart beats that always did.

Historical Note

The Amber Shadows is a work of complete fiction. However, books I found useful in building my own version of Bletch-ley Park, and from which I used various anecdotes, include: Marion Hill's *Bletchley Park People*, Gordon Welchman's *The Hut Six Story*, Sinclair McKay's *The Secret Life of Bletch-ley Park*, Michael Smith's *The Secrets of Station X*, Gwendo-line Page's *We Kept the Secret*, Doreen Luke's *My Road to Bletchley Park*, Simon Singh's *The Code Book*, John Pether's *Funkers & Sparkers* and *Black Propaganda*, Bletchley Park Trust's *History of Bletchley Park Huts & Blocks 1939–45*, Asa Briggs's *Secret Days*, Roy Conyers Nesbit's *Ultra Versus U-Boats: Enigma Decrypts in the National Archives* and Tessa Dunlop's *The Bletchley Girls*.

Also generally on World War II and beyond: *Careless Talk: The Hidden History of the Home Front 1939–1945* by Stuart Hylton, *Private Battles* by Simon Garfield, *We Remember the*

Blitz by Frank Shaw & Joan Shaw, *I was Vermeer: The Forger who Swindled the Nazis* by Frank Wynne, *The Amber Room: the untold story of the greatest hoax of the twentieth century* by Cathy Scott-Clark and Adrian Levy, Stephen Walsh's biography of Stravinsky, Margot Fonteyn's autobiography, newspapers, novels of the period, and Alfred Hitchcock movies.

The Eight Bells is now called The Eight Belles – a local landlady told me this was changed relatively recently to reflect the heritage of the wartime dancing girls.

Hut 6 codebreaker Ann Mitchell very kindly told me a story of being offered post-overall-washing water by her billet landlady, for bathing. I am extremely grateful to Ann Mitchell and to Ailsa Maxwell for taking the time to chat with me about their memories of working in Hut 6; however Honey's story is not supposed to be a direct reflection of their experiences.

I should mention that it's highly unlikely Honey would have the amount of knowledge she does about the overall operation of the Park, but there was no way to communicate the detail of the life of the Park other than to take this liberty, one of many liberties. I've changed locations – particularly with regard to where the Polish codebreakers were based, though it's true they were kept from Bletchley Park – film release dates, adding fouettés to Prince Ivan's role in Fokine's original *Firebird*, among other fictions.

I used the *Fashion on the Ration* exhibition at the Imperial War Museum to browse for clothing and cosmetics, particularly for Moira, and it was also my source for discovering the popular Bourjois wartime fragrance Soir de Paris.

There are hundreds of papers relating to Bletchley Park available to the public in the National Archives at Kew, and these were helpful in providing various details, including the story about the RAF man who followed a BP worker at the start of the novel, and other insights into security breaches and procedures relating to the running of the Park.

I am grateful also for the written wartime reminiscences of my late nanna and to my grandma for sharing her memories with me.

The Bletchley Park museum staff and guides were incredibly helpful on the various occasions I visited, and although I was too shy to tell them what I was doing, their accounts have helped in numerous ways to shape the novel. Any inaccuracies or liberties I've taken are not a reflection on this brilliant museum, which I recommend as a must-visit for anyone who has enjoyed the book and wants to know the truth about this extraordinary group of war workers.

CPSIA information can be obtained
at www.ICGtesting.com
Printed in the USA
LVHW02s2139260618
581953LV00014B/1694/P